PRAISE FOR NATALIE K MARTIN

'A significant new voice in Women's Fiction.'

Pride Magazine

'Thought-provoking, emotionally intelligent.'

Daily Mail

T0058717

ALL
WE
LEFT
UNSAID

ALSO BY NATALIE K MARTIN

Love You Better
Together Apart
Wanderlust
What Goes Down

ALL
WE
LEFT
UNSAID

Natalie K Martin

LAKE UNION
PUBLISHING

Published by Lake Union Publishing, Seattle

www.apub.com

Amazon, the Amazon logo, and Lake Union Publishing are trademarks of Amazon.com, Inc., or its affiliates.

ISBN-13: 9781542029551
ISBN-10: 1542029554

Cover design and illustration by Ghost Design

Printed in the United States of America

'Out beyond ideas of wrongdoing and righting,
there is a field. I'll meet you there.' – Rumi

Prologue

Jess

August, this year

'He found her, just lying there.'

My eyes sting as I look down, blinking against another surge of hot tears. I can't stop them from escaping and burning their way down my cheeks before landing on my leg. I try to make sense of those words again and look up at Maddie, who is holding a mug of hot tea towards me. She doesn't say anything as I take it from her. She doesn't have to. I've lost count of the amount of times I've repeated the sentence in the past half-hour.

I roughly wipe another tear from my cheek and shake my head again as Maddie sits next to me on the sofa. Hearing Finn's voice on the phone had felt like walking into a golden memory. Warm and safe. Until the words he'd said ripped away the last bit of family I had left.

Ivy's dead.

My little sister. His words had cut through me like a knife.

'He said she just didn't wake up,' I say, replaying the conversation to Maddie again. I keep a neutral tone to my voice, as if it might somehow help the words to land in a way that makes sense. 'He said she fell asleep and just didn't wake up.'

Maddie sighs heavily. 'I can't believe it.'

'I keep thinking it has to be some kind of weird joke, you know?'

They say the death of a loved one can make time feel like it's stopped. It isn't true. Since Finn called, the world outside has continued to turn. It doesn't make sense to me that I've spent the day doing normal stuff, going to work, stopping at the supermarket on the way home, ordering takeaway . . . and all while my sister had been dead. If only the world *would* stop, I might be able to catch my breath and make sense of it all.

Ivy. My little sister. Dead. The words don't belong in the same sentence and they make my body shiver. I pull the sleeves of my jumper down over my hands as an image of her lying in bed flashes in my mind. I picture her brown skin against white sheets, locked in an endless sleep. Her limbs growing cold, which would never happen in reality. She was always the warm-blooded one out of the two of us. I lift the cup of tea to my mouth, blow on the steaming liquid and then put it straight back down again.

'I always thought we'd sort things out before something serious happened,' I say, but it isn't as if serious things haven't happened since we'd stopped talking. 'I don't know how it's really been seven years.' A frown pulls at my eyebrows.

'I can't believe it's been that long,' Maddie replies.

We'd shared our lives. Ivy and I had made blanket forts and created dance routines as kids. We'd obsessed over pop stars and boy bands, shared bottles of Clearasil and spent Saturday afternoons in Tammy Girl as teenagers. As adults we'd shared a flat and a car. And then it had all come falling down. *Seven years.* Guilt drops in my stomach like a lift in free fall.

'I should've tried harder,' I mutter.

'You did, Jess.'

'Not hard enough,' I reply harshly. 'She's my little sister, and my responsibility.'

I heave a sigh and rub at the headache building in my temples. The lingering scent of lemongrass from our curry dinner floats under my nose from the smeared plates on the coffee table in front of us. Maddie's glass of Malbec is almost empty, and mine still holds a sip of the one unit of red wine I allow myself each night.

I look down at the coffee table. Our MacBooks sit side by side and my ring-bound planner is open in front of me. The rose-gold pen Maddie bought me for my birthday last year still has its cap off, exactly as I'd left it to answer the call from a number I hadn't recognised. I take the pen and put the cap on it to stop it from drying out.

'I'll take care of all this,' Maddie says, leaning forward to close her laptop. 'You don't need to be thinking about work right now.'

'It's always helped before,' I reply, and it's true.

Work has been the one thing that's always been there to catch me. I'd buried myself in it to block out missing Ivy and Finn, not to mention escaping my marriage. The suitcase propping open the living room door is like a sign declaring my almost divorced status, along with all the other boxes and bags dotted throughout the flat, creating trip hazards and bouts of anxiety every time I pass them. It's almost three months since I moved in, and most of my things are still boxed up. My natural need for order and zero clutter was clearly lost along the journey from one end of London to the other when a van full of boxes transported my old life into a new one. The only thing that makes this place feel remotely like home is the macramé wall hanging that had been a wedding gift.

'I just don't want you to feel like you're alone.' Maddie reaches across and puts her hand on my knee, giving it a little squeeze.

'I know I'm not.' I put my hand on top of hers. 'Thanks, Mads. I'm glad you were here.'

The thought of having been alone to take that call makes my insides shudder as I drag myself up from the sofa to go to the toilet. Afterwards, I splash my face with water and look at my reflection in the mirror. My upturned eyes are puffy and red, and tears have left tracks on my cheeks. I close my eyes and press my fingers against them, momentarily relieving the building headache. I can already feel it's one that'll stay with me until tomorrow, but I hate taking painkillers. I take a deep breath before releasing my fingers and catching my reflection again.

I look right into my eyes, so dark I can barely see where the iris ends and the pupil begins. We had the same eyes, Ivy and I. Inherited from Mum. Eyes a man could get lost in, Dad would always say when he reminisced about her. We'd looked similar as kids too, with our conker-brown skin and long, thin limbs, but we couldn't have been any more different. There was just one year between us in age, but we were miles apart in personality. Ivy was the definition of attitude and intensity. She was the mouthy one, who'd talk back and take what she wanted and scream with the unfairness of everything, especially when we were in our early teens. I was the quiet one who took what was given and got on with life, unfair or not. Ivy was like a Tasmanian devil, leaving a riot of upturned chaos wherever she went, borrowing clothes and giving them back with stains and cigarette burns, if I ever got them back at all. Not that it happened too often. My style was far too conservative for her. She was infuriating, and a royal pain in the backside sometimes. And I don't remember ever not loving her.

My eyes swim and I take a deep breath in, counting to ten. I don't want Maddie to worry any more than she already is, so I splash my face again, letting the water wash away any remaining tears. I leave the bathroom and head to the kitchen, where she is stacking the tiny dishwasher.

'Thanks, Mads.' I smile and reach for a glass of water.

She looks at me as I shake out a pharmacy's worth of multivitamins and supplements on the counter. I know what she's thinking. She's thinking that I don't need to take a rainbow spectrum of pills when I'm young, fit and healthy. She's probably right, but keeping myself this way has been my protective blanket for so many years. Mum was only thirty-three when she died and Ivy only turned thirty-five last November. I swallow the pills one by one and Maddie stands beside me, wrapping her arms around my shoulders.

I squeeze my eyes shut and take a deep breath. I know it's impossible, but I wish with everything I have that, when I open them again, everything will be different. I wish I would know what happened to Ivy, where she'd been for the last seven years and what she'd done. Where she worked and who her friends were. I wish I could pick up the phone and ask her. But when I open my eyes, the world is still the same.

Chapter One

Jess

Fourteen years earlier

I huff and lift my knee to hitch the cardboard box I'm carrying up into my arms. My fingers strain under its weight as I quickly shuffle past the tiny kitchen and into the second bedroom.

'Bloody hell, Ivy! What have you got in here?' I ask as I put it on the chest of drawers.

Ivy laughs, dropping a duffel bag onto the floor next to me with a thud. 'Um . . . candles, I think.'

I open one of the flaps and, sure enough, the box is filled with candles in a rainbow of colours, assortment of sizes and variety of scents. She's been collecting them since she was a kid, making Christmas and birthday presents an easy buy. I lift one of them out to double-check the label.

'Jo Malone? Really?' I sniff at it before reading the stylish label that tells me it's *pomegranate noir*. 'Isn't this a bit expensive for you?'

'About three hundred pounds worth of expensive, actually.'

My eyes widen. There's no way on earth my sister would ever spend three hundred pounds on a candle, no matter how much she loves them.

'Noooo, I didn't buy it,' she says, clearly reading the look on my face before grinning. 'It was a present from that guy.'

I lift an eyebrow playfully. 'You'll have to be more specific. Which one?'

'Ha, ha,' she replies with a deadpan voice and rolls her black-lined eyes. 'That older one who was obsessed with sushi. The one with the wax fetish. I told you, remember?'

'Oh, him.' I grimace. 'Ew.'

'This candle was his favourite.' She takes it from me and puts it right in the centre of her windowsill as we both laugh.

I know that, if she has anything to do with it, every available surface in our new flat will be adorned with the flickering of a candle flame.

'What are you girls giggling about?' Dad asks, bringing in the last of the boxes.

He's as fit as ever, despite the greying edges to his hair. We've been traipsing up and down three flights of stairs with boxes, bags and flat-pack furniture, and he's barely even broken a sweat.

'Nothing,' I say, catching Ivy's gaze and trying not to snort with laughter. I'm pretty sure the idea of his youngest daughter pouring wax over the body of a naked man would add a few more grey hairs to his head.

His tall, broad body almost fills the doorway as he shakes his head. 'God help me with you two.'

Ivy laughs. 'He hasn't helped you yet.'

It's a prayer he's offered up more times than I can remember over the years, like when Ivy had snuck out to a party and I'd tried to convince him that her bed hadn't been slept in because she'd slept in mine, and her evident – and first-ever – hangover was a tummy bug. Or the times we used to fight about who got to sit in the front passenger seat of the car. Honestly, I can't imagine what it must be like to bring up two young girls as a single dad.

'Remember that time we swapped your keys around?' Ivy asks and I burst out laughing.

It had been her idea to swap all his keyrings over and he'd spent a solid five minutes trying to get in while we'd sat on the stairs holding down giggles as we watched him through the mottled glass of the front door.

'Hilarious.' Dad tuts playfully.

His face is a little fuller these days, as is his belly, and I look at him with a lump in my throat.

'Are you going to be alright on your own?' I ask.

'Are you kidding?' he laughs. 'I'll finally be able to watch what I want in peace and get to sleep at night without waiting up to hear a key in the lock.'

I playfully whack his arm. 'We weren't that bad.'

'I know *I* wasn't,' Ivy says and the three of us fall about laughing because we all know that definitely isn't true.

I never understood my friends who'd itched to move out of their childhood home as teenagers. They'd wished for the freedom of getting away from overbearing parents, counting down the days until they could go to university or find a job and be able to pay their own rent. But it wasn't like that for Ivy and me. Home was a haven. Dad was fun and kind and generous. He trusted us not to get ourselves into trouble, and he knew I'd be there to make sure we didn't. He did the job of mum *and* dad, and we loved him for it. Now Ivy's back from university, it's a natural time for change. He's got used to having more space and we've grown up. Mum left us a bit of money, so we put it towards a deposit. Our new flat is in Camberwell, so not a million miles away from our childhood home, but far enough to feel like we're making a fresh start. And having a mortgage at twenty-two feels like the right step towards true adulthood.

'Alright,' he says, grabbing the jacket he'd hung on the doorknob. 'I'll nip down to B&Q so we can get on with your wardrobes.'

'Thanks, Dad.' Ivy grins and wraps her arms around his broad belly.

He drops a kiss onto the top of her head and, as Ivy closes her eyes drinking in his attention, I can't help but smile. She has a sense of naivety about her, which is probably why he'd asked me to help look after her after Mum died.

'Nothing to thank me for. You're the ones on cleaning duty.' He grins. 'I'll fetch some fish and chips on the way back.'

I consider telling him that I've decided to go vegan after reading a book that said eating any kind of animal product would basically kill me, but I decide to keep it to myself. I know he's already worried about me getting enough calories and protein without his Jamaican breakfasts of eggs, bammy, dumplings and plantains.

Ivy grins at me when Dad leaves. 'We should throw a house-warming party.'

I roll my eyes. 'You're so predictable. I knew you'd say that.'

'Well, duh. That *is* what you do when you move into a new place, isn't it?'

She stands in front of me in a yellow Care Bears t-shirt that I guess is supposed to be ironic, paired with super low-rise jeans and a spiky choker around her throat. 'Come on. It'll be fun. Remember that time we went to the fair on Clapham Common? You were convinced it would be crap and you had a great time.'

I raise my eyebrows. 'You dragged me on the waltzer and I threw up behind a tree.'

'But you had *fun*.'

I sigh, but I can already see how this will play out. I'll find reasons not to, because I'm the one who looks after the practical things. I had to be. Mum left such a huge gap behind and Dad worked all the hours he could to keep things going. Ivy would sleep with me when she was sick so Dad could rest between shifts, and I'd be the one who folded the laundry and made sure she handed in homework on time, along with finding time to do my own. My being responsible meant that she could be the one to come up with the so-called fun ideas, like going to Thorpe Park or, evidently, having a party.

I look at her as she plays with the ring in her lip. Maybe us moving in together can be something of a fresh start.

'Alright,' I concede, but put my hand up before she can interrupt, 'but only if it's *this* weekend because we're painting next week and the new sofa's being delivered at the end of the month.'

If we're going to have a party, then it should at least be before there's much that can be wrecked in the way of new furniture.

Ivy grins. 'Deal. Oh, it's going to be *so* good. We had the most epic parties at uni.'

I smile and nod as if I know, but I don't. Ivy went off to Sheffield to study hospitality, while I stayed here. I'd got a place at South Bank University and it felt wrong to leave Dad behind. While my evenings over those years were pretty much spent studying at the kitchen table, I know from Ivy's stories that hers were mostly spent necking jelly shots and turning up to lectures barely functioning with the world's worst hangover.

'I'll send out texts straight away. Any hot guys you want to invite?'

'Yeah, sure. They're lining up around the block,' I reply as we head into the kitchen.

It's clean enough, but the perfectionist in me knows that I won't be able to cook anything in here without giving it a thorough clean myself first.

'I don't want to get tied down too early.' I hand a sponge and spray bottle of disinfectant over to Ivy and she takes it from me with a look of amusement on her face.

'Nice. Life's too short to get caught up in a relationship.'

'I mean because I'm focusing on my career right now,' I say and squirt a burst of lemon-scented cleaner onto the tiles behind the sink.

'You've got plenty of time for that,' Ivy replies. 'We're fresh out of uni and we'll never be this young again. This is the time for F.U.N.'

I laugh, scrubbing the tiles. 'I always get a bad feeling when you say that word.'

'It's true. It'll be like *This Life* without all the lawyering, or *Friends* without all the canned laughter, or *Sex and the City* without New York.'

'You'd be Samantha, obviously.'

'But only if you'll be my Charlotte.'

I turn to face her, leaning my forearm against the edge of the sink. 'It *will* be fun, won't it?'

'Are you kidding? Two sisters, sharing a flat in London? It's the stuff romcoms are made of.' She grins and closes the fridge door.

I want to tell her that there's no possible way she could've cleaned the fridge properly in such a short space of time. But I don't. How can I, when she's standing there with that eager grin on her face? She's like an excitable puppy. I just can't help but love her.

'I make an amazing wing-woman too, you know,' she says. 'Just in case you feel like getting a bit flirty.'

I jut my chin out playfully. 'You know what? I may well do that.'

'I like it.' She laughs. 'There's hope for you yet.'

I throw my sponge at her and she ducks, laughing as it narrowly misses her.

'It's not like I plan to have a revolving door on my bedroom or anything. There's only enough room in the flat for one of *those*.'

She playfully sticks her tongue out at me and I laugh back. This feels nice. As Ivy reels off ideas for which cocktails to make and who to invite, I have to admit that I feel a thrill of excitement about the idea of a party now. She has so much enthusiasm, it's contagious. We've always been close, it was impossible not to be, being so near to each other in age. But moving in together feels like an opportunity to go from being sisters to true, best friends. And, if I'm honest, the idea of shedding the mumsy role I've always been in doesn't seem half-bad right now.

Ivy bends down, grabs the sponge and throws it back over to me. I easily catch it with a grin and get back to scrubbing the tiles. She's right, I think. This is going to be pretty fun.

Chapter Two

Ivy

July, nine years ago

What was it about the sun that made everything feel so *good*? Ivy rolled onto her stomach on the lilo and adjusted the towel draped over the plastic material. The coconut oil she'd slathered over her skin sent tropical scented wafts under her nose and she took a sip from her home-made caipirinha as the sun tickled her back. London was positively heatwaving and even though the news blamed climate change, Ivy could only find the positives in it. She loved her city when it was like this.

Ivy sighed with pleasure and propped herself up onto her elbows to look at Jess. 'Isn't this just the best?'

Jess laughed from her deckchair. 'A minute ago you were in *absolute hell.*'

'That was this morning,' Ivy reasoned. 'And I really was.'

She'd woken with a raging hangover – the worst she'd had in ages. She'd had to bolt for the bathroom straight after getting out of bed and had skipped breakfast altogether. If it weren't for Jess, she'd have crawled back under the covers and stayed there, but her sister had lured her up to the flat roof of their building. Jess was like a modern-day Mary Seacole, tending to her with buttered toast and a cup of strong coffee, along with a dose of fresh air. It made being hung-over so much more bearable having her big sister there with her calm, mothering presence. Ivy had lost count of the times she'd been rescued over the last five years of living together. She really did have the best sister in the world. Two hours after waking and feeling absolutely rotten, they were now under the blue sky, coffee had been replaced with cocktails, and Ivy's hangover was all but forgotten.

'So, what exactly did you do to end up in such a state?' Jess asked, flicking through the magazine in her lap.

'Well . . .' Ivy said slowly. Where should she start? 'I had some dates.'

Jess dropped her sunglasses down onto the bridge of her nose and stared at her with wide eyes. 'Some *dates*? Plural?'

'Three.'

'*Three* dates in one day?'

Ivy laughed. 'I can't help it if the world is full of hot men right now. It's not like I had an orgy or anything.' The laugh fell away as the words echoed in her head and the unfamiliar sensation of self-consciousness crept across her cheeks. 'You think it's too much?'

Jess smiled reassuringly. 'Not at all. If anything, I'm impressed you can coordinate more than one guy to date at a time when you can barely coordinate your work shifts.'

Ivy threw the wooden stick from her long-eaten Magnum at her sister.

'I'm joking.' Jess laughed and closed her magazine. 'Tell the truth, I'm a little jealous. I barely rack up three dates a month. Which is fine because I don't have time anyway.'

'All work and no play makes Jess a lonely girl.'

'I'm not lonely. I'm putting my career first. I want to be set up by the time I'm thirty. Three more years of hard grind before I can focus on dating and settling down. There's no point until then.'

Ivy had to smile. It was kind of cute, Jess's idea of the future. Build the career, then meet The One. That dream man who would tick her extensive list of boxes: just the right mix of sensitive and masculine with his hedonistic, wild oat-sowing days behind him, attractive, with an established career and faithful. In Ivy's opinion, it was like searching for a unicorn, and she was certain they were only myths. But, she supposed, if anyone could find this perfect man, it'd be Jess. She was gorgeous. Stunning, really. She had killer legs and boobs that were small enough to get away with not wearing a bra – something Ivy had always envied. Not to mention the fact that she was incredibly smart, had a tidiness obsession that meant the flat was always clean *and* had a good income to boot. And she knew how to look after you when you were sick, or hung-over, which was basically the same thing.

'So, go on,' Jess said, taking her sunglasses off and shifting round to face her. 'Tell me.'

Ivy hesitated about sharing her escapades yesterday. On the other hand, she was dying to tell someone because it was one of those days that just kept unfolding.

'So, remember that Greek guy I told you about from my barista art course? The one who can make those awesome swans and hearts with cappuccino foam?' she asked, and Jess nodded. 'We went for a drink afterwards—'

'But wasn't that the day before yesterday?'

Ivy nodded. It was. They'd gone for a drink to celebrate the last day of the course. Ivy had been adamant she didn't fancy him, despite the way he always seemed to catch her eye. He was too cocky, wore Reebok classics and wasn't tall enough. The list went on. But somewhere between getting their certificates and taking her first sip of wine, she realised she did fancy him. A lot. His banter was good, he was cheeky and flirty, and he'd offered her his hoodie when the evening chill set in.

'We went for a drink and then had a nightcap,' Ivy said with a little smile. 'At his place.'

'Of *course*. What other kind of nightcap is there?' Jess shook her head but smiled back. 'So, what then?'

'It was good.' Ivy grinned. 'Really, *really* good. What he can do with his—'

'La, la, la, la, la!' Jess stuck her fingers in her ears and Ivy laughed.

'Alright, alright, I'll stop,' she said as Jess removed her fingers. 'Jeez, you're such a prude.'

'I'm not. I just don't know why you need to go into detail. We both know what they look like and where they go.'

Ivy rolled her eyes. 'Anyway, I'd totally forgotten about the date I'd arranged with Filip, the Portuguese guy I met at that party last week. So when I woke up, I had to race back home from East London, shower, cram in breakfast and then go to up Camden to meet him.'

'This is the doctor, right?'

'Right.' Ivy nodded. 'And he's so cute. Like, really cute. His smile is perfect, his biceps are perfect, even his teeth are perfect.'

'So why do I sense a *but* coming up?'

Ivy turned to sit up and the lilo squeaked beneath her as she crossed her legs. 'There was no spark. None.'

'Out of ten?'

'One?'

Jess pulled a face.

'I know,' Ivy groaned. 'And it was so frustrating because I mean, the man is gorgeous. I could see the way other women were looking at him and . . .' She shrugged and let her hands fall into her lap. 'There was just nothing there for me.'

'Maybe you could send him my way in a few years.' Jess smiled. 'He sounds nice. And a doctor.'

'He smokes,' Ivy replied, reaching for her pouch of tobacco.

'In that case . . .' Jess grimaced and waved a hand dismissively.

'So anyway, we had a nice afternoon walking around London Zoo, taking the piss out of the monkeys and shrieking at the spiders. It was nice in a refreshingly platonic kind of way.' Ivy smiled. 'But, in the end, it wasn't for me. He's too clean-cut.'

'Okay, but none of this explains why you woke up looking like something from *28 Days Later*,' Jess pointed out.

Ivy sprinkled tobacco into her cigarette paper, crisping the dry strands between her fingers. 'That's Micha's fault.'

'Who's Micha?'

'The Croatian guy in the block next door.'

'Oh my God,' Jess said, shaking her head again. 'This is like some crazy, international edition of *Take Me Out*. The Greek, the Portuguese and the Croatian.'

Ivy laughed, licking her paper and rolling it shut. 'It was fun, though. We just hung out, drinking some crazy Croatian home-made liquor until I don't even know what time. Not a single drop of bodily fluids was exchanged, apart from sharing a shot glass.'

The last twenty-four hours were actually much less hedonistic than they first sounded. She hadn't slept with, or even kissed, more than one of them. If she were in New York, it would've been a totally typical Saturday for a single woman. Last night, before she'd gotten too drunk, she'd stood on Micha's balcony with the balmy evening heat on her skin. The scent of doner kebab had wafted in the air from the shop on the corner, and in the distance the twinkly lights of London's cityscape had shone against the night sky. It had been one of those days where one thing had just flowed into the next and she'd savoured every moment. Even if she had paid for it this morning.

Ivy lit her cigarette and blew a puff of smoke through her mouth. 'So that's how I ended up like I did. Thanks for saving me.'

'I'm pretty sure it's in my job description.'

'I know. But you do it really well and I appreciate it.'

She really did. She'd had so much fun at university, but Ivy had missed her sister, even if she wouldn't have much approved of the study/party ratio. Jess had a way of making everything feel homely. She was a natural caretaker and would make a great mum one day. Ivy, on the other hand, was made to help people forget about whatever was going on, usually with a glass of something chilled and alcoholic, and bring in the good times. They couldn't be any more different. Jess was firmly in the world of early commuting, nine-to-fives and weekends spent recovering from the week. Ivy couldn't imagine anything worse, but it was exactly that mothering, responsible side of Jess that had brought Ivy back from near death that morning *and* had inflated the lilos to make the most of the sunshine.

Jess heaved a sigh that sounded like it had made its way up through the ground and all the levels of their building before finally coming out of her mouth. Ivy stubbed her half-smoked roll-up out on the gritty surface of the roof. Jess needed to let off some steam. Ivy got that she was focused on her career, but she had been ever since they'd moved in together. The last five years had been all work and minimal, sporadic play for Jess. Ivy knew where her strengths lay. She couldn't always be relied on to make sure the loo roll was never empty, but she sure as hell could be the one who provided a healthy amount of *life* to balance all the work.

'Alright,' she said, blowing the last plume of smoke from her mouth. 'Next weekend, we're having a house party. We're both going to get dressed up, paint the town red and have fun.'

'Only you could plan a party when hung-over.' Jess laughed before shaking her head. 'And in case you've forgotten, there's a house-party ban after the one we had when we moved in.'

Ivy grimaced. It had been wild and fun, but Jess had fumed about the state of the flat and they hadn't had one since.

'Oh, come on. That was *years* ago,' Ivy said, rolling her eyes. 'We're adults now.'

'No. Next week is going to be all kinds of madness at work, and—'

'—and that's exactly why you need a night out,' Ivy interrupted.

'What I *need* is a holiday. With a beach and sand. We could probably find a cheap one before the summer's done. Portugal, maybe? Or Tenerife?'

'Sounds great,' Ivy agreed. 'We can absolutely go on holiday, but we can totally *still* party next week. You told me to remind you when you needed to have fun, remember?'

'I remember,' Jess conceded, raising her eyebrow. 'I just don't remember why I'd ever have said such a silly thing.'

'Because you know that without me, you'd be chained to your work desk and letting your life pass you by. I know you're all about your career right now, but these are our twenties! We're supposed to be having fun and doing all kinds of silly stuff.' Ivy grinned. 'Plus, one of my old uni mates is moving back to London and this'll be a great way to integrate him.'

'Ah.' Jess nodded. 'So it's about a guy. I should've guessed.'

Ivy grinned and put her empty glass down. 'It's not *just* about a guy but yep, there is one and yep, he's gorgeous.'

'That's not like you to have a second round with a guy.'

'Well, we never got around to a first one.'

Jess raised her eyebrows. 'Also not like you.'

Ivy laughed. 'I just didn't make it happen yet. But I will.'

'At the party?'

'Why not? Parties are a great place for such things.' Ivy shrugged with a wide grin. 'If we have one, that is.'

Jess tutted and shook her head. 'Fine. We'll have one. But I am *not* cleaning up on my own and it's a closed invite list. No waifs and strays.'

If there was one thing Ivy knew how to do well, it was how to bring people together, create an atmosphere of fun and make the kind of memories you looked back on with a smile.

She crossed her heart with her fingers. 'You're going to have a blast, I promise.'

Chapter Three

JESS

July, nine years ago

There's a clown staring back at me from the mirror with lips painted scarlet red and eyes rimmed with black liner. I groan and shake my head, reaching for a cotton pad from the bag on the chest of drawers.

'Uh-uh.' Ivy whacks the back of my hand with her blusher brush.

'I look like Lily Savage.'

'A middle-aged white man? Really?' Ivy fixes me with a look that reminds me so much of Mum it takes my breath away for a second. But whereas Mum's look would stop us playing up in the supermarket or quieten us down on the bus, Ivy's is much more playful, with a hint of being up to absolutely no good.

I turn to look at Maddie. 'What do *you* think?'

She nods appreciatively from her seat on Ivy's bed. 'You look great. Different, but great.'

I don't usually do make-up, let alone like this. I look back in the mirror and try to see past the bold colour streaked across my lips.

'It's so in your face,' I mumble.

'Which is the point,' Ivy replies, closing the blusher. I realise, as she puts it down into the bowl on the dresser, it's actually mine. 'You look hot. You never know, you might even pull.'

I roll my eyes, brushing the compliment to one side. 'I doubt that very much.'

'Ugh, can't you get some optimism into her?' Ivy says to Maddie, who laughs and shrugs.

'From what I hear the dating pool is pretty slim pickings these days.'

'Exactly. *You're* practically married,' I say before turning to Ivy, 'and *you're* up for anything—'

'And *you're* too picky,' Ivy says, finishing my sentence for me.

'After the last two, can you blame me?'

Ivy and Maddie both nod in reluctant agreement. One date had talked all the way through dinner about his ex-wife and the other had admitted that one of the reasons he'd asked me out was because he'd always had a fantasy of sleeping with an 'ebony' woman. I shudder inside just at the thought of it and sigh. Whatever, it doesn't matter.

'Anyway, I'm focusing—'

'On your job,' they both chime in.

'We know,' Ivy adds with a theatrical roll of her eyes. 'Anyone would think you're working for some huge, soul-sucking global corporation instead of a tiny printing company in Hendon.'

'I will be, soon enough,' I reply.

Hendon isn't quite Canary Wharf or The City, but I'm patient. After getting my marketing degree, I purposefully looked for a small company to work for to get my bearings so I could take a few courses on the side. I'm almost through one on social media, which I know will come in handy at some point, and have another in bookkeeping starting next year.

I look at my little sister as she cackles at something Maddie says, throwing her long, electric-blue braids over her shoulder. She's always been the centre of attention. She was born for it. Ivy pours shots of tequila to get us in the mood before the party starts and the silver chain across her belly glints in the light. With her brown-suede mini-skirt and off-the-shoulder top, she looks like a black Kate Hudson from *Almost Famous*.

'Maybe I should get changed,' I say, readjusting the straps of the plain white vest I've teamed up with a pair of Daisy Duke style shorts.

'Are you kidding? You look fab,' Ivy replies. 'If I had legs like yours . . .'

She shakes her head and Maddie coos in agreement. I look down at my legs, freshly shaven and coated in cocoa butter, before looking back up at Ivy. I know she wouldn't let me wear something that made me look awful, especially to a party. I look in the mirror again. I suppose the red lipstick does sit nicely against my skin tone. I'd never have gone for it myself but I have to hand it to my little sister – I *do* look pretty damned good.

'Thanks.' I smile. 'Anyway. Tonight is all about you.'

'Oh, right!' Maddie nods. 'The guy from uni?'

Ivy grins and hands a glass to Maddie. 'If I have anything to do with it, yes.'

'I wish I had so much confidence when it came to such things,' Maddie says with a grin, and I have to agree.

'I'm telling you, tonight is going to be so epic, I can't even cope.' Ivy grins and nods to my tequila.

I grimace. I really hate shots, but Ivy is right about me needing to find my fun to balance out all the work I've been doing.

'Come on, Jess,' Ivy says, tilting her head to the side and fixing me with that innocent look of hers.

'I'll have the worst hangover in the world.'

'So will I.'

'And me,' Maddie chimes in with a grin.

'Ugh.' I sigh, but the corners of my mouth twitch with a smile. I know I'm going to pay for this tomorrow but the feeling of saying *screw it* for just one night is sitting nicely with me right now.

I pick up my sticky shot glass and we clink them together before I close my eyes and down the tequila.

◆　◆　◆

It might be down to the alcohol running wild in my bloodstream, but his eyes disarm me. The brown outer rims of his irises are stark against the depth of green inside them and, even though I'm sitting down, I feel slightly off balance.

'Mind if I join you?' The curves of his lips change as he speaks with a warm, mellow voice.

I've no idea who this guy is but, then again, I have no idea who most of the people downstairs are either.

'Sure.' I nod and he lets the fire escape door shut behind him before sitting next to me on the ground.

The action of nodding makes my head swim for a second and I take a deeper lungful of the fresh air I'd come up to the roof for. After a rainy start, the sun came out and the party could move from our flat to the shared garden. I'm secretly relieved that everyone can make use of the mismatched wooden chairs and fake lawn instead of being cooped up in a flat we'll have to clean tomorrow. It's not the prettiest of places up here. It's bare, and the surface of the flat roof is sprinkled with grit, a few pigeon feathers and a lot of dust. I'm not sure what this guy is doing up here.

'Cheers,' he says, brushing the palms of his hands across his black jeans.

Despite the vastness of the space around us, this section of wall is the only bit of the roof where you can comfortably sit and lean back against something flat. The music playing in the garden carries in the air and I pick at the label on my bottle of beer. It's flat and warm, and the only reason I took it was to keep Ivy happy. He sits with his back against the wall and his bent legs spread in front of him. His elbows rest on his knees and he holds a pack of Marlboro in one of his hands.

'Want one?'

I turn enough to look at his face, and a wave of disappointment hits me. His eyes are even more startling up close and they make my already mushy insides swirl even more. I really must be drunk, because despite the box of Marlboro, I can't take my eyes off him.

I shake my head. 'I don't smoke.'

'Neither do I, it's a filthy habit,' he says, speaking through the corner of his mouth while he dips his head to touch the tip of his cigarette against the flame in his cupped hand.

'Spoken like a true social smoker,' I reply with a hint of a smile and he chuckles.

'Guilty.' His eyes twinkle at me in the late evening sunshine and my belly flips. 'I'm Finn.'

'Jess.'

'Ah. The sister.'

I raise my eyebrows. '*The sister?* That sounds ominous.'

Finn laughs. 'You've been a bit of a mystery, that's all.'

I'm assuming he's one of Ivy's many, many friends and my forehead pulls into an amused frown. I'm pretty certain nobody has ever described me as mysterious until now.

'I'm not sure I'm any less of a mystery now. We've only just met.'

'True,' he concedes with a nod. 'But the fact that you're up here tells me a fair bit about you already.'

'Oh yeah? Like what?' I ask and turn my body to face him completely.

I cross my legs and let the warm beer bottle rest against my inner thigh. He narrows his eyes at me a little, as if he's sizing me up, and I fight the flush in my cheeks. Thank God my skin is dark enough to conceal it.

'My first thought is, you're getting some fresh air. Maybe you're a bit tipsy?'

I laugh and roll my eyes. 'Wow. I bet Sherlock is quaking in his boots with that observation.'

Finn laughs back. 'I'm just getting started.'

'Oh, really? Go on then.' I raise an eyebrow. 'Read me.'

When was the last time I felt this quick and witty? A while ago, I'm sure. If ever. Even when I'm on top dating form, I rarely feel brave enough to be like this. He stubs his cigarette out on the floor and turns to face me too, mirroring my posture. He puts his hands on his knees and his fingertips graze the bare skin of mine, making my breath catch in my throat.

'Okay,' he says, tipping his head to one side. His jawline is coated with light stubble that reaches down to his Adam's apple. 'So, I'm sticking with the tipsy thing but if that were the only reason, you'd have stayed in the garden with everyone else. Nobody in their right mind goes up to the roof after one too many unless they're willing to fall off it.'

The way his green eyes glint keeps the corner of my mouth lifted into a curious smile. 'Is that right?'

He nods. 'So the fact that you're up here and not down there with everyone else tells me you're someone who needs their own space. Even at a party. Maybe *especially* at a party.'

I tilt my head from side to side. 'Good. But anyone could come to that conclusion.'

'Hold on.' He lifts his hands from his knees and laughs. 'Jeez, you're a tough crowd.'

My lips pull into a close-mouthed grin and I dip my head in a way that tells him to continue.

'So. Where was I?' He clears his throat and looks me right in the eye with full concentration.

The intensity of his stare makes my shoulders tremble with bubbles of nervous laughter and he lifts his palms up again with a look of mock exasperation on his face.

'I'm sorry.' I splutter and swallow the giggles back down as I sit up straight. 'Go on.'

He looks at me with a sceptically raised eyebrow and I hold my face still with neutrality. After a few seconds, he smiles a little and goes back to gazing at me with his startling eyes.

'You're not used to attention,' he continues. 'And you're not sure if you like it, or want to hide from it.'

His words land right in the centre of my chest and my grin falters a little.

'You're shy. A little reserved. Someone who prefers to be behind the scenes instead of out there in the thick of it.' He bends his arms, putting his elbows on his knees and resting his chin on his domed knuckles. 'But every now and again, when the conditions are just right, you like to be seen.'

My chest rises and falls as my breath deepens and somehow quickens at the same time. I keep myself completely still as I stare back into the eyes of this man I've never met before but who seems to see me so clearly.

'You're the one who takes responsibility for things but deep down, you want someone to give you the chance to kick back instead of always being the one to sort everything out. The role of caretaker . . .' The tone of his voice rises as his voice trails off, and he shrugs. 'It's not the one you chose or were made for. Not really.'

I swallow and remember to breathe, waiting for the next observation to come. But it doesn't. The air around us crackles, as if we're a pair of electrodes with streaks of energy passing between us. Is it real, or in my head? The look on his face tells me it might well be the former. The light around us has shifted to that golden, amber tone that the sunset pours from the sky and the sound of trumpets rises from the garden with a jazzy song. The reflected heat from the flat roof seeps up from its surface, into my legs and hips. As Finn and I stare at each other, the heat intensifies, between my legs, into my belly and up the length of my spine. My skin prickles with it until I feel like I'm in a sauna. The light catches the gold lettering of his cigarette pack, and I drag my eyes away from his.

'Give me one of those,' I say, knowing that my impoliteness will wash over him. After everything he's just said, we're way past that point.

That I'm willing to poison my lungs is a testament to how much this man has shaken me up. I try to tell myself that the whole night is a write-off anyway thanks to Ivy and Maddie's persistence with the alcohol as Finn silently pulls one out of the box. He keeps his eyes trained and unwavering on mine. My lips close around the cigarette in a way that feels provocative and completely appropriate and I wonder what my sister and best friend would say if they could see me now.

Finn lights the tip and I slowly pull the smoke in, overcoming the urge to cough. It's only the second cigarette I've ever smoked – my first was in Year Eight at the park with friends and it made me vomit on my shoes. My fingers tremble as I blow it back out and he reaches his hand over to take the cigarette from mine. For a few seconds, we share it, smoking in turns, passing it back and forth between us while I try to process all the things he's said.

'So, how did I do?' he eventually asks.

I nod a few times, trying to sum up the magnitude of it. 'Oh, you know. Not bad.'

He smiles and opens his lips a fraction, the tip of his tongue right there between his teeth. I never noticed until this precise moment just how sensual lips are. How kissable *his* are. How soft and full and completely enticing such a simple thing as a mouth could be.

'That'll do,' he replies with a humble grin.

'So go on,' I say, reaching out for the cigarette and letting my fingers brush against his. 'Spill it. How did you manage to come to all that from a few seconds on a roof?'

Finn shrugs and shakes his head as if he's not quite sure how to answer. 'I've always been good at reading people. Plus, I already saw you downstairs.'

He did? I try to think if I'd seen him in the flat or the garden, but I'm pretty sure I didn't. There's no way I'd have forgotten him. My cheeks get hot as I realise that he must've been watching me closely enough to read me like an open, completely free-for-all book with frightening accuracy.

'I didn't see you,' I reply nonchalantly, and he laughs.

'Well, there's a lot of people here.'

'Meanwhile, you're still a complete mystery to me,' I say, stubbing the cigarette out.

'What do you want to know?' he asks with ease.

After the depth of what he'd said to me, all the questions coming to mind sound completely superficial.

'For someone who's such a people person, what are you doing up here instead of down there?'

He laughs, making his Adam's apple bob up and down. 'They've started playing spin the bottle.'

I pull a face. 'Oh, God.'

'Yep. I thought it best to escape before being asked to put my car keys in a bowl.'

I laugh with a loud snort and instantly put a hand over my mouth, mortified.

'What was *that*?' The skin around Finn's eyes crinkles and creases as he falls into laughter that, even though is about me, is warming enough to smother my embarrassment completely.

Our giggles float out into the balmy air and despite being on top of a building filled with people, in a city of millions, it's hard for me to imagine even a single one of them. The only thing I'm aware of right now is him. And us. Here, on this roof. We both sigh as the last of the laughter fades and Finn motions towards my bottle.

'Can I have a swig? I left mine downstairs.'

'Knock yourself out,' I reply, handing it to him. Just as he puts it to his lips and takes a sip, I add, 'It's warm and flat though.'

He grimaces and shakes his head. 'Jeez. How long have you been nursing that?'

'I'm not a big drinker.'

'Evidently.' He grins and looks away, out at the other apartment blocks and buildings around us.

I study his profile, taking in the shape of his nose and the curves of his lips. There is something about him and his ruggedness that I can't help being pulled in by. He turns back to look at me with a lopsided smile that makes my insides fizzle.

'You know, I got my first kiss with spin the bottle. Her name was Joanna Downs and we were eleven.'

I giggle and put my hands behind me as I lean back, feeling the grit and warmth of the roof's surface under my palms. 'And how was it?'

'Awful. I tried to go in with the tongue like my friend had told me to do, but she freaked out . . .' He shudders playfully. 'Complete disaster.'

'Oh, now that explains a lot. Maybe you're up here so you don't have to relive past trauma.'

He grins back. 'Yeah, maybe.'

I realise the music playing from the garden has stopped as my phone vibrates from my back pocket.

Ivy: In bed already??? Lame! We're going to the pub, then to a club if you wake up and wanna join xx

'Sorry, one sec,' I say to Finn and quickly reply.

Jess: On the roof, not up for clubbing. Have fun xx No luck with your guy??

Ivy: Left already! Also lame. LOL. Don't wait up. xx

I definitely won't. Knowing Ivy she'll not be back until midday tomorrow. I put the phone back in my pocket and turn back to Finn.

'So what do you do when you're not reading people?'

'I think if we're going to go down that road, we need something decent to drink.'

'Oh, so you hate your job?'

'Not at all. I'm a chef and I love it. But I *hate* being thirsty.'

He does that thing again, smiling with the tip of his tongue between his teeth, and a number of scenarios go through my head. I could go down, relieve my aching bladder and then bring drinks up here. Or he could do it. Both options mean pausing whatever this is, and there's a part of me that feels like if we do, the spell might be broken. Like we'd be leaving the warmth and intimacy of a special cocoon behind. Or, the third option is that we go downstairs together to a now empty flat. Judging from the lift of his eyebrows and the way we stand up at the same time, we've both decided to take the latter.

◆ ◆ ◆

'Didn't anyone ever tell you that mixing drinks is dangerous?' I grin, shaking my head in a very wobbly way as Finn pours a small measure of wine into his glass. 'How does that saying go? *Whisky before wine and you'll pay the fine?*'

'I always thought it was *wine before whisky and you'll be fine.* Maybe it's the other way around?'

We both fall into laughter and I take a sip from his glass. 'Who knows?'

'I thought you weren't a big drinker?' Finn asks with a raised eyebrow. 'Now you're just breaking the rules.'

'We can't be good all the time.'

Who am I? I seem to have turned into the kind of woman I've always wanted to be. Maybe it's the make-up and skimpy clothes, but I've morphed into someone who's fun, light-hearted and unapologetically flirty. We're sitting at the little round dining table that's laden with a variety of booze. The flat is a mess but I don't care, which definitely isn't like me at all, and I feel a burst of pride about how Ivy would approve. I'm having far too much fun sitting here with Finn. His laugh is gentle and at odds with the loud, barrelling sound his rugged style might assume. If I had to describe him, I'd call him understated, cosy and a little rough around the edges. His hair is cut in a completely non-defined style and his jaw is coated in light-brown bristles. I try my best, but it's simply impossible not to appreciate his toned forearms as he pushes the dark green sleeves of his long-sleeved t-shirt up to his elbows.

'These are probably a good idea,' he says, pushing one of the many bowls of mixed nuts that Ivy classed as food for tonight towards me.

Usually, I wouldn't eat from a bowl like this. It'd be too unhygienic. God only knows how many other grubby fingers have been in there, but the ratio of food to alcohol in my system is low enough to make the bowl look positively Michelin starred. I prise a cashew from the bowl and pop it into my mouth. The tang of salt hits my tongue, followed by the sharpness of chilli as I suck the remnants of it from my finger. I don't even think about what I might have touched since last washing my hands. All I can think about is Finn. Maybe it's being in such close proximity to him, or that I've drunk more alcohol tonight than I have in the last year. Maybe it's being indoors as opposed to the vastness of the roof, but it feels like my sensibilities have been pushed to one side. A thrill blooms inside as I realise that I'm happy to let them stay there.

The sun has long since set, and the only light around us comes from the paper lamp in the corner. Finn is sitting directly in front of me and, with every move he makes, I get a hint of his aftershave, a mix of something musky with a hint of citrus. It makes me think of hazy summer days that feel endless in both time and possibilities. I stretch my legs out to put my feet between his on the footrest under his seat. He drops a few nuts into his hand and his eyes meet mine. I swallow. There's something about the way he looks at me. How his right eyebrow lifts by just a millimetre and the intensity of his gaze deepens to make it feel like he's zoned out the rest of the entire world to take in our conversation.

'So,' I say, leaning back in my wooden chair. 'Since you're a chef, what's your favourite food?'

'Beans on toast.'

I laugh, shaking my head. 'Really?'

'Sure. It's comfort food at its best. Reminds me of breakfast on a Saturday morning as a kid.'

'That's sweet. Favourite dessert?'

'Apple crumble, without a doubt.'

'With custard?'

He frowns. 'Is there such a thing as apple crumble *without* custard? I don't think so.'

I laugh again and shrug. 'I never much liked it. I haven't had custard since school and it was always thick and lumpy.'

Finn shudders. 'That's a good enough reason to be put off. But proper, silky custard with a tart apple crumble? That's heaven. My aunt has a tree with the best apples I've ever had.'

'So what is it about food?' I ask. 'I mean, why choose it as a profession?'

I'm not exactly adventurous with my nutrition. I learned how to cook when I was young, but it was never a passion.

Finn leans back in his chair and smiles. 'Food is connection. When you eat with someone, it brings you closer together, whether it's with family or friends, or your boss. And it's about memories. I like to cook the things I grew up with – traditional British food. Updated, of course. One day, I'll have my own restaurant and that'll be the theme.'

This man is a bit of a paradox. He has an actual profession, one that he takes seriously from what he's telling me. He has future goals and what seems like a clear path to get there. He sounds just as ambitious as I am. He doesn't seem to fit the mould of the guys Ivy usually hangs out with.

'Is that what you served up in your restaurant in . . .' I shake my head, ignoring the fact that my vision takes a second to catch up with the movement. 'Where was it you said you lived again?'

'Gothenburg,' he says. 'And yeah, beans on toast was on the menu. A kind of re-imagined, posh version of it anyway.'

35

I laugh, trying to imagine him in chef's whites, expertly slicing vegetables and sautéing things I probably would never dare cook myself. It doesn't match at first but, when I think about it, I'd have guessed he did something with his hands. Which he does. It just isn't the carpentry or mechanical work I'd have guessed at. I look at his hands and, sure enough, they look like they might belong to a chef, with a couple of scars, maybe from accidental brushes against the stove or a nick from a knife.

'And how was Sweden?' I ask. 'Is it really the utopia we think it is? Is everyone all happy and healthy and beautiful?'

Finn laughs. 'And shopping at IKEA?'

'Ha, ha,' I reply with a deadpan tone.

'They do all drive Volvos, though.'

'Really?'

He laughs again and I lightly whack his thigh with the back of my hand. 'You're hilarious.'

'I couldn't resist,' he replies, holding a hand up in mock surrender.

'They're always coming out as the happiest people on earth or whatever, so there must be *something* to the stereotype.'

'Well, I definitely *felt* happy there so they must be doing something right.'

'Why'd you come back?'

'I got a job offer here that I couldn't really pass up. Great restaurant, creative menu, whispers of a Michelin star. It would've been silly not to.' His eyes lock on to mine. 'I'm glad I did.'

My belly jumps, double somersaults and triple pikes at the way he says it, because so am I. I reach for my glass, just to have something to distract myself with, but it's a feeble effort that's no match for the tiny strip of skin that peeks out at me as his t-shirt lifts while he leans back to take his phone from his pocket. It's the colour of eggshells and I find myself wondering if he has a smattering of freckles across his shoulder blades or a sprinkling of hairs on his chest.

'Damn,' he says. 'I should be going if I want to catch the last train.'

'Where do you have to get to?'

'Muswell Hill.'

He'll never catch the last train now and a night bus will take forever. I reach for the Pastis and pour some into my glass. It's an awful drink, but if I don't have it, I might well chicken out. Finn doesn't say anything, but I feel his eyes on me as I tilt my head and knock it back. I might have had enough alcohol to knock out my liver tonight, but that shot was exactly what I needed to kill my shyness.

'You could stay,' I suggest. 'If you want.'

It's the first time I've ever said that to a man and, I have to admit, it makes me feel oddly powerful inside. What would Ivy do, if it were her? I barely need to ask the question. If she were here, she'd be cheering me on, telling me to throw caution to the wind and end my dating drought by taking his hand and leading him to my bedroom. It's so far removed from what *I* would do, but there's something in the way he holds himself that brings out a kick of rebellion in me. It makes me want to step out of what I've always done, and do something different instead. I look down and realise that his knees aren't so wide apart any more. They're right outside of mine, sandwiching my legs between his, as if they've moved closer on the suggestion that he stay.

I put my glass down, ignoring the urge to take the invitation back. Because screw it. I'm always playing it safe. Always being responsible. I'd promised Ivy I'd let my hair down and I need this. My heart speeds up in my chest as I put my feet on the ground and a jolt of electricity shoots between my legs as I inch forward in my seat. For once, I want to be the one to have fun, to have the morning-after story to tell.

It feels like there's a magnet between the two of us, closing the gap between our bodies inch by inch until his lips land on mine and I close my eyes to drink in the sheer bliss of it. The sound of traffic through the open window drowns out to nothing until all I can hear is my heart beating wildly in my chest, throat and ears. It feels too good to stop. I don't want to break off our kiss, or move the hand that's firmly, yet tenderly cupping the back of my neck. And so I don't.

Chapter Four

JESS

July, nine years ago

Sharp sunlight burns the back of my closed eyelids, but I couldn't move to get up and close the blinds, even if I wanted to. Instead, I let myself drift back to sleep, ignoring the groaning of my bladder and the dryness of my throat, enticed by the body heat spooning around my back. When I wake again, the heat is gone and I slowly peek one eye open. The blackout blinds have been drawn and the room is in darkness. My eyebrows pinch together as I hoist myself up on one elbow. The other side of my bed is empty, but the pillow is creased and, as I shift the duvet a little, the delicate, barely-there scent of citrus aftershave floats under my nose and – I can't help it – I smile.

I burrow back under the covers and wrap them around me like a cocoon with my smile growing into a grin. I feel physically awful – there's no escaping the hangover – but the heat flushing into my cheeks is delicious. Finn's scent wraps around me and the faint recollection of him dropping a kiss on my forehead at some point this morning sends a shiver across my skin. The memory of his hands on my body both thrills and shocks me.

I had sex last night. With someone I barely even know. A burst of giggles flutters in my chest at the madness of it. It's so unlike me, so outside the realms of my normal that if it weren't for the smell of him on my sheets, I might wonder if I'd hallucinated it. I breathe under the sheets, inhaling the scent of his aftershave and exhaling the warm air back out onto my skin. We might have only met last night, but it's wrong to say I barely know him. I might not know much about his life, but there had been something about him that made him familiar and safe. Safe enough to bring back to my bed.

My body starts to overheat, so I push the covers down and lie on my back, staring at the ceiling. My head is pounding as if it's being picked apart by someone with an axe. My belly is swirling and leaping, both with the remnants of yesterday's alcohol and the flashbacks of last night. I turn my head and see a glass of water that I know hadn't been there earlier. Finn must have poured it out before leaving and, even though it's an act of kindness, I tell myself not to let it mean too much. He's a nice guy, maybe he does this all the time. Straight away, I find myself wondering if he'd be this considerate if we did it all over again, but then I shake my head. If we did meet again, he'd see the real, and sober, Jess isn't the flirty, confident woman he'd met last night.

I hear movement on the other side of my bedroom door. Ivy must be home, which means I must have slept most of the morning away. If she could see me now, she'd be proud. Pulling a guy *and* having a lie-in is not normally how my weekends go. If I tell her about last night, she'll want all the gory details – how muscular he was, how well he kissed, how big was he and, most importantly, was he any good? Ivy isn't shy about sharing details from her sexual conquests, but it's not my style. I don't want to share any of it. Not yet, anyway. Maybe I'll want to soon, but for now, I want to keep it all to myself. Instead, I lie a little longer, trying to let the deliciousness of it battle the hangover brewing inside me. I recall the buzz of my skin as his lips had traced their way up my legs and how tender, yet surprisingly intense sleeping with him had been until, eventually, I have to get up.

I slowly swing my legs from the bed and let my feet rest on the soft rug on the floor. The action of sitting up makes my head throb, and I rest my elbows on my knees, holding my head in my hands until it subsides. I move slowly, pulling on a pair of leggings and a hoodie before stumbling to the door. I open it and am hit by a gush of fresh air and, if I'm not mistaken, the sharp tang of disinfectant spray.

'Ouch. That looks painful,' Ivy says, and I wince, leaning against the doorjamb.

Now that I'm up and about, the hangover has notched from average to raging. Ivy, on the other hand, looks disturbingly fresh.

'How do you look so normal?'

'I'm pretty sure I'm still wasted.' She grins. 'It'll catch me later.'

I must be hallucinating. Why else would Ivy have a black bin liner in her hands? She ties it up and the sound of bottles and cans clinking together floats out into the air. I frown and peek my head around to look at the living room and kitchen.

'You've tidied up?' I ask.

Ivy shrugs. 'That was the deal, wasn't it?'

It was, but I didn't really expect it would happen. The windows are wide open, the dining table is clear and, aside from a messy floor, I might not have been able to tell there'd been a party here the night before at all.

'It's good that you're up,' Ivy says. 'I was just about to vacuum.'

'Okay, now I'm pretty sure I've woken up in a parallel universe,' I reply. If there's one thing Ivy hates, it's pushing the vacuum cleaner around.

She laughs. 'You can talk, with that hangover.'

We grin at each other and I shake my head as minimally as I can without exacerbating my headache. 'It helps knowing I don't have to clean the flat alone. Thanks.'

There are times when Ivy can be a pain in the backside, but there are also times when she's the sweetest sister someone could wish for. This is one of them.

'Well you looked after me last weekend, I figured it's your turn,' she says, putting the bin bag on the floor. 'Breakfast smoothie?'

'I'm getting breakfast too?' I raise my eyebrows. Part of me is wondering if she's done something terrible and is trying to butter me up, but I take her on good faith and shrug. 'I'd kill for a coffee. And eggs.'

'An egg-eating vegan? Must be bad,' Ivy replies with a laugh. 'Don't take forever in the shower, I'm starved.'

Yesterday, I'd resigned myself to a monstrous morning. I'd predicted a hangover and borderline anger at waking and seeing the state of the flat. As I stand under the shower, I feel a strange sense of satisfaction. True, my head is throbbing and my tummy feels unsettled, but I don't have to lift a finger around the flat now and, to top it off, I'd had a luscious night with a fit guy. I'd be lying if I said there wasn't a hint of shame tugging at my conscience. One-night stands have always seemed sordid to me. There was no space for connection or intimacy. Or so I'd thought. Last night had felt intimate, and it helps to quiet that shame back down. I suppose they can't be all bad. Ivy has them all the time. If I told her I'd done the same, she'd probably high-five me and give me some kind of initiatory sisterly medal.

By the time I've finished showering and got dressed, I feel more human. The scent of coffee is thick in the air and Ivy hands me a cup as I walk into the living room.

'Thanks,' I sigh gratefully before taking a gulp and settling on the sofa. 'Wow.'

I look at the plates on the coffee table: scrambled eggs, a couple of my vegan sausages, buttered toast and baked beans with onions and curry powder in them, just how Mum used to do them. It's the total opposite of what I normally eat and, right now, it looks perfect.

'You're welcome.' Ivy grins as I reach for one of the plates. 'So what did you get up to last night? When I last saw you, you didn't look drunk enough to look like *that*.'

Heat flares to my cheeks as I pick up a triangle of toast. I can't quite bring myself to share what went on between my sheets last night, so I shake my head.

'I'm too hungry to talk. You go first.'

'Oh, the party got a bit quiet—'

'—before or after spin the bottle?'

'After. And you know what the neighbours are like about noise, so we went to the pub around the corner.' Ivy picks up a sausage and bites the top off it. 'We played darts – don't ask me how because we were all hammered and I'm pretty sure darts when you're that drunk is probably illegal. And then we decided to go to Heaven.'

'The gay club?'

'It was sooooo good. We met a bunch of girls on a hen night on the way there and had a singing competition on the bus. Even the driver got involved.'

'Only you could do that. If it were me, I'd have gotten thrown off.'

'It's my charm, what can I say. It's probably the same charm that let me steal some poor guy's fairy wings outside the Tube station.'

I shake my head and laugh, loading beans onto some more toast. 'Did you take photos?'

'Obvs.' She rolls her eyes and puts her plate back down before reaching for her phone. 'I kept them on for ages. No idea what happened to them, though.'

I use my hands to shovel toast into my mouth, sending a couple of beans tumbling onto my leggings as Ivy goes through her phone. Sure enough, there she is, standing in a toilet with a pair of fairy wings strapped to her back. We giggle as she shows me more photos and with the food soaking up last night's booze, I already feel so much better.

'Oh, these are from the party,' Ivy says. 'That's a nice one of you and Maddie.'

'Gosh, I don't even remember that.'

'You looked so hot.'

I squint and look closer at the screen. 'You know, you might be right.'

'Ooh, look.' Ivy shoves the phone right up in my face. 'There he is. That's Finn.'

I push her hand away so I can see the screen more clearly.

'I can't believe he just disappeared like that.'

My eyes settle on the screen and my stomach drops. The photograph is blurry, but there's no way I could ever mistake those eyes. I swallow against the ball of beans on toast that seems to have wedged into the base of my throat.

'Are you alright?' Ivy asks. 'You're not going to puke, are you?'

I shake my head a little and stutter. 'I'm fine.'

'Didn't I tell you he was gorgeous?'

Ivy cocks her head, looking at her phone. She did tell me, but I could never have imagined we'd ever use that word to describe the same man. The guys Ivy's into all look like they've been dredged up from a festival and in need of a good wash – all messy-haired and scruffy. Finn doesn't fit that type. I put my plate down and pick up my cup instead, wrapping my fingers around its warmth.

'He's even better looking than he used to be. Like, he's so much more manly now, and I'm pretty sure he was flirting with me, too.'

I shudder inside at the thought. The idea of Finn flirting with Ivy before doing the same with me makes me want to throw my breakfast right up.

'So what happened?' I croak, though I really don't think I want to know.

Ivy pulls a face. 'We caught up a bit and then some of my workmates turned up. I lost him after that.'

'Right,' I say dryly, breathing into my cup.

'Doesn't matter.' Ivy shrugs. 'I'll invite him over for dinner and have my wicked way with him then.'

I feel sick. Not just because the first guy I've found attractive for ages is the very same guy Ivy's been banging on about for the last few days, or because my first-ever one-night stand has turned out to be more complicated than I'd bargained for, or because he might be the world's best player and I'd totally misjudged him. But because, if I tell Ivy now, I know she'll be pissed. Ivy can be generous, but I'm certain that won't extend to me managing to sleep with Finn after five minutes when it's taken her years to get even half as close. And worse, the lovely little morning-after huddle she's created – the cleaning, the breakfast – will be shattered. The good vibes will be replaced by a bad mood, and I know it's selfish, but I want to hold on to that.

'Are you sure you're alright?' she asks, putting a hand on my leg. 'Because you look like you're about to vom.'

Honestly, I feel like I could.

'I'm fine.' I wipe a hand over my forehead. 'Maybe it was for the best? With Finn. It sounds like you had a great night anyway.'

'I did.' Ivy nods. 'But now he's like an itch I can't quite scratch. It's my own fault really. It'll be much easier when it's just the two of us. He's a chef, so I'll woo him with food.'

For the next couple of minutes, Ivy rolls off her plans for a full-on seduction and I'm too thrown by all of it to make her stop.

I know the window of time I have to nip this in the bud is closing by the millisecond, but my hung-over brain is too battered to jolt into action.

'You know what, you're right. I'm not feeling too great,' I interrupt, uncurling my legs from the sofa. 'I need to go back to bed.'

Ivy looks at me with such concern that it leaves a bitter taste in my mouth.

'Do you need anything? Tea? Bucket?'

I shake my head. 'I'll be fine. Thanks, though.'

I go to my room, close the door behind me and climb straight into bed. I am mortified. All the pleasure I'd felt about last night with Finn has dispersed like the air from a popped balloon. If I'd have behaved more like *me* and waited, instead of spontaneously sleeping with him, I'd have been able to just shrug this off because nothing would've happened. Ivy could still do what she wanted and I wouldn't feel like this. My sheets still smell of him, so I turn to lie on my side and thump my pillow back into shape with a sigh. I squeeze my eyes shut. The sooner I can forget about all this, the better.

The vibration of my phone on my bedside table feels far too loud for my head to cope with, and I scowl as I grab it. I raise my eyebrows at the message on my screen.

Sorry for sneaking out, had to get to work. I had fun last night. Let's do it again? Finn x p.s. hope your head isn't too sore!

I'd forgotten we'd exchanged numbers. It's a sweet text, but knowing that he's flirted with Ivy before me makes me wonder if he really is just a player. Maybe if Ivy had had more time for him, he'd have ended up in her bed, not mine. I sigh. This is all much too complicated. If Finn were just some random guy, I'd never have to see him again. Instead, he's Ivy's new target and I know her. It won't be long until he's here, sitting on our sofa while she's seducing him, and I can only hope he won't tell her I got there first because if there's one thing I know, it's that Ivy won't like that. Not one bit.

My head is pounding and my stomach feels sick. I can't deal with this right now, so I turn my phone off and burrow my head under the covers.

Chapter Five

JESS

July, nine years ago

A few days later, I'm curled up on the sofa with a book. My alcohol hangover finally went away after two days of feeling rotten, but the Finn hangover hasn't budged. If anything, it's getting worse. I reread the same page for what must be the fourth time before sighing and closing my book. My eyes flick to the clock. Ivy will be home any minute, and I'll hide in my bedroom for the night while she seduces Finn. And I can't help it, but the thought of it creates a spark of jealousy. It's completely irrational. She's known him for years whereas I've known him two minutes, but still, it's there. Ivy has been totally wrapped up in tonight for the last two days, planning what to wear, what music to play in the background, which sheets to have on her bed. She's followed me around, reading their text conversations aloud for analysis. I don't know if my opinion of his texts being more matey and less flirty are true or simply wishful thinking, because I barely know the guy. Is he the type of man who'd get satisfaction from scoring with two sisters within a week? He might well be. What I do know is that since I replied to his text with a polite *no thank you*, I haven't heard a word from him.

A few minutes later, my phone rings and I see Ivy's name flashing up at me.

'Finn's not there, is he?'

'No,' I reply slowly. Something in her voice makes a drop of dread land in my stomach.

'Damn it. I've been trying to get hold of him for the last half-hour. Benny's sick and I have to cover his shift. Finn should be there already.'

'Well have you tried his mobile?'

'*Obviously*. It's going straight to voicemail.'

'So what should I say when he gets here expecting to see you?' I ask, trying to keep the mild panic from my voice.

'Tell him I'm sorry and enjoy the food?'

I swear to myself and tip my head back, wishing I could say no. But I can't. If I do, Ivy will want to know why and she is *relentless* when she wants to know something, so I stifle a sigh.

'Alright,' I grumble.

I tell myself it might all be fine anyway. Maybe he'll get her voicemails before he gets here, turn around and go home. We hang up and I barely have time to open my book again before the buzz of the intercom rings out through the flat. I trudge over to the handset to answer it, hoping this won't be too awkward.

'Hi, it's Finn.'

'Hey.' I reply into the handset, peering at the grainy black and white image of him standing on the street. 'Ivy isn't here.'

'Oh? We arranged for me to come over.' He turns a little to show me the backpack on his shoulder. 'I'm cooking dinner.'

Only Ivy could invite someone over for dinner and end up having them do the cooking.

'I know,' I reply. 'But she just called to say she has to cover a shift and won't be back.'

'Damn.' He rubs a hand across his short cut hair and then looks into the camera, almost as if he could look right into my eyes. 'Don't suppose you're hungry? We could make use of my night off.'

'I . . .' I hesitate. I am hungry. Ravenous, in fact. But I don't want to tell him that.

'We could talk, too. I've been meaning to call.'

I pause. He can't see me through the camera, but the way his eyes seem to be focused on me reminds me of the night we'd spent together and my cheeks burn. I consider telling him to go back home but at the same time, I don't want to seem like I'm not adult enough to just deal with the fact that we'd had sex. Besides, it's not like I can avoid him forever if he's going to be hanging around with Ivy.

'Sure,' I reply with a little sigh. 'Come on up.'

I buzz him in before taking a quick look in the mirror. My first instinct is to change out of my vest and leggings, but I stop myself. I don't want to look or feel like I've made any effort at all. In fact, it's probably better that he sees me how I usually look, without the make-up Ivy had caked me with at the party.

I hear his footsteps on the landing, unlatch the door and go into the kitchen to look for something to do, settling on pouring myself a glass of water. I tell myself to calm down. It was just sex. It doesn't have to be a big deal. Every animal on earth does it, and it doesn't have to mean anything other than what it was, even if he wasn't quite the stranger I'd thought.

'It's open,' I call out when he knocks on the door.

'Hey,' Finn says and fixes me with his intense green eyes as he puts the backpack on the side.

'Hi,' I reply.

It wasn't just sex. The way my belly leaps like a ballet dancer tells me that. I gulp a mouthful of water to stop the memory of him running his fingers down the length of my body from taking over.

I refill the glass, avoiding his eyes. 'Ivy said she'd been trying to reach you on your mobile?'

'My battery died.' Finn takes his phone from his back pocket. 'I was going to charge it when I got here.'

The kitchen feels smaller with him in it. And even though it has no door and leads right into the hallway, it feels like he's managed to zip an imaginary seal behind him and close the rest of the flat off. My eyes flick to and from his face and a couple of silent seconds tick by. I let myself accept the fact that he is as gorgeous as I remember. At least I hadn't been so drunk to have been mistaken about that.

'It's nice to see you again,' he says with a smile and I simply nod in reply. 'I felt really bad about leaving while you were asleep, but I had to work the next day. I didn't want to wake you up.'

I wave my hand dismissively as if waking up to men who've disappeared from my bed is standard procedure. 'Don't worry about it.'

'So.' He tips his head to the side and his eyes smile at me. 'How've you been?'

'Good.' I shrug and cross my arms over my chest.

His eyebrows flinch and, for a second, he looks vulnerable. He shakes his head an inch. 'Look, Jess. Did I do something wrong? I thought we had a great night.'

'We did.' I nod. 'It was. But that's . . . all it was.'

Finn raises his eyebrows an inch before nodding slowly. 'That's me told.'

'I didn't mean it like that.' I hunch my shoulders to my ears. God, this is awkward.

He drops a small laugh. 'It's alright. Always better to be upfront about these things.'

'Right.'

'It's probably for the best anyway, what with you and Ivy,' I add. 'I guess it goes without saying that we should keep the other night between us.'

Finn frowns. 'Right.'

He looks offended. Maybe he's not used to women turning him down, but at least this way the cut is clean and we can simply move on from it.

He looks down at the floor and shifts on his feet. 'You know what, maybe I should go. I don't want to interrupt your night.'

Something in his voice makes me soften a little. Maybe I really *did* offend him. I'm not used to being so assertive, especially with men. Maybe I came across as rude. I look at him and remember that moment when he came up to the roof and I'd felt that pull. He'd looked at me and told me more about myself than even Ivy could, and I guess I can't just ignore that. Not when it had felt so real.

'Don't be silly,' I say. 'I was only reading and besides, Ivy told me I should enjoy the dinner you were going to cook.'

'Did she now?' he asks with a playful smile.

'She did. It does depend on what you've got in that backpack of yours, though.' I nod towards his bag and suppress the smile that wants to respond to his.

'Well, I planned to make some gnocchi and pan-roasted chicken but you're vegan, right?' He looks at me as he unzips the backpack and I nod, ignoring the hung-over egg breakfast I'd had at the weekend.

'Is that a problem?'

'Nah. I'll save the chicken and make something else.'

Being vegan is definitely becoming more of a thing now, but it's still not always easy to get a decent, *tasty* meal when out with friends for dinner. I usually feel like a nuisance and sometimes I'll end up ordering something with meat or fish just to be less of a hassle and ignore my paranoia about clogged arteries.

'I've got tofu?' I offer and he pulls a face.

'Mushrooms?' he counters and I nod. 'Perfect.'

He takes out a few ingredients from his bag and starts opening drawers and cupboards, as if he's getting his bearings, while I get the speaker to organise the music that, he says, he can't cook without. Despite my initial feelings, I'm surprised at how easily we've slipped into something that feels normal. As if this is just a regular thing to do.

'How do you cope at work without music?' I ask, taking out my phone and connecting it to the speaker while his charges. 'Surely you can't wear headphones?'

'No, but work is something different. There's a hundred different things to focus on.' He laughs. 'At home though, it's no music, no food.'

'Fair enough. What do you listen to usually?'

I open up my music app, picturing him as a guitar music kind of guy.

Finn raises his eyebrows at me. 'I don't think you'd like it.'

'Why not?' I ask. If I look at him and think *guitars*, I wonder what he thinks when he looks at me. 'Try me.'

He nods with an amused smile. 'Alright. Look for a band called Terror.'

It already doesn't sound good. When I'd pictured him being into guitar music, I'd been thinking along the lines of Red Hot Chili Peppers or The Kooks. I don't know who Terror are, but from the name, I doubt it'll be pretty. I press play on a random song and the throbbing sound of electric guitars starts pulsing from the speaker, followed a few seconds later by guttural male growling.

'What do you think?' he asks with a challenging but playful look on his face.

53

'Honestly? It's awful.' I shake my head, turning it off. If this were a date, I'd probably make my ears bleed by pretending to like it but, since it isn't, I can simply tell him how it is instead. 'What even was that?'

'Hardcore.'

'Sounds it.' I laugh and pull a face before searching for some mellow soul that feels infinitely better for cooking to.

'This also works,' Finn says with approval before throwing me a potato from the net he lifted from his bag. 'You're on peeling duty.'

I catch it with both hands and ignore the feeling that this exact scene is probably played out in countless romcoms. 'I thought we were having gnocchi?'

'We are.' He looks at me and grins. 'From scratch.'

I can't help but be impressed. Having seen them being attempted, and failed, enough times on *MasterChef*, I suddenly feel very special at having them hand-made for my dinner.

'So,' Finn says, 'how was your week?'

'My week?' I repeat, giving him a sideways look.

'Yeah, you know. What have you done? Work, life . . . dates?' He raises his eyebrows playfully.

I scoff and shake my head as my cheeks flame.

'What?' He laughs a little. 'I don't pretend to expect that someone like you isn't fighting them off.'

'I don't have guys just *hanging around*,' I reply with a little more heat than might actually be necessary, but now it's my turn to feel offended. 'Just because we . . . I'm not in the habit of doing what we did, okay?'

'You mean having sex?'

How can such simple words do so much with my body at the same time? I close my eyes to block out the memory of it. I've tried to tell myself over the last couple of days that I couldn't remember the details. But I do. Every single one. I remember exactly how he'd smelled and tasted, and the exact pressure of his body on mine. I remember the taut muscles on the sides of his abs, and the grip of his fingers in my hair. I sigh and open my eyes again.

'One-night stands,' I reply.

'Well, any time you want to change that status . . .' He lets the sentence hang in the air and then shakes his head a little. 'Look, if you're worried about Ivy getting pissed off, she won't.'

I snort and start peeling my potato.

'God, this is going to sound so arrogant but I know what's going on,' he continues. 'I've known Ivy for a long time and I know when she's making a play for someone.'

I glance up at him. 'Oh. And what do you plan to do about it?'

My eyebrow raises by itself as I fix him with a stony stare, and Finn seems taken back.

'Nothing.' He shakes his head a fraction. 'I mean, we're just mates, she knows that. I've told her that already. And I mean, I literally just slept with you. I'm not the kind of guy to mess around with two sisters.'

My face softens as I realise I've offended him for the second time in as many minutes.

'I'm sorry,' I mumble in return. 'I had to ask. She's my little sister and you're someone I don't know from Adam.'

He doesn't say anything as he takes a handful of mushrooms to the sink and rinses them under the tap.

'Did I really give you that bad an impression?' he asks, shaking the excess water away.

'Well what do you expect when you just up and leave the morning after?'

'I explained already . . .' His sentence trails as he registers the smile twitching at my lips.

He didn't leave a bad impression – the opposite in fact. I'm just out of practice and slightly thrown off by how he's patting the mushrooms dry with kitchen paper as if they're the most delicate things in the world. He accepts my backhanded apology with a grin and I go back to peeling my potato.

'Alright,' he says, and slices a mushroom in half. 'So now we've got the heavy stuff sorted, tell me about work.'

'You don't really want to know about my work week, do you?' I frown, a little surprised at how easily he's changed the conversation.

'I wouldn't ask if I didn't.' He widens his eyes as if to say, *go on, I'm really interested*. So, I tell him about my job, and he laughs when I tell him about the office manager and her love of passive-aggressive notes reminding us that there's no such thing as a cup-cleaning fairy, and the ancient finance guy who thinks nobody can hear him snoring in the back of the office. I tell him that, even though my first class marketing degree means I *could* be working for a global firm and earning twice the money, I'm happy to be in a family-owned company in Hendon because it's giving me a ton of insight into the world of digital printing, which will be needed when I have my own stationery business one day.

We peel, chop and slice vegetables while he tells me about his new job at a restaurant with a boss who has the temper of Gordon Ramsay but none of the skill.

'He set the restaurant up with inherited money for fun. He's got no idea at all about food,' Finn says. 'I don't even think he likes it very much.'

I put the potatoes into a pot of boiling water. 'So there has to be a good reason to stay?'

'He's pretty well connected,' Finn replies, wiping his hands on a tea-towel. 'And him having no idea about food means I get to design the menu. So I'm also getting a ton of insight, which will come in handy when I have my own restaurant one day.'

I can't help but smile at the fact he used the exact same words I did. It's just as it felt at the party. Finn is easy company and even though he's busy cooking, he still manages to give me the feeling that he's completely absorbed in what I'm saying. I don't know if it's a subconscious decision not to bring Ivy up again, but we don't.

We sit on the kitchen counters with our feet dangling in front of the cupboards, holding our plates as we eat and talk about everything and nothing. We drift from memories of my mum to his childhood by the sea, from his favourite film of all time (*Die Hard*) to mine (*The Breakfast Club*). It feels like a simple continuation of our conversation at the party and we keep talking until we realise it's almost eleven and, unlike Finn, I have to get up for work early in the morning.

'Well that was fun,' he says with a grin, hoisting his backpack onto his shoulders.

A wave of déjà vu hits me and the urge to tell him to stay feels almost stronger than I can fight against for a moment.

I nod and grin back. 'It was.'

'You do realise I've spent my only two nights off so far with you.'

'Well, I'm honoured.' I tip my head and he laughs.

'Remind me again why you don't want to go on a date?'

'Because. You mean a lot to Ivy. It wouldn't be right.'

'Okay . . . but just to be clear, Ivy and I are just mates. There's nothing more to it than that, never was and never will be.'

'I know,' I reply breezily. 'But still. It's better not to make things complicated.'

He looks me in the eye and smiles, shaking his head. 'Why do I have the feeling that meeting up with you would be all kinds of good?'

I look down at the ground to hide my face despite everything in my body wanting to squeal. Ivy could have anyone she wants. Literally anyone. And despite my considerate excuse for turning him down, I find myself wishing that, just for once, I could let myself have something I really want instead of always putting Ivy first. I force myself to keep a neutral face and look back up at him. I don't trust myself not to say *screw it, I'd love to*, so I simply shrug instead. He takes the hint and kisses me on the cheek.

'See you around,' he says, and I only breathe again once he's disappeared down the stairs.

Chapter Six

Ivy

August, nine years ago

Ivy tightened the belt of her dressing gown around her waist and shuffled into the living room where Jess sat on the sofa, painting her toenails.

'Did you remember to open the window?' Jess asked without looking up.

'Yes, of course.' Ivy rolled her eyes. She bit the inside of her cheek. 'I forgot the cotton pads though . . .'

She quickly shuffled back to the bathroom. The room was thick with steam and she quietly cracked open the window. She *had* forgotten the cotton pads, but she'd forgotten the window, too. Ivy called it nagging and Jess called it reminding, but either way, it was frustrating that most of the time her sister always managed to catch her out.

'I've already ordered,' Jess said as she came back to the living room. 'Chicken chow mein for you and tofu fried rice for me.'

'Perfect.' Ivy flopped down on the sofa.

Jess tutted loudly. 'You almost smudged me.'

'Sorry.' She pulled a face at her sister's perfectionism with a hint of envy.

Jess liked to take her time when it came to painting her nails. She'd spend what seemed like forever, making sure she didn't smudge them or have uneven streaks. She'd already started before Ivy had gone in the shower, and was still going. At least she'd moved on to her other foot. Ivy let herself sink into their huge, imitation suede corner sofa.

Ivy took her feet from the spotty pink fluffy slippers that matched her dressing gown and put them on the edge of the coffee table. She looked at the row of nail varnish bottles, wiggling her toes. Which colour should she go for this time? She couldn't use the same as Jess, who had gone for a bright coral pink that only she could pull off.

'How long til the food comes?' Ivy asked, picking the bottle of black varnish from the table.

'Half an hour,' Jess replied with intense concentration. 'You can press play when you're ready.'

Ivy looked at the TV screen. '*New Moon*. Yesssss, I love this one.'

The *Twilight* films were a guilty pleasure that Ivy would rather die than admit to out in the real world. She'd hadn't liked the books, but somehow the angst of a girl torn between love for a vampire and a werewolf translated perfectly on the big screen. Plus, Jess loved them too. Once a month, they'd clear a Sunday evening, order takeaway and have a girls' night, rewatching films they loved: *Grease, The Dark Crystal, The Faculty, Mac & Me*. They'd written down all the film titles on scraps of paper and put them in a tin to make it fair. The rules were that they had to watch whichever film was picked at random, which meant there'd be no squabbling about who got to choose. Ivy grinned and pressed play.

Apart from getting up to pay the delivery guy and the odd comment about how mean Edward was for leaving Bella, and how manipulative Bella was for leading Jacob on, they watched the film in easy silence. These Sundays had become one of Ivy's favourite things about living with her sister. The flat was usually clean for a start, which was pretty much all down to Jess. She'd taken over their mum's habit of doing a big clean on the weekend, vacuuming, dusting and cleaning the kitchen and bathroom to hotel standards. Ivy's job was to do the weekly food shop, an arrangement that suited her just fine. Because they'd plan their film night in advance, she usually stayed in the night before and woke up fresh, unless she'd had to work late. It had become a little ritual where neither of them expected anything from the other except easy companionship.

A breeze blew in through the open window, lifting the edges of the light cotton curtains at the window. They'd had days of wall-to-wall sunshine and Ivy was in full summer mode. In just a couple of weeks, she and Jess would be flying to Tenerife, where she'd booked a studio apartment for a week. Until then, she planned to reap as much from the British summer weather as she could.

Ivy's phone beeped from the coffee table and she picked it up. A wide grin pulled at her mouth as she saw Finn's name on the screen, but it fell away again when she read his message.

'Bloody Finn.' She sighed.

Jess quickly turned her head. 'Why? What's happened?'

'He's being so annoying,' Ivy replied with a groan. 'I wanted to go to this street food festival next week and he says he can't make it.'

'Oh. Maybe he has to work.'

'He's always working.'

'He's a chef.' Jess laughed. 'It's not the most social of jobs, is it? I could go with you if you want.'

'You hate street food,' Ivy pointed out. She would eat a samosa from the back of a pick-up truck, but not Jess with her pickiness about hygiene.

'So go with someone else. It's not like Finn's the only person in the world.'

'It's not just that. He's playing hard to get. Like, *really* hard. I've tried every trick in the book and it's not working.' Ivy sighed again. 'What should I do?'

Jess spluttered. 'You're asking *me* what to do about *Finn*?'

Good point. The look on Jess' face was a clear reminder that, when it came to things like this, Ivy was on her own. But she wanted to go to this food festival and eat everything from Argentinian *empanadas* to Hawaiian *poke* and, damn it, she wanted Finn.

'Ivy,' Jess said, turning slightly on the sofa. 'Have you thought about the possibility that Finn just might not be into you like that? I mean, you're friends. Maybe he doesn't want to ruin that?'

'He told me a few days ago that he really values our friendship and doesn't want to wreck it, yada, yada, yada. Which just drives me nuts and makes me want him even more.'

'Jesus, Ivy. Stalker, much? If he's told you he's not interested then maybe it's time to back off. It's not like you can't have anyone else with a quarter of the effort.'

Ivy raised her eyebrows at her sister's snappy tone. 'Who blew smoke up your arse? I was just *saying*, that's all.' She sighed. 'I think it's because he might be leaving again. It's that thing of wanting what you can't have.'

'Leaving? Where to?'

'Back to Sweden. Apparently one of his friends has been talking about opening up a restaurant for ages and it might actually be happening.'

'Oh, right,' Jess said. 'Well, there you go then. Problem solved.'

'It's a bummer, because he only just moved back.'

'Sounds like he can't make up his mind what he wants. I mean, who moves from one city to another and goes back that quickly? You say he's flirty with you one minute and not the next.' Jess bristled like a porcupine on alert. 'You're probably right to back off. Just what the world needs. Another unreliable man.'

'Like there aren't enough already,' Ivy replied with a laugh.

She'd never been hurt by an unreliable guy in her life – that was the advantage of keeping things casual. But it felt like the right thing to say and, besides, it didn't even matter. She'd tried with Finn, and failed. And really, it was his loss. Jess was right, she didn't have to waste her time with someone who wasn't interested and who, in all likelihood, would be gone within a month anyway. Ivy chucked her phone back on the table and mentally marked the Finn file as closed.

Chapter Seven

JESS

August, nine years ago

So, he might be going back to Sweden. It surprised me how that bit of news had punched me right in the gut, leaving me feeling stupid on two counts. First, for actually believing for a second that he really had been interested in dating me, and second, because if I'd have known he'd be leaving anyway, I might have taken him up on his offer. I might not be a one-night stand person, but it's not like I'm looking for a boyfriend right now, either. At least that's what I tell myself as I reread the guide on Facebook statistics for the social media course I'm taking. Instead, my gaze keeps sliding to my mobile phone.

The flat is quiet. Ivy's at the Notting Hill Carnival and has been for ages. She'd left after breakfast in her tiny shorts and bikini top, braids piled high, ready for dancing in the street. It's not my scene. It's too crowded and far too hot today, and I have to study. I sigh and rub the heels of my palms into my eyes. I've been at this for an hour and my brain needs a break, so I turn away from my laptop and look at my phone again. A frown flickers at my eyebrows and I nibble on the inside of my bottom lip before picking the phone up and typing.

Jess: So. You're moving back to Sweden . . .

We haven't spoken since the night he cooked, but he's been on my mind every day. I don't know whether that's a good or a bad thing. My leg bounces as I wait for him to reply, which he does, quickly.

Finn: Hey, Jess. Maybe, yeah. I've not decided yet. Still looking for that reason to stay ;)

Heat flushes from my face and floods down my neck, into my chest where it settles into the quickening of my heartbeat. It's just a winky face. It doesn't mean anything. But it totally does. I put the phone down and go into the kitchen to pour myself a glass of water, squeezing some lemon juice into it for good measure. It's refreshing and cooling, and I press the glass against my forehead as I lean against the sink. If only it could cool the heat that's been there since sleeping with Finn and has gone into overdrive now I know he might be leaving anyway.

I take another sip of my water. Him leaving might be a good thing. It gives things a natural end date. His friendship with Ivy will probably dwindle and, let's face it, he's just as ambitious as I am. I'm under no illusion that he'll be pining for me when he goes if he's throwing himself into work. It feels like an outrageous line of thought to go down, but it *would* be nice to do what I want. To put myself first for a change and do what Ivy always tells me to do: whatever feels good! Just this once.

I push myself away from the sink and put my glass down before going back the living room and picking up my phone.

Jess: Come over.

◆ ◆ ◆

I'm a bad sister. I know that I've crossed some kind of invisible line but, right now, it simply doesn't matter. I'm in the kind of dreamy haze that only comes from having an afternoon nap and, I have to admit, I kind of like being sober enough to enjoy being wrapped up in Finn's arms. His skin is warm and the beating of his heart is steady against me. My body feels spent, in the best kind of way, and I yawn with a heavy dose of pleasure.

'Was that your way of trying to get me to stay?' Finn mumbles, sending wisps of his warm breath onto the side of my neck.

I laugh. 'I know how it is with work. Some things are hard to say no to.'

'You know what's not hard to say no to?' he asks, propping himself up onto his elbow.

I take a moment to look at the face gazing down at me. His green eyes are mellow and look as if they're about to tell me something profound. I swallow and shake my head.

'Ice cream.'

We both laugh and he drops a kiss on my eyebrow as if it's a completely normal thing to do.

'We can head out and get some, if you want?' I suggest.

'Only if we come straight back.' He grins back.

Ivy won't be home until well into the night and my body is already responding to the idea of more time in bed with Finn. I nod with a wide smile and he throws the light sheet all the way back with a sudden burst of energy.

'I'll just grab a quick shower.'

He drops another kiss onto my face and I lie on my back, stretched out like a starfish, as he goes into the bathroom. The air flowing in through my window is warm, landing on my skin like a tropical breeze, and I let my mind drift towards the end of next week when Ivy and I will be in Tenerife. Truthfully, it feels like I'm already on holiday as it is, such is the contentment in my belly right now. Ice cream will be a great addition to it. I roll onto my side and sit up slowly, reaching my arms up high over my head in a deliciously satisfying stretch, but my eyes narrow at the sound of keys in the door.

I quickly glance at my clock. There's no way it could possibly be Ivy already. It's not even dark yet and she always goes to the after-parties. Always. I sit poised on the edge of my bed and my heart jumps to my throat when I hear the door click open.

Shit.

I quickly pull on the vest and shorts I'd been wearing before Finn came over, my pulse thudding loudly in my ears. The shower is running and while Ivy will obviously assume it's me in there, that'll change when it's Finn who steps out of the bathroom instead. I open my door to see her kicking off her trainers in the hallway.

'Ivy,' I stutter. 'What are you doing here?'

'Erm, I live here.' She laughs.

'I mean, how come you're back so early?'

'Tired, and I've got a huge blister. I can't dance any more.' She stops and turns to look at the closed bathroom door, and my stomach drops.

'Ivy, I—'

'Ohhhhh.' She grins. 'You've got someone here, haven't you? Get *you*. I didn't even know there was someone on your radar.' She links her arm in mine and leans into me. 'So, who is he?'

Her whispered voice is low and conspiratorial and it only makes me feel worse. I swallow against a sudden dry throat as the shower stops running. Her eyes are full of glee and excitement at the prospect of meeting the man her sister has secretly snuck into the flat.

'There's something I need to tell you,' I start, but the rest of the words won't come out.

My shoulders sag a little as I realise there's really no way to soften this. As our mum used to say when one of us had done something wrong, I've got some serious explaining to do. The bathroom door clicks and steam billows through the open door. I keep my eyes on Ivy as she frowns and blinks as if she's just seen a cat riding a bicycle.

'Finn?'

Ivy laughs and shakes her head a fraction as she stares at him. And I can't help it, I stare too. There he is with his low-slung jeans and beads of water clinging to the skin of his bare torso. Even in this situation, I can't help but appreciate the lines of the body that Ivy's been lusting over the last few weeks but that has just been in my bed.

Finn's eyes widen, flicking from Ivy to me, and back again. 'Ivy. Hey. What are you doing here?'

'What is with you two? I *live* here, remember.' She laughs and the fact that she hasn't quite yet made the connection only makes the unease in my belly feel even worse. 'The question is, why are you here?' She turns to me with her face pulled into light confusion. 'And what about the guy you've been . . .'

Slowly, the amused look on her face falls.

'You and . . .' She drops her arm from mine and looks back at Finn. 'Are you serious?'

I try to answer, but my throat has dried up and I don't know quite what to say.

'We just . . .' Finn tries, scratching the back of his neck before shrugging a way that says he can't find the words either.

Ivy shakes her head and turns away as a shocked laugh falls from her mouth. 'Wow. Just, wow.'

She walks into the living room, obviously stunned, and I stare at Finn. This isn't how it was supposed to go. She was supposed to have come back hours from now when Finn would have been long gone and I'd probably never see him again. It's only now I've had that thought that I realise it's not actually the outcome I want.

'What is going on?' Ivy asks, turning around with a stony face.

I close my eyes for a second and wipe my hands across the back of my shorts before opening them again.

'Well,' I start. 'Finn came over . . .'

'Why?' She frowns, looking at him. 'You knew I'd be at Carnival all day.'

Finn scratches his neck again. 'I know.'

'So you came to see Jess, then? Not me?'

Finn nods and shoves his hands into his jeans pockets. If I didn't know any better, I'd say he's not sorry. His eyes look a little sheepish, but he doesn't look like he's about to deliver an apology.

Ivy shook her head. 'I don't understand. *Why?*'

'Because I like her.'

His tone is matter of fact, as if it makes perfect sense, and despite myself, my heart blooms in my chest.

'Since when?'

'Since the start.'

'But she's my sister!' A look of hurt and embarrassment passes across Ivy's face as she turns towards me. 'And he's my . . . it's *Finn!*'

'I know,' I groan, my mouth pulling into a grimace. 'I'm sorry.'

'After everything I told you about him?' Ivy shakes her head and I see the tears in her eyes before she blinks them away. 'You knew how I felt about him. You told me to back off. You went behind my back.'

'That's not fair,' Finn interrupts, shaking his head. 'We're mates, Ivy. We've never been more than that and you know it. I've been totally upfront about that.'

I shrink in my skin because I can see the humiliation burning on her face, and I can feel it too. Finn telling her he wasn't interested in private is one thing, but saying it again here and now, in this situation, will be like pouring acid into a wound.

'Whatever,' she snaps back. 'You should go before I get really angry.'

'Angry about what? We haven't done anything wrong.'

'Finn,' I cut in, 'she's right. Maybe you should go.'

It's the complete opposite to how I'd seen this evening panning out, but this is the reality of the situation. I knew Ivy would react like this if she found out and his defiance, as reassuring as it is to hear, definitely isn't helping. He looks at me as if to say *really?* and I nod as if I've got all of this under control. I don't, and he doesn't look happy about it, but after a couple of seconds he goes into my room to grab his things. It's as if someone's put one too many blocks on a Jenga tower and it's all starting to crumble. He stops in front of me on his way out and I pray he doesn't go to kiss me. Instead, he gives me a small smile before heading out of the door. The air in the flat is still, but charged, and I take a deep breath before going back into the living room where Ivy is standing.

'Look, I know this is shit. It's a crap situation, and I'm sorry.' I fold my arms across my chest and sigh, looking away. 'I am.'

Ivy flops down onto the sofa and puts her elbows on her knees. 'I don't get it. Since when would Finn start coming here to see you? And how did you end up in bed together?'

I sigh again, knowing that all of this is going to sound so much worse because she didn't know about it from the start.

'I met him at the party. You said you thought he'd left early, but he'd found me up on the roof.'

'Okay . . .' Ivy says slowly.

I sit on the far end of the sofa. 'I asked him to spend the night.'

'What?'

The confusion on her face is evident, and I can't blame her. That I've had Finn in here behind her back is one thing, but the idea of me asking someone to stay the night is another thing entirely.

'I was drunk. And I didn't know it was him until you showed me the picture the next day.'

'From the *party*?' Ivy shakes her head. 'So the time he came over to cook dinner, you two had already slept together? What was it, like a second date for you two? It was supposed to be a date for *me*.'

'Course not,' I reply hotly. 'Nothing happened. As soon as I realised he was the guy you'd been talking about, I stepped back.'

'Yeah.' Ivy scoffs. 'Looks like it.'

'For God's sake, Ivy. Not everything is about you. It wasn't planned. I didn't know it was him.'

'And today? You can't use that excuse; you know damn well who he is. We were talking about him two days ago when you told me to back off, remember?'

My skin prickles with shame because of course I remember telling her to do just that while we'd watched our Sunday film together.

'So what was that? Were you trying to get me out of the picture so you could have him for yourself?'

'No! Come on, Ivy. You know I wouldn't.' I hunch my shoulders to my ears. 'But then you said he might be going back to Sweden and, I don't know. It just made me feel . . . I don't know. I hadn't planned him to come over. It just happened.'

'You're not the *it just happened* type.'

'Well maybe I am.' I put my hands in my lap and look at Ivy with a small shrug. I can't keep skirting around it. 'I like him. A lot.'

It surprises me to admit it. When I'd messaged him, I really had thought it would be just a one time, second time thing. But somewhere between opening the door to see him on the other side and him leaving again, I realise that I never really stood a chance.

'And he likes you too,' Ivy grumbles in a way that makes my hackles rise.

'Is that so hard to believe? He didn't want you so that means he can't want me?'

'I know what I *can't* believe. I can't believe you lied to me. To my face. Multiple times.'

'I didn't say anything because I knew how you'd react and it wasn't supposed to matter. Finn told you he wanted to stay just friends and he's leaving soon. It was a total non-issue.'

'A non-issue? You lied!' Ivy shakes her head and her face crumples. 'You should have told me. I'd never have lied to you like that.'

Tears are brimming in her eyes and frustration pricks at my skin, overriding the urge to apologise again because I always do. I always put her first.

'Ivy, even if I'd have told you the very next day, we'd have had the exact same fight because you always think everything is about you. I didn't know who he was when I met him. And he didn't mention you in any way that might have made me realise. You're just pissed off because he chose me and not you, and you've never had to come second before, for anything, ever.'

'Well that just goes to show how well you really know me,' Ivy replies, her voice dripping with sarcasm.

'I didn't plan to like him, Ivy. But I do. For the first time in a long time, I really like someone.'

The words come out of my mouth before my mind can put a filter in place and, just like I did right before I messaged Finn to come over, I feel a little thrill inside because it's true. Finn is the first man I've met who's made me feel like this.

'I told him nothing could happen between us because I didn't want it to ruin your friendship,' I continue. 'But there *is* something there and I want to know what it is. I know you're pissed off, but I have to see where this goes.'

'You don't even know him,' she scoffs. 'You're really going to put him before me?'

'It doesn't have to be like that,' I reply, exasperated.

Ivy always does this. It's always extremes with her, there's rarely a middle ground and I'm always the one who has to make the compromise.

'Whatever.' She gets up. 'I can't listen to this crap.'

She barges past me and I drop my head back, fighting the urge to scream with frustration.

'You can forget about Tenerife, too,' she says curtly, before going into her room and slamming the door behind her with so much force it makes the wall shake.

Chapter Eight

JESS

August, nine years ago

'I'm telling you, Mads. She's pissed. Like, really pissed.' I sigh down the phone and sit on my bedroom windowsill.

'I can't believe she's banned you from Tenerife,' Maddie replies.

Music is blasting from Ivy's bedroom and the washing machine has been running all day. I'm pretty sure she's packing, throwing bikinis and crop tops and shorts and sun lotion into her suitcase.

'She hasn't banned me,' I explain. 'We both decided it was better for us not to go together, that's all.'

The sun warms my thigh as I sit on the ledge. I won't lie, I'm gutted about our holiday. I'd been really looking forward to it, counting down the days at work until we were due to fly out in the early hours of tomorrow morning. But honestly? I'm also kind of glad not to be going. It had already been a huge compromise for the both of us in terms of where to stay. I didn't want to be in the crazy resorts full of drunken teenagers, and Ivy didn't want to be out of the action in a quieter part of town. I didn't want to spend every night getting wasted and Ivy wasn't interested in a hiking tour up Mount Teide.

'At least this way, she gets her perfect holiday,' I say grudgingly.

'And you get to spend time with Finn,' Maddie replies. 'Though if it were me, I'd have told Ivy to stay home and taken him with me on holiday instead.'

'It's a cheapo last-minute booking – non-transferrable and we'd lose our money if we cancelled.'

Maddie sighs. 'I know you're dressing this up like you're okay about it, but still. I think it's a bit out of order.'

'I know. But spending seven nights and eight days cramped in one room together definitely won't help. Besides, it's not like we're not speaking at all. The space will do us good.'

Ivy hadn't spoken to me for an entire day after our fight, and it was the longest day of my life. The only thing that made it bearable was knowing she'd eventually calm down. It wasn't like she was in love with Finn. I'd never have gone there if she had been. He'd been a misguided crush, an infatuation that had ended as quickly as it had started. I hadn't mean to sound so harsh when I'd told her she was only angry because he'd chosen me over her, especially because I know that what really hurt her was not knowing what was going on. She hasn't fully defrosted yet, but I'm sure it's nothing a week's holiday can't help with.

'So what are you going to do with your week off?' Maddie asks.

I could've told work the holiday had fallen through and gone in anyway, but the weather forecast looks great and Finn's wrangled a few days off. Funnily enough, I'd had Ivy's voice in my head telling me not to be such a workaholic and make use of the time instead.

'No idea. Chill out, I guess.'

'And have lots of new couple sex.' Maddie laughed and I shook my head, smiling. I don't know if I'd class us as a new couple, we're still getting to know each other, but of course we were going to do plenty of that, too.

'I'm just looking forward to things calming down a bit.' I read-just myself on the ledge. 'I hate things being so all over the place with her.'

'Well, for what it's worth, I think it's great you're giving it a chance and not letting the fight with Ivy wreck things before they've even started. You deserve this.'

Maddie makes it sound like a conscious choice, but it isn't. Me being the disruptor is a new, strange twist to the dynamic with Ivy and it's not something I'm comfortable with at all. I've asked myself a lot whether I'd have told Ivy about it if she'd have come home hours later and missed Finn completely. The answer changes every time I ask the question.

Later that evening, I knock on Ivy's bedroom door. It's almost midnight and the music that had been blaring from her speaker earlier is now barely audible in the rest of the flat.

'Come in,' she calls, and I step into her room.

Her suitcase is packed and closed, with a small bag sitting on top of it. Ivy pushes one of her drawers shut with her leg and looks at me as I stand in her doorway.

'You all packed?' I ask with a small smile.

'Just about.'

'What time's your taxi booked for?'

'I cancelled it,' she replies, opening up another drawer. 'I'll get the night bus to Victoria station instead.'

'Oh, right.'

Ivy had balked at the cost of parking our car at Gatwick for the week and scoffed at my idea of taking a taxi, so we'd made yet another compromise. We'd settled on a cab to the station, and then the Gatwick Express to the airport. Except, now she was going alone, she was already doing things her way.

'It's cheaper.' She shrugs and pulls her braids back from her shoulders and up into a bun.

We stay silent for a few seconds and even though I'm sure we'll both have a great week, my insides tug with a hint of apprehension. We've had arguments before of course, and I know we'll come through this one intact, but I suddenly wish we weren't putting so many miles between us. Ivy's eyes catch mine and her face softens an inch.

'I'll be fine,' she says.

I nod and swallow the lump in my throat. 'I know.'

Mum had always told us never to go to bed on an argument. This week we've managed only a few strained words between us but her getting on a plane and going abroad like this feels wrong.

'I really am sorry,' I add for what must be the millionth time.

'I know. Me too.'

I'm reminded of the times when Mum or Dad would stand between the two of us after breaking up an argument and tell us both to apologise. The words would be said, but it wouldn't really be sealed until we were told to *now hug and make up*. I guess Ivy feels the same, because even though neither of our parents are here to say it, we do it anyway.

Chapter Nine

JESS

September, nine years ago

The sun beats down onto my already flushed face, lighting the inside of my eyelids in a soothing, balmy orange colour. The scent of the grass around us fills my nose and blades of it press into the back of my arms as I lie on the ground. The sweetest of kisses lands on my neck and I squirm as I laugh, opening my eyes.

'There she is.' Finn's face hovers above me, his mouth pulled into a lazy grin.

I smile as he bends down, planting another on the place where my collarbones meet at the base of my throat and sending currents of delicious warmth right down to my toes.

'I can't believe you just did that,' I say, stretching as I roll over onto my side and prop myself up with my elbow.

'I didn't hear you complaining.' He grins back and my heart gallops in my chest.

'I'm not.'

What had started as a picnic in a deserted spot on Hampstead Heath had quickly descended into a full-on, teenage-style make-out session. The space between my legs surges with heat at the memory of Finn's fingers in my jeans and I shake my head, catching my bottom lip between my teeth as I look at him. His long legs are stretched out as he lies on his side, his feet bare in the late summer heat. Even his toes are worth looking at. I laugh at myself and shake my head again.

'What?' he asks with a smile.

I shrug. 'Nothing.'

But we both know it's not nothing. The way we smile at each other and the depth in his green eyes tells me that this is everything.

I lie back in the grass, resting my head on our rolled-up jackets, and look up at the sky as Finn drops his head to rest on my chest. The world around us feels distant. The quiet hum of traffic barely permeates my consciousness and, despite being in London, I have the feeling that we're somewhere deep in the countryside with just the insects in the grass around us for company. I play with Finn's hair with one of my hands and a rush of that *I can't believe how lucky I am* feeling bursts in my chest. It's only been a month. I tell myself it's much too early to be thinking about it being love, but the feelings I have convince me otherwise. Finn draws circles on my thigh, his fingertip scorching my skin through my jeans, and I try to let myself settle into this contented feeling.

A plane flies high above us, and immediately my thoughts turn to Ivy. I sigh so heavily that Finn's head rises and falls with the force of my breath. I miss her. What was supposed to be a week's holiday was extended as she deliberately missed her flight home. Apparently, she was having such a great time in Tenerife that she wanted to stay on and had even managed to find a bar job. It was all so spontaneous and quick and, despite her saying it was nothing to do with the fight about Finn, I can't help but think that I must have hurt her more than I'd realised. Especially because it came after telling her that we were officially dating.

I sigh again and Finn rolls over to face me, moving his head to rest on my stomach so we can see each other more clearly.

'You okay?'

I shrug as best as I can while lying down. 'Just thinking about Ivy.'

'I'm sure she's having a blast.'

'Have you spoken to her?'

'Nope.'

That's another thing. If she really wasn't bothered about it all, surely she wouldn't have just dropped her friendship with Finn? I know she's always been a bit flaky with keeping in touch with people, but still.

I sigh again. 'I don't know. She said she's alright with all this, but . . .'

'You don't think she is?' he says after I leave the sentence hanging.

'She's not exactly rushing to get back.'

Finn laughs. 'Come on, can you blame her? She's in Tenerife. It's hot and she's probably having the time of her life.'

'Maybe. But it doesn't stop me from feeling like the world's worst sister.'

'Look,' he says, shifting to sit up. 'We haven't done anything wrong. Ivy and I have known each other for years. If anything was ever going to happen between us, it would have done ages ago. I don't feel bad for what's happened between us, and neither should you.'

'You don't get it,' I say, rubbing a thumb over the indentations of grass on my skin. 'There are certain people that are off limits. You were one of them.'

'And now look at us.' He takes my hand and grins.

I look away and shake my head.

'Jess, come on.' He rubs his thumb across my hand and I shake my head. 'Don't do this.'

I'm trying not to. I'm trying to just let things play out without jumping into the future, but it's easier said than done.

'We've had such a nice day and I have to get to work soon. Let's just enjoy it, yeah?'

And yet another thing. Finn's work, it's all consuming. We barely see each other as it is. When I finish work, he's already in the thick of evening service prep and when he *has* come over afterwards, it's been after midnight when I've been in bed for two hours already for a 6 a.m. wake-up. My weekends are taken up with studying and, despite his assurances that he's staying, he talks about his friend's restaurant in Sweden a lot.

'Yeah.' I swallow and try to fix a smile onto my face. 'You're right. Sorry.'

I'm trying to give this a chance, but with Ivy now gone and our contact being so significantly reduced, I'm not sure how to balance out the high price that this might have cost.

Chapter Ten

Ivy

September, nine years ago

Ivy took one last drag on her cigarette before flicking it against the wall in the tiny alley. Its amber tip fizzed as it landed in a small puddle leaking from under one of the huge metal bins. Music blared through the door that she'd wedged open to stop herself from getting locked out. She turned to look down the alley. Out on the main street, a seemingly never-ending stream of people paraded past against a backdrop of neon lights so cluttered and strong they could probably be seen from space.

The Veronicas Strip was every bit as mad as she'd seen on *Tenerife Uncovered*. It was like an adult playground where anything went and everything was available, on tap. Bad behaviour was allowed and even encouraged, and nobody seemed to have any problems living up to expectations. Right on cue, a girl staggered into the alley and retched, sending a stream of vomit splashing loudly onto the ground. Ivy grimaced. When she'd first arrived, she'd stopped every time she'd seen someone passed out or throwing up the copious amounts of alcohol they'd drank to see if they needed help and offer a bottle of water. By now, she knew it was a pointless thing to do. At best, they'd be carted off by their friends to continue drinking or, at worst, stagger back to their room to sleep it off and do it all over again tomorrow. Still, Ivy hovered for a few seconds until a group of equally drunken girls came into the alley to rescue their friend. Ivy shook her head with a small laugh and headed back inside.

The air in the back of Shooters always smelled of grease from the fry-ups and chips served during the day to the same people who'd stumbled out the night before. Ivy passed shelves holding giant-sized cans of baked beans, hot dogs and chopped tomatoes, industrial sized bottles of ketchup, salad cream and mayonnaise, and bags of sesame-topped burger buns. It definitely wasn't fine dining, but the owners knew their customers and what they wanted – plenty of alcohol and fatty food to soak it up with. As soon as she stepped behind the bar, she was back in the thick of it. Ten shots of tequila for a group of guys who'd had countless shots already, a gin bucket for some girls who looked suspiciously sober and endless re-servings of beer.

'And one for the fit barmaid.'

Ivy looked down at the shot glass being offered by her work-mate Emma and laughed.

'Who's it from?' she asked.

Emma put the glass down and nodded towards a man prop-ping up the bar with sweat dripping down his forehead and the all-too-common redness of someone who'd majorly underestimated the Canarian sun. Ivy put the pint of Carlsberg she'd just pulled down on the bar. Its foamy head sloshed over the top of the glass and ran down her fingers. She quickly wiped her hand on her skirt, took the money for the pint and returned the change at warp speed before looking back over at the man. His England World Cup t-shirt was drenched and his eyelids were heavy with the weight of booze.

'He's so far gone he probably doesn't even know where he is, let alone what he's looking at,' Ivy said, picking up the sticky glass and raising it in a salute towards the man.

She knocked it back, barely wincing as the sweet anise liquid hit the back of her throat. Somewhere in the back of her mind, the memory of Jess's voice prompted her to chase it down with water. It wasn't bad advice. They were always being bought drinks by customers and it was the only way to stop herself from getting trollied after an hour.

The bar attracted a fairly typical crowd of 18–30s, with the scales being tipped more towards the younger end. They had regular guest DJs, smoke machines and strobe lights that, once you stepped away from the bar, were the only light source that allowed anyone to see the person they'd been snogging for the last half an hour. The shifts were long and most of the day was spent catching up on sleep, but it was fun. Everyone was there to have a good time and let loose, shaking off the stress they had to deal with back at home. Being constantly surrounded by people on a mission to enjoy themselves was contagious, and working with Emma was a guaranteed laugh. The people they served were on a high from freedom at having escaped the nine-to-five, even if only for a week or two.

'Aye, aye,' Emma said in her broad north Lancashire accent. 'Lover boy's just walked in.'

Ivy looked out from the elevated bar towards the entrance where a group was making their way in from the street. With them were three guys dressed in identical aqua blue polo t-shirts with lanyards around their necks.

'You mean Will?' Ivy flicked her long black and red braids over her shoulders. 'It's just a bit of fun.'

'Well, duh, he's a rep. You can't trust that lot as far as you can throw them,' Emma said, and Ivy nodded in agreement. 'Shagging a rep is like getting a medal of honour and they're only too happy to dish them out.'

Ivy laughed and took a tube of gloss from her back pocket to streak it across her lips.

'Still,' Emma continued, 'you could do a lot worse. He's fit as.'

'Yeah, he is.' Ivy grinned as they got to the bar. 'Beer?'

She looked him over as he sipped his Heineken. He was tanned with a shaved head, a wide grin and a scar across one of his eyebrows that gave him the look of a loveable troublemaker. He'd brought a group in on Ivy's first-ever shift and she'd noticed him straight away. Emma was right about his popularity though, because Ivy hadn't been the only one to notice him. Will and his colleagues were constantly propositioned by the tourists they were paid to look after. Ivy didn't mind. She wasn't looking for a boyfriend and their friends with benefits arrangement suited them both.

'They're all looking a bit worse for wear,' she said, nodding towards his bedraggled group, including the girl she'd just seen throwing up in the alley. 'What have you done to them? It's not even midnight yet.'

'Booze cruise.' Will winked.

'Ah. Boat, bumpy waves and booze.' Emma mock-gagged. 'I dunno how you lot do it. I'd be puking my guts up the whole time.'

Will laughed. 'Well you'd fit right in with everyone else then.'

Ivy shook her head. Boats were her limit, especially combined with alcohol. Will put his glass on the bar and leaned forwards, looking her in the eye.

'So, we still on for later? This lot look ready for bed already, I think I'll be getting off early.'

Ivy nodded. 'Alright, if you don't pass out before the night's done then feel free. I'll text you when I'm finished.'

A few hours later, Ivy stepped through the open door to her tiny balcony and leaned against the iron railing. The tang of salt wafted under her nose as a breeze blew inland and she lit a cigarette. She looked through the gap between two hotels across the road. Beyond the blocks of concrete, she could see the ocean. The sun was starting to peek over the horizon, sending beams of golden light across the shimmering water. The usually lively and brash resort was always peaceful at this time of the morning. No more loud music, drunks or neon lights. Just the rustle of wind shaking the leaves of the palm trees lining the street and the light clinking of metal on metal from the restaurant below as some seasonal worker sorted through cutlery for breakfast service.

Ivy blew a plume of smoke through her mouth and turned to look at the small studio apartment she rented. The kitchenette at the far end was separated from the living space by a chest of drawers and a tiny, uncomfortable sofa with itchy fabric. Closest to the balcony was her bed, made from two singles pushed together and currently occupied by Will. Him staying over wasn't a new thing – it made sense since they both finished work so late. And true to his promise, he'd shown up sober, more or less. He was fun and when he wasn't living up to his image as a cocky holiday rep, she sensed that he was probably a real catch underneath. She'd been surprised to learn that he was heading back to finish his master's degree in engineering when the season ended, and he'd go back to being an upstanding citizen with his days of getting eighteen-year-olds to play a drunken version of kiss chase around the pool well behind him. He'd probably make someone a nice, fun husband – something she definitely had no interest in having.

Will stirred in his sleep, and Ivy turned back to look down at the street. She'd wake him up soon. He'd be needed to ferry his group back to the airport and besides, she wanted her place to herself again. Since touching down at Reina Sofia airport, Ivy had discovered independence. Freedom. What had started as a week's beach holiday was developing into something much more.

She thought back to the flat she'd shared with her sister, filled with the lives of two people with wildly different tastes. Jess's neatness and need for order had competed with her wild and messy way of living. Ivy pictured her sister at home, fast asleep. Was she with Finn? Maybe. Ivy took a drag on her cigarette. She had to admit, being here made the whole thing easier to deal with. It wasn't that she still had a crush on him. It was just that being here felt much more her.

Ivy looked at the ocean, stretching way out into the horizon. The season here would be over soon, but the owner of Shooters also owned a beach-front cafe, and had already offered her work there to see her through the winter if she wanted it. It was tempting. The idea of going back to autumn in London didn't exactly make her want to jump for joy. Jess wouldn't like it, but this wasn't Jess's life. It was hers. Plus, her sister had made it pretty clear that they should do what they wanted by going after Finn.

Ivy stubbed out her cigarette. There wasn't even a choice to make, really. She had everything to stay for here. She'd made a new group of friends, had the sun on her skin and could swim in the sea every day. Ivy had discovered a valuable lesson in life. Jumping on a plane alone had done more than just change her physical location. It had also opened the door to things she might have never experienced otherwise, and now she'd had a taste of it, she wasn't ready to stop just yet.

Chapter Eleven

JESS

April, seven years ago

I close the front door to our childhood home behind me and step out into the spring sunshine. Delicate pink blossoms fall to the ground like confetti, the sky is cloudless and the bakery on the end of the road has smothered the entire street with the scent of fresh doughnuts. The perfection of this spring day makes me angry, as if it's taking a jab at me and rubbing the beauty of it in my face. I squeeze my eyes shut and tilt my head backwards to stem the flow of tears.

I knew this was a bad idea, right from the start. Keeping something this big from Ivy was always going to be a bad idea, but Dad insisted, and now it's too late to take it back because of the words his doctor had said earlier today. *The cancer has spread.* Just repeating them to myself sends my heart leaping off a cliff. I don't know how I'm supposed to put that in an email or a text message because, how can you? These last six weeks have been bad enough, wondering how Dad could really be sick when he seemed so fit. Six weeks of hoping there might be a way through it and praying the disease that'd already taken Mum wouldn't take my dad too.

And an eternity of feeling jealous of Ivy for being protected from all this, angry at having to deal with this alone and wishing she were here all at the same time. I get that Ivy's off having fun. And I get that Dad didn't want her to worry unnecessarily. Except it turns out that worry *was* necessary, and I know Ivy. She will absolutely lose her shit with this.

I round the corner and make my way to the bus stop. One thing is clear, Dad doesn't want chemo, he doesn't see the point. Pancreatic cancer has such a low survival rate and that's without it having spread. At least he wouldn't be fighting it for ages like Mum had, he'd said with a dry laugh. He has weeks if we're lucky, and Ivy's somewhere in Spain, having the time of her life. I rub at the worry lines that etched into my forehead the day he went for his tests and have deepened ever since. Guilt tries to yank me back to the house as I step onto the bus. I'd rather be there with him, but Dad won't hear of it because he's *not dead yet*. That's just another reason I wish Ivy were here. She'd be able to pierce through that. She'd make the idea of us being there more about company and fun instead of the way I do it that probably only reminds him of his sickness.

As the bus takes me home, the tears and frustration that have built up give way to tiredness. My collarbones sag, pulling the tense muscles around my shoulders with them. I reach a hand behind my neck and squeeze it with a sigh. The quiet anonymity of being on public transport in the middle of the afternoon and the time it takes to make the journey to Camberwell acts like a decompression chamber. I see my life as it is right now, and it feels empty without my free-spirited sister around. The flat is less cluttered without her discarded clothes strung around the place, and my nail varnishes don't get gloopy and ruined because of her inability to screw the caps back on properly. But watching certain films and TV shows are boring without the running commentary Ivy always used to give.

And I laugh less. A lot less. Especially now. I need her here to help me deal with all of this.

I get off the bus and catch sight of the Sainsbury's across the road. Despite having cooked lunch and preparing a reheatable dinner for Dad, I haven't eaten a thing myself since an apple for breakfast. My appetite disappears when I'm with him now, as if all of my energy and attention are purely based on his survival, not mine. But now, with that familiar orange sign in front of me, I picture a simple dinner of fresh pasta and salad, followed by huddling up on the sofa for an early night. I step inside the supermarket and grab a basket, when my mobile phone vibrates in my bag.

Nick: Hey, Jess. Just checking you're still ok to meet up later? Nick x

I stop and reread his message. I'd completely forgotten about our rearranged date. We've been out twice already but this last one has been shifted and moved three times between his work commitments and my sapped energy after visiting Dad. I read his message a third time, gnawing on my bottom lip. Do I really want to do this again? It's over a year since Finn left. Or, depending on the viewpoint, since I let him go. In theory, it's enough time to have moved on and everything is different now. For one thing, there's no need to consider anyone else's feelings for Nick and no potential for anyone to get hurt. I've reached the metaphorical glass ceiling of the little family printing company in Hendon and there's no need for me to work as much as before. I've finished those part-time courses and, until Dad got sick, my evenings and weekends were finally mine again. Not to mention the fact that Nick works a corporate, nine-to-five job instead of spending his evenings and weekends in a kitchen. It hasn't been the simplest of things to arrange this last date, but there also haven't been mounting and ever-present arguments about work bubbling in the background. Dating would be altogether much easier with Nick than it had been with Finn. And the chances of Nick being offered a dream job in Sweden are slim.

It would be so easy.

I shake my head and reread Nick's message. It isn't fair to use Finn as a comparison. I'd let Finn go. I'd had to, even with his assurances about wanting to stay. I didn't want him to resent being held back for a relationship. It would only have killed us in the end. There's a fresh slate with Nick and the potential foundations for something good. But still, my body is exhausted and my mind is wired, and I honestly don't know if I have it in me to socialise with anyone, even him. I ought to reply that I'm too tired, and ask to rearrange one more time. He's such a nice guy he probably won't mind. But I don't. My hate of letting people down stops me.

Jess: Hey, yes for sure. Looking forward to it x

I put the basket back, shelving my internal plans for a quiet night in, and make my way home.

◆　◆　◆

A few hours later, Nick and I are in a Highgate pub playing pool. Framed black-and-white drawings of hunting hounds and horses dot the walls around us and a lamp hangs low above the table. I furrow my brows and guide the smooth wooden cue between my fingers to nudge the tip against the white ball. I follow its trajectory, connecting with the green barrier of the table before ricocheting and hitting the eight-ball with a satisfying crack. I stand back up with a wry smile as the black ball sinks into the corner pocket.

'Are you sure you're not hustling me?' Nick laughs with a shake of his head.

'I *might* have underplayed my pool skills.'

He holds his pint glass up towards me. 'Well, congrats. You royally kicked my butt.'

I grin and tap my half-empty glass of gin and tonic against his. 'Twice, no less.'

I've won both games now, and the reluctance I'd felt about meeting up has melted away. We've laughed and gently mocked each other with every potted ball, and Nick has a kindness about him that has scooped me up like a warm hug.

'I have to admit, I didn't think you'd be all that good,' he says, laying his cue on the table.

I have to laugh as I shake my head. 'Don't let the clothes fool you.'

'Fool me, no. Distract me?' He unbuttons the top of his Ralph Lauren shirt. 'A little.'

Dating always used to feel like such a disappointment. With Nick though, it feels like smooth sailing and, despite feeling less than enthusiastic when he'd texted earlier, I'm actually having a nice time. Maddie had given me a much-needed pep talk and I'd taken my time to get ready, getting myself into the mood. My cream sheer vest, black pencil skirt and heels are a classic combination that accentuates my curves and long legs, which is great for a date but has left me feeling slightly overdressed. I'm the only person with melanin in this room, and I self-consciously check that the clips holding in the sides of my frizzy Afro hair haven't failed me. I don't want to look like someone who's just stepped off the boat, as my nan always used to say. There ought to be a stuffed stag's head on the wall to complete the interior design. It definitely isn't the kind of place I'd have opted for, and it doesn't seem to match Nick either, but it's around the corner from his house and it *is* our third date.

I've been out of the game for a while, but not so long I've forgotten the expectations of where date number three ends. He looks me up and down, and I unashamedly accept the boost it gives me. I feel about a million times better than I did this afternoon.

'My male pride is making me want to suggest best out of three,' he says. 'What do you say to a top-up instead?'

I lift my half-full glass and shake my head. 'I'm still good for now, thanks.'

The last time I'd been drunk was with Finn, that night at the house party, and, with Ivy gone, it feels like I'm still somehow paying the price for it now. Nick signals the barman for another before turning to look back at me.

'So, how did you get to be so good at pool?'

'We had a table in the pub around the corner from our flat,' I explain. 'Me and Ivy would go all the time. It was our thing.'

I like the way the edges of his eyes crinkle as he smiles back before pulling his wallet from the back pocket of his jeans to pay for the beer. He takes his freshly pulled pint and motions to the brown sofa in the corner of the room where we'd left our jackets. We settle into the leather material and, despite the easy smile on his lips, he glances at me with an unsure look in his eyes.

'I wasn't sure if you were keen on meeting up again. Our last date was a while ago.'

I grimace. 'I know. I'm sorry, I just . . .'

I hesitate before telling him about Dad. It's only our third date and I'd wanted to avoid getting heavy, but his eyes are so kind and I feel bad for him thinking my being distant was because of him. My thumb glides across the smooth surface of my glass and I take a breath before looking at him.

'My dad's sick. Cancer. It's been . . .' I shake my head. 'Well, I've been a bit all over the place to be honest.'

'God, Jess.' His face pinches and he puts his glass on the table in front of us. 'I'm sorry. How serious is it?'

'It's terminal.' I swallow. 'We thought he might be able to fight it but we got the news this morning. It's pretty aggressive.'

Nick takes my hand in his and gives it a squeeze. 'I'm so sorry. I lost my dad to lung cancer a few years back. I know how hard it is.'

I nod a thanks. Despite the awfulness of what I'm telling him, my body relaxes with his kindness. His palm is warm, and his thumb is making reassuring circles on my skin.

'I'd have understood if you'd have wanted to shift it again.'

'No, I'm glad we met up,' I say with a smile. 'It's nice to have some normality.'

'You've got your sister though,' he says. 'You're not dealing with it alone, at least.'

I take a sip of my drink and shake my head at the mess of it all. 'She doesn't know yet. She's been living abroad for a while and Dad wanted to wait until . . . well. Until he got better, I suppose.'

Nick lets go of my hand and drapes his arm around my shoulders instead. 'Listen, if you need anything, just let me know. I can help with stuff around the house, give him a shave, that kind of thing. Like I said, I've been there. It's tough to do it alone.'

'Thank you. That's really kind,' I reply with a smile.

God, he's so nice. If ever there were a poster-boy for the perfect man on the perfect date, it would definitely be Nick: politeness personified, attractive, sensitive and not at all pushy. How many other men would volunteer to shave your sick dad's beard? Nick is the kind of guy your nan would like and your best friend would drool over.

His thumb grazes my skin, trailing up the nape of my neck, and I let my head tilt back. The tips of his fingers press lightly against my skin, making the tiniest of circular movements. From the outside, it looks like a simple neck massage but on the inside, it feels intensely intimate. It's like a spark plug, firing up a part of me that only now realises just how much I've craved touch like this. His thigh presses into mine with comforting warmth and I let myself settle into the crook of his shoulder. I haven't slept with anyone since Finn. It was a conscious choice but my God, it's been a long time.

I'm not sure if it's been down to his good manners or my being out of practice, but our previous dates have ended with a polite kiss on the cheek. This time though, he leans over and puts the most innocent of butterfly kisses against my cheek and it sends a jolt right between my legs. He kisses me again, a little closer towards my lips. And again, this time with his lips brushing the side of my mouth.

It's nice. And gentle. And while my body doesn't burst with a ball of flaming, sexual desire, it *does* remember how to respond, without any input from me. It's the complete opposite to how it was with Finn, where everything would come alive, like moving from a world of black and white to Technicolour, but it feels nice. It feels safe.

I turn my head to kiss Nick back. I know that, if I go to his place, it won't be just about the sex. Nick is that guy I'd always wanted to find. Someone who wants to settle down and live an uncomplicated life. He gives me the feeling that he's someone I can rely on. That being with him would be straightforward. That if this does develop into something, it would be on stable ground, which is exactly what I've always said I'd needed after Finn.

Chapter Twelve

IVY

May, seven years ago

Ivy rolled her eyes at the sound of her mobile ringing and unzipped the small pouch around her hips. She already knew who it would be.

'I can't talk right now, Jess,' she said quickly. 'I'll have to call you back.'

It was the third time in the last half an hour she'd called and Ivy had seen missed calls on her phone all week. It had been a hectic few days with the new work season starting and she'd been meaning to call Jess back, but every time she'd remembered it had been much too late at night.

'I promise,' she added, hitching her clipboard under her arm.

'Ivy . . .'

A flash of unease rippled in her body at the strange tone of her sister's voice. 'What's wrong?'

'You need to come home.'

'Why?'

'It's Dad . . . he's sick.'

'Sick how?' Ivy shook her head as an announcement played out over the tannoy in the airport terminal.

'He's got cancer.'

'What?' For a second, the noise in the terminal around her disappeared as her ears rang and her pulse thudded loudly inside her head. Ivy clutched the mobile phone tightly in her hand. 'What kind of cancer?'

'Pancreatic,' Jess replied flatly. 'It's bad.'

Ivy blinked, trying to make sense of it. 'How bad? What did the doctor say?'

The new cluster of pale-faced people wheeling suitcases through the arrival doors felt as disorientating as the words her sister had just told her. Ivy took a breath. Cancer wasn't an automatic death sentence these days. There was so much research on it. It didn't have to be how it had been with their mum. Dad would start treatment and fight it, and in a year's time he'd be a cancer survivor with an inspiring story to tell.

'Jess?' she prompted, holding up the clipboard with her free hand to display the name of the company she worked for to the pasty Brits walking through the doors. 'When does he start chemo?'

'He doesn't want to.'

'But . . . why?'

Ivy's heart pounded and she shook her head, trying to dislodge the news as if by shaking it off, it simply wouldn't be real.

'It's too late for chemo. Ivy, you need to come home.'

A day and a half after their phone call, Ivy slid into one of the pine chairs in her dad's kitchen and put her elbows on the table.

'You're not seriously hung-over right now?' Jess asked, standing with her hand on her hip.

'Of course not.'

Ivy dropped her head into her hands and tried not to heave as Jess put a cup of milky tea under her nose.

'It looks like one to me,' Jess said knowingly.

In normal circumstances, it would be a fair assumption to make, but not this time.

'It's food poisoning,' Ivy replied with a sigh. 'I ate mussels last night.'

She hadn't been able to eat after taking Jess's call at the airport. Somehow, she'd managed to switch into holiday rep mode on auto-pilot, shepherding her new coachload of holiday-makers to their resort and giving them their orientation meeting. She'd called her dad in her half-hour break and he'd tried to sound normal, as if everything was okay. How she'd made it through the bar-crawl that night without breaking down, she didn't know. Reality had only hit when she'd finally made it back to her studio apartment in the early hours of the morning. She'd spent the next few hours in tears, staring out of her window at everything and nothing until her next workday started. The idea of food hadn't existed in her mind until Jess's voice had popped up in her head, telling her to make sure she ate something before going to the airport to fly home.

'Here,' Jess said, putting a glass of water on the table. 'Drink this.'

Ivy scrunched her nose as her sister used a pipette to drop some green liquid into it. 'What is it?'

'Swedish bitter herbs. It'll help with your stomach.'

She doubted it. Ivy almost wished it was a hangover – they were easy enough to cure with a little hair of the dog. She took a sip from the glass, wincing at the bitterness as Jess sat in the chair next to her.

'Thanks,' she said, letting her shoulders droop as she looked around at the kitchen.

It was exactly how it always had been. The wooden clock carved into the shape of the island of Jamaica still hung next to the fridge, and, as ever, an insane number of packets of cream crackers were stacked by the microwave. It was a place where everything seemed to have stood still while changing at breakneck speed.

Ivy sighed deeply. 'I can't believe it.'

'I know.'

'I can't believe there's nothing they can do,' she said, shaking her head. 'There's so much funding into cancer research and so many treatments out there. Not to mention all the alternative therapy. You know all about that stuff, you could convince him.'

Jess was always trying weird things out in the name of health. When they'd lived together, she'd eaten raw garlic cloves because some doctor on an internet documentary had said it was the best thing to do to prevent illness.

'I tried,' her sister replied, 'but the diagnosis just came too late.'

Ivy shook her head again. Until she saw him for herself, she was going to cling on to the hope that something could be done.

'Maybe we should make some breakfast?' she asked. The idea of eating made her stomach churn but he'd need to keep his strength up.

'He doesn't eat much any more,' Jess said.

'Since when does Dad not eat much? He's only just been diagnosed; it can't be that bad already.'

'The morphine makes him sick.'

'Okay . . . well a cup of tea, then?' Ivy suggested.

Jess sighed. 'The morphine runs out first thing and the Macmillan nurse is usually running late because they're so backed up and it's better to let him sleep. Though how he gets any with that stupid machine beeping all the time, I don't know.'

Jess rubbed her hands across her face. She looked tired and stressed. Her skin had always been flawless, but now she had dark circles under her eyes. It was a different version of the Jess that Ivy had lived with. That Jess had always given the impression of never really needing anyone's help and always having things running smoothly. This one looked like she needed a big bowl of soup, a hot-water bottle and a week in bed.

'Look, Ivy. It's great that you're back,' Jess said, throwing her a weak smile. 'There's so much to get into, but just . . . you need to know that Dad doesn't have much energy right now.'

'Okay,' Ivy replied slowly, trying not to let defensiveness creep in. What exactly was her sister trying to say? That she shouldn't be *too much*? 'So what should I do then?'

Jess shrugged. 'Drink that water so you feel better? Go take a shower?'

It felt a lot like being mothered. Again. She'd only been back a few hours and they'd slipped so easily into their assigned roles. Jess was right, though. Ivy couldn't go up and see her dad in this state, so she slugged another mouthful of the herbal water before going into the living room. She'd dumped her suitcase and crashed down here after getting in from the airport. It made more sense than being upstairs and waking them up with the constant toilet flushing.

Ivy rifled through her suitcase in a room full of memories. The walls were covered with photographs – images of Jess and Ivy as kids with missing teeth and teenagers with too much make-up, and other extended family. She and Jess had a dozen cousins in total, and some of those even had kids of their own. Whenever there was be a big family do, like important wedding anniversaries or christenings, she'd always be momentarily shocked by the sheer amount of people. She wondered how many of them knew about her dad. Ivy sat on the floor and picked up the silver frame on the side table next to the phone. The picture of them on holiday was taken just before their mum had gotten sick. They'd been to Florida and Jess had been mobbed by mosquitoes so badly that she'd had her legs slathered in ointment and bandaged afterwards. Ivy stared at her mum and dad, standing behind the two sisters. They'd been such young parents and she'd assumed they'd always be around. She'd never have thought she'd be in the situation of neither of them being alive before she turned thirty.

Ivy put the frame back down and frowned at the stack of NHS letters and a Macmillan leaflet on the shelf under the table. It seemed like an awful lot of letters to have considering he'd only just been diagnosed. She took the letters out and scanned the top one with the frown deepening on her forehead. Bitterness flooded her mouth as she flicked through to the one behind it, and the one behind that until the downstairs toilet flushed.

'What is this?' she asked as soon as her sister walked into the living room, holding the letters up in her hand. 'Why do these letters date back to last month?'

'Oh, God.' Jess rubbed a hand across her forehead.

'Some of them are from six weeks ago. You said the diagnosis was last week.'

Jess dropped her hands and sat on the arm of the sofa with a sigh. 'I tried to tell him he should tell you.'

Ivy blinked. *'What?'*

'He didn't want to worry you. You were just about to go to Portugal.' She shook her head. 'He wanted you to enjoy your holiday.'

'Are you serious? That was ages ago, Jess. Why didn't *you* tell me? *I'd* have told *you.'*

'He made me promise not to. And honestly, at that stage we thought he'd be okay.' Jess sucked her bottom lip into her mouth and blinked a few times. 'I wanted to tell you. I didn't want to keep it from you but Dad insisted. And then last week they found out it's spread and I couldn't keep that from you.'

Ivy dropped a sarcastic laugh. 'Oh, well thanks for the honesty. Come on, Jess. *Six weeks?* I'd have come home straight away if I'd known.'

'Exactly. That's what he didn't want.'

'I had a right to know,' Ivy replied hotly. 'I could've been here to help with stuff.'

'You think I wouldn't have wanted that? I've been dealing with this all by myself while you've been partying and surfing in Portugal and Spain.'

'I've been working, and I dropped everything as soon as you called,' Ivy shot back, struggling to keep her voice down. 'I found out *two days* ago. You've known about this for almost two months.'

It burned her chest, right in the middle of it, deep in her breastbone. That's two months she'd missed out on because, once again, she'd been the last to know what was going on. Tears pricked at her eyes and she rubbed them away with the back of her hand.

'He wanted to protect you.'

'From what?' Ivy hissed.

'From *this*,' Jess snapped back. 'From flipping out and getting upset.'

'He's my dad! Of course I'm upset,' Ivy replied, her head spinning with disbelief.

'Yeah, well, so am I. Where's *my* protection? Who's looking out for *me*?' Her sister's voice rose before she stopped, took a deep breath and blew it out shakily through her mouth. 'Look, Ivy. It wasn't my idea and it wasn't what I wanted, but you're here now. Please, let's not fight.'

Ivy threw the letters on to the sofa and shook her head. 'You really do have a natural talent for lying, don't you?'

'Come on, Ivy. That's not fair. I *wanted* to tell you.'

'But you didn't. Instead, you lied. Again.'

Hurt flickered on Jess's face, but it was true, whether she wanted to hear it or not. Only this time, Jess hadn't lied about a guy. It was about their dad, lying upstairs with who knew how long left to live. Keeping it a secret hadn't protected her from anything, it had only made her lose time.

Jess looked up at the ceiling and sighed before looking back at her sister. 'This is about Dad right now, not you. He doesn't need this.'

'You're unbelievable, you know that?' Ivy grabbed her toiletry bag and some clothes from her open suitcase. 'I need a shower.'

'Don't wake him up,' Jess called behind her.

She had to get out of that room before she flipped completely. It was bad enough to learn her dad was sick, but knowing she could've been here ages ago to spend time with him was even worse. Ivy went up the carpeted stairs and stopped at the top, staring at the door to her dad's bedroom. It was slightly open, enough for her to see the end of the bed and the slight curve of his feet under the covers. She put her head down and hurried to the bathroom, closing the door quietly behind her. She stood for a second with her head pressed against the back of the door. It was madness, this whole thing. That she was back here to effectively say goodbye to her dad felt like some kind of cosmic joke she couldn't understand.

She pushed herself away from the door and turned the shower on. Ivy looked at her reflection as she peeled off her t-shirt and shorts. Even with her dark and tanned skin, she looked pasty and absolutely wrecked – an accurate reflection of how she felt inside. She wound her hair up into a bun and stepped under the shower where she stayed for far longer than she'd planned to. By the time she turned the water off, the bathroom was hidden in a billowing cloud of steam and Ivy felt a touch more human. After slathering her skin with cocoa butter and pulling on a fresh vest and jeans,

Ivy wiped a hand across the mirror above the sink and looked at her blurry reflection.

'You can do this,' she whispered to herself.

She had to. There was no choice, even though the idea of going into her dad's bedroom was making every single cell in her body revolt. It was stupid, but she had the thought that if she just walked past his door again and went back downstairs, it would mean that everything was fine, like he was just having a lie-in. Ivy heaved out a sigh and gripped the edge of the sink with her hands before pushing herself away from it. Hearing Jess's voice in her head, she swung open the window to let the steam out, and then went out into the hallway before she could let the fear kick in.

Ivy hovered outside his bedroom door for a moment, took a deep, quiet breath to steel herself, and then pushed the door open. Her dad was lying on his side, fast asleep. She wasn't sure what she'd expected him to look like, but he still looked like *him*. It helped to calm her nerves as she crept into the room and slowly sat on the bed, making sure not to disturb him. He had some kind of machine strapped to him, with a tube disappearing into his sleeve – medication, Ivy guessed. The bedside table was piled high with stacks and stacks of medication. A plastic beaker with a straw stood next to his clock radio, along with a picture of Jess and Ivy as kids with him and their mum. On the floor by his bed was a small bin with an open plastic bag in it. The room was a curious mix of the scent of the aftershave he'd always worn that had seeped into every available piece of fabric in the room, and the unmistakable, sickly smell of vomit. Ivy took the bin and quietly went back into the bathroom to empty it.

When she came back in, the machine strapped to him beeped, just as Jess had said. Ivy held her breath, waiting to see if he'd wake up. He didn't, and the relief at him not having to wake up in pain was quickly replaced with panic that he wouldn't wake up at all.

She lowered herself as close to him as she could, until she heard the light puff of his exhale. She stayed in a half-bent position, listening to him breathe a few more times to be sure, before sitting back up again.

For a while, Ivy sat there with him, half-hoping he'd wake up, and half-hoping he wouldn't because she didn't know what to say. He'd still sounded normal on the phone yesterday. She'd expected him to be up and about, not lying in bed like this. Jess had told her the spread was aggressive and doctors were giving him a week, two at most. In the confines of his room, it felt like both a blip and an eternal amount of time. Everything was still. It had always been quiet on this side of the house with none of the traffic noise that there was on the other. His radio was off, which, when Ivy thought about it, might be the first time she'd ever known it to be silent. All she could hear was the periodic beep of his machine and the odd twitch of his feet under the covers, which came with increasing regularity. She guessed the morphine he'd had overnight was leaving his system. Ivy looked at the clock. Jess had said the nurse would be likely running late, but it surely couldn't be long? Maybe, if the pain was too much, she could get some marijuana instead. It was easy enough to get and definitely wouldn't make him sick like Jess said the morphine did. He might even eat and feel better.

A few minutes later, his eyes opened and he slowly turned his head. His eyes were cloudy, but the skin around them wrinkled with recognition. He'd lost so much weight.

'It *is* you,' he croaked. 'I thought I'd died already.'

'Dad!' Ivy went to playfully whack his arm but quickly thought better of it. 'Don't say things like that.'

'Pass some of that water, will you?'

Ivy grabbed the beaker from his nightstand as if his life depended on it, and held it to his mouth. A ball the size of a melon choked in her throat at the effort it took him to sip through the straw. He couldn't have taken more than a tiny mouthful before he dropped his head back onto the pillow and his machine beeped again.

'When did you get back?' he asked.

'Early this morning.'

'Mm. I'm glad you're home. Means a lot.'

'As if I wouldn't,' she whispered.

She wanted to tell him she'd have come back six weeks ago if she'd have known, but decided against it. What good would it do now? She'd never have imagined he could possibly get to be so weak, especially when he looked like he always had. Apart from being skinnier, he didn't look like he was dying. She thought about the mass of cells that had spread and taken over his body, and squeezed her hands into fists. Ivy took a breath and pushed the thought away. She would not, could not, lose it in front of him. It wouldn't be fair.

'So tell me about your travels,' he said.

Ivy raised her eyebrows. 'Really?'

'Of course. It's better than listening to this stupid thing beeping non-stop.' He laughed a little and Ivy squeezed his hand.

He hadn't travelled much, though he'd always wanted to. He'd married young and then found himself unexpectedly widowed with two young daughters. When would he have had the chance to see the things he'd wanted? Ivy told him about the majesty of the palace of Alhambra, with its pristine gardens and intricate architecture, the monkeys on Gibraltar and the soul-tingling silence of the deserts in Almeria. Until now, she'd thought she hadn't seen all that much. The travellers who passed through the hostel she'd worked at for a while had passports full of visas and stamps. She had a whole list of places she wanted to see, and so far, she'd only been in Spain and Portugal. But as she told her dad about the flamenco dancing she'd seen in Seville and the cobbled streets of Lisbon, she realised that she was effectively showing him things he'd never get the chance to see for himself. It all felt so unfair, and it weighed in her chest like a block of concrete.

Forty minutes later, his eyelids grew heavy and Ivy kept his hand between hers as he fell back asleep. She hoped he was dreaming of the sun and heat of Spain. Anything to distract him from the relentless beep of his empty medicine regulator. She shook her head and rubbed her eyes with one of her hands. She was exhausted, even without the food poisoning.

Ivy looked out through the window. It was the start of a bright spring day and the urge to get a gulp of fresh air pulsed through her body. It hadn't been like this when Mum was sick. She'd been in the hospital and then the hospice. Her parents hadn't wanted them to see her dying. It had been a couple of days after their last visit that she'd died in her sleep, something that Ivy had always felt a little grateful for. She knew that wouldn't be the case this time. Death was already here, seeping in through the gaps under the doors, carried in with every open and close of the letter box. She was exhausted after just an hour. What must it be like for him? And for Jess? She'd said nobody had been supporting or protecting her. She'd had to deal with all of this alone, along with keeping a secret she hadn't wanted to. No wonder she'd seemed so exhausted.

Ivy kissed the back of her dad's hand and pulled his blanket up from the bottom of the bed to cover the rest of him before leaving the room as quietly as she could. She held her breath and quickly ran down the stairs, almost slipping on the carpet, not sure if she needed to vomit or cry or both. Ivy flung open the front door and stepped outside, gasping with her hands on her knees and pulling the air down deep into her lungs before heaving and coughing back out again.

'What happened?' Jess ran out behind her. 'Ivy?'

She looked at her sister, the only other person in the world who could possibly understand the feelings boiling inside her. The sadness and anger and desperation for things to be different. The tears she'd been holding back flowed like open floodgates and clogged her throat.

'He's dying, Jess,' she croaked, the words feeling acid on her tongue.

Jess's chin trembled as she pursed her lips together and nodded. 'I know.'

Ivy reached out and grabbed her sister, burying her face into her shoulder while simultaneously offering hers for Jess to do the same.

Chapter Thirteen

Ivy

May, seven years ago

The next day, Ivy walked into the kitchen where Jess was stood at the sink rinsing lettuce leaves.

'Nick'll be here with the food in a minute,' she said, looking over her shoulder.

Ivy leaned against the kitchen counter. 'What's he like, this Nick?'

'He's nice.'

'Nice?' Ivy raised an eyebrow and piled her hair up into a bun. Nice didn't exactly set the world on fire.

'He's a nice guy. Normal. Considerate. Kind.' Jess flashed her a smile.

It all sounded very underwhelming compared to the way Jess had spoken about Finn that day when Ivy had come home to find him in their bathroom. Ivy had been surprised when Jess had told her curtly on the phone that they'd broken up, after the way she'd defended their sleeping together in the first place.

'Is it serious with him?' Ivy asked.

Jess shrugged, taking the colander full of lettuce to the wooden chopping board. 'I guess.'

As conversations went, this felt very different to the way they'd spoken about guys when they'd lived together. Back then, it had been a bonding thing. Now, it only seemed to show Ivy just how much things had changed. Her sister wasn't giving the impression that she wanted to go into a whole lot of detail about any of this, and the closeness they used to share felt very far away.

Jess started chopping the lettuce and then stopped. She put the knife down and looked at Ivy. 'Actually, I wanted to talk to you about something.'

The look in her sister's eyes made Ivy uneasy, and she automatically crossed her arms, ready for whatever was about to come.

'Go on.'

'I've got an appointment with an estate agent to value the flat.'

Ivy frowned. 'Why?'

'Because you don't live there any more and I don't want to be there on my own. And once Dad . . . well, it'll be too much to deal with.'

'Well, you can't just sell it. Rent it out, or get Nick to move in.'

Jess sighed. 'It doesn't make sense to keep it. It needs so much work done to it and I can't *handle* everything on my own.'

'But—'

'But what?' Jess threw her hands up. 'You're not here, Ivy. You're not the one who's dealing with all the stuff that goes with owning a flat. You don't pay for the insurance, the mortgage or service fees. You don't have to be the one to call the plumber when a pipe's blocked – you're not here!'

'So I'm being punished for leaving?' Ivy shook her head. 'It's my home!'

'A home you don't even live in!'

Ivy groaned and pushed herself away from the counter. 'Oh my God, you just don't get it, do you. It's not *just* a home, it's . . . it's . . .'

What was it exactly? Ivy didn't know. Considering she'd barely even thought about the place since leaving, she was surprising herself with the intensity of what she was feeling right now. Things had turned out great in Spain, but the flat was like a trump card she could play if things went belly up. If Jess sold it, that'd be gone.

'Look,' Jess said, 'I don't want to get into this right now. Nick'll be here any minute and Dad doesn't need to hear us arguing.'

'Fine, but my name's on the mortgage too, Jess. You can't sell it without my approval.'

Jess sighed. 'It's just a valuation, there's no need to be so dramatic.'

Frustration rose in her chest. She hated it when Jess spoke like this, like she was being totally reasonable and Ivy was acting out of control when all she was really doing was voicing her opinion and standing up for herself. The doorbell rang and Jess swore under her breath.

'Nick's here. Look, can we talk about this later? It's just an idea, nothing's set in stone.'

As far as Ivy was concerned, there was nothing to talk about.

◆ ◆ ◆

Two weeks later

'Fucking funerals,' Ivy hissed under her breath.

She hated them. She hated the sadness, the grief, the distant family, the tears and the blackness. She hated the coldness of them. The sky was clear blue and the sun had shone all day like it had something special to say, but it was still cold in this room, in her bones, in her heart. Ivy nodded to the young guy behind the bar and signalled for another drink. He poured out another measure of rum and she took it, sinking it in one long gulp. She put the glass back down on the bar, and signalled for another, barely wincing any more at the burn at the back of her throat. It got less intense with each shot.

'Oh, Ivy. How are you holding up?'

Her forehead wrinkled as she squinted her eyes at the face in front of her. Female, ancient, with a big black hat and lipstick that seemed to bleed from the rims of her mouth into the lines of her face. Who was she? Ivy snorted and shook her head. She had no idea. In fact, as she looked around the hall, she had no idea who most of these people were. Her vision swam as she looked from table to table, filled with flowers and people sitting and talking and eating and drinking. Reggae played loudly on the speakers, mixed by some distant relative moonlighting as a DJ, and the air was thick with the mixed scents of curried goat, jerk chicken and rice and peas. Ivy ground her teeth together. The only person who wasn't here, who *should* be here, was her dad. She shook her head again to correct herself. The only *people* who should be here were her mum *and* dad. The woman, whoever she was, was still talking and Ivy had no idea what she was saying. She didn't really care. She looked at the clock. When could she leave and get the hell away from all of these people?

The woman in front of her was *still* talking. 'I remember when—'

'Look, lady. I don't know who you are, but can't you just leave me alone?'

That seemed to have done the trick. The woman straightened up, haughtily frowning before bustling away. Ivy shook her head, swearing to herself as the woman made a beeline straight for her sister. She watched as the woman stood prim and upright with her hands piously clasped in front of her and, even from the other side of the room, she could see the way Jess's shoulders sagged. Nick was standing next to her and Ivy imagined the conversation between them. Nick would probably be telling her to leave it alone, diffusing the situation. He had that way about him. Maybe that's what had attracted Jess to him, because it wasn't his personality. He was totally nondescript. Nice, but not the kind of guy you'd remember years down the line. At least Jess had someone by her side instead of being all alone like Ivy was. She sighed as Jess snatched her arm away from Nick when he tried to hold her elbow and braced herself as her sister stalked over to her.

'Before you say anything, I just asked her to leave me alone. She kept going on and on about I don't know what,' Ivy said, holding her glass out in the air.

'I think you need to eat something and drink some water,' Jess hissed quietly.

'I already have a drink and I'm not hungry.'

'Well, you need something to soak up all that alcohol. You're drunk.'

'Aren't you a regular Miss Marple.' Ivy rolled her eyes and sank the amber liquid in one gulp. 'Yes, I'm drunk. What of it?'

Jess sighed and blinked. The two sisters stared at each other for a few seconds and the scowl fell from Jess's face.

'Ivy. I know today has been shit—'

'Understatement.'

'—but you can't do this. You can't just be rude to people. Not here, not today. These are Dad's friends and family. *Our* family.'

'Pfft. I don't know most of these people. And I can do what I want, he was my dad.'

'He was my dad, too.'

Jess had a look on her face and a tightness around her mouth that Ivy knew meant she was skating on thin ice. It had been thin enough already, since she'd come back. Jess had done everything, putting the plans their dad had already made into motion, organising the funeral, calling banks and pension funds and insurance companies with the news that their customer – their dad – had died. And Ivy had done nothing. Jess hadn't let her. She'd made her feel as if she might mess things up, as if she couldn't be trusted to place an order at the florist or get a suit dry-cleaned. As if she wasn't capable of organising things, when she'd managed to organise a whole life for herself in a foreign country. Even Nick had been involved, arranging the cars and a suit for Dad to be buried in. All Ivy had been left to do was cook and clean, and it hadn't been enough to let her escape the reality of the situation. It hadn't distracted her from the fact that their dad had died in the room right above the table they'd eaten at for as long as she could remember. That now, there were no parents. They were orphans. And worse, she was an orphan without a home, or she would be if Jess really did get her way with selling the flat.

Jess sighed deeply. 'Please, Ivy. Just eat something and sober up.'

'Why? Nobody else is. Look at Uncle Leon, he's even more drunk than I am.' Ivy nodded to some cousin of their dad's, sitting on his chair with his chin in his chest as a consequence of the open bar.

'Oh, God.' Jess shook her head and, horror, even laughed a bit.

'See. Totally acceptable.'

Jess looked back at her with raised eyebrows in a look that said she didn't agree.

'Jess, please. Just get off my back and let me do things my way for once.'

'Please.'

Jess sighed with a shake of her head. 'Just don't be rude to the other guests, okay?'

Ivy watched her sister as she threaded her way back through the tables towards Nick. There was no doubt it was hard on Jess, too. She never asked for help or liked to admit that she might not be coping. Ivy knew it was a trauma response to dive into distractions. Jess had been doing it ever since their mum had died, and it had gone into overdrive since Dad had followed. Ivy understood it, but it was driving her mad. Jess's way of taking over reminded her of all the times she'd been made to feel like a kid, even though there was only a year between them. Jess was great at organising things and being responsible, but she'd had nowhere near the same amount of life experience that Ivy had. It was Ivy who'd gone out into the world, stood on her own two feet in a country where she knew nobody and couldn't speak one word of the language. Clearly none of that mattered.

Everyone in this room had offered her their condolences, but not in the way they had to Jess. Jess had been the one to look after him when he was sick, to make the phone calls and put the notice in the paper. Ivy knew that, in their eyes, Jess had been left alone to do it all because Ivy had been swanning around in Spain having the time of her life. They didn't know that Ivy had been deliberately lied to and kept in the dark. That Jess had made that decision to keep the secret, whether their dad had demanded it or not. They didn't see that Jess was about to shatter the last bit of familiarity that Ivy knew by selling the flat they'd shared and, in all likelihood, the house they'd grown up in too. The people in this room didn't see the stuff that Ivy had to deal with. All they saw was Jess, the sister who'd sacrificed her childhood to step into the role of mother, and then cared for their sick dad. Ivy wondered how it would be if they knew about Jess's capacity for lying right to her face, not once, but twice. If they'd known that she was the one who'd caused the fracture between them that had opened the door to her leaving in the first place, and then deliberately kept that door shut until the last minute.

Ivy stalked away from the bar, past the picture of their dad with his honorary glass of Wray & Nephew Rum standing next to it, and pushed open the swinging doors. A few people stood in the lobby of the venue they'd hired, and she recognised none of them. There was no comfort in them being here. If anything, she wished they'd all just disappear.

Ivy pushed her way through the door to the toilets and closed one of the cubicle doors behind her. Her chest ached as frustration pushed against her ribs like a pressure cooker and her hands shook as she prised a wrap of cocaine from her bra. She peeled it open and carefully placed it on the edge of the cistern. The white powder was already pressed and cut, in anticipation of needing to have it with her as support for this god-awful day. It had been ridiculously easy to get and far too difficult not to use, and she used her little finger to separate a bit of the powder before bending down and sniffing it in one short, sharp go. She winced at the sting behind her eyes and swallowed against the bitter, chemical taste at the back of her throat. Ivy leaned against the cubicle wall and closed her eyes.

God, this hurt. It was like losing Mum all over again. And it wasn't just an emotional pain, it was physical too, clawing right at her breastbone. In fact, it was worse than with Mum, because this time she hadn't been spared the end. She hadn't been prepared for his condition to worsen so quickly. His breathing had deteriorated to the point where he seemed to only take a single breath every five minutes, and it rattled at the back of his throat. His legs and arms had twitched, as if he'd wanted to escape his bed. Ivy had learned that Hollywood was the biggest liar in the world. Death wasn't the way they showed it. There was no simple slipping away with a peaceful smile. It was painful and it was messy and it went on for far longer than was humane.

Tears cascaded down her face as someone else came in and Ivy stayed as silent as she could, waiting for the cocaine to land and numb the feeling back down. The spotlights in the ceiling started to grow little halos around them, and Ivy put a hand on her heart.

I'm sorry, I'm sorry, I'm sorry.

She repeated the sentence, knowing that, if he could see her now, he'd be pissed. Or disappointed, which was always so much worse. But the truth was, she didn't know how to get through this day otherwise. The toilet in the next cubicle flushed, and she sniffed, scrubbing the tears from her face. He wasn't here any more, so it didn't matter. She could do whatever she wanted knowing there wouldn't be a watchful parent somewhere. The realisation of it would've made her heart break, if it weren't for the cocaine in her system that made it all feel that much more bearable.

Ivy coughed, repackaged her stash and opened the door, in desperate need of water to wash the taste in the back of her throat away. She bent down to drink straight from the tap by the sink, just as Jess came out from another cubicle. Ivy stood back up and wiped the back of her hand across her mouth as her sister washed her hands.

The muffled sounds of people outside filtered through the door and Ivy wished she could teleport herself away instead of having to go back out there. Jess turned off the tap and stood with her hands on the sink, looking down into it.

'I'm sorry. About earlier. This whole thing is just a lot,' Jess said.

Ivy swallowed. 'I know.'

'You'd think it'd be easier the second time around.'

'At least you've got Nick.'

Jess took a paper towel from the dispenser. 'Yeah. That's true.'

'I don't have anyone.'

'You never wanted anyone.'

It wasn't strictly true. She just didn't want someone in the way other people did. As far as Ivy was concerned, modern relationships were set up for failure. There was too much temptation and too many restrictions. You never stood a chance. She loved intimacy, and she loved sex. She loved the feeling of falling in love. But she wasn't about to give up her freedom for it. She sniffed. Now that she was bolstered by the coke, the loneliness she'd just felt in the cubicle seemed a little less acute.

Jess scrunched the paper towels up and threw them into the bin before wiping her fingers under her eyes as she peered at the mirror. She looked at Ivy's reflection and the soft look on her face hardened as her eyes narrowed.

'What is *that*?'

Ivy frowned. 'What's what?'

'That shit on your nose.'

Ivy leaned forwards to look more closely in the mirror and quickly rubbed the remnants of white powder from the inside of her nostril.

Jess straightened up and stared at her. 'Tell me that's not what I think it is.'

'It's not what you think it is.'

Her sister shook her head, sending her dangly earrings swinging by her neck. 'Can't you just make an effort? For one bloody day? It's Dad's funeral, for God's sake.'

'Yes, thank you, Jess. I'm well aware of that,' Ivy snapped back.

'Are you? Are you actually aware of anything other than yourself? What the hell were you thinking? I need you to just bloody *be* here. For once, Ivy.'

'For what? So you can tell me how useless I am? How you're so much more capable of things than I am?'

Jess shook her head. 'What are you *talking* about? When have I ever said that?'

'You kept Dad being sick a secret from me! I think that says it loud enough.'

'How many times do I have to tell you, it was what he wanted. He wanted to protect you, like he always did. Like *I* always did, because God forbid Ivy ever has to deal with anything tough in this life.'

'You kept him from me!' Rage boiled in Ivy's belly, bolstered by the cocaine and alcohol. She could almost feel her anger running through her veins, sending her pulse thumping in her ears. 'And now you're trying to tell me it's somehow my fault?'

Jess laughed sarcastically. 'Look at yourself. Is it any wonder you get treated like you do? You had Dad wrapped around your little finger. Being the fucked-up one who needed all the extra love and attention but never did anything to earn it.'

Ivy's eyes stung. 'That's not true.'

'Isn't it?' Jess jutted her chin out, her chest rising and falling as she breathed heavily. 'Even at the end, you get some hero's return after swanning around without a care in the world to get the last bit of time that he had.'

'That is *not* fair. You keep on saying that but you seem to ignore the fact that you kept it from me. How was I supposed to know?' Ivy said, clenching her fists by her sides.

'Yeah well, I've got news for you, Ivy. Life isn't fair. It never has been, but you don't see *me* running around getting shit-faced, blaming everyone and everything for my problems and shoving crap up my nose, do you? When are you ever going to grow up?'

'God, when did you become such a bitch?' Ivy spat the words out with her heart ramming in her chest. 'I mean, seriously. All you've done since I've got back is remind me of how fucking

119

inadequate I am. Like I don't even have a place in this family any more. You're even selling our flat, like it's nothing.'

'Because I don't want to be the one who always has to sort things out. I'm sick and tired of having to do *everything*. It was always me who had to sort things out around the house, pay the council tax, take the car for its bloody MOT. And then you decide to stay in Spain and leave me with a mortgage to pay.'

'Nobody asked you to do those things. You did all that by yourself, without ever asking for help or even *giving* me the chance to do any of it, just like you've done with all of this.' Ivy shook her head. 'It never even crossed your mind that I might have actually wanted to be involved in my own dad's funeral, did it?'

Her blood rushed in her veins. The pressure building inside was so tangible she could really feel it, brewing up from her toes and pushing up through her legs.

Jess rolled her eyes. 'Oh, please. You could've if you'd really wanted to, but you chose to be out every single time there was something to be done. It's the same old with you. There's always some reason for you not being where you're supposed to be, or doing what you're supposed to be doing.'

'I wasn't here because of *you*!' Ivy shouted. 'I missed the last part of Dad's life because of you. And if you'd never slept with Finn, I probably would never have even left in the first place.'

'God, not this again.' Jess tilted her head back. 'How many times do I need to apologise for that? Isn't it enough that we split up?'

'You just don't get it do you? You *lied* to me. You made me feel and look like an idiot. I'd never have done that to you. I went to Tenerife alone because of what *you* did.'

Jess's eyes swivelled as Ivy spat the words at her, but it was true. If she hadn't come home to find Finn in their flat that day, they'd have gone on holiday together and then come back as planned. She might never have been in Spain and instead, she would have been able to spend the last bit of Dad's life here, with him.

'This is *your* fault,' Ivy seethed. *'Yours, not mine.'*

'No, Ivy. I didn't force you to put that shit up your nose, or to stay in Spain, or to be such a constant mess. Take some fucking responsibility for yourself for once.'

Ivy shot her hand out and slapped Jess right across the face. The tips of her fingers stung as they connected with her sister's cheek with such force that Jess's head snapped to the side. For a few seconds, they stood in silence with just the sound of their breathing and the reverberation from music though the walls between them. When Jess slowly turned back, her eyes were swimming with tears and wide with shock.

In all of the fights they'd ever had, things had never got physical. Ivy looked at her sister, in her respectable black trousers and black silk vest with her hair pinned up. The elegant one. The clever one. The one who always got the best of whatever there was to be had. The shoes, until they were outgrown and handed down to Ivy. The clothes, until they were outgrown and handed down to Ivy.

'You're a joke, Ivy,' Jess said, her hand still on her cheek. 'You always have been.'

'You can't *stand* the fact that I actually *live* my life and have fun, can you?'

'What you do isn't fun. It's destruction. How do you think Dad would feel if he could see you now? Coked up at his funeral, you're a disgrace.'

Ivy squared her shoulders back and sniffed. 'I'd rather be a mess than a hypocrite, acting like I never step a foot wrong when I'm just as messed up as everyone else.'

'Go to hell, Ivy.'

'You know what. I like who I am, even if you don't. You don't have to like my life or the way I live, because it's mine, not yours.'

Ivy put her hand around the cold steel of the door next to her and looked back at her sister. 'And by the way, Dad fully approved of the way I live my life, so all this shit you're putting on me is yours. Not his.'

Ivy swung the door open and left, without looking back.

Chapter Fourteen

Ivy

August, seven years ago

'How long's the coach ride?'

'Have I got time for a quick smoke?'

'What's the plan for tonight?'

'Where can I change my money?'

Ivy stood in the blazing sunshine with a smile as neat and pristine as her uniform. London felt very, very far away. Here, all that mattered was fun, happiness and the prospect of an amazing week ahead. After ushering everyone onto the coach, Ivy climbed up the stairs and into air-conditioned heaven. She grabbed the top of the front seat for balance as the bus pulled off. This was the part of her job she loved the most – surveying her new group, although in reality they were usually made up of the same sort of people.

There was always the group of teens on their first holiday alone, already wasted from drinking straight after check-in. Then there was the couple who fitted the 18–30 age range but were only here for the cheap flights and accommodation, and would likely turn their noses up at any of the activities or excursions Ivy would offer. And, of course, there'd be that one person who would go a little extra and end up with a tattoo, injury or STI to take home as a souvenir.

Ivy bent down to pick up the microphone from her seat to launch into her welcome speech.

'Oi, oi. Tits are out already!'

Ivy looked down at her chest and the view of her cleavage that was hugely exaggerated thanks to her V-neck t-shirt. She stood back up and readjusted her top. The man who'd catcalled her leaned on his arm-rest with an amused look on his face.

'Well now,' she said calmly. 'Thanks for identifying yourself as twat of the week so I don't have to. Now that we all know who you are, we can get on with things. Welcome to Malaga.'

Everyone fell into laughter, including the man she'd just insulted. From her very first day, she'd learned that there was always one guy who liked to fan his peacock feathers and push boundaries. Nine out of ten times, he'd be happy to exchange in a little self-humiliation disguised as banter.

'My name's Ivy and I'll be your rep for your time here in Malaga,' Ivy spoke into her mic, reciting the words she knew by heart.

The man who'd called out to her held her gaze and kept that grin on his face throughout. He wasn't anything great to look at. His type never was. His eyes flicked down to look again at the breasts he'd already gotten a peek at, not that there was much to see. She wasn't one for dabbling in the client pool anyway, unlike some of her colleagues. Men like him usually racked up a huge tally of notches on their hotel beds. Ivy was the last person to judge when it came to sex, but she wasn't a complete idiot, no matter what Jess thought.

What she did wasn't fun, it was destruction. It was three months since their dad's funeral, and Jess's words still stung.

With her speech done, Ivy took her seat at the front of the bus, dropping her head back against the fuzzy material. Bloody Jess. What was it about sisters that got under the skin so easily? Jess didn't see the 5 a.m. starts, or the fifteen-hour days Ivy worked. She hadn't seen the determination it had taken to get through the surprisingly tough recruitment process for this job and she knew nothing about the real responsibility that came with being a holiday representative. It didn't matter, anyway, because Ivy had the best of both worlds. She was actually getting paid to show people a good time. She loved watching them relax as soon as the sun hit their skin. The relief of a week or two in the sun shone from their faces, their shoulders loosened and their foreheads de-creased. It felt good to know she was part of it, that she had some part in making sure they got exactly what they'd paid for. It was a dream that felt more real than what she'd left behind.

On some level, Ivy knew she'd need to sort things out with Jess. It had been a brutal fight. The worst they'd ever had. She hadn't stuck around. She'd booked a flight back that very night and hadn't spoken to her sister since. Ivy looked outside the window as the coach drove along a coastal road and the sea stretched out like a sapphire blanket.

Being here in Spain meant not having to be there, dealing with the fallout of her dad's death. She swallowed. It still didn't seem real, though the memory of his coffin being lowered into the ground told her it was. The way she saw it, she had two options. She could either sit and wallow in it, and let life make her sour inside the way it seemed to with Jess, or she could do what she'd always done – live her life to the fullest and enjoy every single second.

Six days later, Ivy stood with her back pressed against black metal railings and squinted her eyes against the sun. She looked out at the inflatable yellow dinghy sitting alone in the lake farther upstream. It was an overcast day, but sweat trickled down the side of her neck as she gripped the railing behind her. She craned her neck a little to look down. Only two-thirds of her feet stood on solid ground; the tips of her trainers were already off the surface of the bridge.

'Smile!'

Ivy turned and laughed at Emma, holding a digital camera out in front of her face.

'Smile?' She pulled a face. 'I think I'm about to throw up and pee my pants at the same time.'

Emma cackled as Ivy reached down to tug at the harness strapped around her waist and between her legs. Her stomach somersaulted as the man behind her checked all the fastenings and the rope attached to her harness. It was a ritual for the reps to get hammered the night before their one day off a week, but as she stood teetering on the edge of the bridge, Ivy thanked God she'd had the sense to stay home last night and save herself the embarrassment of throwing up on camera.

When Emma had suggested bungee jumping earlier in the week, Ivy had said yes straight away. She'd always wanted to try it, and the fight she'd had with Jess had added extra fuel. If Jess knew she was planning to jump seventy feet from a bridge, she'd freak out and tell her she was mad, that it was all too unsafe and risky and didn't she know people died while bungee jumping? Knowing she would disapprove made the idea just that bit more appealing. Technically, there was a one in five hundred thousand chance that she wouldn't live to tell the tale. But instead of seeing risk, Ivy saw the four hundred and ninety-nine thousand chances to experience something spectacular.

Emma gave Ivy a reassuring grin, having already done her jump. Ivy was beyond grateful for a friend like her, and that they'd managed to stay together after Shooters. They'd gone for drinks one night back in Tenerife, plotting what to do with themselves once the summer season ended. Transitioning to holiday reps made the most sense and Emma had just as much of a thirst for fun as Ivy did. It had been pure luck that they'd both been placed in Malaga. Emma had a resistance to the mundane that easily matched hers, making it easy for Ivy to stop herself from thinking about the life she'd left behind and concentrate on the new one she was building.

At least here, she was respected for being herself. It was a requirement for the job, even. True, she worked around the clock, sometimes racking up eighty hours a week, but they played hard too. Once their jump was done, they would drive the two hours back home to get ready for a night out that would involve an innumerable measure of alcohol and, if they were lucky, a pill to go with it. It was like being in Never-Never Land with the absolute permission to live up to the thrill-seeking, fun-scouting aspect of her personality without feeling like she was being *too much*. Nothing here was too much.

The man behind her started shouting in rapid fire Spanish, and Ivy blew a puff of air out through her mouth. The centre of her palms tingled and her mouth ran dry as she caught his countdown.

Uno. Dos. Tres.

She spread her arms wide and closed her eyes. Before she could think twice, she bent her knees, pushed from her feet and launched herself out into nothingness. For a second, it felt like flying as the air rushed over her body, her face and between her outstretched fingers. She snapped her eyes open with her heart caught in her throat and her stomach in free fall. Ivy whooped as the water came up close to her face and the world turned on its axis as she swung underneath the bridge and back up the other side. It was like being on an enormous swing and she burst into uncontrollable laughter. Her heartbeat had never sounded so loud in her ears and her throat burned, but her entire being felt alive.

This was what life was about. She was here to live, experience and *feel*. She simply wasn't made for anything else.

Chapter Fifteen

Jess

November, five years ago

I rub my eyes and close my laptop as Nick stands in front of the open fridge. His long fingers drum against the door and his broad back rises and falls with his breath. It's almost nine on a Saturday morning and while he was out for a 5k run, I put the finishing touches to a draft business plan. I hold my breath as he takes out a small cardboard box of ridiculously fresh-looking blueberries and a glass tub of pre-chopped honeydew melon and pineapple.

'You think I'm nuts, don't you?' I ask, letting the breath out in one go.

Nick looks at me as if I've just asked the most stupid question on earth. 'What kind of question is that?'

'It's quitting my job. It's a pretty big deal.'

'It is, but I think it's a great idea.' He holds a piece of pineapple towards my mouth.

'You do?' I lean forward and take it with my teeth.

'I do,' he replies, popping a chunk of melon into his mouth with one hand and heaping the rest of the fruit into a tall NutriBullet cup with the other. 'So to answer your question, no. You're not nuts. It's a little impulsive, maybe.'

A flicker of unease makes me cross my arms over my chest. 'I know.'

Impulsive isn't a word that's normally associated with me. Careful and considered, yes. Impulsive? No.

'That being said,' Nick continues, adding a spoonful of ground flax seeds to the cup, 'you're probably the most sensible, level-headed person I know. So even if it *seems* impulsive, we both know it's not. You've been unhappy at work for ages.'

'Tell me about it,' I mutter back as he pours coconut water from a carton into the cup and screws the blade onto it before blitzing the fruit together.

This summer I finally left the tiny company where I'd been working to go big. The title of Marketing Manager for a global real estate company and the hefty salary that came with it felt like a great move. I'd wanted to get all the experience and insight I could for the business I'd own myself one day. Instead, I spend my time sharing a soulless, open-plan office in a crowd of Henrys, Charles and Dickies who answer the phone with an exuberant *how the devil are you?* I've never felt less at home anywhere in my life. I miss the lunches I'd have with my ex-colleagues, and the inane chat we'd lapse into on a slow day. The things my new co-workers talk about fly right over my head and I spend my time away from work dreading having to go in and my time at work eager to go home. I feel frustrated and alone. Nick has been great, listening to my moans of dissatisfaction and wishes for things to be different. He's as understanding and helpful and kind as ever. But he's not my sister. It's her birthday in a couple of weeks, and even though we haven't spoken since the funeral, I'll send her a message. I'd love to do more than that and maybe call her. She'd totally get my frustration with work. Then again, she's probably too busy having fun to even answer. She'd posted a rare picture on Facebook of herself, sunbathing by a pool somewhere. I don't get the impression that she's unhappy with anything in her life, and of the two of us, I'm supposed to be the one with my life together.

Nick pours the now purple liquid into two tall glasses and laces one of them with my omega oil blend.

'Thanks,' I half-smile as he passes the glass towards me.

'Besides,' he continues, 'I can't think of the last time you didn't spend an entire evening on your laptop. So if going full time and all in means less of that, it can only be a good thing.'

'It's not that bad,' I mumble as he takes a long slug from my smoothie.

'I've managed to watch *Sons of Anarchy* from start to finish because you haven't been there to complain about it.'

'No you haven't.'

'I have,' he replies, but his voice still carries a hint of light playfulness about it.

'Wow. You might be right then . . . things *have* been full on lately,' I reply, shaking my head.

It's the understatement of the century. Since Dad got sick, it feels like it's been one thing after another – sorting through the house after the funeral, getting it refurbished and into a rentable state, starting and finishing a bookbinding course, not to mention job hunting and interviews and then actually starting the new job. It's easy for Ivy to say I take on too much responsibility, but it's the only way I know how to make sure the things that need to be done, get done.

I rub my fingers across my forehead. Maybe this really is a stupid idea. I can't add starting a business to everything else. I barely know how I'm functioning as it is.

'Hey,' Nick says, taking the glass from my hand before pulling my body in towards his. He kisses the top of my head and I let him wrap me in a hug. 'You've got this, Jess. If this'll make you happy, then you should do it.'

I wrap my arms around his back and lay my cheek on his chest with his heart beating steadily under my ear. It *would* make me happy. Being my own boss, doing what I love and sharing it with Maddie, one of my favourite people on the planet. I picture us taking the small but thriving business we've built online to the next level and a shiver runs through me.

'I don't know,' I say, peeling myself from Nick's arms to smooth my hair back into its bun. 'It's pretty risky. Don't you think it's too risky?'

'I think there's only so long you can go on like you are before you burn yourself out.'

'But we've just signed a mortgage. And what about the bills?' I ask.

Nick laughs and shakes his head. 'Why does it sound like you're trying to talk yourself out of it?'

'I'm not,' I mumble. 'I'm just saying, it's a lot to cover each month.'

'Yes, it is.' He takes my hands and pulls me back towards him. 'But we can more than manage.'

After Ivy left, I surprised Nick, and myself, by asking him to move in with me. I couldn't stay in Dad's house after the funeral, and the idea of coming back here alone was just too much. The things Ivy had said hurt, and I didn't want to be alone. It helps that Nick is a great guy to live with. He cooks and cleans and knows how to do laundry. It's a kind of stability I hadn't known I'd needed, but this place doesn't feel like *ours*. With Nick's hefty salary and my inheritance money from Dad, we've just put a deposit on a new place in Hammersmith. I'll put this place up for rent. After the fight at Dad's funeral, I don't have the strength to deal with Ivy about it right now. And, as Nick pointed out, it means a steady stream of income that, thinking about it, could be a lifeline if things don't work out and I end up with no money coming in.

Until I'd uttered the suggestion to Nick just now, it hadn't felt like a risk at all. It had felt like the obvious thing to do. Maddie and I have always dreamed about going self-employed together *one day*, and we were both mad about stationery. Last year, we'd designed some printable planner inserts and put them for sale on the internet, just to see what would happen. They were an instant hit, and what was a tiny sideline hobby is growing with a steady and not insignificant passive income for us both. Dreamy chats about leaving our jobs and making an actual company out of it started becoming more and more earnest, and peaked yesterday when Maddie got the news that her job was at risk of redundancy for the second time in five years. We'd sat on her sofa with a bag of vegetable chips and a bottle of kombucha I'd made and failed at making taste nice. Once her angry tears had dried up, we'd started googling how to draw up business plans. It had felt thrilling. Exciting. But now, the excitement that had flickered in my belly was quickly being replaced with doubt.

'It'll mean a huge pay cut,' I say.

'You've got savings, and some left over from your dad,' Nick replies.

'We might not even make any money at all,' I continue, ignoring the way my head feels like a traitor to my heart for doubting myself.

He squeezes my hands. 'You already *are*. Look at how many orders you're getting every day. You can do this.'

I look up at him. 'You think so?'

'Absolutely.' He nods.

He sounds so certain that my doubt starts to fade. Nick knows his stuff. As a business consultant, it's his job to understand current market trends and what works versus what doesn't. He's one of the top consultants at the company he works for and there's even talk of him being opted for partnership. He knows what XOXO is all about and, even though he's always been supportive of Maddie and me, it's different when we're talking about it being my sole means of income. He grins at me and it bolsters my confidence. He's such a steady, careful and considered man. I trust he wouldn't say it if he really didn't think it were true.

I lift my chin and give him a small smile. 'Thanks for the encouragement.'

'Anytime. Just promise me one thing,' he says.

'Go on.'

'Once you're all set up and running, the twenty-four-hour working has to stop. I want us to spend more time together. I know things have been like this because you've both been working full time, but once the business becomes your main focus, that'll change. I miss having weekends with you.'

I look at his chest and nod. 'I know. You're right.'

This is a conversation we've been having more and more lately and, as much as I hate to admit it, he's right. Our weekends used to mean time off to spend together, but once our website went online, that changed and I'm more likely to be found hunched over my laptop updating our storefront and coordinating with Maddie on insert mock-ups and social media.

I know that something has to give. I know I have to find the same spark I feel when it comes to work, and apply it to Nick. I look at his bicep, tanned but still pale against my brown skin, and the curve of his shoulder. My eyes take in the dip at the base of his throat and move up to his square jaw. He's a good man. He really is. He was such a rock when Dad died, not to mention after the fight with Ivy. Even now, when the reality of the situation hits me and I think about how long it's been since I've spoken to my sister, Nick always seems to plug into how I'm feeling. He's exactly what

I always knew he would be: reliable, loving, kind. A man to really settle down with.

His thumb makes small circles on my shoulder, just like on our third date in that Highgate pub. I know from the slight amount of pressure on my skin that he'll drag it across my collarbone and down towards my breast. I try to think back to the last time we had sex, and a bolt of embarrassment hits me as I struggle to remember. It must have been a couple of weeks at least. Have I really been so tied up with work?

'I'm sorry,' I say, blinking as I look up at him.

'I know.'

I close my eyes as he kisses me, and I concentrate on the feeling of his lips on mine. His hands wind around my bum to hoist me up and I wrap my legs around him, pushing the thought of the business plan out of my head. My arms wrap tightly around him as he carries me to the bedroom and the part of me that wishes he'd divert to the sofa instead stays quiet as he carefully negotiates the door frame so we don't bash into it.

See, I tell myself as he lowers me onto the bed. *This is nice.* It's how it always is with Nick. His touch is soft and tender and my body responds to it in an equally soft and tender way, almost without my input at all.

The memory of Finn's stubble raking across my shoulder and firm grip on my thigh comes from nowhere and hits me with such force, it makes me shiver. My heart gallops and I open my eyes, relieved to find brown eyes looking back at me, not green. I sit up halfway to pull my vest over my head in one go, and throw it as far away from me as possible. I hear it land in the corner of the room, and imagine the memory of Finn going with it.

I'm here. I'm here and present, with Nick. And it's . . .

Nice.

Chapter Sixteen

Ivy

November, five years ago

Ivy wandered through the near-empty streets with the breeze tingling her bare arms. It had been yet another summer of madness, and working the resorts in Malaga couldn't have prepared her for the intensity of being a rep on the party mecca of Ibiza. The planeloads of people landing on the island seemed to go ten times harder and all in, more determined to get absolutely wrecked by any means possible. Now though, it was much quieter. Calmer. She never thought she'd say it, but after a long summer of being with other people, it felt like sweet relief to have some time to decompress.

Ivy crossed her arms and looked up at the sky, clouded over and grey. The wind was chilly, and it flapped the light cotton of her long skirt around her legs as she walked until she reached an intersection of streets. She'd said she was leaving the apartment to get coffee but the truth was, she'd simply needed to get out. She'd needed to put some distance between herself and Emma, whose new boyfriend was responsible for dealing a big chunk of the pills being consumed in beach bars and clubs across the island. It was ironic. Ivy had always thought she'd love to be around someone with a constant source of the drugs she loved to party with, but now Emma was talking about getting involved and trying to rope Ivy in with it too. They'd been talking about getting out of the holiday rep game. It was getting exhausting to be so 'up' all the time and selling pills made good money, fast. But all she could hear was Jess's voice ringing in her ears.

What she did wasn't fun. It was destructive.

Ivy didn't agree, but she knew that if she got involved with this, Jess would be right. Droplets of rain began to fall, softly at first, speckling the ground with darker patches of grey, before intensifying. Splashes hit her forehead, shoulders and arms as the rain came heavier and faster. She ducked into the doorway of a cafe and wiped her face with her hands as she stepped inside.

A guy behind a little coffee machine greeted her, and she returned it with a distracted smile. A band was playing in the back of the cafe and her ears were filled with a sound she'd never heard before. She kept her eyes on the man sitting in the middle with a domed, steel instrument sitting on his lap. His fingers and thumbs brushed over it, creating a sound that reminded her of the steel drums she'd heard play at the Notting Hill Carnival, except that this was softer.

The cafe was tiny, with just a handful of low circular tables, surrounded by cushions on the floor in all colours and sizes. Ivy turned to the barista and ordered a coffee before picking her way through the small crowd to the last unoccupied table. She sat cross-legged on the floor and untied the scarf around her braids, letting them fall to her shoulders and flicking droplets of rain on her arms. A clap of thunder crashed outside as Ivy settled herself into her seat. Along with the man with the strange drum, there was one with a clarinet, another with a guitar and another on a keyboard. All four were wearing loose clothes, kaftans and linen. They looked like the hippies at the market, selling jewellery and crystals.

With a perfect cup of coffee in her hand, warmth on her skin and the aroma of something spicy cooking in the air, Ivy let herself get carried away with the music. Candle-lit lanterns sat on every table and multicoloured glass baubles hung from the ceiling. She sunk herself into the cafe's relaxing atmosphere, listening to the music and pushing all thoughts of Emma and drug dealing to somewhere that simply didn't matter.

When the band finished, Ivy clapped enthusiastically, along with everyone else. A few more people had crammed into the cafe, drawn in either by refuge from the rain or the sound of the drum. She looked at the table next to her, only just noticing the empty instrument cases to one side of it and when the band made their way over, she smiled widely at them. It took just minutes for Ivy to know who they all were and where they came from. Working with people and helping them to feel at ease was something she did naturally anyway, and working as a rep had only enhanced it.

An hour after the concert had ended, Ivy put her empty cup on the brushed bronze table and readjusted her legs.

'So that's what you do? All year round?' she asked Matthias, the particularly attractive guitar player.

'Yep. Pretty sweet, no?' he replied.

Ivy nodded. 'I'll say.'

Summers in Europe, playing concerts and busking around the Mediterranean, followed by winters in Asia. Sweet was the right word to describe it. They all sounded like her kind of people, sun-seekers who wanted to live a little differently than the rest of the world. Except, they had a profession. One that could take them anywhere and didn't involve running on empty while chaperoning drunken teenagers. The feeling of freedom she'd gained in Tenerife four years ago felt far away. She knew, deep in her bones, that she didn't have another holiday rep season in her. She had a little money coming in each month from the rental of the flat back in London, but it wasn't enough to sustain her life here without a salary.

'So what about you?' Matthias asked. 'Will you stay on Ibiza all winter?'

Ivy shrugged. 'I don't know. Maybe. I've never stayed the winter here before.'

'You're not missing much. I mean, it's nice not to have so many tourists around and everything but the weather gets cold and rainy.'

'Sounds wonderful,' she grimaced in return. 'I'm not made for that kind of weather.'

'With your roots, I'm not surprised.' He laughed. 'You should come with us.'

Ivy looked at him. He was cute, with his dark hair pulled back into a man bun. Cute, and obviously deluded.

'To Goa?' she asked with a small laugh. He nodded and she laughed again. 'Yeah, right.'

'Why not?'

Ivy shook her head, her face pulled into a searching frown. 'Because . . . because it's India. I've never really wanted to go there.'

'It's Goa. It's barely India at all. You'll probably see a lot of the same people from here at the beach parties and drum circles there.'

Ivy doubted it. She stayed in the party district in the south and rarely ventured to the hippy-lands of the northern end of the island.

'The thing that makes Goa better than this place, though, is that we don't get the wasted teenagers over there. Not really.'

Ivy tilted her head with a small nod. An Ibiza without the booze tourism would be nice. As would the sunshine.

'India,' she muttered. 'It's cheap there, right?'

'Oh, yeah. Like, three euros a night for a place to stay cheap. You can get a really good meal for half that.'

The money from the flat rental each month wouldn't go far here, but in India, she'd be able to go for the winter, live like a queen and still be able to fly back to Europe for whatever was waiting for her next year. If Jess were here, she'd freak. Going to India with a musician she'd literally met just an hour ago would be seen as plain reckless. But the more Ivy considered it, the more it seemed like a great idea and she'd been in Europe long enough. It was time for a change.

◆ ◆ ◆

Two weeks later

Humid air rushed across Ivy's face as she sat in a taxi, holding on to the headrest while the car careered around a corner. Her nose was assaulted with a mix of incense, burning plastic and an underlying note of something lush and tropical. It reminded her of the scent her nan used to bring with her when she'd visit from Jamaica and open up her suitcases. A rosary dangled from the rearview mirror, tapering off into a jewel-encrusted cross, and a woman sang in a high-pitched voice through the tinny radio. It was late afternoon, and after a day of travelling, Ivy had landed in Goa.

She looked out of the window as they drove past buildings plastered with advertising and houses painted in bright purples, greens, pinks and yellows. Shops that looked like they were constructed entirely from tarpaulin jostled for space with more palm trees than she'd ever seen in one place before. There was rubbish everywhere, with plastic bottles and bags scattered along the roadside and she'd never seen so many mopeds in her life. Everyone seemed to be on one. She'd even seen an entire family on one, with the mum sitting behind the dad with a toddler in her arms, while another, slightly older child stood at the front between the dad's legs. Ivy rubbed a hand over her eyes. They were tired from too little sleep, itchy from too much dust flying in through the window and overwhelmed by all the new sights whizzing past her. She sat back and looked through the windscreen instead.

Ivy took a deep breath and opened the window to the maximum, more for the idea of fresh air than the heat brushing against her face. She'd never been carsick in her life, but this weaving in and out of traffic, narrowly avoiding motorbikes and buses . . . she gawped as the car moved to make space for a cow. This was a complete one-eighty from the resorts of Spain. Over an hour later, the taxi dropped her off at the guesthouse Matthias had recommended and Ivy stood, looking at her surroundings. Like everywhere else she'd seen, the ground was littered with rubbish and discarded palm leaves. The dense smell of smoke filled the air, along with a hint of spice, and the guesthouse in front of her was painted a bright, acid green. She took a step, stopped at a loud, squelching sound and looked down. Her face pulled into a grimace at the brown splodge of cow dung under her Converse. Ivy wiped her foot on one of the palm branches on the ground. It wasn't much different to stepping in puddles of alcoholic vomit, and she'd done that more times than she cared to remember.

Ivy looped her hands into the straps of the backpack she'd bought only a couple of days ago. It seemed a much better fit than coming here with a suitcase and was a perfect way to start this new chapter. She wiped the rest of her shoe clean, and went to find the guesthouse reception.

Chapter Seventeen

JESS

November, five years ago

I step through the revolving doors of my office building and out into the cold afternoon air. I stand still for a second, wrapping my scarf around my neck and deciding where to go for lunch. Eating in the canteen is absolutely out of the question. I need to get as far away from this place as possible. It's a week since I handed in my notice, and it feels as long as the two months I still have yet to work. I cross the street and round the corner. I might be being dramatic, but I really do feel better with every inch of physical distance away from that place. The only thing keeping me going is the countdown I've started towards being able to finally do the thing that really makes me happy.

'I'm telling you, Mads. I'm reaching my limit,' I say into my headphones as I unwrap my humous and chipotle wrap. 'I'm running out of external meetings I can escape to.'

The Pret A Manger I've taken refuge in is far enough from the office that it's unlikely I'll run into anyone – a key consideration for lunch locations these days.

'You're lucky to be somewhere you actually like,' I add before biting into my wrap.

'Ehh, it's not that great here either to be honest. Now that I've said yes to taking the money and running, I feel bad for everyone else who's waiting to be interviewed for their own jobs.' Maddie sighs. 'Can we please just fast forward to us working side by side at home? Or better yet, in our fancy future office with a decent coffee machine and daily delivered bagels and doughnuts?'

I laugh and swallow my food down. 'That's what you're manifesting is it? Krispy Kremes and Nespresso?'

'You'd better believe it.'

I almost hear her grin down the phone, and I *do* believe it. Not only is she into all that universe having your back stuff, Maddie is also vocal and proud about her love for sugar. She refuses to get sucked into the stevia and coconut blossom alternatives I've tried to ply her with over the years.

I go to take another bite of my wrap and stop, holding it in mid-air.

'Fuck.' I whisper. 'It's Finn.'

'What? What do you mean, it's Finn?'

My eyes are wide open and staring at the man who's just walked in and is now hovering in front of one of the sandwich displays.

'I mean, it's *Finn*.' I whisper loudly and drop my wrap to hold the microphone closer to my mouth. 'He just walked into the Pret where I am.'

'Wait a minute, you're eating at Pret? What about—'

'Forget that,' I say quickly. On any other day, my eating out for lunch instead of bringing in my own, home-made food that I know is organic, unsalted and unsweetened would be headline news. 'Fuck, Maddie. It's *Finn*.'

'Are you sure?'

'Of course I'm sure.'

As if I could ever forget him. My heart beats wildly in my chest as he stands just a few feet away. I stare at the back of his head and shiver at the memory of running my hands across his short hair. His shoulders are broad under his denim jacket, tapering down to his waist in a shape I'd recognise from a mile away.

'What's he doing?' Maddie asks, and I can picture her heading out of her open-plan office and into the lift lobby where she can talk more freely.

'Choosing a sandwich.'

'Has he seen you?'

'Not yet,' I reply, keeping myself absolutely still as he selects his sandwich and a bottle of Coke, and goes to join the queue. 'But he will.'

I'm sitting at a table right next to the bank of tills and he's chosen the line that will end up with him paying for his food pretty much right in front of me. I swallow against a dry throat.

'Shit, Mads. What should I do?'

Why is he here, in this very Pret instead of the countless others within spitting distance? I can't help but stare at him as he waits in line, even though I know it'll probably make me stand out even more. I'd thought these feelings swirling in my body had gone, but instead he's managed to rob me of breath and control the pace of my heart just by being in the same room.

'Maddie, I've got to go. I'll call you back,' I say as he gets closer.

'You'd better. I want all the details.'

I hang up and quickly wipe a hand across my mouth to make sure I don't have sauce on my face. There are just two people in front of him now and all he has to do is look a little to his left to see me. I don't know how to sit. If I should pretend I haven't seen him, or dig out my Kindle and pretend to read. It takes a second more until he shifts his focus and lands his gaze squarely on me. The recognition lights up his green eyes and, if I didn't know any

144

better, I'd say he's just lost his breath too. He lifts a hand and I do the same, waving back as my skin flushes with heat. The wait until he's at the till feels ridiculously long but far too quick as he looks from his sandwich to the cashier to me. By the time he's paid, I feel a nervous wreck.

'Jess,' he says, standing in front of my table. 'Wow. This is a surprise.'

'I know.' I laugh nervously and shift in my seat.

There wasn't supposed to be another meeting, ever. He was supposed to be in Sweden living his best life as a head chef. What was he doing here?

'How are you doing?' he asks and I nod.

'Yeah, good. I'm just on my lunch break. You?'

'Also good. I thought you worked in Hendon?'

'I moved jobs. I'm leaving soon though. Setting up a business with Maddie.'

His smile widens and it lights up my world. 'Oh, wow. Congrats.'

'What about you?' I ask. 'I thought you were in Sweden?'

He goes to answer, but his phone beeps and a flicker of irritation passes across his face. I want to know everything that's happened in the last four years. Where was he working? Living? Has he met someone? Is he happy? His phone beeps again. I want to know who it is and why it's irritating him so much.

'You can sit, if you want?' I offer, moving my things a little closer towards me to make space for him.

Before he can answer his phone beeps again and he shakes his head. 'Sorry, one sec.'

I watch as he shifts his sandwich and Coke into the crook of his arm to use his free hand to check his phone. I look at his long fingers, remembering how they'd looked entwined in mine and feel a longing so strong I have to take a sip of my water to stop myself

145

from acting on it. Now that he's here in front of me, the squabbles we'd had over work getting in the way and incompatible lifestyles seem unimportant and the decision I'd made to be magnanimous in telling him to accept a job nine hundred miles away suddenly feels like the stupidest one ever made. Finn swears under his breath and looks away for a second, the muscles in his jaws flexing under his skin. He looks back at me with a sigh and shakes his head.

'I'm sorry. I need to go.' He looks down at the phone as if he wants to throw it through the window.

His voice tells me that he wants to stay and I'm not ready to say goodbye again. Not yet. It feels too randomly coincidental that he should walk into this cafe at the exact time I'd be here. He stands there staring at me, as if his feet are glued to the ground. I know he wants to stay, but his phone beeps again and he shoves it back in his pocket. He glances away and then back to me with a look on his face as if he's weighing up his options.

'I don't suppose you're free later? After work, maybe?'

I nod straight away. 'Sure.'

Nick and I don't have any plans that I know of.

Finn grins. 'Great. There's a pub on Dean Street – The Crown & Two Chairmen? We could meet there, around six?'

'Sounds great.' I grin back.

I know that nothing will happen between us. There's too much water under our bridge for that and besides, I'm with Nick. But this is Finn. There's no way we can leave things like this.

At six o'clock, I'm sitting in the pub after watching the hands drag around the clock for the entire afternoon. I've told Nick I'm meeting up with an old friend and he didn't ask for details. I'm oddly nervous, as if I'm waiting for a blind date to turn up despite it being someone I've known for years. I deliberately resisted the urge to detour after work and buy some lipstick, and instead have simply shown up exactly as I am and as I was at lunch.

At six-thirty, I'm starting to feel uncomfortable with sitting here and not ordering, so I ask for a glass of tonic water with a slice of lemon and try not to look like someone who's being stood up.

At five to seven, my tonic water is empty and I've been texting back and forth with Maddie for the last ten minutes to avoid the look of sympathy from the barman.

At five minutes past, I shake my head and try not to let disappointment overwhelm me. Or anger at actually being stood up with not even a text to excuse it. It's a side to Finn I hadn't expected but as I sling my bag over my shoulder, I shrug the thought away. Maybe it's for the best that he hasn't turned up. I've got so much to focus on. A new business and career. A stable relationship that's actually going somewhere.

I leave the pub and tell myself that him not turning up is a reminder to enjoy what I have at home. A man who would never dream of turning up to anything even five minutes late and would absolutely never not text or call to cancel. A man who's been talking about marriage, using the word *when* not *if*. He's there and waiting for me and I know that all I have to do is take it. Because, really, what am I waiting for? I cross the street and head away from the pub quickly, in case Finn might just suddenly appear out of nowhere like he had at lunch.

No more looking back. It is time to look forwards.

Chapter Eighteen

Ivy

January, four years ago

Ivy stood with a towel wrapped around her body and looked at her gleaming bathroom. She couldn't help but smile to herself with the irony of it. Jess would piss herself laughing if she could see how clean it was. The truth was, she'd been scarred by her first bathroom experience in Goa. After travelling for so long, she'd planned to shower and sleep. Instead, she'd balked at the shared guesthouse bathroom. Ivy wasn't sensitive at all. She liked to think she could deal with most things, but the smell coming from the tiled toilet hole in the floor had made her heave. She'd washed herself under the dribbling shower, wrapped herself in her towel and stepped out into the hallway, just in time to see a woman coming from the toilet with bare feet and a long, layered skirt that dragged on the floor behind her. Ivy had held her pee in for the rest of the night and gone room hunting the next morning. She'd wanted to text Jess to tell her about it.

> Hey, sis. I know we haven't spoken for a while but here's a
> photo of this super gross toilet and by the way, I'm in India!

She could laugh about it now, but since then, she'd become almost obsessive about cleaning the bathroom, which was handy, because after moving into her own little bungalow, she'd gotten sick and spent three days in a row attached to the toilet. Luckily, she'd met Lisa, a friend of Matthias and a seasoned Goa traveller. She had connections with everyone and had helped Ivy to find a cheap place to stay, along with a moped for half of what the other backpackers paid. Lisa was a hula hoop and fire poi performer in Goa, and kept it going back in the real world, giving workshops to circus acts and corporate companies who wanted their employees to *let loose* and *have fun*. She lived in Copenhagen and did well enough out of it to be able to escape the European winter every year. Ivy couldn't imagine her doing anything else and was glad to learn she wasn't really a banker or lawyer back home. From her unkempt hair and the mandala tattooed right in the middle of her chest, to her dusty bare feet, Lisa came across as genuine and authentic, unlike so many of the people around them. There were a lot of toothy smiles and lingering hugs being doled out all the time, and Ivy still didn't quite trust it.

◆ ◆ ◆

Ivy went into her bedroom and slathered herself with fragrant coconut oil from a recycled water bottle, covering every inch of her skin from her toes to her scalp. She ran her fingers through her braids too, for good measure. It blew her mind that she could get organic, locally sourced coconut oil from the side of a road for a ridiculous fraction of what it cost back in Ibiza. Plus, her skin was totally dehydrated from the alcohol and surprise token of MDMA last night, and was greedily soaking it up. She'd partied at Shiva Valley with her new friend Lisa, and not only had the night been epic, her hangover this morning had been minimal. Not a bad trade-off at all.

Ivy went to look in the rusted mirror propped up on the rickety table in her bedroom. She'd dropped the make-up within a couple of days of arriving. Nobody wore make-up here. From what she'd seen, and smelled, it was already enough if someone wore deodorant. She definitely wasn't about to go so far as to ditch her roll-on, but she liked the idea of leaving behind the make-up that she'd always worn back in Spain. Besides, her skin looked fantastic thanks to the coconut oil anyway.

She tied an elaborate choker around her neck, fumbling blindly with the clasp. It wasn't like anything she'd have worn in the past, but she'd made it herself after spending two days in a macramé workshop. It was actually way more technical than she'd expected, but she'd had fun and it turned out she had a natural flair for it with quick and nimble fingers that worked at speed. Ivy stepped back from the mirror, bending her knees so she could get an overall view of her reflection. She was wearing a pair of short denim cut-offs that barely covered more than her bikini bottoms, a crocheted top with sleeves that stopped just below the elbow and a pair of black biker-style ankle boots she'd bought in one of the boutiques on the main road and were now coated in the red dust that covered everything here.

Her phone beeped, and she opened the Facebook notification. Someone had tagged her in a photo from last night and she quickly liked it before closing the app and then re-opening it again. Ivy clicked through to Jess's profile. A smile twitched at her lips as she read the latest update: *Owner of XOXO stationery – with Maddie Johnson*. She'd actually done it. Throwing herself headlong into work and studying at the weekends had paid off. Maybe she should comment with congratulations, or send a message.

Ivy's phone beeped and a message popped up on her screen.

Lisa (Hula Hoops): You're gonna miss the sunset, hurry up xx

She was running late, and quickly typed out a reply.

Ivy: Just getting ready. See you in 15 xx

The sun setting wasn't just the beginning of the evening here. It was an event. A celebration. And anyone who was anyone in Arambol would go down to the beach to pay homage. Ivy put her phone into her little bag along with her tobacco. She'd write to Jess when things calmed down a bit. They had a lot to sort out, and Ivy guessed she was run off her feet with the new company.

She hung a leather necklace with her key on it around her neck, tucking it under her top. She'd been lucky to find the only key she had to unlock the padlock for her little bungalow in the sand a few days ago after dinner at a beach cafe. She doubted she'd get that kind of chance a second time around, so wearing it as a necklace was the best option. Ivy went around the two rooms, sticking her arm through the ornate bars to close her windows. She wasn't sure if they were there to keep out people or monkeys, having been told that she could be broken into by either. The place she was renting was a little behind the busy main road, and she didn't want to be lax enough to find out.

The air was warm and muggy, and carried a million and one scents as she made her way down the main road. There was the smell of exhaust fumes from the motorbike that had just driven past, the sweet scent of incense burning from shops, the unmistakable aroma of hash coming from almost every direction, the cinnamon coming from The German Bakery, not to mention the spices from the restaurants and cafes. Ivy remembered thinking that Tenerife was like an adult playground, and had to laugh. It had nothing on Arambol. She smiled, shaking her head at a shop trader trying to entice her in to buy tie-dye t-shirts. In the short time she'd been here, she'd already learned the basics of hula hooping, thanks to Lisa, learned to macramé, had singing classes, been to a two-day djembe workshop, had a billion cups of chai, more spliffs than she could ever count and danced every single night. There was always something being offered, and she couldn't see how she'd ever get bored. It was so far removed from the life she'd lived in London, she couldn't ever imagine going back.

She thought about Jess, in the cold British winter. She'd probably hate everything about this place, but still, there was a part of Ivy that wished her sister could experience it. If anyone needed to feel freedom and let loose, it was her. Ivy crossed the street, narrowly avoiding a couple of motorbikes riding past. It still blew her mind that they hadn't spoken for so long. If anyone would have told her that she'd have fallen out with Jess like this, she'd have thought they were mad. They'd always been so close. Until they weren't. She'd thought about writing an email or sending a postcard, and had even bought a couple with the intention to reach out. But she'd never got around to writing them. The memory of their dad's funeral made her cringe inside. They'd said such awful things to each other, and since Jess hadn't reached out either, she guessed it was all still too raw for her as well. The one-line birthday emails were enough for now and there was no rush. They were both doing their own things – Ivy was here, experiencing a new way of life, and Jess had her new company to focus on. Besides, they had their whole lives ahead of them. The time would come when they'd sort something out.

She took a side road and waved at two children playing on the corner. They were barefooted, with gold bangles on their wrists, and the youngest one had a black smudge in the centre of her forehead, right between her eyebrows. It was easy to forget she was in India sometimes, with the majority of people around her being

Western and living what was a relatively affluent lifestyle of three meals out a day and nothing more to do than the pursuit of pleasure. When she'd first arrived, Matthias had described Arambol as a paradise. She hadn't been able to see it through the ammonia tang wafting from an open toilet and the litter everywhere she'd looked. But now?

Ivy reached the edge of the beach and walked along the water's edge in her boots, letting them sink down into the sand. The beach was already full. Sunset was a time when everyone came together – the stoned hippies and the yogis, the old-timers and the psy-trancers, the tantricas and the healers. There was space for everyone. Those who wanted to flap their hands instead of clap at a concert, those who wanted to wake and bake and those who wanted to dive into spirituality. It was like a huge, mismatched family. And Ivy felt right at home.

The rhythmic pulse of music was already ringing out from the drum circle and the sellers had set up their makeshift stalls showing off jewellery and offers of massages. The contact dancers were rolling around in the sand and street dogs that had been sleeping all day in the heat were waking up, ready to prowl around for scraps of food. Ivy stopped and looked at the sky, covered in a blanket of pinks and greys. The sun rarely touched the horizon here at sunset, disappearing behind a thin film of cloud instead. Maybe that was what was so special about it. Regardless, it was a tradition she was happy to get involved with, celebrating the end of another day.

'Ivy, over here!' Lisa's voice called out and she turned to see her with a few other people sitting by the drum circle.

She held her hand up in a wave and made her way over with her face fixed into a grin and the warmth of the air on her skin. Matthias had been right. It was a paradise, and Ivy had never felt more free.

Chapter Nineteen

JESS

January, two years ago

From: JessPalmer@xoxo.com

To: Ivy Palmer

Subject: Invitation

Hey Ivy,

It feels so weird to write this in an email to you, but I wanted to let you know I'm getting married! To Nick, obviously. He proposed a while back but we've finally settled on a date this June. I saw a couple of photos of you on Facebook, so I know you're in India. It's not exactly close but I'd love it if you were able to come. I know it's been a long time but the idea of getting married without you there feels wrong.

A lot's happened . . . it'd be great to catch up. The invitation's attached . . . hope you can make it.

Love,

Jess

xx

Chapter Twenty

Ivy

January, two years ago

Jess was getting married? Ivy reread the email, flicking the tip of her roll-up into the clay ashtray on the table in front of her. *Married?* She leaned back against the low wall as someone stepped across her folded legs to leave the cafe. She was upstairs in Dreamland Cafe, where pretty much every backpacker and tourist around came at some point. She came here almost every day for a proper, machine-made cappuccino, a smoothie and panini, and until about two minutes ago, she'd been happily chatting with Lisa about going to Hampi for a few days and a change of scenery. Now, the only change of scenery happening was in her mind as she tried to picture her sister back in London with an engagement ring on her finger. Ivy opened the photo attachment because she knew Jess, and there was no way she'd never show off the ring.

'Bloody hell,' she muttered, staring at what looked like a black diamond. If such a thing even existed.

'Hello? Earth to Ivy?'

She turned to Lisa and blinked. 'Sorry. What?'

'Are you alright?'

Ivy turned her sticker-covered laptop to her friend and re-lit the end of her roll-up.

'Far out. That's some ring.' Lisa's thin eyebrows raised towards her hairline. 'Whose is it?'

'My sister's,' Ivy replied, turning the screen back towards herself. 'She just got engaged.'

Jess had said that Nick had proposed a while back. A few years ago, Ivy would never have believed that Jess would be engaged to someone she barely even knew, let alone that she'd only know about it 'a while' later. There were things about her sister that Ivy did know from social media, like the business she'd set up with Maddie and how successful it seemed to be. And of course, she knew Jess had moved in with Nick. Jess was living the life she'd always wanted. Man, house, business. The only thing missing was kids, and Ivy felt a pang in her chest at the idea. What if Jess did the same thing after getting pregnant? Ivy might one day open an email to see a surprise niece or nephew that had been born months ago.

Ivy looked up as one of the staff put her panini and smoothie down on the low table in front of her. She closed her laptop with the image of Jess's ring in her mind. She hadn't spoken much about her life back home with Lisa. It wasn't the way things were done here. It didn't really matter what your life looked like back home. The here and now was all that was important. Ivy stirred the straw in her peanut butter and banana smoothie.

'Okay,' Lisa said, scrolling through her phone, 'so there's an overnight bus for Hampi that leaves on Saturday that looks good. I've got a couple of friends who are planning to get there next weekend, too. You'd like them.'

Ivy nodded absent-mindedly. 'Yeah, sure. Sounds good.'

It was her third winter here and while it had been fun, it wasn't the same as before. The cafe was full, as usual, with a deep and meaningful discussion about the point of existence happening in one corner and two people working side by side on shiny MacBooks in the other. There was a woman breastfeeding a kid who looked old enough to be in school, and a man intently studying the *Lonely Planet* guide for Delhi. On the other side of the cafe's small roof terrace, one of the girls who'd played in the same band as Matthias last season was strumming on a ukulele and singing with someone else. It all looked the same, but reading Jess's email had been like throwing a rock at an already cracked window.

When she'd first come here, she'd thought she'd found an adult playground with endless possibilities. It had felt like the absolute opposite to all she'd hated back home. It had looked like the life she'd really wanted, and she'd had an easy entry too, thanks to Matthias being so well connected here. But this third time was different. The dynamics of his band had changed and alliances had shifted, and for the first time, Ivy saw the dividing lines of cliques and groups wherever she went. Walking into a cafe meant choosing sides, which was another reason she came here so much because it felt like Switzerland – completely neutral. But even that was getting boring. Was it adventurous to go to the same cafe every morning? To stay in the same house every time, rent the same moped and eat at the same places? Some of the people here had been doing that for five, ten, even twenty years. How different was it really to being back in Tenerife with the Brits who booked the same hotel for the same two weeks every year, or getting off the Tube and getting the same breakfast baguette and coffee order from Starbucks every single morning?

She'd left to do something different. To show that *she* was different. Except now, she couldn't help feeling that really, she was the same as everyone else. And if that was the case, then what had been the point?

Ivy pushed her smoothie away as a well of frustration rose in her. She needed to do something, otherwise she'd spend the whole day dissecting and analysing how she'd lived her life since leaving England.

'Hey,' Ivy said, interrupting Lisa's scrolling through bus times, 'didn't Moshe say something about a party tonight?'

'His weird friend is throwing it. You don't want to go, do you?'

'Why not?' Ivy shrugged. 'It's not like I've got other plans and I really need to shake some stuff off. Will you come?'

'I can't. I've got that performance gig over at that hotel.'

'Oh yeah. I forgot about that.'

'But I can come to yours after and we can go together if you want? They're a weird bunch,' Lisa said, pulling a face. 'I wouldn't go alone.'

'Hey, I'm from Camberwell. Trust me, I can look after myself.' She laughed, pulling her smoothie back towards her.

Jess's email had thrown her, but she wasn't in the right mood to reply to it now. She'd do it later, when she knew how to.

Later that night, Ivy felt her feet melt down into the ground and closed her eyes. The breeze on her body felt like velvet and when she opened her eyes again, the sky was on fire with streaks of orange.

'Got any more?' she asked, turning to the man standing next to her. What was his name again? She couldn't quite remember, but he had the most insanely gorgeous dimples.

'Are you sure? It's strong stuff,' he replied, lifting his eyebrows.

'I'm a strong girl,' Ivy replied and leaned her mouth close to his ear. 'I can take it.'

She grinned as he opened the tiny resealable plastic bag in his hand and Ivy sucked the tip of her finger to coat it in the small pink powder. Music from the speaker in the house filled her ears as she put her finger into her mouth, filling it with acrid bitterness.

Her hips rolled from side to side as she took the hand of the man whose name she didn't know, and started to dance. She was no stranger to drugs, but this was like nothing she'd had before. It wasn't just a high filled with energy and the need to dance. The man she was dancing with knew more about her than maybe anyone else, because she'd literally felt her heart opening up as the chemicals had hit and they'd spent an unknown amount of time talking about life and the universe. She'd had the weirdest feeling that she'd been there before. Not just like a déjà vu, but an actual out-of-body experience where she'd seen herself standing here, in this house, with this man, surrounded by people at this party.

She felt alive and soft and dark and mysterious and sensual. She remembered who she was and why she was here, something Jess's email had made her forget. The man she was dancing with pulled her into him and Ivy sighed as a wave of pleasure twirled from her toes, up through her legs and back, right up to the crown of her head. His fingers played with the skin on her lower back and Ivy closed her eyes, letting his arms wrap around her like a blanket.

◆ ◆ ◆

The next morning, the helicopter-like drone of a mosquito buzzing in her ear woke her with a start. Ivy's eyes flickered open, revealing a patchwork of brown roof tiles. Her tongue was stuck to the roof of her mouth and she swatted at the mosquito as it came back towards her face. She turned to see a man lying next to her on the thin mattress. His head was turned away from her and his hair was shaved into a mohawk, tapering into long, chunky dreads. He was lying on his belly, completely naked, with a smattering of blonde curly hairs on his lower back. Ivy shook her head an inch.

Who the hell was he? He had a huge tattoo of a bird between his shoulder blades, another with Hebrew letters on the side of his ribs, and he wore a big silver ring with a skull on his middle finger. Ivy turned to look back up at the ceiling. Come to think of it, where was she? She sat up slowly and looked around her. They weren't in a room at all, but on a big balcony, and the mattress wasn't on a bed, but on the floor. It looked like every other place in Arambol, but Ivy knew she'd never been here before. The air was uncharacteristically cold on her skin, which meant she was probably farther inland than the main street and backpacker village she lived in. Three other people she didn't recognise were lying passed out on a second mattress and big, patterned sheets hung on the wall in psychedelic colours and prints. Countless bottles of beer, vodka and rum were on the floor along with strands of tobacco and a smattering of loose cigarette papers.

She got up as quietly as she could, standing up on legs that felt weak, as if they'd danced all night. The pads of her big toes felt sore on the cold tiles, and that wasn't all. Her breath caught in her throat at the feeling between her legs. She looked back at the man she'd woken up next to. They hadn't had sex. Had they? The feel of her skirt against her bare skin told her she wasn't wearing knickers and she turned to find them crumpled up and abandoned at the bottom of the mattress. Ivy quickly grabbed them and looked for the money belt she always wore, finding it wedged up against the side of the mattress. She popped open both pockets. Her phone and little wallet were still there, as was the condom she always had with her, just in case. That wasn't a good sign.

Ivy swallowed, looking at the man again. What the hell had she taken last night? No matter how wasted she was, she'd always, *always* been able to remember to use a condom, and to know who she'd slept with. If she had no idea who this man was, then how could she know she'd even been safe about it? Unless he'd been sober enough, or cared enough, she might have just done something monumentally stupid. Her heart began to pound in her ears.

How did she even know she'd wanted it to happen in the first place? The man stirred and Ivy quickly left, making her way inside and heading straight for the open front door at the other end of the hallway. She stuffed her knickers into one of the pockets of her money belt and prayed that she wasn't too far from home.

Goosebumps bubbled on her skin. Two other houses and a well stood in front of her, with no landmarks to tell her where she might be. A path ran through one of the front gardens and Ivy followed it, hoping it would take her to a street. She crossed her arms over her body, feeling exposed in her little vest, and trod lightly as stones dug into her bare feet until she stepped out onto a small road. A field stretched along the other side of it and the air was hazy in that way she'd never seen anywhere else but in Goa. Ivy turned left on instinct and walked on the tarmac as quickly as she could. A Western girl walking on the street at the crack of dawn without shoes and looking worse for wear was the same in India as it was back home. Ivy had done the walk of shame before, but had never actually felt shameful about it. Until now.

The image of his tattoos and that ring came back to her mind, and she walked faster. What the hell had happened last night? She pulled her eyebrows together, trying to remember. She'd gone to the party Lisa had warned her against that had actually been pretty tame. And then she'd left with a group of people she didn't know, getting a ride on one of their bikes. Ivy remembered riding on the back of it with her arms stretched out like wings, not paying any attention to where they were going at all. She remembered one of them offering her some super strong pink stuff from Holland, but after that? Her mind drew blank.

From behind the mental fog, she recognised one of the guest-houses up ahead. It was the one Matthias had been staying at when she'd come here for the very first time. He'd been nice. Too nice, of course. He wanted a fun but quiet life of travel and music, and Ivy was like a chaotic whirlwind – his words. He'd said them kindly, but she knew the drill. Men like him didn't fit with women like her. And last night, whatever the hell had happened, only proved it. At the end of her first trip here, Matthias had left to travel to Rajasthan and she'd gone to Vietnam, and last year, they'd barely exchanged more than a few polite hellos. She'd barely seen him this time around. She'd been so into the party scene that she hadn't been to a single concert. They moved in completely different circles. She'd barely even seen daylight and now here it was, blinding her with full force.

This wasn't walking across the coconut grove alone at night, or going on three-day benders. For years, she'd felt limitless, drinking everything, taking everything. But now, as her teeth chattered against the fresh morning air and her body throbbed, all she felt was sick. She'd blacked out. No recollection, no knowledge, no nothing. She thought back to that hung-over morning after her three dates in one day, and how she'd laughed with Jess about it all. That had been fun. This was destruction. Her sister had been right and far from it being yet another reason to be mad at her, it only made her wish that Jess would be on the other side of her front door with toast and coffee and her ability to make Ivy feel okay.

Ivy turned onto the main road with a relief so great, her body almost sagged as she walked. The street was empty at this early hour, but the bike that belonged to the owner of Dreamland was outside the cafe. She rubbed a hand across her face and through her hair, hoping she didn't look as messed up as she felt, and stepped inside. She couldn't go home. She didn't want to be alone in her bungalow right now, but being alone and in company felt right. It felt safe.

'Someone had a fun night,' he said as she got to the counter. 'Espresso?'

'Please.' Ivy nodded, feeling both relieved that she looked normal enough not to have any unwanted attention, and shocked that he couldn't see the way her world had just lost its footing.

She took her coffee up to the empty terrace and sat in the very same spot she had just yesterday, reading Jess's email. The toasted scent of her espresso sat under her nose, but she couldn't drink it. Her throat felt tight and constricted and she began to shiver. She drew her knees up to her chest and wrapped her arms around her legs, letting the tears flow down her cheeks in the privacy of being alone with the security of knowing that someone was downstairs.

She didn't hear the woman coming up the stairs, or see her sitting in front of her. She only became aware that she was there when the warmth of her hand landed on Ivy's arm.

'Are you okay?'

Ivy looked up to see a pair of intense green eyes scanning her face. They were startlingly familiar and comforting in a way that made her tears intensify, pouring from her eyes with so much force there was nothing she could do to stop them. The woman didn't hug her, or do anything apart from sitting there with her hand on Ivy's skin. It was such a warm and soothing touch, it reminded Ivy of her mum and Jess, and her heart hurt with the weight of it all. Eventually, the tears started to ease and Ivy became aware of herself again. Her cheeks burned from the tears and a headache pounded behind her eyes. Her vest was wet, clinging to her belly with sweat and the material of her skirt was dark, stained with her tears.

She turned to the woman who'd sat with her and shook her head. 'God, I'm sorry.'

'Nothing to be sorry be for,' she replied with a smile.

Her face was friendly and framed with grey, wavy hair cropped just above her shoulders. Her skin was smooth, making it difficult to place her age but Ivy guessed she was somewhere in her late fifties or early sixties.

'Looks like you're having a rough start to the day,' the woman said with a small smile and Ivy snorted an involuntary, dry laugh through her nose.

'The worst.' Her throat closed again and she shook her head. 'I'm a mess. How am I supposed to turn up at Jess's wedding like this? I can't do that.'

She'd have stuck out anyway, with her dreadlocks and the almost fully tattooed arm, not to mention the ornate gold hoop through her septum. But now, she felt like an outsider even to herself. She'd always told herself she had everything under control. Clearly, she didn't.

'Jess is my sister,' Ivy explained. 'She emailed me yesterday that she's getting married.'

The woman nodded, but didn't say anything, so Ivy filled the gap.

'We haven't spoken in years. And the last time we did it was . . .' Ivy shook her head. 'It was awful. *I* was awful. Our dad had just died and there was just so much anger, you know?'

'I have two older siblings,' the woman said, still with her hand on Ivy's arm. 'I think I can relate.'

Ivy stared at the ashtray on the table. 'Well, she's getting married and her email was an invitation to the wedding.'

'A peace offering in disguise?'

'I guess.' Ivy nodded and chewed the inside of her lip, remembering their dad's funeral. As if she could ever forget. 'I can't go. She'll have planned everything to the absolute max. It's her big day and I don't want to ruin it. Because in all likelihood, that's what would happen. It's what I do.'

The woman gave Ivy's arm a slight squeeze. 'I'm sure that's not true.'

'Are you?' Ivy replied, raising a sceptical eyebrow. 'I've spent a long time being wrecked. I don't even know what I've been doing with myself these last couple of years. I thought I was having fun and doing something that meant something. But then I read Jess's email and I felt so lost. Like, what's the point? What's changed in *my* life? Nothing.'

She knew she wasn't making much sense, but it was the first time she'd been able to verbalise the feeling that had been growing day by day with intensity. Something about this woman made it possible for the scramble of emotions to become something even vaguely coherent in her head. If only she'd have met her yesterday, Ivy might not have gone on such a bender. She laughed to herself, shaking her head.

'What's funny?'

'I always thought I was one of those people who had perfect timing for things. Being in the right place at the right time.' Ivy smiled sadly. 'I was just thinking it would've been good to have met you yesterday. Last night, I . . .' She shook her head and swallowed the ball in her throat. 'I can't remember what happened. Not really.'

She squeezed her eyebrows together, as if it might help her remember, but all she could see was that mohawk and dreadlocks.

'I blacked out and, when I woke up . . .' Ivy sighed, tears stinging the back of her eyes again.

'Did something happen?' the woman asked softly.

Ivy shivered. She couldn't be sure. She'd been too wasted. And who would believe her anyway? She was a party girl. She loved a good time, loved drugs, loved men. She didn't have any proof apart from that knowing feeling she'd had as soon as she'd woken up. She felt *used*. Ivy swallowed. She couldn't say the words. Didn't even know how to. Instead, the woman simply nodded and gave her arm a reassuring squeeze as if she understood anyway.

'I can't bring all of this to Jess.' Ivy groaned. 'Not after years without speaking and definitely not on her wedding day. I need to sort myself out. I need to get out of *this*.'

'Where would you go?'

'Home. England, I mean. I don't actually *have* a home there any more.' Ivy shook her head. For someone who'd felt like they'd had everything, she suddenly realised she had nothing.

'Well, I have a little place in Cornwall that's sitting empty right now and a lot of land that needs working.'

Ivy frowned and looked at the woman in front of her. Who was she? Maybe she didn't even really exist. Ivy had clearly been over the top high last night – she could be hallucinating this for all she knew.

'It's not much,' the woman continued, 'but it's a pretty little village. A perfect place to get yourself sorted, really. And I've been meaning to get someone to help at my yoga studio for a while now.'

Ivy looked at her with questioning eyes. 'Why would you help me? You don't even know me. Nobody does stuff like this, not even here where it's supposed to be all free love and peace on earth.'

The woman laughed a little. 'Oh, us lot from the old guard are still here. You just have to know where to find us.'

She could be a total wackjob. A serial killer who preyed on vulnerable people. Arambol had its fair share of weirdos. But Ivy knew she wasn't. She felt like someone Ivy had known her whole life, sturdy and safe.

'No, but seriously,' the woman continued, 'I've been there, *right* where you are. I've woken up from things I don't remember and even more I'd rather forget. I know how bad it can make a person feel.'

Ivy looked at her, dressed in a simple vest and leggings. Her skin was tanned and glowing in that healthy kind of way. Ivy couldn't imagine her being in any kind of state like the one she was in.

'Can you get yourself a ticket back?'

Ivy nodded.

'Are you an addict?'

'No,' Ivy replied quickly. 'It was always just for partying but after last night, I know I don't want any of that any more. I can't.'

'So what *do* you want?'

'I want to be . . .' she shook her head, trying to find the right word and almost laughed when she found it. 'I want to be normal.'

She really did. Ivy knew in that moment that this was her get-out-of-jail-free card. She might not be so lucky next time and end up dead in a ditch somewhere, high and alone.

The woman's eyes searched hers for a few seconds, as if she were scanning Ivy's body and soul for a lie, before she blinked again and smiled. She didn't know where this woman had come from, but a wave of gratitude flooded her body. Maybe by coming to the cafe instead of going straight home, she'd put herself in the right place at the right time after all.

'None of us are normal. That's the beauty of being human.' The woman smiled. 'But if you want to try, I'm willing to help. What's your name?'

Gratitude filled her eyes with tears as she smiled at the older woman in front of her. 'I'm Ivy.'

The woman's eyes narrowed slightly, as if there was a hint of recognition there, before flicking it away and returning Ivy's smile.

'Nice to meet you, Ivy. I'm Ruth.'

Chapter Twenty-One

Ivy

January, two years ago

Rain flecked the small cabin window as soon as the plane dipped below the clouds. The constant dark blue sky that Ivy had been sat in for hours had now been replaced by a muggy grey, and the patchwork of fields below looked brown and dead. Houses and buildings started to come into view, thousands of feet below her. Suburbs grew into a sprawling metropolis with the buildings clustering closer and closer together, and there in the distance was a long and winding river. The Thames sparkled, despite the overcast weather, and Ivy let her head rest against the hard window frame. A long, slow exhale left her mouth. It was as if she'd been holding her breath for the entire nine hours she'd been sitting in the plane. She was home.

It was only now that she saw the familiarity of it through the window that she realised the feeling of freedom she'd thought she'd found after leaving England wasn't real. This, seeing the O2 Centre, Docklands and Canary Wharf, felt like freedom. She was back. She could stop running. She looked at the skyscrapers as they flew over The City. The Gherkin and Lloyd's building were surrounded by buildings she was sure hadn't been there when she'd last seen the London skyline. And there was the London Eye, Big Ben and the green oasis of Hyde Park. With every familiar landmark they flew over, a little more tension left her body. Somewhere down there, Jess was getting on with her life, preparing for her wedding. It still felt as unreal as the idea of her coming back. She'd shoved thoughts of returning to England into a mental drawer labelled *screw that, never again*. But meeting Ruth had changed everything and, in the week since she'd been offered that lifeline, Ivy had got busy, posting an ad offering her small bungalow in a Facebook group, along with everything in it. Ruth had flown back a couple of days before Ivy, leaving her to daydream of England, grey pavements, cold weather and mugs of hot tea with buttered toast and chatty morning radio shows.

She hadn't told Jess she was coming back. The last thing Ivy wanted was a repeat of the fight they'd had, because if Jess had thought she was a fuck-up back then, she'd only be convinced of it now. Better to wait until she had an idea of how things were going to pan out and get herself sorted. Right now, she had nothing to show for herself at all, unlike Jess with her new home, new business and soon-to-be-new husband.

◆ ◆ ◆

Hours later, Ivy woke to the sound of her alarm ringing in her ears. She pulled her headphones out and rubbed her eyes before looking out of the window. Hedges and bushes blurred in front of her. This was her third and final bus ride and she'd fallen asleep for most of it. She'd been on countless buses over the years, overpacked with people, winding up and down mountain roads. She'd sat with chickens flapping their wings in the arms of locals and, one time, a man had brought an actual goat with him. She'd had constant bouts of diarrhoea on one, and a travel-sick child leaning over her lap and throwing up out of the window on another. This was altogether much more comfortable.

Ivy yawned loudly on the empty bus as it followed the curve in the road. The heating was on full blast, creating a feeling of humidity in the air as rain battered the windows outside. She looked straight down the aisle through the windscreen as the sea came into view in the distance, roaring with white-tipped waves. Ivy yawned again, reaching up to stretch her arms above her head. It was almost twenty-six hours since she'd left her bungalow to go to the airport in Goa – half a world away. By now, a taxi, two planes, two coaches and a regional bus later, she felt as foggy as the windows.

The bus slowed down as it entered a village. Ivy zipped up her hoodie, gathered up her backpack and made her way down the aisle to stand next to the driver's plexiglass window. She held on to the yellow metal handrail above and peered out at the surf shops and cafes against a backdrop of darkened sky.

'Is this Treppin Bay?' she asked.

The bus driver nodded. 'And the last stop. Hope you've got a brolly in there.'

'Nope. But I'll live.'

The slight drizzle she'd landed in at Heathrow was a full-on downpour here. She had no umbrella, no rain jacket and her battered Converse were ripped at the sides by the toe creases. According to the directions she'd been given, she had a further ten-minute walk ahead, but it was fine. She was actually looking forward to getting a bit soaked and letting everything she'd left behind get washed away by the rain. Thankfully, the bus stop was right outside a shop where she could get a few supplies. She had no idea what, if anything, would be waiting for her at the house. Ivy thanked the driver, tucked her shoulder-length dreadlocks into the collar of her jacket and pulled her hood over her head before stepping off the bus and ducking straight into the shop.

Bright lights lit up a white and cream space, and there was a slight smell of spilled milk. The teenage girl sitting behind the counter glanced up from her phone for a millisecond before looking straight back down again. Ivy was surrounded by things she knew just on sight and grabbed a basket, eager to fill it. She'd got used to settling for usually unsatisfying alternative versions of what she really wanted. She'd never have expected to be so happy to see proper pickle again. Ivy wandered through the shop, picking up a two-pint bottle of full-fat milk, a box of tea, eggs, thick-sliced bread and actual salad cream, one of the things she'd missed the most. She stopped in front of the magazine rack, looking at the shiny covers. *Cosmopolitan, Glamour, Elle* . . . she'd never bought one in her life, but Jess had always loved them. Ivy thought they were waste of money, but she'd still flick through the pages once her sister had finished with them. She picked one at random and put it in the basket, along with a jar of marmalade and a can of beans. Her stomach growled as she placed the basket on the counter. The food she'd eaten on the plane felt a long time ago and she was looking forward to having a couple of slices of toast and a boiled egg with a cup of tea.

The girl behind the counter scanned each item with a barely disguised boredom that Ivy could relate to. She'd had to work plenty of similar jobs before herself.

'I'm supposed to pick up a set of keys?' Ivy said, putting her debit card into the reader.

'Oh, you must be Ivy?' she asked and Ivy nodded. 'Ruth left them with me earlier.'

The girl opened up a drawer under the till and handed over a small envelope with her name on it, written in neat, capital letters and underlined in black ink. Ivy flicked her thumb under the seal and shook out the single brass key inside, along with a handwritten note.

Hello, lovely. Get settled in, sleep well and drop by to see me tomorrow. I'll be at the studio from 8am. Ruth x

Ivy put the note back into the envelope and slipped it into the bag of groceries.

'Long trip?' The girl nodded at Ivy's backpack.

'Since yesterday.' Ivy laced her grimace with a smile as she punched in her PIN. 'I'm glad it's almost over.'

'Where are you coming from?'

'India.'

'Backpacking?' The girl perked up a little, the boredom giving way to curiosity. 'I want to travel when I've finished my A levels. Have you been gone long?'

'Seven years, give or take,' Ivy replied. It sounded like an awfully long time.

'Cool.' The girl ripped Ivy's receipt from the machine and handed it over. 'I'm Zoë, by the way.'

Ivy took the receipt and slipped it into a little canvas tote bag along with everything else and Zoë nodded towards the window.

'You'll be better off taking the small footpath to get to the house. It's way quicker than taking the road, especially in this. It's just behind the Cove Cafe and it'll come out pretty much right by the door.'

'Thanks for the tip.' Ivy grinned back.

Zoë shrugged, slipping back into bored-teenager mode and Ivy headed out into the rain, following the instructions she'd been given. The wet seeped through her jacket, ran down her face and crept in through her shoes as she trudged along the footpath. Wind blew in through her collar and bit at her bare fingers. Her breath grew shallow as she followed the path uphill, and she ground her teeth. It wasn't good that someone her age got out of breath just from walking a few steps up a slope. She was tired of feeling tired, always wrecked from the night before. After avoiding cold winters for so many years, Ivy tilted her face up towards the sky as she walked, letting the bitter weather splash against her skin.

The path ended at a wall and Ivy stopped, staring at a small cottage. Its white lime-washed exterior stood in stark contrast to the grey sky and muddy fields surrounding it. Ivy walked through a gap in the wall and followed a path laid with small circular stones to the front door. She wiped the rain from her face with her free hand before taking the key from her pocket and slipping it into the lock.

Musty air greeted her as she stepped inside and found a switch by the door. Light filled the small space, revealing an open-plan kitchen and living room with white-washed walls and rows of empty shelves built in on one side. A two-seater sofa sat by a fireplace, along with a small coffee table. Ivy closed the door behind her, dropped her bags to the floor and slipped out of her Converse. The floor was cold beneath her wet feet as she stepped lightly through the house, discovering a small bathroom, complete with bathtub, something she'd gone for years without. At the back of the cottage was a small bedroom with just enough space for a bed and chair, and wardrobe space built into the walls.

Ivy hugged her arms around herself as she walked back to the living room.

She stood still, listening to the rain and wind lashing the windows. She was in a tiny cottage in the middle of nowhere with just the bare essentials. She'd never been to Cornwall in her life and the only people she knew was a woman she'd randomly met in Goa and a teenager from the village shop. But Ivy had never felt more at home.

◆ ◆ ◆

The next morning, Ivy crossed the field behind the cottage and made her way to the yoga studio as the map drawn on the back of Ruth's note had told her to, and came to a barn. There, behind the huge glass door, was Ruth. Despite being in Treppin Bay and staying in Ruth's cottage, Ivy had been half-worried that she'd made the woman up out of desperation.

'Ah, she's awake,' Ruth said, looking up as Ivy walked in.

She looked exactly as she had that morning in the cafe in a vest, leggings and no shoes. It was comforting to see she wasn't one of those who turned out to be a completely different person out of the Arambol bubble.

Ruth wrapped her in a hug. 'It's great to see you. How was the journey, all okay?'

Ivy nodded as Ruth held her at arms' length, looking at her in the way a mum would look at her child. 'All good. Long, but worth it.'

'The best things usually are.' Ruth's face creased into a smile as warm as the central heating circulating around them. 'How'd you sleep?'

'Like the dead. I'd have slept right through if it weren't for the rain.'

'It's been going pretty much since I got back,' Ruth said, closing the folder she'd been leafing through and looking out through the panoramic windows at the front of the barn. 'Welcome back to England.'

Ivy laughed a little. 'I never thought I'd ever say this, but I'm kind of happy for the cold.'

The phone behind the desk rang and while Ruth answered, Ivy looked around the reception. The simple exterior of the barn hid the beauty of the space inside. She hadn't known what to expect from the studio, but it hadn't been this. It felt terrible to admit it, but Ivy had thought that with Ruth's age, it might be more . . . homely. Less stylish. Instead, everything she could see had been done to a high standard, with exposed brick walls and dark wood floorboards. The air was scented with incense and the recessed lighting made the whole place feel safe. Like a sanctuary. Especially on a stormy day like this.

Ivy heard the faint voice of a woman talking through the closed door in front of her, along with a loud whooshing sound. She shivered and crossed her arms over her chest. It was as if the entire world around her had just breathed out at the same time, and it was as nice as it was unsettling.

'Sorry about that,' Ruth said, putting the phone down.

Ivy looked back at her and then stopped as her eyes readjusted to the framed mosaic of photographs on the wall behind Ruth's head. She blinked and put her hands on the oak reception desk, leaning on them to look closer, barely able to believe what she was seeing.

'Finn?'

Ruth turned to look too, and Ivy's eyes stayed fixed on the photograph. It was definitely him. Much younger, but still Finn.

'He's my nephew,' Ruth smiled, turning back to face her. 'How do you know him?'

'You're his aunt?' Ivy shook her head as if she were trying to rejig the information into a format that made sense. 'We've known each other for years. Since uni.' She shook her head again and laughed a little. 'He used to date my sister.'

Ruth's face brightened a little in realisation. 'Your sister was *his* Jess?'

She nodded, dumbfounded. 'Yeah, I guess she was.'

His Jess. Those two words said it all. It still amazed Ivy to think she'd ever been so convinced she could win him over, or how much of a fuss she'd made about him and Jess getting together.

'What are the chances?' Ruth smiled. 'You'd be surprised how many crazy connections I've made with people while travelling.'

'The six degrees of separation thing, I've had that too,' Ivy said, referring to the theory that everyone in the world was linked by six social connections or less. Still, it was a shock when the connection was this close.

Ruth looked at the studio around them. 'So, Ivy. Have you ever worked in a yoga studio before?'

Ivy pulled her eyebrows together and shook her head. She'd had loads of jobs: bartending, waitressing, olive picking and selling in markets. She'd even helped out at a nursing home for a while, reading to residents who were so far gone with dementia, they'd had no idea whether she was there or not.

She'd tried to make a good impression today to replace the bedraggled state Ruth had met her in. She'd showered, washed her hair and put on the best of what she had: a pair of black jeans and a thin jumper. She'd even used the Benefit eyebrow shaping pencil she'd bought way back when, and her honey-scented lip balm. Ivy had always been able to make money and wasn't afraid of hard work. It was ironic that after years of being surrounded by hippies and bendy yogis, she'd never even been inside a yoga studio, let alone worked in one.

'I've worked in a backpacking hostel, if that helps?' she said, finding the most comparable thing she could from her lengthy CV.

'Probably.' Ruth smiled with a dismissive wave of her hand. 'It doesn't matter, it's all fairly easy to pick up.'

'I feel like I should tell you, I've also never even done yoga before.'

What was she *doing*? Ivy picked at the skin on her thumb. Anyone would think she was trying to sabotage herself on purpose, telling the owner of a yoga studio she was being interviewed by that she had absolutely zero experience in anything to do with the world of yoga whatsoever.

'I must be the only person in the world who hasn't,' Ivy added with what she hoped was an excusable smile.

'Oh, you'd be surprised. Work on the land won't start for another couple of months, so you'll have plenty of time to pick things up. Come on.' Ruth stepped out from behind the desk. 'Let me show you around. Your shoes go there.'

Ruth pointed to a row of shelves against the wall and Ivy pulled off her trainers, slotting them into an empty space.

'You can wear socks or slippers, but no shoes are allowed beyond this point for anyone. Not for anyone, not ever.' She looked down and lifted her perfectly pedicured feet for effect.

Ivy nodded. 'I'm used to being barefoot. Prefer it, actually.'

A smile of approval crossed Ruth's face and she led her to the doorway of a second room leading off from the reception. She flicked a switch, sending soft amber light from solitary bulbs hanging from the exposed ceiling beams. Ivy stepped inside, her bare feet landing on the heated floorboards. At the other end, another panoramic window showed the view down the hill, overlooking the village and out to the sea, rolling with furious, messy waves. Two big plants stood by the window and rows of long cushions and cork bricks were stacked into yet more storage shelves.

'This place is amazing,' Ivy said, turning on the spot. 'I still can't believe all this is real.'

'It's real, alright. You asked me in Goa why I'm helping you?' Ruth said, and Ivy nodded. 'Someone helped me once, and I owe her all of this because of it. I was an alcoholic – still am, albeit sober.

She helped me, and you could say I've made it my life's work to keep paying it forward.'

Ivy liked that idea, and knowing that Ruth had gone through something similar herself made all of this feel even more special. She didn't know why Ruth had been put in front of her, or what the connection with Finn meant. But she did know that being here, in this room where the air carried the faintest hint of body sweat, she felt still. It reminded her of that feeling after a storm had raged through and the only thing left was quiet. She'd spent a lifetime trying to discover that quiet for herself, with little success. Now, it looked like she might have found it.

Chapter Twenty-Two

Ivy

February, two years ago

Ivy closed the door of the cottage behind her and looked up at the silver moon. When was the last time she'd been up and out of the house at quarter past six in the morning? She pulled the collar of a coat she'd found in the wardrobe up around her ears and jammed her hands into the faux-fur-lined oversized pockets. Catching a bus, plane or train didn't count, and neither did hailing a taxi to get from a club to an after-hours party. Ivy yawned, sending her breath curling into the dark air like wisps of smoke. Frozen grass and clumps of earth crunched loudly beneath her feet as she trudged across the field. It felt as if the rest of the world was still fast asleep.

There was the tiniest part of her that wanted to stop and say *stuff this*, turn around and scurry back to the warmth of the cottage and her bed. Instead, she clenched her teeth to stop them from chattering in the freezing air. After shadowing Ruth for a while, learning how to use the studio software and understanding how things went, she'd been given her own set of keys. This morning, she was responsible for opening up alone. Going back to bed wasn't an option.

Ivy's belly tied in knots. She'd done all kinds of jobs before and this would probably be among the easiest of them all, but still nerves were flickering inside her like a defective light bulb. With each footstep, keys clinked against each other in her pocket. They were the only two keys she possessed – one for the studio and the other for the cottage. Both were places owned by someone who'd taken her in on a gut feeling of trust. It was a new, sweet and slightly intimidating feeling, but she liked it. Jess wouldn't believe her eyes if she could see her now. Maybe she'd tell her about it, when she got around to replying to her email, which she would. Once things had settled down and she could be sure that she wasn't going to be a chaotic influence in Jess's orderly life.

Ivy carefully made her way down the steep slope to the studio with one hand trailing along the damp, cold grass behind her for stability. She slid a couple of inches in her wellies and made a note to get boots with decent grip as soon as she could. It would've been much easier to take the road, but at this time in the morning, every extra minute was precious. She'd had some serious jetlag and coming this way meant she could have almost a quarter of an hour longer in bed.

Ivy got to the bottom of the slope and brushed the dirt from her palms before cupping her hands in front of her mouth and blowing on her fingers. That was something else she'd need – a decent pair of gloves. Her fingertips were burning after being exposed to the air for just a few seconds. The studio was lit up by lamps set into the gravel-covered ground, sending soft yellow light up the external brick walls. The nerves in her belly grew as she took the key from her pocket and slid it into the lock to open the full-length glass door. She stepped inside, letting the warm air wash over her face, and unzipped her coat. It was time to get to work.

She found the list she'd left on the desk the day before and set about brewing tea in the big silver urn. She plumped the cushions on the sofa in the room next to the entrance and rearranged the magazines on the table. She turned up the heating in the big practice room, lit candles and incense, unloaded clean glasses from the dishwasher and opened the windows in the toilet and shower room. Then she sat in the chair behind the front desk and took a sip of lemongrass and eucalyptus tea from the glass in her hand. It was surprisingly good.

'Right,' she said to herself with a little sigh of determination.

Ivy looked at the Mac. She'd felt silly admitting to Ruth that she had no idea how to use it. In a time where it felt like everyone had Apple everything, Ivy had kept her clunky old laptop from university. She wished she'd had a fancy, expensive MacBook too so she'd have a little more confidence behind her. Instead, she turned the piece of paper over and followed the instructions to open up the studio software, stumbling over keys that were in a different place than she was used to. When she finally navigated her way through the software menu and brought up the information for the morning class, she pushed the small keyboard away with relief.

She took a final check of her list. Everything was done and class wasn't due to start for another fifteen minutes. The sky outside had brightened as dawn approached. Ivy took another sip of her tea, which, although tasting good, was no substitute for her usual strong morning coffee. Her thoughts turned to the packet of tobacco in her coat pocket. She was missing that, too. She could quickly nip behind the studio for a quick smoke, but she promptly remembered the rules of the studio: no shoes beyond the hallway, no strong perfume and no smoking. She didn't want to reek like an ashtray, because it wasn't as if she'd be going home when class started. Her initiation this morning wasn't just about opening up the studio. Today, she would also go to her first-ever yoga class.

Twenty minutes later, Ivy sat on a cushion in the back corner of the yoga room with her legs crossed and her eyes closed. She'd always thought that people who woke up at the crack of dawn to go and exercise were a little nuts, which meant that the six people sitting around her in this room must be too. She'd woken up, stumbled out of bed and come here because it was her new job. But them? They'd all arrived looking as if they'd been up for hours already, fresh-faced and smiling as they came into the studio and signed in.

'Feel your hip bones rooting down into your cushion and allow yourself to sink into your seat.'

Ruth gave her instructions in a clear, calm voice, but Ivy's attention wandered. It felt like they'd been sitting for an age, but it couldn't have been more than a couple of minutes. She opened her eyes a little and snuck a look at the woman next to her, sitting ramrod straight, with her eyes closed and a look of serenity on her face. Ivy closed her eyes again and pinched her eyebrows together in an effort to concentrate, which would be easy enough if only she knew how to create more space between her vertebrae as Ruth was instructing. Right now, she'd settle for a little more space in the elastic of her sports bra that was digging into her ribs. Ivy held down a sigh. There was a reason why she'd stayed away from things like yoga and meditation and sport in general. She simply didn't have the capacity for it. She lacked the concentration and commitment to learn. Jess, on the other hand, would get up and run, or go to the gym before work or on a Saturday morning.

'Keeping your eyes closed, raise your arms over your head . . .'

Ivy snapped her mind away from Jess and back into the room as Ruth instructed her to bring her hands together in front of her heart. Maybe the crabbiness was from missing her cigarette and coffee, but she was relieved they were finally about to start moving.

It had always looked so easy when she'd seen people doing yoga at sunset on the beach, but for the next hour, Ivy struggled to keep up as the rest of the class glided from position to position. She seemed to have forgotten which side of her body was right and which was left, and her skin quickly beaded with sweat. By the time Ruth told them to lie on their backs and rest, Ivy almost cried with relief. Despite only being there for a few minutes, she actually slept. As she rolled onto her side and sat up again, she yawned. The crabbiness she'd felt at the start of class had gone, replaced by a feeling of tired calm.

By the time class was over and everyone started to roll up their mats, Ivy's stomach was growling.

'So,' Ruth grinned, almost gliding across the floor towards her. 'You're still alive.'

Ivy laughed, crouching on the floor and rolling the rubber mat tightly with her hands. 'Barely.'

'Coffee?'

'Absolutely. I'll need a bowl of the stuff,' Ivy replied, slowly standing up. Her thighs already told her she'd pay for this tomorrow.

Half an hour later, Ivy, Ruth and three of the students sat in a beachside cafe down in the village. The universe had been listening to Ivy's every word, because in front of her was a large bowl of milky coffee with a double shot of espresso. It was so big that Ivy had to use both hands to hold it. She inhaled the slightly bitter aroma before taking a sip and ignoring the craving to have it accompanied by tobacco.

'So you've just got here from India, right?' Hannah, the girl Ivy had snuck a look at during class, asked.

'A few days ago.' Ivy nodded with a smile and put her bowl back down. 'Wish I'd have made the effort to go to yoga while I was there so I could've been prepared.'

Everyone laughed, including Ruth.

'Honestly, you all make it look so easy.'

'It's called a practice for a reason,' Ruth said with a smile and the others nodded. 'It takes time to get used to it.'

'Oh, God, I remember my first class,' Hannah said with a laugh, holding a tiny espresso cup in the centre of her palm. She was around the same age as Ivy, with short brown hair and big, innocent-looking doe eyes that conflicted with the cackle of a laugh she'd just given. Ivy took an instant liking to her.

'I actually thought I was going to die,' Hannah continued. 'It felt like my ribs were being prised apart. They probably were in a way.'

The general consensus around the table was that it would get easier and as the group exchanged memories of their first time in a class, Ivy sipped her coffee. She was in awe of Ruth. With the much-needed caffeine hit being delivered to her bloodstream, Ivy was able to think back to the glimpses of Ruth she'd had in class. She'd been so there. So present. Even with the discomfort of her body contorting into all sorts of strange positions, Ivy had felt Ruth's support from start to finish.

'A few of us are going to the cinema tomorrow night if you want to come?' Hannah asked and Ivy raised her eyebrows.

'There's a cinema in the village?'

Hannah cackled again. 'No. It's in Wadebridge, a bit of a drive. We'll have dinner afterwards, too. It'll be fun.'

And a good way to meet people, Ivy thought. She'd spent the entire time she'd been here in Treppin Bay cooped up in her cottage. She'd needed some time to adjust to being back in England, in the cold, in a different time zone. She'd sat in front of daytime TV, unpacked her backpack and taken a couple of walks on the beach, but now it was time to get out and make friends. It was always going to be a trial, coming here. For all she knew, she could've hated it. She might not have got on with Ruth and had to leave. Instead, she'd allowed herself to settle in slowly. Her little cottage didn't feel like a temporary place. For the first time in a long time, Ivy had started to think about small things she could buy make it feel more homely. Despite the nerves and reluctance to be up so early today, she'd done everything that had needed to be done and, as she sipped her coffee, she realised that, actually, she felt pretty good. Which was a big difference to how she'd been feeling just a short while ago.

Ivy grinned and nodded. It was time to meet the locals.

Chapter Twenty-Three

Jess

June, two years ago

She hasn't come. It's the morning of my wedding, and Ivy isn't here. I sit in front of the mirror in my hotel room, staring at my made-up face. It reminds me of the party the night I let Ivy cover me with make-up. The night I met Finn. The night everything changed. Only this time, everything is different, including the make-up. Maddie has done it so well that you can barely even tell it's there – exactly how I like it.

'You ready?' Maddie asks.

I stare at her through the mirror. Her red hair is up in a gorgeous chignon and she's wearing false eyelashes that on anyone else would look ridiculous but, on her, just work. I take a deep breath and nod, getting up from the chair, and use my palms to smooth the crinkles in my dress. My wedding dress.

'This feels weird,' I say quietly to Maddie.

'Nervous?'

'A little. But it's not just that. It's the whole thing. Getting married . . . the wedding.'

She looks me dead in the eye. 'Are you having second thoughts?'

'I don't know,' I reply. 'Is it normal to feel like this?'

'Probably.' She smiles and tips her head to one side. 'I'll let you know – if Chris ever decides to make an honest woman out of me.'

They've been together for so long they might as well be married. I look around at the room Maddie had booked us for last night. My hen party was a low-key one: massages at the spa in the hotel followed by a few drinks with a couple of friends and our staff, and a pre-wedding yoga class organised by a friend of Maddie's. I feel refreshed for what's deemed to be the biggest day in a woman's life instead of hung-over and tied to a lamp post – though I think that's usually reserved for the men. A fleeting image of Nick tied to one in the middle of nowhere, naked with his eyebrows shaved, pops into my mind and it's such an unlikely one that I almost laugh out loud. He'd gone to Prague with some friends two weeks ago for his stag do. He's probably already at the registry office feeling even fresher than I am.

'I don't know, Mads,' I sigh and put a hand over my stomach. 'I feel a bit sick.'

'Here, sit down,' she says, and hands me a bottle of water from the mini kitchen. 'What's going on?'

I unscrew the bottle and chug a mouthful back.

'Is it because of Ivy?'

'She never even replied. I'm getting married and she just didn't reply.'

'Maybe she didn't see it?'

'Or maybe she just hates me more than I thought.'

'Don't be silly. She's your sister, she doesn't hate you,' Maddie says, sitting next to me. 'You know Ivy. She doesn't check anything, ever.'

'Who doesn't check their emails?' I shake my head, remembering the way she'd slapped me at Dad's funeral. 'I think she's still mad at me and I don't blame her. What I did was unforgiveable.'

'You did what you thought was best.'

I dig my stockinged toes into the plush grey carpet. It was no excuse. I'd written emails and Facebook messages and WhatsApps, but I'd always stopped short of sending them. I know how volatile Ivy can be and always told myself it was probably still too raw and she needed more time. Besides, it looks like Ivy is having an amazing time. All the photos I ever see on Facebook are of her somewhere hot and gorgeous, with dazzling sunsets. I'd hoped a wedding invitation might be something good to break the ice with. To say, *look, I know things have been crap between us but you're good and I'm good and maybe we can sort things out?* Instead, I find myself here, about to get married with no family on my side at all.

'It's not just that,' I say, shaking my head. 'I don't have anyone here, Mads. No mum to give me advice, no dad to give me away and no sister to try and get off with the best man.'

'*I'm* here. I can do all of those things. Apart from the best man bit. I don't think that'll go down well with Chris.' She grins and I return it.

'Sorry. I didn't mean to sound ungrateful, it's just hit me, that's all.'

I'd be lying if I said I hadn't had little doubts, but they'd always been just that – little. Until this morning, I'd told myself that it was okay if Ivy didn't come, because we have so much to sort out and a wedding isn't the time for that. And since I woke up in this plush hotel suite, I've been trying to tell myself that what Nick and I have is real. That he's a great guy and while the intimacy we once had has lessened, it can always be recaptured. I've made a point of carving time in my diary for date nights and weekends away. I'm not one of those women who have silky lingerie in the back of their drawer, because I know that keeping a relationship going means making an effort. I actually wear them for him on a regular enough basis. So why am I remembering the way Finn had looked at me that day when I'd seen him in Pret, or worse, how he'd not bothered to turn up?

'If you don't want to do this, you don't have to,' Maddie says, taking my hand. 'We can flag down a cab and you can take me on your honeymoon instead.'

I put a hand on my chest with my fingers splayed wide and close my eyes, taking a deep breath. This tightness in my chest is nothing new. It's simply stress and nerves. I had it the day Maddie and I signed a lease for office space, and it was there when I tried my wedding dress on for the first time. It's nothing new, and it doesn't matter, because I know how to deal with it. Security, reliability and routine – the magic trio. I have someone who embodies all of those things, waiting to marry me across the road, and I'm determined to make this work.

I open up my eyes and fix a smile on my face. 'I'm good. Let's go.'

Chapter Twenty-Four

IVY

August, two years ago

'Did you hear about that girl on the news?' Hannah asked as she stirred a pot full of bolognese. Her big, doe-like eyes were wide, peeking out from under a severe, straight-cut fringe.

Ivy shook her head and squeezed the garlic press in her hand. 'What girl?'

'The one who's got done for smuggling drugs? From Spain to Morocco, I think. I never understand how people can get themselves into such crazy situations,' Hannah said, putting the wooden spoon down. 'Like, how can they *not* think they'll get caught?'

'Beats me,' Ivy said, shaking her head and sprinkling the garlic over slices of baguette topped with butter and herbs.

Hannah's cottage was lovely. It was about the same size as Ivy's, but somehow Hannah, her husband and daughter were all able to fit in. Ivy looked at the photos on the fridge door. She hadn't believed it when Hannah had told her she had a kid, and a fifteen-year-old at that. When she wasn't in her yoga clothes, Hannah wore fishnet tights with Dr Martens and Guns N' Roses t-shirts. She drank wine and had a laugh that could probably be heard in London. If things were different, Ivy was sure they'd have egged each other on, necking shots and sharing a duvet on the sofa to groan through their hangovers. Instead, Ivy had been invited round for Thursday night spaghetti bolognese where she'd be sipping grape juice and sharing a table with her new friend's husband and their daughter.

'I love your house,' she said as Hannah put a handful of dried spaghetti into a pot of boiling water.

Hannah laughed and raised her eyebrows. 'It's a mess! I can't even make any excuses, it's like this all the time.'

Ivy shrugged. 'It's homely. You can tell there's a family living here.'

'I don't know how other people manage to keep things all spick and span.' She poured herself a glass of red wine. 'Sure you don't want one?'

Ivy hesitated for a second, and then shook her head. 'Better not.'

Hannah pulled her lips to one side, swirling the wine in her glass. Ivy could see it on her face – the question of whether she was an alcoholic or just teetotal, especially because it was the third time now that she'd turned down a drink in a social setting.

'I'm not an alcoholic or anything like that,' Ivy quickly said with a light laugh.

'Oh, God. Was I just looking all judgemental?' Hannah's cheeks flooded red. 'I didn't mean to.'

Ivy shook her head. 'No, not at all. I just wanted to put it out there so you don't feel awkward about me always saying no.' She laughed to herself at the idea that her saying no to anything was even a reality. 'I just prefer to have my mind clear these days.'

Hannah smiled and nodded. 'Good for you. I'd go mad if it weren't for a tipple now and then.'

'Today was one of those days.' Ivy grimaced.

'Oh?' Hannah leaned against the side of the fridge with her shoulder and took a sip of wine. 'Wanna talk about it?'

Ivy shrugged shyly. 'It's silly, really. I slipped in the mud and my muscles hurt from gardening. I think I just freaked out a bit. I mean, I've never gardened a day in my life before now.'

'Big adjustment after being on the road for what . . .?'

'Seven years.'

'I can't even imagine.' Hannah laughed through her nose. 'I was born here, grew up here and have settled down here. God, that makes me sound so boring.'

She pulled a face and Ivy smiled.

'I don't know. You're kind of lucky, really. You've always belonged somewhere.'

'I didn't have much choice after getting pregnant so young. But if I'm honest, I don't think I'd have left even if Libby hadn't come along. I'm a family girl at heart. Need them around me all the time. It must be tough without family for you.'

'I've got a sister,' Ivy said, taking her glass of juice from the side. She'd already told Hannah that her parents had died years ago, but she'd never mentioned Jess before. 'She lives in London.'

'Oh, I hadn't realised. Will she be coming to visit anytime soon?'

'I doubt it.' Ivy hesitated and played with the glass in her hand. 'We don't talk any more. We had a huge fight years ago. You grew up here, right? So you must know Finn Jackson, Ruth's nephew?'

'Oh yeah, I know Finn. He was in the year above me at school.'

'I met him when I was at uni through a friend and we reconnected afterwards. I had a *huge* crush on him.' Ivy laughed a little at the memory. 'Turned out that he liked my sister much better. I pretty much walked in on them together.'

Hannah pulled a face. 'Ouch. That explains the fallout.'

'Not really. I mean, I was really embarrassed about it all, especially because Finn knew I fancied him too. Honestly, I don't think I was that bothered about them getting together, I just hated that I didn't know about it. And then our dad died and . . . ugh.' Ivy jutted her lower jaw out and sighed. 'It was a mess. We had a huge, huge fight and we never really came back from it.'

Ivy felt a softening in her chest and stomach as she spoke. She wouldn't tell all of this to just anyone, but sharing it with Hannah felt good. It felt nice. Apart from Ruth, she hadn't shared anything so personal with anyone, not even Emma or Lisa. The friendships she'd made over the last few years had been built on fun, partying and shared travel experiences. This felt like it could be something better. A real friendship.

'She's married now anyway,' Ivy said, 'and from what I gather she's doing really well. She has a successful business and her life looks pretty perfect.'

Ivy frowned to herself. It was that perfect-looking life that was stopping her from replying to Jess's email. She'd felt awful for missing the wedding, but it had just felt too impossible to go. Jess had uploaded the most gorgeous picture of her and Nick to her Facebook yesterday. As predicted, she'd made a stunning bride with a simple and elegant gown and a smile that showed the whole world just how happy she was. It had only confirmed to Ivy that not going, and bringing all her mess with her, had been the right thing to do. She had sent a wedding gift and hadn't heard anything back. It wasn't like Jess not to reply to something like that. She was probably angry at her for not showing up. Putting that on top of everything else between them was just much too much, and Ivy didn't even know where to start with a response.

'I don't know. Lately, I've found myself thinking a lot about stuff, you know?' Ivy continued. 'I think I might have been a bit of a brat about a lot of things.'

'How long is it since you've spoken?' Hannah asked.

'Five years.' She grimaced at the face Hannah pulled. 'I mean, we email each other at Christmas and on birthdays, but we haven't actually spoken or opened things up to talk. I meant to but it's like I just blinked and the time disappeared.'

'Maybe now's a good time to try and make contact?'

'Yeah, maybe. I still need to get myself really settled and everything first.'

She'd never been more settled at any other stage in her life than now. She had a great job, a house and a growing community of friends. She wasn't drinking or smoking and she went to Ruth's yoga classes pretty much every day. But still, it all felt too new to really show Jess that things had changed. That she'd changed. Especially when she'd just spent that morning considering running back to her old life.

'Well, you're always welcome in this madhouse,' Hannah said with a caring smile as the front door opened.

Ivy waved at the fifteen-year-old carbon copy of Hannah that came through the door and slung her school backpack on the floor. She wanted some of this. She wasn't ready for a family of her own. Far, far from it. The idea of letting any guy near her after that last night out in Goa made her shudder inside. But seeing Jess's new profile photo had triggered something inside her. She wanted a bit of what she had. She wanted something that felt like home.

Chapter Twenty-Five

JESS

October, last year

It's after nine at night, and my fingers are still tapping across my keyboard. A cup of now lukewarm ginger tea and a small bowl of banana chips sit on one side of my MacBook and my open planner is on the other. All but two of the twelve things on my list have a line through them. I take a pause from typing, sit back in my chair and loosen the thick French side plait that I'd put my hair in that morning.

Maddie and I have spent the bulk of the day interviewing people for a new social media position and, even after having done it countless times, it never gets easier or less tiring. There's been so much talking and observing that my brain feels like mush, but still, I have a little smile on my face. Seven interviews and an hour of comparison meetings later, we have the newest member of our team and growing family. I go back to finishing my email and as I hit send, I hear Nick coming out of the bathroom.

'Still going?' he asks, bringing the scent of his shower gel into the room with him.

Nick puts his fingers in my hair and scrunches it in his hand to give me a mini head massage before bending down and softly kissing the side of my neck.

'Nick, I'm working.' I laugh a little and squirm against the tickle of his lips on my skin.

'You're always working,' he mumbles back, kissing me again. 'And tonight is date night.'

'I know, I'm almost finished. Just give me ten more minutes.'

In reality, ten more minutes won't get me through the rest of my list, but we've already given the trip to the cinema a miss so I could get through the work I need to before tomorrow. There are expectations about where tonight will lead. For a moment, I wish it wasn't quite so organised, that we could be more spontaneous with our intimate time instead.

'I can think of something better to do in those ten minutes,' Nick says, and closes my laptop.

It's the act of spontaneity I've just wished for, but all it does is light frustration in my chest.

'Nick! I was in the middle of something important.'

He puts his hands on the table next to me and bows his head with an undercurrent of annoyance.

'What can you *possibly* be doing that needs to be done now? At nine in the evening?' He pushes himself away from the table.

He's still wet from his shower and stark naked apart from the towel wrapped around his waist and the anger in his voice.

'I need to—'

'You don't *need* to do anything. Whoever you send your next email to won't even see it until tomorrow, because it's nine o'clock at night.'

'Nick, I'm a boss. I have a company to run.'

'Do you think Maddie's glued to her laptop too right now, or do you think she's on the sofa enjoying an evening with her boyfriend?'

'I don't know,' I reply, exasperated and irritated at the same argument that keeps replaying.

'Remember when you wanted to quit your job to start this business? I told you back then that this wasn't part of the deal. I told you I wanted us to have more time together.'

'We do,' I point out. 'We just had a weekend away, and we have date nights every week that wouldn't happen if I didn't arrange them.'

'You only arrange them because if you didn't, they wouldn't happen at all.'

His looming over me makes me feel claustrophobic, and I get up from my chair to walk past him to the kitchen to get some space. We're always going to the cinema or the theatre and we take as many holidays and trips away as calendars allow. And while it might not be the most passionate, intense time together, it *is* still time.

I pour myself a glass of water. 'My job isn't like yours, Nick. I don't get to just leave things until tomorrow and the next day and the next. I don't get to just leave it all in the office; we're still building things up.'

'It's been four years, Jess. How long do you need to break your back for until you can enjoy life? *Our* life?'

It wasn't that easy. It *has* been four years, but things haven't stabilised in the way I'd thought. We're growing constantly, our revenue is going up month by month and instead of being able to take my foot off the brake and let everything coast, it feels too fragile. We can't take our focus away now. *I* can't take my focus away now.

Nick stares at me with his mouth set into a scowl and his eyebrows pulled tightly together, shaking his head.

'If I'd have known this was what being married would be like—'

'You'd have what?' I interrupt, jutting my chin with the all-too-familiar defensiveness that sets in when this topic comes up. 'You'd have never proposed?'

For a couple who'd rarely argued before, it feels like that's all we've done since he'd put this ring on my finger. His shoulders are rising and falling with his breath and his jaw is clenched.

'Actually, no. I wouldn't have. I didn't sign up for this.' He lifts a hand towards me and drops it again. His voice is strained, as if he's fighting against throwing his words at me with rage.

I know I should leave it. We've had this argument enough times for me to know it'll die down. It always does. Tomorrow, he'll tell me he understands how important work is to me, I'll make an extra effort to make up for tonight and ensure that nothing coincides with date night again, no matter what. I should just leave it because he's right. It has been non-stop lately, but for some uncharacteristic reason, I can't keep myself in check.

'So why propose then?' I probe.

'Yeah.' Nick laughs with sarcasm. 'Good question.'

His words stab me square in the chest but my pride stops the tears from building in my eyes.

'I don't think you have any idea how it feels to be constantly pushed away by my own wife unless it fits into a pre-planned schedule,' he says with a low voice that lands with unease on my skin. It's the kind of voice that's thick with disappointment. It cuts deep.

My heart pulls in my chest and I cross my arms over my body. 'Nick . . .'

'Is there someone else?' he asks, and I widen my eyes, shaking my head.

'Of course not! How could you ask me that?'

'Because what else am I supposed to think when I spend my evenings alone waiting for you to notice I'm here?'

I rub the tips of my fingers across my forehead. Half of my frustration is not knowing how to explain the way I feel. The connection between us has changed. It's true I'm not keen on sex these days, but I don't think he is either, not really. He might come up and kiss my neck but it's mechanical. We don't explore each other any more or gaze into each other's eyes. If we ever really did. The last few times I'd had the feeling that we were only doing it because it's what couples do, and not because either of us actually wanted to. Because it was date night and scheduled and expected. I don't know what changed after getting married but I do know that I can't say all of that without us falling into a deadly ravine.

Nick shakes his head and looks at me with defeat in his eyes. I don't want to hurt him. I don't mean to. But even if I took him by the hand now and led him into the bedroom, I know it wouldn't change things. He's using sex as the symptom of something being wrong, but he doesn't seem to be any more able than I am to look at the big picture and acknowledge the issue that I'm almost too scared to say even to myself. That maybe this was all a big mistake.

He drops his hands to his sides. 'I'm tired.'

His hair flops into his eyes and my heart lurches. I didn't mean that. It hasn't been a mistake. I look at the ring on his finger that matches mine. Who was it that said marriage isn't supposed to be easy? It couldn't feel any harder right now. It's nine thirty on a Tuesday night and he's right. Nobody will look at the next email I send until tomorrow because the culture Maddie and I have built in the office means that our staff value and get to enjoy their downtime. A voice inside my head screams at me, wondering why I can't seem to do the same myself.

'I'll be in in a sec,' I say quietly.

Our argument has gone far enough, further than it ever has before. If it goes much further, it'll be just like the fight with Ivy at Dad's funeral and we might say things we regret. As tough as this patch is, it can still be saved. I just have to try harder.

'Don't bother,' Nick says with a shrug. 'I'll sleep in the spare room.'

I go to reply but he turns his back on me before the words get to leave my mouth and I slump against the kitchen worktop wondering where it all went wrong.

◆ ◆ ◆

A few days later, Maddie and I are walking back from viewing an empty shop we'd hoped could be the very first XOXO store. It was a huge disappointment and far too expensive for what it was, but it's a gorgeous autumnal day that actually lives up to what social media sells it as: sunny, crisp and ripe for Maddie's favourite drink of pumpkin spiced latte. We duck into a coffee shop and while it's normal for me to opt for something without caffeine, it's definitely *not* normal for her to bypass the pumpkin latte.

'Since when do you drink hot chocolate?' I ask, taking both our cups from the girl with a lotus flower tattooed right over her throat.

Maddie blows through the tiny sip hole and glances at me sideways. 'I'm pregnant.'

'Oh my God!' I squeal, causing the other customers to stare at us as we make our way back out into the sunshine. 'What? How?'

'I think you know how,' she replies with a laugh as we stand outside.

I roll my eyes with a grin. 'You know what I mean.'

She grins back. 'It's really early days. I'm only four weeks in. We're not telling anyone yet, obviously, but there's no way I couldn't not tell you.'

My eyes brim with tears and I pull her in for a hug. This is big. Huge. Maddie and Chris have been trying for a couple of years and she had a miscarriage a few months back. It isn't something she talks about any more until it becomes too much or she gets her period with a bout of extreme self-loathing. I get it. Not talking about the things that hurt is self-protection, plain and simple.

I wipe a tear away with my finger. 'How's Chris?'

'Nervous. He's fussing over me like mad and won't let me lift a finger.' Maddie grins and tucks her red hair behind her ear. 'It's really sweet. Not sure he can keep it up the whole way through though.'

We both laugh and start walking back towards the train station. That bit of news has completely made my day and put a whole heap of sunshine on what's been an otherwise glum week.

'Jess, I wanted to talk to you about cutting back a bit. Nothing major, but we just want to make sure I'm not overdoing things until we know we're in the clear.'

I nod vigorously. 'Of course.'

'Really? You're alright with it?'

I look at her as if she's just sprouted another head. 'Are you kidding, of course I am.'

'Well, the thing is,' Maddie says carefully, 'I was thinking maybe we could look at getting someone in as an assistant? I mean, I plan to work throughout but I'll need maternity leave and I don't want you to be swamped with everything. Who knows, maybe you'll get preggers too. We should have a plan to keep things going, in any case.'

'Makes sense,' I say with a smile and the relief on her face is clear. 'I mean, come on. We both know things can't continue as they are. We're growing and we need the support.'

Maybe *I* need the support too. Nick has barely spoken to me since our argument and the tension in our flat is getting thicker by the day.

She takes a sip of her hot chocolate and looks at me with a raised eyebrow. 'Well that was suspiciously easy. I'd have thought the workaholic in you would try to convince me to let you do it all yourself.'

'I'm not that bad,' I reply and she snorts so loudly that the man walking a couple of steps ahead visibly flinches.

'Alright, alright.' I say, my voice thick with sarcasm. I sigh. 'Nick and I had a huge fight the other day. He says I work too much.'

Maddie nods with understanding but, thankfully, doesn't say anything back.

'I don't think we'll be close behind you with the baby news any time soon. If ever,' I continue and tap my finger against the cardboard lid of my cup.

It's another thing Nick's been talking more and more about. I'd always seen myself with kids somewhere down the line, but Nick wants them sooner rather than later. I get it – we're not getting any younger. But he's been putting pressure on, which hasn't exactly made me want to drag him into the bedroom. I can't tell Maddie that, though. She's been trying for so long, it would feel insensitive.

'He said he regrets marrying me,' I add instead.

Maddie pulls in a sharp breath. 'Really, he said that?'

'In as many words.' I sigh quietly. 'He's slept in the spare room the last few days and we've barely spoken since.'

'Oh, Jess. I'm sorry. But you guys have argued before, you'll be fine.'

Will we? I'm really not sure. It's nothing I can put my finger on, but the space between us has changed and I don't know if it can go back to how it was.

'He asked if there was someone else.'

'Is he mad?'

'Clearly. But I know he's right. About me working too much.'

'It's definitely something to look at, the work–life balance.'

I concede with a nod. 'I know. That's why I agree with you about getting someone in to help.'

'You guys will be fine. As for work,' she bumps me with her shoulder, 'we're doing really well, Jess. Like, a billion times more than we'd expected. So maybe it's okay to kick back a bit. Take a holiday, spend time with Nick, and get back to a good place.'

'I've always wanted to go to Bali,' I say with a smile back.

There's no way we could go before the end of the year, it's always such a busy time for us. But January? I squeeze Maddie's arm back as we turn into the Tube station feeling a touch more optimistic. Bali, with Nick. I could make that work.

Chapter Twenty-Six

IVY

November, last year

Ivy tracked her finger across her mousepad and clicked on the *buy tickets* button. A shiver of excitement ran through her, quickly followed by nerves that were so strong, she would've clicked on an *only joking, I don't really want to go* button if there'd been one. She went to her email and opened the confirmation, her eyes scanning the page. London Heathrow to Mumbai, Mumbai to Goa, leaving in a few days' time. Ivy pulled the sleeves of her hoodie farther down her arms as doubt gnawed in her mind. Was she mad? She'd been so quick to get out of there and vowed never to return. She searched through her inbox to the course booking confirmation she'd received a few days earlier.

This time next week, she'd be ready to immerse herself in yoga teacher training. Two hundred hours of practice over four weeks. It was absolutely the right thing to do. It wasn't far away from the hippy village she'd made her winter home for three years, but Ivy had no intention of going back to her old haunts. Besides, the main reason she was going was because Ruth would be there too. She led a teacher training course there every year – it was why she'd been there at the same time as Ivy in the first place. Ivy had been mulling it over for weeks and, as usual, left it until the very last minute to decide. It was lucky Ruth was the organiser of it all because technically the course was full and Ivy would've had to wait another year until the next round otherwise. It felt like coming full circle, somehow. Going back to the place she'd fallen apart in to be put back together again. She'd never felt stronger than she did right now. She could do this. Ivy grinned to herself and closed her laptop.

If anyone would've told her that she'd be spending her thirty-fifth birthday morning going to yoga, she'd have laughed in their face. Unless it was beer yoga or wine yoga or whatever else was on trend that included alcohol. But here she was, making her way across the field behind her cottage to the studio with the winter sun hung low in the sky. Its pale yellow light bounced off the frozen grass as if a fairy had scattered the ground with glitter. The ropes around the horse enclosure on the neighbour's field looked like strips of sour sugar-coated sweets. She smiled to herself. That was the kind of thing she would have only noticed if she was high before.

How far she'd come in less than a year was even more obvious on her mat. She moved through Ruth's class with ease, able by now to follow her cues without having to look to the front of the room all the time. These days, she practised with her eyes closed and her breath deep. After feeling unstable on her feet in the beginning, she now felt rooted. Instead of her muscles screaming at her in torture for being twisted and moulded into unnatural positions, they now found something like release. It felt special to start her birthday off like this. She didn't know quite what it was, but Ivy had the feeling that she was right at the edge of something. She almost felt how she had right before bungee jumping from that bridge in Spain in a past life.

By the time class had finished, any doubts Ivy might have had about flying to India had all but disappeared. Things would be very different, this time around. *She* was different. She hadn't touched any drugs and while she *had* drunk a bit of alcohol, it was all very respectable. Her need to get completely hammered was long gone. She'd stopped smoking and had a house she could call her own, one she'd decorated in a way that felt homely and cosy. She'd be going back to Goa looking very much the same – still with her long brown and multicoloured dreads piled up high on her head, tattoos, piercings in her lip and nose – but inside, she'd changed.

'Coffee?' Ruth asked, and Ivy grinned.

'Absolutely.'

Some things, though, had remained the same. She was still an unashamed coffee lover and the post-class ritual of caffeine and a croissant was something she never missed. After the balmy warmth of the yoga studio, the air outside was bitingly cold, making for a brisk walk down the hill to the cafe.

'Mad to think I'll be in thirty-odd degree heat in a couple of days, isn't it?' Ivy said, hunching her shoulders up to her ears and shrinking the tips of her fingers into the sleeves of her coat to keep out the cold.

'Don't, or I might have to throw you in the sea out of pure jealousy,' Hannah replied with a smile. 'I'm only letting you go on the promise that you'll bring some of that sun back with you,'

At this time in the morning, everything was glittery with dew. Steam evaporated from the tops of the hedges in a fine mist and traces of spiderwebs glistened in the sun. Winter in the countryside was beautiful, but Ivy would be lying if she said she wasn't looking forward to having the sun beating down on her skin. For now, she settled for the warmth of the cafe as they stepped inside.

It was the hipster cafe in the village, with dark wooden tables, white tiles on the walls and blackboards with the entire menu handwritten in chalk. It also made the best coffee and always reserved a table for them by the window. They piled in, unwrapping scarves and taking off hats, and Ivy blew on her fingertips. Zoë, the girl who'd served her at the shop when she'd first arrived, had switched jobs and now worked here as a barista. Ivy waved and went to the counter as the others sat at the table.

'I've booked my tickets,' she said with a grin. 'I'm leaving on Wednesday.'

Zoë grinned back. 'Take me with you?'

'Are you up for eleven hours of class a day?'

'Nope.'

Ivy laughed.

'But I really do want to travel after my A levels this summer,' Zoë said, carefully putting an almost overflowing cup of coffee on a matching saucer. 'Maybe, if you've got time, I could get some tips from you?'

With her long, glossy black hair and made-up face, she could easily pass for being in her early twenties. But at that moment, seeing the blush rising in her cheeks and the sheepish look on her face, Ivy was reminded that Zoë was barely an adult yet.

'Well, where are you thinking of going?' Ivy asked.

Zoë shrugged. 'Anywhere but here.'

It was funny. For Ivy, Treppin Bay had become her home. A safe place filled with people she'd quickly got to know who greeted her on the street. It was the perfect antidote to a life spent on the road, in tiny guest rooms and hostel dorms. But for Zoë, it was the dullest place on earth that only came alive in the summer with the yearly influx of tourists. Travel was a great way to expand your mind, for sure. But without direction, it could become what it had for Ivy – aimless and an endless pursuit for something that could never really be found externally. She didn't want that for Zoë.

'Sure,' Ivy nodded. 'I can hang around after everyone's gone, if you want?'

It was something that took no effort and might actually be a big influence on Zoë. Ivy ordered and made her way back to the table. It wasn't even lunchtime, but today was a good day. Her chest felt warm with contented happiness. She slid into her space on the bench at the wall and took her phone from her pocket. Her smile froze for a second as she saw the email notification on her screen.

From: Jess Palmer

Subject: Happy birthday

Hope you're having a nice day. Still miss you. xx

She *still* hadn't replied to Jess's email with the wedding invitation. It was ridiculous really and taunted her daily, but the weight of all the things that needed to be said simply couldn't be put into an email. It felt so impersonal. Instead, Ivy had been toying with the idea of going to London for the day, and maybe arranging to meet for lunch or dinner. She never did hear anything back from Jess about the wedding gift, but getting this email felt like the door might still be open. She planned on taking the time at her teacher training to think about what to do.

Ivy looked up as Zoë came over with their order and her face flushed at the single candle stuck into a double chocolate chip muffin. As they broke out into a pretty-well-tuned *happy birthday*, she laughed, burying her face in her hands.

Her birthdays while travelling had always been celebrated with a huge night out and there'd been plenty of people singing around her. Dozens, sometimes, in bars, on beaches and, once, on a yacht. She'd always got hugs and slobbery kisses. But this was the first time since leaving England that she really felt it was real. She looked up, teary eyed but laughing, and blew out the stripy red and white candle, trying not to feel embarrassed at the rest of the customers who were clapping too.

'Thanks guys,' she choked, picking up the muffin and holding it in a salute.

'This is from all of us,' Hannah said, reaching under the bench and pulling out a long, tubular package.

'Did you stow that away in advance?' Ivy laughed.

'With help from Zoë.' Hannah grinned. 'We couldn't very well bring it with us and ruin the surprise.'

Ivy took the package and unwrapped it eagerly, pulling out an expensive yoga mat.

'You'll need that for all of those two hundred hours,' Hannah smiled, and Ivy pulled her in for a hug, before moving around the table to hug the others too.

She sat back down, shaking her head. 'You guys.'

'And this is from me,' Ruth said, handing her a slim gift, wrapped in recycled craft paper.

Ivy unwrapped it and smiled at the black notebook in her hands. It was sprinkled with tiny silver speckles of paint that looked like stars in a pitch-dark sky. Ivy flipped it over and read the words on the front *Grow through what you walk through – Journal.*

'You'll need a notebook for all the classes you'll be planning when you get back.' Ruth smiled.

Ivy held it to her chest. 'Thank you.'

She'd been right about it being a good day. The warm contentedness in her chest settled as she put her gifts down beside her, picked up her coffee and took a sip. There were no big birthday plans, no party or dinner. She'd simply spend the day at home, reading the yoga philosophy books she'd bought in preparation for her course, have a long soak in the bath and maybe take a look at the local animal shelter's website. Maybe it was a consequence of feeling more settled, but she'd found herself thinking more and more about adopting a pet. A cat, or maybe a dog. She wasn't exactly lonely, but it would be nice to have someone to look after.

Ivy held the big cup of coffee in her hands, enjoying the weight of it as she always did, when the cafe door opened and closed.

'Ohmygod – Joe?' Hannah called to the man who'd just walked in.

His face lit up in recognition and Ivy held her cup suspended halfway to her mouth as he waved back to Hannah. His smile was wide and his presence seemed to take up the entire cafe. She sipped at her coffee as Hannah stood up halfway to hug him from the table.

'What are you doing back home?' Hannah asked, gesturing for him to sit. 'Are you meeting someone? Come, sit.' She turned to the table. 'Everyone, this is Joe. Dan's cousin.'

Ivy nodded a greeting, hoping her cheeks weren't as red as they felt. There were definitely advantages to the amount of melanin in her skin, and this was one of them. She shuffled to the side to make room for the cousin of Hannah's husband.

'Dan didn't tell me you were coming back?' Hannah said.

'It was a last-minute thing. I busted my knee and thought it better to come home and get it seen to here.'

Ivy listened in on their conversation. His voice was deep and smooth, and it did things to her insides that no other man's voice had ever managed to do. Zoë quickly came over, barely able to conceal the adoration in her eyes, but if he noticed the way she simpered at him, he didn't react with anything other than a genuine smile as he gave his order. Ivy took another sip of her coffee.

'Oh, it's Ivy's birthday,' Hannah said, turning to face her. 'Ivy, Joe. Joe, Ivy.'

'Happy birthday.' He smiled again.

A lock of hair fell into his brown eyes and heat crept down Ivy's throat and into her breasts. Never mind being in the sun in two days' time, it felt like he'd brought it in the cafe with him.

She smiled back and lifted her cup to her mouth again, but was unable to look away from his dark eyes. 'Thanks.'

Ivy kept drinking, grateful her cup was big enough to hide her face in. She kept herself in conversation with Ruth and the others, but was certain she could feel Joe's eyes on her. For the first time in her life, it made her feel self-conscious, especially in her yoga clothes.

'I need to get going,' Hannah said a few minutes later. 'You two should chat. Ivy's off to India in a few days, you were just there, weren't you?'

He shook his head as she stood up, taking her coat with her. 'Sri Lanka.'

'Yeah, that's right. Sri Lanka is the surfer's paradise, right?' Hannah turned and dropped a kiss on Ivy's cheek. 'Happy birthday.'

Ivy smiled up at her, watching her leave until the very last minute to avoid looking back at Joe, which was the strangest thing because every single part of her wanted to study him in detail.

'So, what's in India? Are you just going to travel?' he asked, and she turned back to look at him.

God, he was beautiful. All bronzed skin and laid-back, sun-kissed vibes.

'No, I've done the travel thing there already. I'm doing yoga teacher training.' Ivy looked down at his hands, strong and muscular, before looking back up to his face. 'What was in Sri Lanka?'

'Surfing. I'm an instructor over there in the winter.'

He leaned back against the backrest of the bench and widened his legs. How funny, that they were both winter-sun chasers who'd found themselves in a place with a lot of winter and not enough sun. He looked like the kind of guy who could be at home anywhere. Like he could just rock up any place and find people to hang out with. His clothes were plain and a little dishevelled, his white long-sleeved t-shirt pulled up to his elbows and his jeans faded in a way that didn't look factory made.

'Is that how you hurt your knee?' Ivy asked, glancing at his leg. 'Surfing?'

He nodded. 'It's not the first time. It's a recurring thing.'

'Maybe you should try yoga.'

'Yeah, I've been told that before, usually by yoga teachers.' He smiled back. 'We did have someone who started doing it at our place but I'm usually too impatient to get out into the water.'

She raised her eyebrow with a grin. 'You're a glutton for punishment, clearly. Besides, yoga's the perfect warm-up for surfing.'

'Do you ride?' His eyebrows lifted.

'I've tried a couple times. Not sure I'd define it as surfing though,' she replied with a laugh, remembering how she'd fallen from her foam board time and time again. 'I'd wanted to look all cool and sexy and ended up looking like a drowned rat.'

He laughed and it felt like golden sunlight streaming on her skin.

'But I plan on giving yoga classes for surfers when I start teaching.'

'And when will that be?'

'A couple of months. Why, are you going to join?'

His eyes danced as he shrugged his shoulders an inch. 'I might. Depends if the teacher's any good.'

Ivy felt the way his words landed, and it tugged in her lower belly. It was a feeling she hadn't had since . . . well. A long time. She'd been certain that she wouldn't ever want to feel it again. To imagine the thought of another man's hands on her body had made her shudder inside. But as she looked at Joe again, she felt a glimmer of something. It was crazy, really. She didn't know him at all. Maybe it was the connection to Hannah, but he felt familiar in a way she didn't understand.

Ivy grinned back. 'Well, I can't guarantee that.'

Their eyes locked for a few seconds before he tore his gaze away and checked his watch.

'I've got to head off to my doctor's appointment. I only came in for a coffee to go.'

Was it possible to miss someone before they'd even gone anywhere? Ivy nodded as he pulled a black beanie hat down over his curly hair. He shrugged his coat on and then looked at her, pulling his bottom lip into his mouth. His thick eyebrows pulled together and his forehead wrinkled as if he were running through something in his mind, before letting his lip go.

'This is kind of random, but would it be weird to ask for your number? You know, in case you need some surfer input on your training.'

He raised his eyebrows and Ivy barely managed to contain the grin on her face.

'Surfer input?'

Joe threw his head back and laughed. He looked back at her and shrugged with an embarrassed smile on his face.

'It was the best I could come up with at short notice.'

Ivy laughed back and put a hand against her flaming cheek. How she'd managed to sound so cool, she'd never know. His question had been like yet another birthday present that had fallen into her lap. She nodded and took his phone from his hand to give him her number.

It was unlike any other birthday she'd ever had before. But so far, it was turning out to be one of the best.

Chapter Twenty-Seven

Ivy

December, last year

Ivy's eyelids fluttered at the sound of Ruth's voice, gently guiding her mind back to her body. Crows cawed from the palm trees around them and the sound of metal on plates tinkled from the restaurant that was attached to the yoga shala. Somewhere along the way, Ivy had drifted away from Ruth's instructions and she had found herself back on the morning she'd woken up on a balcony just a few miles away, with no recollection of the night before.

She'd seen it all, even the parts she thought she'd forgotten. She'd seen the guy's face, with his lip piercing and the Burning Man style clothes he'd worn. She'd seen herself dipping into that bag of pink powder again and again. She'd seen herself spinning out of control with nobody around who knew her well enough to tell her to stop. She'd seen herself clearly enough to know that, even if someone *had* been there, she probably wouldn't have listened to them anyway. She'd been hurting. It was as simple as that, and it was the first time she'd been able to see it without heaping shame or anger at herself for getting into that situation in the first place.

The last three weeks had been brutal. She'd expected the physical work, the muscle ache and strength building. It was the inner work that had knocked her off her feet. Despite being busy in class or studying every day, for the entire day, she seemed to have so much more time for memories to make their way up to the surface. Her mum in that hospice. Her dad in his bed. The look on her sister's face when she'd slapped her at his wake and everything that had come afterwards.

Ivy swallowed, hearing her breath rush in and out through her nose. For the first time in as long as she could remember, she felt calm. It was like that feeling when you've come home after a long day on your feet and you take off your shoes. Like a whole load of tension has been taken away, leaving space behind it. She'd felt hurt and angry for a long, long time. Not just after waking up on that balcony, or when their dad had died or that she hadn't known about it. Not even just after the fight with Jess. It was only now, being in total calm, that she could pinpoint it all to the day their dad had told them their mum had died. Tears pricked the back of Ivy's eyelids and she let them seep from the corners of her closed eyes. Not being able to say goodbye hurt, in ways she hadn't understood at the time. She'd been too young to fully grasp the idea of someone just going away, forever. It had been like having the ground fall away, right from underneath her at a time when she'd needed it the most. When her dad got sick, it was like it happened all over again and somehow, that unrooted, ungrounded feeling had become her comfort blanket. It was why she'd craved it so much.

A few days ago in class, Ruth had talked about letting go of things that didn't have a purpose any more. For a while, the life she'd lived had all felt great. Going from one place to another with no strings, no responsibility, no *grounding* had been thrilling. Amazing, in fact – that's why she'd done it for so long. Except, at some point, it became less fun and more destructive, just as Jess had said. And if the fun was gone, then why had she done it for so long?

Maybe she was getting caught up in all the good vibes she'd been immersed in the last few weeks and months. Maybe it was the non-stop texts with Joe and the way just seeing his name on her screen made her heart flutter. Maybe it was the knowledge that she was able to be just a few minutes' walk from her old haunts and life, and not want to go back to any of it. It might have been everything combined, or none of it at all, but Ivy knew that something had shifted. She wouldn't be going home the same person who'd left.

She took a deep breath into her chest and held it for a moment. The early morning sun was already warm on her skin and the sound of the sea rolling in and out on the beach filled her ears. She didn't want to punish herself any more. She wanted to feel good and happy and settled. She wanted to put things right, and, maybe, close that circle completely and sort things out with Jess.

Ivy slowly let out her breath and, when her teacher told her to, she opened her eyes.

Chapter Twenty-Eight

Ivy

March, this year

Ivy smiled as her students rolled up their mats. She'd just finished teaching her Friday night class, and her heart felt light. It had taken a while to find her confidence, but she had and with every class she gave, it grew a little more. Out of all the jobs she'd had, this was the first one she really, truly loved. It was funny. For someone who'd had such a deep resistance to anything needing commitment, she was now doing something that almost certainly meant lifelong learning and absolute dedication.

As Ivy opened the windows to let some fresh air in, a couple who'd randomly dropped in came over with their mats rolled up under their arms.

'That was *so* good, thank you!' the girl said with a grin. 'I was just saying to Smith this morning that I wanted to find a good class while we're here.'

They made a beautiful couple, with her caramel skin tone and sprinkling of freckles and him with his unusual grey eyes and floppy dark curls.

'Aw, I'm glad you liked it.' Ivy grinned. 'I'm covering a class tomorrow morning at six if you want to join. What was your name again?'

'I'm Effie.' The girl nodded at her boyfriend. 'He's Smith. And we'll be there, for sure.'

'*You'll* be there,' Smith said with a playful raise of his eyebrows. 'I might be in the water already.'

'You definitely want to catch the class before getting in, especially when it's still this cold.' Joe's voice was like honey in Ivy's ears as he joined them. 'Makes a difference.'

If she had a champion in Treppin Bay, it was Joe. Their contact had been pretty much non-stop since she'd given him her number in the cafe on her birthday. He'd become her best friend, spending most evenings together, eating and socialising. He came to almost all her classes and was a walking advertisement for her. He'd been responsible for getting the surfer class going, telling his friends about it, and had arranged for her to give special warm-up classes for the surf school in the summer. He was the birthday gift that just kept on giving and as the four of them chatted a while longer, his eyes caught hers and she let herself linger in his gaze.

'Dinner?' he asked once Effie and Smith had gone to the changing rooms.

The way he looked at her from under his ridiculously long eyelashes made her gooey inside.

She nodded as he followed her out. 'I'll come over when I'm done here.'

Nerves exploded in her belly like a series of fireworks on the fifth of November. They continued to pop and fizz as she closed up the studio, checking the windows were closed, tidying all the equipment, loading the used tea glasses in the dishwasher and checking for any last-minute emails in the system. Ivy now more or less managed the studio, giving Ruth more time to devote to teaching and giving workshops. She loved it, and keeping things running smoothly was one of Ivy's top priorities, after Duke.

She opened the door to the massage room where her little dog shot out and circled her legs with his tail wagging. It had been love at first sight when the scrappy puppy had curled up by her feet on the beach in Goa. He'd found her on the second day of her yoga training and followed her around everywhere. She'd let him sleep in her room and there was no way she could leave him behind. It had been a costly adoption, with a lot of paperwork and vaccinations, but she was completely devoted. Leaving him in here while teaching had been a real test and he'd whined throughout her first few classes. Now that he knew she would always come back, he waited quietly and it always lifted her heart to see how happy he was to see her afterwards.

'I think tonight might be the night, Duke,' she whispered, picking him up and walking towards the front door.

A pulse of excitement ran through her. There surely couldn't be many men who'd wait three months to sleep with a girl. That alone made Joe someone very, very special. It was also the first time that Ivy had ever waited for so long too. There was something nice and, dare she say it, old-fashioned about just spending time together and getting to know each other. She'd never done that before, not with anyone.

Ivy stepped out and took a lungful of the fresh seaside air as she locked the door. She put Duke down and they set off for the ten-minute walk to Joe's caravan, her heart pumping faster with each step. She wasn't sure she'd ever been so excited about meeting up with someone she'd just seen half an hour ago. She wasn't bored by him, not one bit, and her palms tingled as she saw the amber glow from his van. She wished she'd had the sense to shower first. And shave. Ivy swore to herself, stopping for a second. Her cottage was in the other direction and if she turned back now, it would be another hour before she knocked on his door.

Duke whimpered at her as he always did when they stopped mid-walk and she looked down at him.

'You're right, I'm being silly.' She shook her head and continued walking. It wasn't like Joe had said anything to make her think that tonight would be any different to the countless others they'd spent together.

'Knock, knock,' she said, poking her head through his door.

Duke jumped up the stairs and Ivy caught the scent of tomato sauce as she followed him in.

'Hey.' Joe grinned, pushing a spatula around a pan.

It was a small space with a tiny sink, two hob plates and a sliver of a countertop that doubled as a desk and kitchen worktop. His van was just wide enough to hold a double mattress that was also used as a sofa, which he'd put on top of a self-built platform. A small electric heater radiated warmth into the van and two surfboards with sharp, curved fins hung side by side from the ceiling, suspended in a wooden frame.

'Hey.' She smiled back.

Was it just her, or was it all looking tidier than it usually did? It being such a small place, Joe kept it in pretty good condition but something was different. Ivy shrugged her denim jacket from her shoulders and put it down on the bed where Duke had already made himself comfortable.

'What's cooking?' she asked nonchalantly while discreetly inspecting the place a bit more.

She was pretty sure the bed had a different, fresher-looking set of sheets to the ones she'd seen a couple of days ago. She lowered herself to sit on it and ran her hands across the blue cotton material of the duvet cover.

'Penne arrabbiata,' Joe replied, looking at her. 'The sauce still needs a while.'

He'd showered too. His damp hair was now loose, his curls skimming his shoulders. He looked ridiculously good.

'What's a while?'

'Half an hour, maybe a bit longer. The more the tomatoes cook, the better it tastes.'

Ivy's heart beat wildly in her chest as the air around them crackled. She had no idea if it was just in her head, or if he could feel that buzz of electricity too. It had been building up ever since he'd walked into that cafe last winter, over the weeks she'd been in Goa for her training, in every class he'd come to since and during every minute they'd spent together.

The van felt like a cocoon, wrapping them in complete intimacy. He had the best pitch in the caravan park, with nobody parked next to him and a view of the Atlantic from his door. It couldn't be more romantic. Ivy had the feeling that the sauce would probably cook all night. She took a breath as he took the one step towards the bed, putting his hands either side of her body on the mattress.

They hadn't even kissed. They'd cuddled and snuggled and he'd dropped cute little pecks onto her head or shoulder, but they hadn't *kissed*. She had no idea what he tasted like or what his tongue felt like, but she wanted to. He stayed there, his face just a few inches away from hers, looking into her eyes. His pupils grew smaller in his brown, marble-like irises.

Her forehead flickered with doubt and Joe's matched it.

'Are you okay?' His voice was gentle and probing and Ivy couldn't help but feel penetrated by it. 'Is *this* okay?'

Joe knew what had happened back in Goa. After her training, she'd realised that keeping it a secret was a form of self-punishment and denial, so she'd told him. It hadn't been easy, but he'd listened and hadn't judged her. Sharing something so personal and raw had cemented them together in a way she hadn't really expected, and he'd even encouraged her to go to a counsellor to start really processing it. He looked like one of those typical airhead and often arrogant surfer guys, but he was the opposite. The fact that he was actually asking her permission was proof enough. It was like a dose of nurturing she'd never have expected. For the first time ever, she was being asked if this was really what she wanted.

His warm breath rushed from his mouth to hers, sending waves of pleasure from her lips down into the depths of her belly. Ivy lifted her hands, letting her fingers rest on the back of his neck and looked him deep in the eyes. She had a feeling that it wouldn't get much better than this.

It was okay. It was more than okay. It was a full-bodied yes.

Chapter Twenty-Nine

JESS

April, this year

It's been a long day and the last thing I want to do is cook, but it's Wednesday, which means it's my turn. Weirdly, Nick isn't home yet and while I've been making it a priority to reduce the 'work' and increase the 'life' end of the scale, it feels like it's only tipped everything in the opposite direction when it comes to my husband. Nick's been in the office a lot more than usual lately, going in extra early and coming home extra late. I'm the last person to mind. I understand better than anyone how important work is. We've argued enough about it this past year. But as I chop through some lettuce, it's hard not to feel anger bubbling in my belly. I'd left the office on time because that's what we'd agreed. I'd stopped at the supermarket on the way home despite it being packed and the fridge being full, because I'd decided to make his favourite meal of lentil shepherd's pie. Unless he's back in the next five minutes, I'll have to turn the oven off to keep it from burning.

By the time he walks through the door, the lentil shepherd's pie is almost cold, the salad is wilting and I'm at my laptop.

'Hi,' I say evenly, looking up.

'Hey.'

I look back at my screen to press send on an email and close everything down, with the sound of his briefcase being put in its usual place by the door behind me. Next comes the sound of him kicking off his shoes and I wait to hear the padding of his feet as he walks over where he usually drops a cursory and totally impassionate kiss somewhere by my ear. Instead, there's silence and when I turn around, he's leaning against the kitchen counter with his hands gripping the edges.

I rest my arm on the back of my chair to look at him. 'What's wrong?'

Nick's eyes drag away from mine and down to the floor. 'We need to talk.'

Things haven't been great between us. Not at all. But still, my stomach drops at those words because they're universal in relationships and they're usually never good when strung together.

I close my laptop. 'Okay.'

'I got offered a promotion,' he says, lifting his head to look up at me again. 'Heading up an entire new department.'

'That's great news.' I smile, but I'm shaking my head with confusion at the same time, because he doesn't look happy about it.

'It's in Singapore.'

The smile drops from my face. 'Oh. Wow. That's . . . amazing.'

Nick pulls his tie loose. 'I want to go.'

'Okay,' I reply slowly.

My mind floods with practicalities. Do I want to move to Singapore? My business is here, and it's doing amazingly well. I wouldn't be able to run it from there, would I? I'd never been to Asia. And even though I only really have Maddie here, it feels so far away. What if something were to happen and I had to get back quickly?

'I don't,' I say simply.

He nods and pulls his eyebrows together in a deep frown. 'I figured that might be the case.'

'I mean, I have the business and—'

'The business,' he mutters under his breath and turns away, shaking his head. The muscles in his jaw flex. 'If you'd put in just 10 per cent of what you put into your business into our relationship . . .'

He shakes his head again and my hackles rise in defence.

'What's that supposed to mean?'

'It means that I have been trying and trying. And I know you have too. I can see how you've tried these last few months but . . . come on, Jess. Is this a marriage to you? We don't talk, we don't laugh, we don't have sex. What are we doing?'

I wish I could answer, but I can't because he's right. I can't remember the last time we slept together, even with our scheduled date nights. It's like that side of our relationship has just fizzled completely.

'I don't think your heart is in this any more. And I don't think mine is, either.' He rubs a hand through his blonde hair and breathes out loudly through his nose. 'I think we should get divorced.'

My breath catches in my throat and my eyes prick with tears as my mouth opens, but I can't object. To do that means fighting for it, but what is there even left to fight for? It's as if our marriage is like a balloon that's been found behind the sofa, weeks after the party. The air's gone out of it. Nick has been with me through the worst part of my life – losing Dad and Ivy within a matter of weeks of each other. He'd ridden in like a knight in shining armour, and I'm not exaggerating when I say I don't know how I'd have managed without him. He was dependable and comfortable and our relationship had been too, for the most part. He'd become my family. But in doing that, he somehow stopped being my husband.

'I want more than this, Jess.' He leans back against the counter again and shakes his head. 'I deserve it. And so do you.'

His words make the tears spill from my eyes and I wonder how long he's been sitting on them. Maybe this promotion has given him the opportunity to finally say the words we've been skirting around for so long. He's right that we need more than this. There *should* be more than this. More passion and fire and just *more*. The difference between us is that he's finally been able to tell me that, whereas I hadn't been able to.

'The job starts next month,' he says calmly. 'I don't want to make this messy.'

'Okay.' I nod my head, surprised at how calm I sound. 'Me neither.'

'I'm sorry,' he says.

'Me too,' I reply.

But what are we apologising for? Not being enough for the other, or wanting more? It had been enough at one time. I know it had. I try to search my memory for the place where it had started to go wrong, but I can't find it. Our whole marriage feels like a magician's trick. One minute it was there and the next, it was gone.

Chapter Thirty

Ivy

April, this year

Ivy swallowed her nerves as she walked into the beer garden of The Anchor. It was a gloriously sunny day with blue skies and a cool breeze wafted the scent of hyacinths from the neighbour's garden. There were a few people sitting at the picnic tables, but her eyes settled immediately on who she was looking for. Gravel crunched under her feet as she walked over to his table and he turned, doing a double take as he registered that it was her.

'Hi, Finn,' Ivy said with a small smile.

He stood up with a look on his face that said he was half-shocked but half-expecting her to be there. Ivy stood for a second with her hand clasped around the strap of her bag. Would it be awkward to hug him? She had the feeling that it would be more awkward not to. He seemed to have the same thought process as his eyes skipped around her face. Ivy stepped towards him and closed the gap, deciding a hug was the only thing to do.

'I'm so sorry about your dad,' she said, standing on tiptoe as she'd always had to do with him.

He pulled back and nodded. 'Thanks.'

When Ruth's brother, Finn's dad, had been hospitalised from a heart attack two days ago, Ivy knew it was only a matter of time before Finn came back. From what Ruth had told her, things weren't looking good. This pub belonged to his dad so, depending on what happened, Finn might even stick around for good. Ivy had worked hard to become part of this community and she didn't want to have bad blood with anyone, least of all Finn.

She sucked in a breath and slid onto the bench on the other side of the picnic table. It was newly oiled and gleaming under the sun, and she rested her elbows on its smooth surface to look at Finn. His forehead was etched with lines and he looked exactly how she had felt when she'd made that awful journey home when her dad was sick.

'How is he?' she asked, even though she already knew from Ruth.

'Not good.' Finn grimaced. 'Not good at all.'

'You'll let me know if there's anything I can do?'

'Thanks.'

Ivy smiled a little. The gaps of no contact aside, they'd known each other for years. From meeting him through a friend at university to reconnecting when she'd lived with Jess, he'd been both a peripheral friend, and a closer one. Looking back on it, she could see it was some strange sense of entitlement that had told her she could get something more out of it. God, she'd been cocky back then. She'd been embarrassed when she'd found out he'd got with Jess, for a multitude of reasons, but it all felt so trivial now that he was in front of her again. It felt like a lifetime ago. It *was* a lifetime ago.

'How've you been?' he asked, twisting his bottle of beer around in his hand. 'You look good.'

'Thanks. I am,' she said with a suddenly shy smile. 'I feel better than I have in years.'

She pulled her knees up to sit cross-legged on the bench, adjusting her boyfriend-style jeans to accommodate her new position. Ivy looked down at the seashell anklet she'd brought back from her teacher training.

'Ruth told me you're teaching yoga now.'

Ivy looked back up, letting her smile lose its coyness. 'I love it.'

'Good for you.' Finn smiled. 'You deserve it.'

'It still blows my mind that she's your aunt.' She shook her head. 'It's so random.'

Finn nodded. 'Yeah, it is. She was pretty stoked about it. She's convinced it's the universe *conspiring to bring us all back together*.'

'Who knows?' Ivy laughed. 'But it is nice to see you again. How are *you*? Aside from your dad, I mean.'

'I'm alright.'

But Finn looked desperately unhappy. She could see it in the slump to his shoulders and in the lack of any kind of spark behind his eyes. His whole being felt flat.

She tilted her head to one side with a small smile. 'Really?'

'On balance? I'm alright. There's a few things to deal with back in Sweden, but right now I'm just focusing on Dad.'

'Understandable,' she replied with a nod.

Finn scratched the back of his neck and his gaze skipped around her face.

'So, how's Jess?'

Ivy looked down with heat flaming in her neck. She moved the collar of her shirt away from her skin. 'I don't know. We haven't spoken in years.'

Finn's eyes widened. 'Really?'

'We had a huge fight after Dad died and just haven't sorted it out yet.'

At this rate, she wasn't sure if they ever would. Despite feeling confident on her yoga course, the empty silence about the wedding gift felt louder than ever. She knew she only had herself to blame, because she hadn't gone to the wedding, but still. She hadn't quite been able to muster up the courage and close the gap.

'I had no idea,' Finn said quietly. 'I'm sorry to hear that.'

His face paled a little and Ivy guessed he might be thinking about losing his own dad right now.

'What about you? Are you still in touch?' she asked, changing the subject.

He shook his head.

'She got married.'

Finn blinked, stunned. 'Wow.'

'Yeah, I know.'

Finn and Jess had split up years ago, but a flicker of disappointment registered on his face. Jess had told her she'd liked him. A lot. Ivy had to wonder what might have happened if she'd have reacted differently to finding him at her flat that day instead of letting her ego take over. Her sister and Finn might have actually ended up together.

'She emailed me an invite and it was actually her getting married that made me realise I needed to get myself sorted out. Put down some roots.'

'You? Roots?' He raised his eyebrows.

'I know. Who'd have thought it?' She laughed a little. 'So what happened with you two? She never told me and only said it didn't work out.'

'Well.' Finn shrugged. 'After you decided to stay in Tenerife, she just felt guilty the whole time and, in the end, she said she couldn't do it.'

Oh, God. She felt like that rose from *Beauty and the Beast* as it dropped its last petal. Completely sorry and sad.

'But you wanted to?' Ivy probed.

He nodded a little. 'Sure. I guess it was just bad timing. She was working all the time and studying when she was at home, and I was working mad restaurant hours. It wasn't easy.'

'And then you got the job in Sweden?'

'I'd have stayed for her, but Jess was convinced it would be too much of a sacrifice. Combined with you leaving, I think it spooked her.'

Ivy bit her top lip. 'I'm sorry. I wish I could change things.'

Finn shrugged again. 'Hey, don't be. I didn't mean it was your fault – it wasn't. We've all moved on and she's married now anyway. Don't beat yourself up about it.'

'Still. If it were to happen all over again, I'd do it all differently. I'd be totally behind you both, 100 per cent. I'd have taken you both with me to Tenerife, or you'd have gone together and I'd have stayed. You might never have gone back to Sweden.'

'I don't know,' Finn said, curling his fingers around his beer bottle. 'There are things that have happened I wouldn't want to take back.'

'Yeah, I guess you're right.'

It was a tricky one. On one hand, Ivy had come to believe that things happened for a reason, no matter how hard the road. For the first time in her life, she truly felt at home. She had a job she loved, a community of friends, a house and – she was sure – love. Her body bloomed with it at the merest thought of Joe. Things with him were deep and new and terrifying and absolutely magical. She'd never believed in such things before, but she was starting think she'd found her happy ending after all – an ending she'd never have found if things had been different.

Finn went to take a swig of his beer before stopping and giving her a small smile. 'You were right, by the way. It's nice to see you again. I've kind of missed your craziness.'

'Well, you might be disappointed. I'm a lot tamer these days.'

And she was happier for it. The Ivy from a few years back wouldn't have been able to have had that conversation so easily, but the air had been cleared, and now sitting with Finn in a beer garden on a gorgeous spring day felt like being back at uni or in London, before things spiralled. The wounds she had with Jess ran much deeper and after all these years, they might not be so easy to heal.

Chapter Thirty-One

Ivy

Ivy's fingers groped the inner lining of her crocheted bag as she searched for her keys. She shook it, hoping to hear the jangle of metal before turning to Joe with a hapless grin.

'Erm . . . I don't have my keys.'

'Seriously?' Joe laughed with a groan and tilted his head back before looking at her with a reluctant smile. 'You, Ivy, are like a gremlin.'

'I think you mean the cute one. A mogwai.'

'No, I mean a gremlin. The mischievous ones that can't help but make you laugh. Remind me next time not to let you have so much champagne.'

'I've only had a tiny bit.' Ivy laughed.

She'd had three half-filled flutes of bubbly to celebrate their friends' wedding. Compared to how she used to drink, it was barely anything at all but she'd noticed how giddy it had made her. Joe took her chin between his thumb and index finger and she lifted herself up onto her tiptoes to press her lips against his. He tasted of liquorice and champagne, smelled of the sea and wax with a hint of wood smoke. She wrapped her arms around his neck and pulled him closer, until the back of her bare shoulders pressed into the smooth, aged wood of her front door.

Joe broke away and touched his forehead against hers. 'We could always go back to mine.'

'Too far.' She kissed him again.

It was delicious. *He* was delicious. Especially in the dark jeans and linen shirt he'd worn today. It had added an air of respectability to his rugged surfer look. She let her eyes roam up to his tousled, sun-bleached hair and there, dangling right next to his head was a loop of thick string. Ivy smiled and stood on tiptoe, reaching out to close her fingers around the rough twine attached to her spare key from the lantern fixed to the wall.

'Ta-da,' she sang, throwing him a grin.

Despite wearing her key around her neck in Goa, she had managed to really lose it once and had learned the hard way to always bunker a set, just in case. The key slid into the lock and the door gave as it heaved open.

Ivy dropped the key on the table by the front door and turned back to look at Joe. He really was unlike anyone she'd ever met. The way he made her heart flip meant that she simply couldn't imagine being with anyone else. She didn't want to be. Joe was like all of her favourite things, wrapped up in human form. He'd come into her life with his tanned skin and salt-dried hair like a warm summer breeze, full of laughter and sunset swims and bonfires. Joe was like a *not-safe-for-work* Peter Pan, forever playful and refusing to see the world through jaded eyes. He made being in a relationship easy.

Ivy lifted the delicate lace hem of her dress and pulled it over her head. The soft fabric brushed her foot as it landed on the floor with a soft sigh.

Joe closed the door behind him, his gaze fixed on her body. 'No knickers, either? When did you lose those?'

She shrugged, standing naked in the middle of her kitchen. 'Who said I had them on to begin with?'

The summery dress she'd worn was respectable enough to be completely naked underneath without attracting attention, but sheer enough for Joe to feel her bare nipples as they'd danced in the grass. They'd been teasing each other all day with lingering kisses and barely-there skin strokes in an extended foreplay that had been leading right up to this point.

The bracelets around Ivy's wrist jangled as she tugged at her hair scarf, releasing the pile of long dreads to tumble around her shoulders. The corners of Joe's lips lifted into a half-grin that made goosebumps shimmer on her skin. Ivy watched as he unbuttoned the shirt that had given him that delicious hint of respectability, her eyes tracing the taut muscles of his abs as the material fluttered open. His tanned shoulders flexed as he shrugged it down over his arms and let the shirt fall to the floor.

Ivy kept her eyes locked on his as he walked towards her and, when he was close enough, she hooked a finger into the waistband of his jeans, pulling him closer.

Enough teasing for one night.

◆ ◆ ◆

Joe sighed in his sleep and readjusted his arm, tucking it under his head as a pillow. A surge of warmth pumped right into Ivy's chest as she watched his eyelids twitching as he slept. He was so infinitely easy to be around. When he was there, time felt different. As if being with him made it somehow speed up and slow down, all at the same time. She stroked a lock of his hair as he slept soundly, covered with blankets on the thick rug on the living room floor. When she'd moved here, she'd been sure she'd stay alone for the rest of her life. But then came Joe. And tonight, just like every night, he'd made her feel drunk with happiness.

Ivy rubbed at her burning eyes. Why was she still awake when Joe had fallen asleep as soon as they'd settled under the covers? Even after a night of dancing, champagne and sex, she'd spent a solid hour tracking the moon's trajectory across the sky while he'd slept. Ivy gently lifted Joe's arm and slid out from under the blankets. She stood slowly before tiptoeing across the floor to the kitchen with the warm air on her naked skin and the cold floor under her feet. Duke yawned, watching her from his rug in the corner. She crouched down to rub his head and smiled as he licked her wrist.

'Can't sleep either, huh?' she whispered, cupping his ears in her palms and dropping a kiss on the soft fur on his head.

She got up, took a glass from the draining board and filled it with water. She stood by the sink and stared out of the window. The distant sound of the Atlantic waves crashing on the beach mingled with the crickets chirping in the grass surrounding the cottage. An apple tree stood under pale moonlight in the garden. She looked at its solid trunk, picturing its roots going deep down into the earth. There was something reassuring about knowing that it would still be here long after she'd gone. The moon glinted through its branches, a perfect semi-circle in an otherwise dark sky.

Days didn't get much better than this. She replayed it all in her head as if she were watching a film: arriving at the small, flower-filled village church for a short but touching ceremony, sitting down for speeches and food in the grounds of a local hotel. It had been a day filled with laughter, surrounded by friends and giddy on the tangible love in the air. There'd been a moment when they'd been sitting with Finn and Ruth around the fire bowl when Ivy had felt the biggest contentment ever. She so wished that Jess had been there to complete the picture, but Ivy had the feeling that she would be, soon enough. She'd been mulling over how to bridge the gap for long enough and wanting to feel like she was the best possible version of herself to go to her sister with. She'd looked at Jess's life on Facebook and Hannah's life here, and had wanted the same. It was just a couple of days ago that she'd realised she had it too. She had a little family of her own, a career she adored and a lovely house to live in. This was the best she'd ever been, and it was enough to feel able to reach out to Jess. Email was too impersonal after so many years, but a letter would do. She'd post it tomorrow.

She yawned quietly and took a tub of pills from a cupboard and looked at the label. After years of popping pills left, right and centre, she hated even taking paracetamol these days, but they were supposed to be driving to Devon in a few hours for a little mini break and she wanted to be fit. If there was one thing she missed about her old life, it was being able to fall into a stoned coma. Without a little help, it was likely that she wouldn't sleep until the sun had peeked over the horizon. She thought about it for a second, looking at Joe sleeping peacefully on the floor. It would be worth it.

She gulped a couple of them down with the rest of the water. With any luck, she'd fall into a deep sleep, wake up refreshed without a trace of the champagne as a hangover. She crept back over to the other side of the open room with Duke alongside her and quietly slid back under the blankets. The warmth of Joe's body invited her in to nestle herself like a spoon into his chest. She wrapped his arm around her with a smile. Duke sniffed the ground next to her before plopping himself down and nuzzling his nose under a fold in the blanket. With Joe's heartbeat behind her and Duke's in front of her, Ivy closed her eyes.

A perfect end, to a perfect day.

Chapter Thirty-Two

JESS

August, present day

New Year Goals:

- Open a shop on the high street
- Get featured in Cosmo/Elle/Glamour
- Reach 150K Instagram followers
- Holiday in Bali with Nick

I lean against my kitchen counter, looking at the list I'd found after rummaging through boxes in the bedroom. I'd been looking for an old planner, hoping to find some notes from a meeting. Instead, I'd found this. And as I stand here making a drink to take to work with me, all I can think of is why didn't I add the one thing on there that really mattered: *sort things out with Ivy.*

I still can't believe she's dead.

I still can't understand how it's really been so long since that fight. The acidic words we'd spat at each other just a few hours after burying Dad have been stuck on repeat in my mind, intensifying at night and holding back any possibility of sleep. Last night, in the darkness of my bedroom, my anxious mind had latched on to the mortality of my family unit, and the fact that I'm the only one left. It had taken every last ounce of control not to let the thoughts spin into a web of panic until the sun had finally risen.

The sun is bright in my eyes as I step out of my block and I rummage in my bag for my sunglasses. After three sleepless nights and two full days of crying, they're extra sensitive to the light. The breeze is warm but I welcome it. My head feels cotton-wool thick and absolutely not up to the task of running a business today. In fact, I wonder how I can possibly be trusted to run a business when I've failed so epically in my private life. *How* could I have missed the chance to sort things out?

As I walk the five minutes from my flat to the office, I turn it over and over in my mind. The truth is, there'd been plenty of opportunities. Every time a birthday or Christmas email was sent, every time I'd had a bit of news to share or rewatched a film we'd always watched together. There'd been an opportunity every single day over the last seven years. It's as plain and simple as that, but my mind keeps digging into it, turning it over and over and scratching it behind my eyes.

Stepping into the refurbished industrial unit Maddie and I have turned into our office helps to quiet it down at least. This I know. This I can handle. On one side of the unit is the warehouse, from where our products are shipped out, with a small corridor separating it from the office. The space is filled with white desks topped with a kaleidoscope of stationery items, potted plants and laptops. It feels calm and safe, and just being in it loosens anxiety from my chest.

'Jess, hey.' Lily, our office manager, stops tapping on her MacBook and looks up. I stop by her desk as she pushes her round glasses farther up the bridge of her nose. 'I wasn't expecting you to be in today.'

'Neither was I.' I tilt my head with a wry smile.

'Better to have something to do, right?' Her Gold-Coast accented words are full of empathy and she stands, picking up a pastel blue cup from her desk. 'Coffee? I'm due a refill.'

'I've got my matcha.' I hold up my Thermos, which is still more than half-full of the adaptogen-laced tea I'd made. 'But thanks.'

It's been years since I touched coffee. I'd read an article saying that women who drink it are one and a half times more likely to develop breast cancer and given it up straight away.

'I'm really sorry for your loss, Jess.' Lily lowers her voice as we reach my desk, her face filled with concern. 'You'll let me know if you need anything?'

'Thanks, Lily.' I smile. 'I really appreciate it.'

She nods and continues off to the kitchen, and I drop my things on my desk. I sit in my chair and dig my heels into the carpet to pull myself in towards my desk. Its pristine orderliness is like a wave of calm. My *daily greatness* to-do jotting pad sits to the side of my keyboard with a pen on it, ready for action. A bowl of gold-finished bulldog clips and three matching ring binders stand next to rose-gold-finished in-trays. I pull my hair back from my face to settle myself into what I know. Except, the meetings, phone calls and emails across the day don't distract me from questions about Ivy. Like, why was it Finn who'd called? I hadn't thought their friendship would rekindle, especially since ours hadn't. And he'd said they were in Cornwall. What was she doing there, of all places?

'Ugh, I'm done for the day.' Maddie yawns and closes her laptop shut. 'And so are you.'

I lean back in my chair and rub my eyes with the heels of my palms. 'I just want to finish this first.'

She peers at me from her chaotic desk opposite mine.

'Nope, you're done,' she insists. 'There's nothing you can be doing now that can't wait til tomorrow. Chris is taking his parents to see a show tonight, I'm flying solo. Let's go grab some dinner?'

My stomach growls in response.

'I *am* a little hungry,' I admit.

'A little?' She laughs. 'I saw how you wolfed that bagel down.'

I smile reluctantly and my stomach growls again, a touch louder for extra effect. The avocado and hummus bagel I'd gulped down is the first real food I've eaten since Finn called and I realise how ravenous I am.

Twenty minutes later, we're sitting on stools surrounded by chatter and squished into the corner of a tiny restaurant off Brixton Market. The windows are steamed with condensation and the air is heavily fragranced with the scent of garlic and lemongrass. The girl behind the bar places two huge bowls of pho in front of us and Maddie and I eat the first few mouthfuls in silence.

'I found the list I'd made at that New Year's intention setting workshop we went to last year,' I say while I chew my food. 'This year, I was supposed to fall in love again and go to Bali with Nick.'

'Ah,' Maddie says, straightening up and wiping a napkin across her mouth.

'Yeah.' I poke my chopsticks in my bowl. We continue eating in silence for a few more seconds. 'And do you know what *wasn't* on the list? Sorting things out with Ivy.'

Maddie puts her chopsticks down and looks at me. 'Oh, Jess.'

'Looking at that list was like being punched right between the eyes. Everything else had been done. The magazine exposure, the social media reach. I've spent the last few years doing everything I could to get our business off the ground, and meanwhile, everything else suffered.'

'That's not true.'

'Isn't it? Nick was always on about how I worked too much, and I buried myself in it rather than reaching out to my sister who was God knows where with God knows who.' I shake my head and push my bowl away from me. 'Do you realise I don't know any-thing about her life apart from some tagged photos on Facebook?'

'I'm going to be really controversial here and say that Ivy could've reached out to you as well,' Maddie points out. 'You invited her to your wedding, remember?'

'And I shouldn't have let her not coming stop me from reaching out again, but I did.'

'Jess, I know you're hurting and I know all this doesn't make sense right now, but I've been here with you the whole time. I know all you've ever done is your best. You can't keep beating yourself up.'

Her words are sweet, and on some level I know she's right. But I'm pissed at myself all the same and I'm even more pissed with Ivy for dying. And I know I shouldn't say that. But I am.

Chapter Thirty-Three

JESS

Present day

Two days later, I'm driving a rental car down a narrow country lane with hedges and blackberry bushes feeling much too close on either side of me. I swallow at the nausea rising in my belly. Getting car sick as the driver is a new one on me. I've never been good in cars, and especially not on windy roads like these, but I wonder if the swirling and leaping of my stomach has more to do with nerves and less to do with motion.

I let the window down a little more before reaching a hand into the bag sitting on the passenger seat. My fingers rummage until they close around a pack of mints and I pop one into my mouth. It instantly helps and I smooth my hair with my hand before bringing it back to the steering wheel. A green camper van with surf boards fixed to the roof appears up ahead and I slow down, almost creeping into the ditch beside the road. It roars past with a few inches to spare and I puff the air from the side of my mouth as I turn the car back on the road. Everyone says that driving in the city is the worst, but the roads here are tiny and unforgiving, with hidden turn-offs and sharp corners. The road slopes downwards and the hedges grow shorter, widening the view in the distance to reveal the sea, bright turquoise and sparkling like a jewel under a blue sky. The free fall of my stomach continues as I slow down, entering the village.

My head turns left and right as I search for The Anchor, the pub I'm supposed to go to. And all I can think as I drive down the main street is: *this was where Ivy lived?* I'd have expected her to end up in East London, or Manchester, or some party island in the Mediterranean, not a little village in Cornwall lined with surf shops and cafes.

I spot the pub I'm looking for a little farther up the road, and decide to park up by the beach. I drive slowly towards the cluster of other cars and vans. Sand crunches under the tyres until I stop, turn off the engine and open the door. Seagulls squawk overhead and a light breeze winds its way around me, causing the delicate lace-trimmed collar of my blouse to flutter as I step out of the car. The air is tinged with salt and I stare out at the long, wide stretch of beach curving out towards cliffs on the far side. I tuck the whip of a curl behind my ear and look at a group of wetsuit-clad surfers wading out of the water, carrying their boards under their arms. Sunbathers are dotted on the sand, soaking up the warm rays of sunshine poking through scattered clouds. I turn on the spot, looking in every direction. There are people everywhere – on the pavement, at the bus stop, getting changed by their cars, walking dogs and sitting at tables in the beachside cafes. A hint of something being barbecued floats along the breeze and I realise that I've never stepped foot on a British beach until now. It's actually pretty nice.

I duck my head back inside the car and grab my handbag, deciding to leave my suitcase in the car until the owner of the Airbnb I'm trying to book gets back to me. It seems that Ivy chose to settle in a real tourist destination and finding accommodation hasn't been easy. I quickly check my phone but there are no messages waiting, so I decide to find the pub and get on with the inevitable task of meeting Finn.

I close the car door and turn around at the sound of barking to see a little black dog bounding towards me. He's running with such determination that I can't help but smile at the way his feet seem to struggle to keep up with his speed. I laugh as he sniffs around my feet with his tail wagging so hard it looks like it might fall off.

I crouch down, holding my hand out for him to sniff, and his nose tickles my skin. 'Hey, there. And who are you, little guy?'

I love dogs. I always have, even though we'd never had one at home. Dad was dead set against pets in the house, but any time I saw a dog on the street, I'd ask to stroke it no matter how big or scary-looking it was. As far back as I can remember, any future vision of adult life always included a dog as a companion, but Nick was allergic, in a big way. My heart melts as the little pup sniffs and licks my hand in turns.

'Duke!'

A man's voice shouts in my direction, but the dog doesn't react. Instead, he tries to jump up into my lap, flicking grains of sand and grit onto my black jeans.

'Hey, Duke. Stop!'

I look up and see the dog's owner jogging over towards us with a leather leash in his hand.

'It's fine,' I call out to the man as I scratch behind one of the dog's ears. 'Hello, Duke. Nice to meet you.'

The man sighs as he reaches us and shakes his head. 'Damned dog. He doesn't listen.'

'Really, it's fine,' I repeat, and stand up to face him.

He looks like a surfer, with jaw-length tousled hair and a muscular body dressed in a vest and board shorts. But he looks washed out and exhausted, with a grey pallor behind his tanned skin. He looks at me with a frown for a second, as if he recognises me, before shaking it away.

'He's ruined your jeans. Sorry about that.'

I look down at the smears of mud and sand. The silk coral blouse I'm wearing only narrowly escaped the same fate, but I shrug and brush the dirt away.

'It's alright. They're just clothes.'

The man nods and I watch as he bends down to clip the leash to Duke's harness. His movements are awkward and fumbling, as if he isn't really used to doing it, and I wonder how on earth the two of them have ended up together. He doesn't look like he should have a little dog. A husky or German shepherd maybe, but not a cute, small and inquisitive thing like this. The relief on his face having clipped the leash is obvious.

'He probably shouldn't be off the leash so close to the road,' I say softly, crouching back down to stroke the dog as he sidles up next to my leg.

'I know. I'm still getting used to him.'

I raise my eyebrows. 'Dog-sitting?'

A look passes over his face and it's as if the clouds have rolled in, and he stiffens. 'Something like that.'

I nod. I've always been able to tell when someone doesn't want to talk about something, and the vibes he's giving off as he looks past me are loud and clear.

'Well,' he says, tugging at Duke's leash and nodding at my jeans again. 'We'd better be off. Sorry again about your trousers.'

I shrug and shake my head at the same time. 'Good luck with the dog.'

He walks past me, towards the street with little Duke in tow, leaving me feeling strangely alone despite being surrounded by people. I wonder if he'd known Ivy. Maybe that was why he'd looked at me so strangely. Aside from a man sitting outside a cafe down the beach, I'm the only black person I can see. Maybe he'd assumed that I was her family – assuming that she'd told people about me at all. I shake my head. I wouldn't be thinking this if Ivy and I were white. I could be anybody, and maybe he was just having a bad day, looking after a dog he had no idea how to care for. I brush off my jeans again and head towards the pub, walking across the flat, densely packed sand.

The Anchor pub looks like it's been here for centuries, with bumpy, white exterior walls, black lanterns and a mildewed roof. This is where I'm supposed to meet Finn, five years after we'd bumped into each other on my lunch break. I'd told Maddie that I'd be fine, but nerves are tingling in my belly. I have the feeling that the nausea I'd felt in the car was less to do with motion sickness and more to do with seeing him again. I take a deep breath and swallow against it. I'm here for Ivy. Nothing else really matters, not even Finn. I look down at my watch. I'm half an hour early, which was exactly how I'd planned it. I want to be able to find a comfortable place to sit and feel prepared.

I push my hand against the black door and step into a big, square room. It takes a moment for my eyes to adjust. From the outside, it appears to be a traditional pub but inside, it feels distinctly Scandinavian. It looks newly refurbished, with a lingering smell of fresh paint in the air, and the long bar is covered with planks of sun-bleached driftwood. There's nobody behind it, and I drop my handbag on its smooth surface.

A young girl comes out from behind the bar and asks for my order. I'm hungry, and the scent of frying onions and garlic wafting from the kitchen only makes my mouth water, but instead of food, I make an uncharacteristic choice and order a white wine. I instantly regret it as she pours a much bigger glass than I'd anticipated. I rarely ever drink white wine, especially when it's only four in the afternoon, but a mineral water feels far too weak for a meeting like this.

I look around at the room again. Photographs of the bay are dotted along the walls, and two thick columns stand in the centre of the pub stretching from the ceiling to the floor, scuffed and pockmarked with age. It's fairly busy already, but a long, wooden table is free, so I pay and take my wine over to the far side of the pub.

I take a sip of my wine and check my phone. Still no message from my Airbnb, but there's one from Maddie, asking if I arrived safely and if I've met Finn yet. My thumbs fly over the screen as I reply before taking another sip. The unfamiliar acidity is sharp on my tongue. I can't remember the last time I drank white wine. Red has far more health benefits and tends to taste nicer, too. I look up at the sound of scratching across the floorboards and smile as Duke trots over towards me.

'You again,' I say, reaching down to stroke his head.

Maybe it's a measure of how lonely I feel, but the sight of this little dog wagging his tail makes me feel like I've found a friend. I read somewhere once that stroking cats and dogs releases certain hormones that make people feel happier. He definitely brings a smile to my face and is a useful distraction from the realisation that I have no idea what I will say to Finn when he gets here. It's been so long, not to mention the fact that he'd basically stood me up the last time we'd seen each other.

I pick at my pink-painted fingernails and take another gulp of wine as Duke settles against my feet. The door behind the bar opens, and my heart stops, actually missing a beat. There's no question that it's Finn standing there. We still have another twenty minutes until our arranged time to meet, and it takes me a moment to understand that he's early because he works here. His eyes lock with mine and, for a second, it's as if there's nothing standing between us. No history or missed chances. Until I remember to breathe, and, more importantly, remember why I'm here in the first place.

The wine is now streaming around my bloodstream, causing my head to feel a bit light. He looks so familiar, as if it's just yesterday that we'd bumped into each other and arranged to meet for a drink that had never happened. If he's nervous, it doesn't show as he walks over towards me. I set my glass down on the table. Should I get up, or will he sit down? I decide to stay where I am as he stands in front of me with a slightly confused look on his face.

'Jess, hey,' he says.

'Hey,' I say back.

His awkward smile mirrors mine and he leans in towards me. I go to hug him while he goes to land a kiss on my cheek, resulting in his lips ending up somewhere around my eye. The contact of his lips on my skin brings back the belly flip-flopping that, until now, had been quietened with the wine. He drops a small, nervous laugh and steps back shaking his head.

'You're early. We said four thirty, right?'

I nod and smooth my hairline down with my hand. 'We did. I just . . . got here quicker than I'd expected. Is that okay?'

'Yeah, sure. Of course.' Finn slides onto the bench opposite me. 'You found us alright then?'

'Yep. It was all pretty straightforward. The rental has a satnav.' I put my hands in my lap. My voice feels too high and a little shaky and I don't know why I'm talking about the satnav.

He lets out a little puff of air and shakes his head again, as if he's dazed. 'You look . . .' He nods. 'You look good.'

'Thanks.'

The bottom of my blouse is sticking to my back and my jeans are a little muddy from my encounter with Duke on the beach, but I suppose to Finn, I look how I always did.

'You look the same,' I say and immediately regret it, hoping he doesn't take it as an insult.

He half-laughs. 'Few more grey hairs here and there.'

We smile shyly at each other for a few seconds and I wonder how seeing him can simultaneously feel just like the old days and like we are meeting for the first time. He rests his elbows and forearms on the table, interlacing his fingers. His nails are pink and clean and evenly cut.

'I want to say it's good to see you again but . . .' he sighs. 'I never imagined it would be like this.'

I nod. 'I know.'

I feel the same. I hadn't imagined it would feel like this to see him. To feel like home. Like I've just bumped into my very best friend. The fact that it's only happening because of Ivy dying wedges a ball into my throat that I push back down with a gulp of wine. Duke sighs loudly from his place next to my feet and Finn leans back to look under the table.

He smiles. 'Figures he found you.'

I look down at the dog lying on his belly with his head between his front paws. 'Why?'

'Duke. He's Ivy's.' Finn shakes his head an inch. '*Was* Ivy's.'

'Oh.' I feel the weight of his body sink further onto my foot and my heart tugs in my chest. 'So the guy who was walking him . . .?'

'That's Joe. Ivy's boyfriend.'

'I met him on the beach just now.'

'He's gone to work so Duke'll hang here for a bit. We're still trying to figure out what to do with him.'

I've only been here for five minutes and it's starting to dawn on me that I really know nothing about my sister's life. I'd never have thought she'd end up in England, by the coast, or that she'd have a dog and a boyfriend. Ivy had always loved men, but she'd never let one stick around for too long. I take a long sip of my wine. By now, it tastes less acidic and actually quite good. Finn looks at me and it's just how it always was, as if his eyes are made of magnets because I can't look away. It takes me a moment to realise that the nerves that had been building all day have gone. They disappeared the moment he appeared and sat down in front of me.

My mobile phone buzzes on the table as an Airbnb notification pops up on my screen. I can read enough of it to see that my request for booking was unsuccessful. I sigh and rub my fingers on my forehead.

'Everything alright?' Finn asks.

'The Airbnb I wanted has already been booked.'

He pulls a face. 'It's the last week of the summer holidays. I'm surprised you even found somewhere with availability.'

I'm usually so well organised. I've never travelled anywhere for an overnight trip without knowing exactly where I'd be laying my head when I got there. I've had last-minute trips before and still managed to sort out accommodation and entire itineraries before arrival. This isn't like me, and I can't even put it down to the emotional shock about Ivy. My attention has been much shorter than usual for months. Maybe even since Nick and I separated.

'I'm sure I'll find somewhere,' I say, trying to push my brain into action.

Finn looks back at me with his eyebrows pulled into a sceptical look. 'You'll have your work cut out. You *might* get a place at Dobbo's caravan park, if you're lucky, but somehow I don't think it's your style.'

I open my mouth to protest, but stop myself. This is Finn. I'm sure he knows as well as I do that sleeping in a cramped caravan with cold, dribble showers just won't work.

'Maybe you could . . .' He tails off and shakes his head. 'Never mind.'

'I could what?' I probe, digging into his eyes with mine.

The part of me that's hoping he won't offer that I stay at his is in direct conflict with the part that's hoping he will. It would actually be nice not to be alone.

'I was going to suggest that you could stay at Ivy's place.'

My jaw drops a little. 'Oh. Really?'

I'm a little relieved that he didn't offer his sofa but at the same time, the idea of staying at Ivy's is . . .

'I mean, it's sitting empty right now. It was just an idea,' he says quickly. 'And a stupid one, obviously. Forget it. Maybe you can stay at mine?'

Now that he's offered it, I shrink back a little into myself. I'm not sure it'd be a good idea. Finn and I are a whole other chapter by itself and, even though I don't want to be alone, I'm not sure I've got the emotional bandwidth to deal with that along with everything else.

'Don't you think it's weird?' I ask. 'Staying in her house. What if I'm not, you know . . .'

Finn looks at me and pinches his eyebrows together, waiting for me to elaborate.

'What if I'm not welcome?' I laugh nervously and shake my head. 'That sounds stupid, I know. And it's not like I believe in ghosts or anything like that, but things weren't good between us. I don't know if I'd feel welcome, staying there.'

'What? Of course you would. She'd want you to.'

I snort through my nose. 'She hated me.'

'She didn't.'

'And how do *you* know?'

'Because we were friends and she'd changed. A lot. I'm pretty sure she'd be fine with you staying there instead of having a mouldy caravan at Dobbo's.'

I fix him with a sceptical look, but his eyes are sincere.

'Also, I don't know how you feel about this or how long you're planning on staying, but Ruth was talking about going through her things. There might be stuff you want, or whatever. If you're up to it, of course. And no problem if you're not.'

I swallow. I hadn't thought about any of this when I'd booked my train ticket. Going through Ivy's things. Staying at her house. I'd only thought about the funeral service.

'I don't know,' I say, but it's not like I've got many other options.

Finn spreads his palms flat on the table. He has a blue plaster wrapped around his left middle finger.

'Okay,' I say with a nod. 'I'll stay there.'

He nods back. 'I'll call Ruth for the key and I can take you up there, if you want?'

'That would be great,' I reply, pushing the glass with a mouthful of wine left in it away from me. 'The wine was pretty strong.'

'Have you had lunch?'

'I had something on the train.'

The carrot sticks and hummus I'd bought at the station's Waitrose back in London are no match for the alcohol. This is one of the reasons why I don't drink white wine. The ball of acid is sitting right at the top of my stomach and crying out for carbs.

Finn shakes his head with a knowing look on his face. 'Fancy a plate of pasta? It comes with salt and everything.'

An involuntary laugh drops from my mouth as I remember the way he'd looked at me as if I were mad when I'd told him I cooked without it. Finn grins before going back into the kitchen and I run both hands up my face and over my hair, letting a shaky breath sigh out between my lips. I hadn't expected it to, but being back with Finn feels just like old times.

Chapter Thirty-Four

JESS

Present day

I sit in the passenger seat of the hire car while Finn drives. Even after a bowl of penne coated in thick pesto with grilled courgettes and bell peppers to soak up the wine, I wasn't sure it was a good idea for me to drive. The earthy smell of cows floats in through the open window along with the sweet scent of hay, and I turn to look at Duke, sitting in the back.

'What do you think he makes of all this?' I ask.

Finn takes his eyes off the road for a second to turn and look at me. 'Who, Duke?'

I turn back around and face the front. 'I mean, do you think he knows that she's . . . you know.' My voice lowers, as if I can protect him from the truth.

'Who knows?'

Dogs are smart. They're emotionally intelligent, more than some humans. More than *most* humans, probably. They're able to sense moods and the tiniest of alterations in body chemistry, like the ones who can tell if someone's about to have a seizure. I suppose that, of the three of us in this car, his life is the one that's probably changed in the most immediate way. He belonged to Ivy, and now he belongs to Joe. Or Finn. Or whoever.

I glance back over at Finn and look at his profile. He really hasn't changed. He still has that smattering of stubble across his chin and jaw, still that same nondescript haircut that suits him so well. But he feels different. I'd noticed it as soon as he'd stepped out from behind the bar. The Finn from back then was loose, always with a laugh on his lips. The version of him sitting next to me feels tense and stiff. And even without this whole situation, I have the feeling that laughter isn't something he's done much of for a while.

The drystone wall on my side of the road gives way to a thick hedge and a cottage comes into view. Its white-washed walls are bright against the sun, criss-crossed by creeping plants reaching up towards its tiled roof. Finn slows down and turns, easing the car through a wide gap in the hedge into a makeshift driveway. We bump over wide, deep tyre tracks that have set into mud and a shiver runs down my arms at the thought that they might have been left by the ambulance that came to take Ivy away. I look again at Finn, but he keeps his sights set firmly on the cottage in front of us as he stops the car. Duke jumps up and climbs over the handbrake and gear stick, right into my lap. He sticks his nose out of the window with his tail wagging so hard it sends wafts of cool air onto my skin.

'So, here we are. You good?' Finn asks with an unreadable face, and I nod.

As soon as I open the door, Duke shoots from my lap and runs around the garden. I get out and stare at the cottage. I'd never have expected her to live somewhere like this. The tiny box windows are coated in purple paint and a giant tree laden with pink-red apples stands with a rope and swing dangling from a low branch. The path alongside the driveway is paved with small stones painted in mosaic patterns and is sheltered by a wooden structure covered in creeping, winding plants. I'm surprised by the big pots of mint, coriander and basil plants. Ivy had managed to kill even cacti and aloe plants when we'd lived together. A pair of black wellies stand by the door and I try to imagine her pulling them off before going inside. It's not easy to imagine a version of her that would even own wellies to begin with.

Duke barks relentlessly, running from the door towards us and back again on a loop.

'Alright, alright,' Finn says, fishing a key from his jeans pocket before looking at me. 'He hasn't been back here since.'

I look over my shoulder at the sprawling land to the side of the house with a sudden urge to run back to the car, get in and drive all the way back to London. But I don't. Instead, I watch Duke run through the crack in the door before it's even fully opened.

'Watch your head,' Finn says.

I instinctively copy him, ducking as I step under a low frame that I could actually easily fit under, and into an open-plan kitchen and living room. The air inside is musty and streaks of light beam in through the small windows, catching the odd dust mote dancing around in space.

Her style hasn't changed. It's updated a little, maybe a bit more refined, but the space around me is undeniably Ivy. It's a mish-mash of colours, with the kitchen cupboards painted in a light blue but every single handle being completely different to the other. A garland of fairy lights hangs across the window behind the sink and the living room is full of a collection of colourful cushions, a mustard-yellow two-seater sofa and a massive, multicoloured tribal patterned rug. And of course, candles are everywhere, on every possible surface.

'Wow,' I say quietly.

The overloaded bookshelf in the corner is a surprise. Reading wasn't a hobby we'd shared. It had always been *my* thing and deigned too boring for my wayward little sister. A big painting of a bright mandala hangs on one of the walls and the air carries the slightest hint of sweet incense. The whole place feels warm and inviting, like being wrapped in a big hug. I'd expected to feel weirded out by being here, but I don't. I can feel her in everything I see, and it brings a tidal wave of tears that spring from my eyes before I can stop them.

'I'm sorry.' I hiccup and cover my mouth with my hand.

I try to gulp the cry back down but it only seems to make it stronger, dredging it up from my feet. Finn puts his arm around my shoulders and gives me a squeeze. I let him guide me to the sofa where I drop into a seat, and he disappears into another room before coming back with a handful of tissues.

'I knew this was a shit idea,' he says.

The sofa dips as he sits next to me and I take a tissue from his hand to bury my nose in it.

'It's not that,' I reply, wiping a hand across my cheek. 'I'm just a bit . . .'

I drop my head as another tear rolls out and slides down my cheek. I don't know how to explain how I feel.

'There's just so much *stuff.*'

Finn nods in a way that tells me he understands I'm not talking about material possessions, but history.

He looks down at his hands. 'I know.'

I slide my shoes off, suddenly exhausted from the journey and the wine and now this, being here. I sit back in the velvety sofa, so deeply that my feet lift off the floor. Duke has been sniffing around the entire place since we walked in and now, with his search coming up empty, he flops down in front of the unlit fireplace. All three of us sit in silence. I stare into space, noticing small things, like the statue of a fat man with an elephant head on a shelf and photos pinned on a cork board. A collection of leather and suede tassel bags hangs behind the front door, and emerald-green curtains frame the living room window. Small potted succulents and cacti sit on the windowsills, along with a big monstera next to one of the beanbags. The more I look, the more I seem to sink back into the sofa. I don't notice Finn getting up, but at some point I become aware of a hot cup of tea in my hands.

I blink slowly, as if I'm waking from a trance. 'Sorry. I don't know where I went.'

He smiles. 'It's alright.'

'Finn,' I say, shaking my head a little. 'How did Ivy end up here? Of all the places in the world, why did she choose this one, where you are?'

He turns his head and looks at me. 'It was one of those weird, coincidental things. She randomly met my Aunt Ruth in Goa. By all accounts, Ivy was in a bad way and, Ruth being Ruth, she offered to help.'

I frown. 'What kind of bad way?'

His mouth twists. 'Drugs, I guess. And I don't know what else.'

Something inside my chest sinks and drops, right down into my belly. I nod. 'I figured. She'd been a mess at Dad's funeral.'

'Yeah, she told me about that.'

'So Ivy just randomly met your aunt and came here?'

'Pretty much. By the time I moved here, she was already doing much better,' he continues. 'She was teaching yoga at Ruth's studio and was pretty much settled. She was doing really well, Jess.'

I look at the space around us again. As chaotic as it looked on first glance, it also looks very lived in. A true home.

Finn shakes his head again. 'The way she died . . . I thought it was a sick joke. Mixing sleeping pills and alcohol. It's stupid, and she should've known better.' His voice has an edge of anger to it and he sighs. 'I don't mean that she was stupid, I just . . . you know what I mean.'

I do. I'd already guessed at the results from the coroner, so when Finn had texted me about it, it hadn't been a shock. It was the thing I'd been most afraid of for her. That she would pay the price for her love of drugs and partying in the end. I just hadn't expected it to be so soon, and now that I know she'd actually stopped using drugs and had settled down, it's even worse. That she'd stopped taking drugs only to die with them in her system is just too sad for words.

Finn rakes his hands across his face and sniffs. 'I have to get back. Will you be alright? You could come and hang out at the pub, if you want?'

'Thanks, but I'll be fine,' I reply. 'I've got a ton of work to do.'

Finn nods knowingly and gets up. I wonder if he's being taken back a few years too because this was how it always was with us. One or both of us always had to work and in the end, the work always won.

When Finn leaves, I wander from the living room to the bedroom. It's calm and surprisingly bare. There's nothing electronic, not even a digital clock, and the only decoration is another monstera plant in the corner and a big wall hanging in the shape of a sun woven from cream rope. It's the oddest thing. I have one just like it, in the shape of a crescent moon, hanging in my living room. It had been a wedding gift, I think from a boho-lifestyle magazine that had run a feature on one of our wedding planners. Given how different mine and Ivy's tastes are, there's something comforting about knowing that when it came to some things, we might not have been so different after all.

When I go into the bathroom, I have to stand stock still to take it in. It's clean. Sparkling, in fact, and a surprised laugh falls from my mouth. The walls are covered in rectangular black-and-white tiles and a stripy rug is laid in front of a gleaming bath. The glass door of the shower is streak free and a wicker laundry basket stands next to the toilet. A black bowl sink sits on top of a white cupboard and fresh air is flowing in through the open window.

'Trust you to get clean after you move out,' I say, and tut into the space around me as I wipe a tear from my eye.

I can count on one hand the number of times Ivy had taken a sponge to the bathroom in the flat we'd shared. By contrast, there's no end to the number of times we'd argued about her lack of ability to see a dirt ring in the bath.

I notice a streak of pink reflected in the mirror and turn around to see Ivy's kimono hanging on the back of the door. A lump of what feels like cement wedges itself right into my throat as I take the hem of it between my finger and thumb. The silk is almost translucent against my skin, and feather soft to the touch. I lift the material a few inches, looking at the pattern of tropical flowers and birds printed on it. The memory of Ivy's smile when she'd lifted it out of the box after unwrapping it for her twenty-second birthday is like a stab to my heart and it brings the tears back to my eyes, only this time without the laugher.

Chapter Thirty-Five

Jess

Present day

Early the next morning, I stand in the kitchen waiting for the kettle to boil. The cleanliness of Ivy's kitchen wasn't the only surprise in this cottage. Her cupboards are full of organic tea and jars of nuts, seeds and muesli, and I shake my head. Who was this version of Ivy? Where was the one who drank instant coffee and smirked at anything that wasn't processed? It's disorientating, being here with one foot in her life and the other in mine. I've been up for an hour already and have taken a break from work and obsessively checking my inbox for news of the John Lewis deal.

I turn towards the cork board pinned to the tiny strip of wall that separates the living space and kitchen. My eyes sting, just as they had when I'd looked at the photographs yesterday. It feels so strange to see Ivy in this way.

My eyes focus on a photo of her sitting cross-legged in the grass with a group of people, holding Duke in her lap. Her smile is big. Huge. She has rings through her nose I've never seen before, her hair is in dreadlocks and she has an arm full of tattoos. In another, she's sitting in the pub in town between Finn and an older woman who, I guess, must be Ruth. I let my eyes roam around the board to the pictures where she's younger, with a less healthy look about them. There's one of her in a club wearing a mini-skirt and vest with a cowboy style belt around her waist. She's holding a bottle of bright-pink liquor in her hand and there's a blonde girl standing next to her wearing the exact same thing. In another, she's on a beach surrounded by hippies, wearing what looks like a tiny, shredded leather skirt and a bikini top made from what looks like string.

I pick up the framed photo standing on the table next to the phone. Somehow, I know that this is the most recent one of her. She's standing with her arms wrapped around the man I'd met on the beach and then again in the pub. Joe. Her boyfriend, the one who'd woken up to find her. They look so in love, and it breaks me.

Tears fall from my eyes and I sit on the arm of the sofa, letting them drop and scorch burning trails on my skin. I cry in a way I haven't until now. I miss her. So much. And I hate myself for the times when I'd wanted to get in touch but decided not to, telling myself I'd do it another time because I've missed out on knowing this Ivy. One who taught yoga, adopted a dog and had finally learned to clean a bathroom. I cry as I picture her scrubbing the bathtub and somewhere through the tears, I feel the cold wetness of a dog sniffing at my legs.

Through the smallest of openings, my eyes see Duke. I drag my hand across my face, wiping the trails of tears, and look over to see Finn holding the door open with one hand and Duke's leash in the other.

'Sorry,' he says. 'I knocked a few times but you didn't answer. And I heard you crying, so . . .'

I can't see him properly through my stinging eyes, but his voice feels like a blanket landing on my shoulders. I sniff, wiping my hand under my nose.

'I can come back later. Or not at all, if you need to be alone.'

'No,' I croak. 'It's okay.'

Duke whines, standing on his hind legs and putting his front paws on my knees. His little tail is wagging behind him and I wonder what he makes of this woman crying in what's actually *his* living room. I wipe my eyes again before letting out a big sigh.

'I thought I'd see if you fancied a walk?' Finn asks with that hallmark mellow voice. 'I've got to go down to Ruth's too, but if you're not up for it . . .'

'That'd be nice,' I butt in.

Getting out in the fresh air would do me some good.

'Sure?' Finn asks, dipping his head a little. 'I can come back later.'

'No, it's fine,' I insist, sniffing again and rubbing the back of Duke's head as he drops back down onto all fours. 'I just needed to get that out, you know?'

He nods. I have no idea if he really does know, but I'm thankful that he's here. I'd have gone out myself eventually, but the inclusion of a dog walk is one I could never pass up. They always manage to make things seem doable.

I look up at Finn through slightly clearer eyes. He's wearing the same jeans as yesterday with a fresh t-shirt and a thin, unzipped fleece, but I'm still in my pyjamas of an old pair of leggings and a t-shirt. I cross my arms over my chest self-consciously and clear my throat as I stand up.

'Just let me get cleaned up.'

◆　◆　◆

We've been walking for almost half an hour, and neither of us have said much. After getting dressed, he'd offered me some green tea in a Thermos and then we'd set off in silence. I have the feeling he's been giving me some time to recover and decompress, and I'm grateful for his silent but reassuring presence. I sneak a look at him, telling myself I'm actually taking in the view. Duke's leather leash hangs around his shoulders and he's holding the ends in his hands. His eyes flick towards me, as if he can feel me looking at him, and I quickly shift my gaze to the view behind him instead.

It's a beautiful morning, the kind I really love, with an azure blue sky and hazy, wispy streaked clouds that look like they could be cut in half with the tip of your finger. The sun is faint on my skin, adding just enough warmth to the otherwise chilly air to give the promise of a gorgeous summer day, but not quite enough to take off my running jacket. The ground is covered with a carpet of lush, short green grass and the sound of the sea rolling in and out of the bay fills the air around us. I take a deep breath of it in, pulling it deep down into my lungs. It's a perfect tonic, clearing away the rush of feelings that had overwhelmed me earlier.

The hill gets steeper and I welcome the slight burn in my thighs. A seaside walk is a great alternative to a run, especially with Duke's endless energy. I smile as he scrambles up and over the almost moss-like hilly mounds with an enthusiasm that hasn't slowed since we left the cottage. The mounds make tough work for his little legs and he almost falls back down as he negotiates the next one. Finn lets out a grunt of laughter and we look at each other with mirroring looks that say *silly dog*.

'So,' he says eventually, glancing at me. 'Wanna talk about it?'

I raise my eyebrows and blow air from my mouth. 'Which part?'

He twists his lips, as if he's considering the options. 'What's with your back?'

'What do you mean?' I frown.

'You've been doing weird twisty things with it since we left.'

Have I? Maybe I'm not the only one who's been stealing glances as we've been walking. For some reason, the thought creates a tingle of warmth in my chest.

'I woke up like it,' I explain. 'The sofa's a bit soft.'

'Why did you sleep on the sofa?'

'I can't sleep in the bed where Ivy died.'

'But she didn't,' he says, and my eyes swivel towards him.

'You said she had.'

Finn shakes his head. 'She died in her sleep, but not in bed. They were in the living room.'

My eyes widen as I picture her being found on the sofa I'd just slept on.

'On the floor, Joe said,' he adds quickly.

'Oh,' I say, letting the word get carried out towards the sea. 'Right.'

I'm not sure that makes things any better, picturing her on the cold floor instead, but I already know I'll be sleeping in the bedroom tonight.

The grass around us becomes lighter in colour and taller in length, and I look down at our feet tramping across it. Our pace mirrors each other, left foot with left, right with right. A memory floats across my mind, of the way our feet had looked, entwined at the end of my bed – a memory I didn't even know I'd saved. I swipe it away with a blink of my eyes. I'd been nervous about seeing Finn again, mostly because of what he represents. A past version of me, of Ivy. Of everything. Honestly, I hadn't factored in the possibility of the attraction that had pulled us together in the first place still being here, even though it had been there just as strongly on the day he'd left me waiting in that pub. Still, I hadn't expected my heart to leap whenever he looks in my direction, to feel clamminess in my palms. And if I had, I would've been absolutely sure I'd have been able to ignore it.

I tread on an uneven clump of grass and my ankle twists a little to one side in my trainers – they are great for runs around central London but clearly useless in hilly fields. Finn reaches out, grabbing my hand in his to steady me. The warmth of his palm against mine sends a sweet, sharp electric current right up my arm and into my core.

His eyes catch me almost as steadily as his hand does, holding me up against the rush of energy flushing across my body. I'm hyper aware of his fingers closing around the side of my hand and my heart is thudding in my chest so loudly, I'm sure he can hear it. It feels like it's pumping out of my chest and through my clothes, spurred on by the contact of his skin on mine. But I drop my hand and stuff it into my pocket. I don't want things to get complicated.

Duke is barking ahead of us, sending little yelps of delight out into the air, and I take advantage of the narrowing path to walk behind Finn. The firmness of earth shifts to sand as we follow the path uphill until Finn stops a couple of metres ahead of me. He stands with his hands stuffed into his pockets, emphasising the broadness of his shoulders, and turns his head as I catch up with a final step to stand next to him. I use a hand to shield my eyes from the sun as I look out into the distance.

Waves ripple in from the horizon across an expanse of sea that, on this side of the bay, looks as turquoise as the Mediterranean. My eyes follow the waves, surging inland and swelling until they break on the rocks and collapse into white foam. A lighthouse stands on one of a group of smaller islands farther down the shore and a flock of sea gulls shriek overhead. Duke is already down on the small patch of sand between rocks and grassy dunes, sniffing the ground with so much enthusiasm it's as if he's found treasure.

'Wow,' I say, though the word is an understatement.

I've always been a beach person. My idea of a perfect holiday always, always involves a beach, preferably with a good book to go with it. It was something Nick and I had in common and finding the perfect stretch of sand was central to holiday planning, so I'm not exaggerating when I say that this view is right up there.

'England,' I say. 'Who knew?'

Finn lets out a small laugh. 'Not bad, huh?'

It looks completely swimmable, though I have noticed it's about 100 per cent quieter than the wider stretch of beach in town.

'Where is everyone? Where are all the surfers?' I ask. I don't know much about the sport, but even I can see that the waves coming in were made for a board to slide down.

'See those rocks?' Finn points. 'They're fairly lethal.'

'Fairly?' I look at him and he smiles with a shrug.

'Only for nutters and people with a death wish. Every now and again someone decides to try and go for it, usually an out-of-towner.'

I look back at the rocks. They do look especially unforgiving, jutting out and breaking through the white water pounding into them.

'And?'

'It rarely ends well.'

I've never understood people who do things like that, throwing themselves out of planes and off bridges. For me, life is something to hang on to. To do otherwise feels like a contradiction to our basic instinct to survive. I look again at the rocks and wonder how many people he's talking about, but I don't ask. I don't need to add any more thoughts of death to the ones I've already got going on.

'Of course, it means it's much less popular than the main beach and much nicer for a walk.'

I nod in agreement. The beach in town had been packed yesterday, full of sunbathers and surfers and people playing football. And even though it's too early and cold for it to be as busy just yet, it still feels nice to be on this side of the bay, away from everything else.

We make our way down the grass-lined dunes to the beach. I can already feel the sand making its way into the soft, porous material of my trainers and after a few more steps, I stop to take them off. The sand is cold and refreshing under my feet, gliding across my toes. A couple of steps later, Finn stops too to pull his Vans from his feet and turn up his jeans. We hold our shoes in the hooks of our fingers and make our way down the hill, our feet submerging into the sand as we go.

I kick the sand with my feet. 'How come you ended up back here and not in Sweden?'

'Short version?' Finn looks at me with a sad pull around his lips. 'My dad died recently. I didn't want to sell the pub. Too many memories.'

'Oh, Finn . . .' I sigh. 'I'm really sorry to hear that.'

He shrugs back at me in a way that says *it's okay*. It's one I've come to use myself when talking about my parents and the thought crosses my mind that I might, one day, use it in response to questions about Ivy. It feels unthinkable, and I push the thought away.

'There's been a lot going on. I'm not sure I've really come up for air yet,' he continues.

'So what's the long version?' I venture, taking us back to the past.

I'd told Maddie I didn't want to dig into the past with Finn, but it's here, staring us in the face, and I don't want to spend the next few days on tiptoe just to avoid the truth.

Finn breathes out a puff of air and swings Duke's leash to wrap over his shoulders again. 'Well, the long version . . . I don't even know how far back to go with that.'

'Last time I saw you was in London.'

I've somehow managed to keep a neutrality to my voice that I absolutely don't feel inside, but his face pinches a little with what I think looks like shame, guilt or maybe even both.

'Yeah. London.' He clears his throat. 'I owe you an apology for that. It was *not* cool of me to leave you there like that. I'd had to book a last-minute flight back to Gothenburg.'

'So you were still living there when we'd seen each other?'

He nods. 'I was just in London for a few days but I'd had to get back. I've got a daughter there.'

My jaw drops an inch. 'You're a dad?'

'Yeah. There'd been some drama with her mum and . . .' He shakes his head. 'Well, I'd had to get back.'

I can't believe Finn's a dad. Whenever I'd imagined what he might be up to, being a parent wasn't in there. It's hardly a weird thing to think at our age. Most other thirty-six-year-olds around me are settled with babies, human or animal. But Finn? That's a big thing to have happened. Probably *the* biggest thing that can happen to a person, really.

'Nuts, right?' He laughs a little. 'It took me a while to get used to the idea too.'

'Congratulations,' I say, still a little stunned. 'What's she called?'

'Emilia. She'll be six soon.'

So she'd already been born when he stood me up. Maybe it's a good thing he hadn't turned up, because although I'd fight to my last tooth to deny it, there's a part of me that thinks things might have turned out very differently. I might never have continued see-ing Nick, and it would've meant complicating Finn's family life.

'So you made a proper life and family in Sweden then,' I say evenly, trying to keep the strange hint of jealousy from my voice.

'I guess. The restaurant job was great. I was still there until I'd had to come back here. I met Maia and, well, we didn't plan to have a baby but you know . . . things happen.' He rubs the back of his neck. 'She'd been adamant about keeping it and I wasn't sure. I was *not* in any place to be a dad. Does that make me sound awful?'

He looks at me from under his long lashes and I shake my head. It might have done, if it were coming from anyone else, but it's coming from him, and I know he's not a heartless kind of guy.

'No, it doesn't,' I say with a small smile. 'It's just the way life is, sometimes.'

'Well, we had Emilia, obviously. And we tried to do the family thing for a while but it was pretty rough. I worked a lot, and we fought a lot. I was in London for a couple of days when I bumped into you, and Maia had been going ballistic.'

I nod in understanding, remembering how his phone had beeped constantly and how harassed he'd looked about it.

'I'd had to get back, so I flew out that night. We broke up for good not long afterwards. I moved out but stuck around for Emilia. I worked too much to really see her though and now I'm back here, I'm not sure when the next time will be.'

Finn stops walking and bends down to pick up a stone from the sand. He frowns and rubs the sand off before swinging his arm over his head and throwing it far out into the sea. He stares at the water.

He shakes his head and turns to look back at me. 'You know what's funny?'

I shake my head. '*Is* there anything funny about all this?'

'It's taken me not being able to be a proper dad to Emilia to realise I really wanted to be one in the first place.'

My heart drops at the tone of his voice. 'But you can go back to visit? Or she can come here.'

'It's not so easy with Maia. I left her, alone with a kid. I'm pretty sure she still hates my guts, and I can't say blame her. The whole thing was just . . .' he shakes his head. 'It wasn't her I wanted to be with. We should've called it off way before things developed like they did.'

The way his green eyes briefly fix on me takes my breath away. *It wasn't her that I wanted to be with.* What did that mean? And why had my stomach fluttered like it was full of a swarm of butterflies? My heart wants to ask the questions, but my throat closes, keeping them inside.

'She's with someone else now anyway. An engineer with money. Em is well looked after, which is the main thing, I guess.'

The tone of his voice makes me instinctively link my arm through his.

'I'm sorry,' I say.

'Not your fault, Jess. I've come to terms with my mistakes.'

My fingers curl around his arm we walk, just like before. Right foot with right, left with left. I could let go of him, but I don't, and he doesn't seem to mind. Our shoulders bump together now and then, and for a while the only sounds around us are the rolling waves, the squawk of gulls and the occasional bark of delight from Duke. The calmness of our surroundings helps to clear my mind in a way it hasn't been for what feels like an eternity.

'And what about you,' Finn asks eventually, pulling my attention back in. 'What've you been up to?'

'Oh. Well, I'm not a mum.' I smile weakly. 'I did get married, though.'

Finn nods. 'Ivy told me.'

'I wasn't sure that she knew. I'd sent an invitation by email but she never replied.'

'Oh, she knew. Your wedding was the catalyst for her getting herself sorted out.'

'How do you mean?'

'It was just something she'd mentioned in passing a couple of times.'

'I can't imagine how it could've done that. She never turned up or even replied to the invite.'

'She said she sent you a present?'

I frown and shake my head. 'She didn't.'

'Well, she said she did.' Finn shrugs and I return it.

Who knows why she'd say that, because she hadn't. We'd had loads of gifts, from dining sets to photo frames and a wine-tasting holiday. There hadn't been anything from Ivy amongst them.

'So, how is married life?' Finn asks. 'Your husband didn't want to come with you?'

'He's in Singapore. We're getting divorced,' I reply flatly.

'Sorry to hear that,' he offers with a pull of his lips to one side.

'It's alright.'

'So. Do you feel up to sharing the long version? Or is that it?'

'The long version . . .' I take a deep breath. 'Well. I met Nick just before Dad got sick. He's a really great guy but it just didn't work in the end. I think we got confused somewhere along the line and he became more of a best friend. Next to Maddie of course. We have a business together.'

'Right, you told me when we saw each other last. Stationery, right?'

I nod, but the frown pops back onto my face. I'd replayed our conversation in Pret in my head over and over again, and I'm pretty sure I hadn't told him what our business was.

'Yeah. Diaries, calendars, stuff like that.'

Finn grins. 'Makes sense. You were always a bit of a stickler about your notepads.'

I smile. 'I know what I like, that's all.'

'And how's it going, the business?'

'Good.' I nod. 'Really good. We've applied for a shop lease and we're growing all the time. But the better the business did, the worse my marriage went. Nick got a promotion to partner and to open a new division in Asia. When he told me, there was no question of him not accepting it, and no question of me leaving my business to go with him. So that was it.'

'That's rough,' Finn says, rubbing a hand across his bristled chin.

'It was just doomed from the start.' My stomach flips as I admit it. 'I should've stopped things before they got so serious.'

Finn opens his mouth to say something, but seems to think better it and looks out to the sea instead.

Chapter Thirty-Six

JESS

Present day

She's just like Mum.

Ruth's limbs are stocky instead of lean, her hair is grey and wavy and her skin is pale with the hint of a tan, not brown. But there's something about Finn's aunt that reminds me of my mum. She wraps me in a warm, strong hug and I find myself melting into it with a comfort that flies in the face of us having just met about three seconds ago.

'It's lovely to finally meet you,' she says into my ear before pulling away. She looks at me with a sad but amused smile and shakes her head. 'Gosh, you're the spit of Ivy.'

'Really?' I ask. 'Everyone always said we were like chalk and cheese.'

'She's old and confused,' Finn laughs. 'Don't mind her.'

'Less of the old, thank you,' Ruth retorts, and pulls him in for a hug too.

Her fingers spread wide across his broad shoulders, the tips of them white with the pressure of her hug. To be held like that by family suddenly feels like the most precious thing in the world, and

I'm once again reminded of the fact that I'll never get that again. I remember reading somewhere once that grief can feel like being out on a canoe in the middle of the sea, at the mercy of changeable weather. If our beach walk was like sailing under a sunny sky then this feels like being pulled in by dark clouds looming on the horizon as my belly drops with a pang of longing. Ruth ushers us inside and I swallow the feeling, using her kindness as a sweetener to help it go down.

'Have you had breakfast?' Ruth asks, crouching down to pet Duke.

'Not yet, we've been out walking this one,' Finn replies.

She smiles as she stands back up, and Duke trots through the house as if he's been here many times before. 'I've got a load of fruit, if you're hungry?'

'Starving.' Finn looks at me. 'Jess?'

My politeness wants me to say no and insist that I can wait until I get home, but my stomach gurgles loudly under my vest before I get the chance.

'We'll take that as a *yes please*,' Finn says with a smile and my cheeks burn as I take off my jacket.

'You have a really beautiful home,' I say as we go through to the kitchen.

'Thanks,' she replies, looking briefly at me over her shoulder. 'I love it here. It's like a personal retreat.'

I can second that. The walls and ceilings are painted white, the floorboards are stripped back and pale and the furnishings are in a palette of creams, beiges and light greys. It's calming with a feeling of extreme cleanliness that's more than just being dust and dirt-free. I tread self-consciously, hyper aware of the grains of sand that are most definitely stuck to my socks despite me brushing as much of it away as I could. Her kitchen is small, with a wooden table and bench sofa on one wall, and cupboards and an old-fashioned range cooker on the other.

'Tea? Coffee? Herbal?' Ruth offers, handing me a huge slab of wood with a loaf of bread and carving knife on it.

'Herbal would be great, thanks.' I set the chopping board down and sit on the cushioned bench.

The oak table looks old and a wave of fragrance from a potted plant with tiny purple flowers wafts at me from the centre of it.

'You should try her chai,' Finn says. 'It's amazing. Black tea, though.'

'I can make yours with red bush, if you don't do caffeine?' Ruth asks, and I nod with a grateful smile.

She grins in a way that lights up her face, and I find myself trying to place her age. I'd say she's in her early sixties, around the same age Mum would be.

'You can cut a few slices for toast,' Ruth says to me before turning to Finn, 'and you can make us a fruit salad.'

'Already on it,' Finn says, pulling a tea-towel from the rail on the cooker and slinging it over his shoulder. He inspects a bowl of fruit on the side. 'Mm, watermelon.'

'No melon. It shouldn't be mixed with other food.'

I raise my eyebrows with surprise. I'm usually the one who comes out with sentences like that.

Finn groans. 'Can't we have it on the side?'

'*You* can.' Ruth takes a carton from the fridge and looks at me. 'I only have oat milk, hope that's okay?'

I nod with a wide smile, glad not to have to be the awkward one who needs special ingredients for once.

'What about you, Jess?' Finn turns and looks at me with a raised eyebrow and the hint of a grin on his lips. 'Will you live dangerously and have watermelon with your breakfast?'

'That depends,' I reply, looking slowly from him to Ruth. Now that I've met her, I can tell they're family. They have the same nose and the same intense green eyes. 'Why shouldn't I be having it?'

Finn drops his head in an *oh no, here we go* type of way and turns back to the melon. His long-sleeved top is thin, and I can see the dips and curves of his shoulder blades as he cuts into the fruit.

'According to Ayurveda, melon should never be eaten with anything else. Combining it with other food creates a kind of fermentation that causes bloating and gas, and is bad for you in general.' Ruth pours the oat milk into a pan. 'As is mixing fruit with dairy, which is why we've got coconut yoghurt to go with the fruit salad.'

'Jess, meet my Aunt Ruth, bad-food mixing specialist. Ruth, meet Jess, chronic food under-seasoner.'

I tilt my head to one side and roll my eyes as Ruth laughs.

'I fear my skills are being wasted this morning,' Finn says with a playful sigh.

'Oh, come on. It's only a fruit salad, it's hardly haute cuisine,' Ruth replies.

I smile at the exchange between them, drinking in the loving bickering of this family dynamic. It's been such a long time since I've been this up close and personal to it, and I settle onto the bench, carving thick slices of heavily seeded bread. The air around me is infused with the scent of cardamom and cinnamon, and Duke is curled up on a rug by the door, worn out by our walk. Ruth moves with consideration and the air of someone who's completely grounded in themselves. She reminds me of the apple tree I'd seen in Ivy's garden. Sturdy and stable. She's wearing a white t-shirt with turned-up, loose jeans, and a leather strap around one of her ankles. Her toenails are painted a dark cherry red, and she's wearing a silver necklace with an iridescent pendant. If I'd have seen her on the street and had to guess what the inside of her house would be like, I would have guessed something exactly like this. Everything about her screams health and wellbeing.

Finn, on the other hand, looks a little out of place. His height and broad shoulders seem far too masculine for a space like this, and as Ruth sets some bowls on the table, I find myself wondering what his place looks like. I imagine an abundance of wood and metal, with a big, open kitchen full of pots and pans and herbs and spices.

My phone buzzes in my pocket. It's been going all morning and I've managed to ignore it until now, but each vibration is like a little tug in the back of my mind that things are waking up, back in my world. Responses to the barrage of emails I'd sent after waking would be coming in, creating that never-ending chain reaction of read and reply. I figure a quick look won't hurt, just to make sure it's nothing urgent, but I don't want to appear rude. Ruth returns to the table with two pots of chai, and Finn brings a glass bowl of glistening fruit salad. I leave the phone in my pocket and we tuck into breakfast.

Finn's fruit salad is tangy and sweet, and Ruth's chai is creamy and spicy. I don't know if it's deliberate, but nobody ventures onto the topic of Ivy. It's there though, I can feel it, waiting to be brought up and I'm grateful for the simplicity of sitting and eating food with easy conversation. Maddie would be proud of the gratitude list that's building in my head for today, and I take it all in as some kind of armour for the funeral tomorrow. I know I'm going to need it.

I wonder if Ivy had sat in this very spot, with Finn and Ruth in front of her like this. She must've done. The sun is streaming in through the open window and the back door opens onto a lush green field with a clear view of the sea in the distance. It feels startlingly normal for me to be here, even though the reason for it is anything but. I put my hands around the glazed blue cup and take a sip of chai before looking at them both.

'Thanks for a lovely breakfast, and for this,' I say with a little smile, looking around at the kitchen. It would have been a very different morning had Finn not popped round.

'Ah, you're welcome. It's the least I can do.' Ruth lifts her eyebrows a little, creating the tiniest of wrinkles across her otherwise smooth forehead. 'It's still an incredible shock.'

Finn nods in agreement and rubs his fingers across his lips.

'How are you holding up?' she asks with a voice thick with kindness that wraps around me like a blanket.

'Oh, you know.' I shrug a little and shake my head, looking down into my chai again. 'I'm fine, I guess.'

It feels like a lame answer, but the word *fine* has a sliding scale of meanings, from struggling to okay to coping. From the emotional rollercoaster that's been the theme of the morning so far, I'm not sure which one fits best. I found it so strange after Mum died, how sometimes I could almost forget that it had happened and that everything was exactly how it always was. Until I'd be reminded that it wasn't, blindsided by hurt. It was the same when Dad died, and it's the same now.

'I hadn't really known what to expect coming here, but it looks like Ivy really made a good life for herself.'

It could've been much worse. She might have been alone, in a place where nobody knew or cared about her. Knowing that she ended up in a good place can never really make up for my guilt over not patching things up, but it does help.

'She worked hard at it. I don't think it came easily at the start, but creating a good life *was* her life in the end.' Ruth's eyes glisten with tears and she swallows a sip of tea. 'I've not met many people with such determination.'

I lean back against the back of the bench. 'Finn told me she was teaching yoga?'

She nods back. 'At my studio, next door.'

'Ivy. A yoga teacher.' I shake my head a little. 'It's the last thing I'd have expected.'

'She was totally unconventional,' Ruth says with a chuckle. 'She made it her own and managed to get people in who'd always ran a mile at the idea before, like this one here.'

She nods towards Finn and I raise my eyebrows.

'*You* do yoga?'

He's clearly kept his athletic body if the muscles I'd seen flexing under his top earlier were anything to go by, but I'd never imagined him as the downward dog type.

He shrugs with a grin. 'I tried it. It's not for me, but Ruth's right. Ivy was a good teacher and got a load of the surfers into it, too. Joe brought them all in.'

'They were a pair, if ever I saw one. Pretty perfect together, actually,' Ruth says with a smile before nodding a little. 'Yep. I'd say she made a good life for herself. A well-deserved one, too.'

It makes my chest glow with warmth, hearing about Ivy in this way. I smile sadly.

'I wish I'd have been able to see it for myself.'

The look on Ruth's face mirrors mine as she puts her cup on the table. 'Oh, you will. There'll be a lot of people at the funeral tomorrow and more at the wake, I'd imagine. Some of her friends have organised a party.'

'A rave,' Finn corrects.

'Really?' I ask, trying not to let the distaste show on my face. 'A rave?'

Who organises a rave as a wake, especially for someone who'd spent her whole life doing it before turning things around?

'I'm sorry to do this, but I've got to get to work,' Finn says with a grimace before looking at Duke. 'Could you look after him, Ruth? Joe can't today and the pub just isn't the right place.'

'I can't, sorry. I've got private classes all day.'

'Damn.' Finn sighs reluctantly and tilts his head back.

I look at the little dog sitting in a ray of sunlight streaming onto the floor. It must be so unsettling for him to be dropped off from person to person and place to place.

'I'll watch him,' I pipe up.

'Really?' Finn asks, and the relief is evident.

'Sure. I'll be happy for the company and he'll probably feel more at home there anyway.'

'Do you have to rush off, too?' Ruth asks me as Finn kisses her cheek.

I shake my head. My inbox must be exploding by now, but it feels more urgent to stay here, sitting in the warmth and hearing about Ivy from a woman who feels so much like my own mother did.

'Thanks, Jess. You're a godsend.' He stops beside me and kisses my cheek, just like he had with Ruth.

His lips land as softly as a butterfly on a leaf. The way I tip my head and nestle into him for a brief, fleeting second is completely instinctual. His citrusy scent fills my nose like a comfort blanket that I'd once had and since forgotten about.

I look up into his piercing eyes and match his smile. 'Welcome.'

He squeezes my shoulder and then leaves us in the kitchen as he makes his way out and I turn back to Ruth. Her mouth is pulled into the hint of a smile that makes my cheeks flare. If she and Ivy were close, as Finn said, she must know the history between us.

'This is going to sound mad,' I say with a shy smile. 'But you remind me of my mum. I don't know why, because from the outside you couldn't be more different, but . . .' I lean back in my chair and shake my head.

'It doesn't sound mad. Ivy said the same thing, actually.'

'Really?'

Ruth nods. 'Yep.'

A shiver runs along my spine. That Ivy had felt the same feels somehow strangely creepy and beautiful at the same time.

'She spoke about you a lot, you know,' Ruth says, leaning forward and resting her elbows on the table.

'Oh.' I shift in my seat. 'That can't have been good.'

'Well, it definitely wasn't *all* bad,' she replies with a small laugh. 'She spoke about the good things too.'

I raise my eyebrows in a gesture of surprising disbelief. 'Really?'

'Really.' Ruth reaches across the table and takes one of my hands. 'I know this is hard. I've just lost my brother and we'd had our fair share of problems, so I can relate. You can't change the history you and Ivy had, but you can stop letting it affect your future. *She* did.'

But that was always the difference between me and Ivy. She was always able to reinvent herself, to shrug off the things that didn't serve her any more. But for me?

If only it were so easy.

Chapter Thirty-Seven

JESS

Present day

'That isn't Ivy,' I say, almost laughing with relief.

I hear myself saying *it's all been a big mistake* as I look back at Ruth, expecting her to have an explanation as to why we've been led into this small room to see someone who clearly isn't Ivy. But she just stands there with her lips pulled thin. The air smells of nothing, like an airplane cabin, and in the middle of the room is a coffin that looks like a cardboard box and a body in it that doesn't look at all like my sister. Ruth hangs back by the door, and I shake my head at her, as if to say *how can they have made such a huge mistake?* I look at everything else in the room. I take in the pale yellow paint on the walls and the small, stained glass window, the two chairs and a table in the corner. Then I turn back towards the coffin.

She's lying on her back, with her hands on her lower belly, one on top of the other. A twinge pulls in my heart so deep that it makes my knees feel weak, because I'd recognise her hands anywhere. They were smaller than mine, with nails that always grew quicker and a cluster of dark freckles across the knuckles of her left hand. A breath leaves my mouth as I look up at her face. She looks much smaller than I remember, with her dreads wrapped up into a spiralled bun that presses against the top edge of the coffin.

I don't know how long I stand there for as I study every detail. She's wearing a baggy, grey knitted jumper, a pair of jeans and Dr Martens on her feet, which, for some reason, bring the full realisation that this really is my sister. Only she would go to her own funeral in DMs. I tentatively reach out to hold one of her hands. And even though I'd done the same with Dad and know what to expect, the cold slackness of her skin shocks me. I stare at her, and the longer I look, the more I see.

I see her full eyebrows and the small pockmark in her right nostril and bottom lip from a piercing. I see the powder they've put on her face clinging to the tiny hairs on her skin. I look at her, waiting for her to open her eyes, sit up and say *ha, fooled you!* before bursting out into laughter. But she doesn't and she can't. Because I can see that although this *is* her body, there's no life in it. I don't know what it is that animates us, wakes us up in the morning and adds presence to a room, but whatever it is, it isn't here. A shiver runs up my spine and I pull my hand away.

'Jess?' Ruth's voice is gentle as she comes to stand on the opposite side of the coffin. 'Are you okay?'

I look up at her.

'It's really her,' I reply.

She nods back and tilts her head to the side, looking at Ivy in full length. 'Yes. It is.'

I catch sight of something behind Ivy's ear and go to look at it before stopping myself. They'd cut Dad open for his autopsy, and I'd seen the stitch. It was the one thing that had haunted me for weeks afterwards, and I don't want that again.

'It's weird to see her looking so . . .' I search for the right word. 'Dead.' I shake my head. 'She was always so alive.'

I know the words sound basic, but it's true. Ivy was one of the most alive people I knew. Like she'd said at Dad's wake, she really lived her life. Every second of it.

For a while, we just stand there, looking at her. It's like being pulled into a strange void that makes me start to question what I think I know and understand about life. What it's all about. What the point of it is, if this is what it comes down to in the end.

Eventually, I look at Ruth. 'What do you think happens after we die?'

The idea that someone as alive as Ivy could just disappear into nothingness feels just too tragic for words.

'Well,' Ruth replies. 'I suppose that, in my view, we're energy, just like everything else in the universe. I think that our consciousness or spirit or soul makes a home in the body that we're in and afterwards it goes back.'

'Goes back to where?'

Ruth shrugs. 'For me, nothing is ever really wasted. It's simply broken down and redistributed. I think that energy is the same. Either we disperse into the collective bigger energy, or we come back again, into another body for another try at life.'

'Reincarnation?'

'Maybe.'

I look down at Ivy. I don't know what I believe. Even after losing both parents years before ever having expected to, it's one question I haven't found an answer to. I've never found a faith or religion to cling to. Mum and Dad had been raised in the Jamaican evangelist Church. For them, there'd been no question that there was a heaven where they'd be reunited with everyone they'd ever cared about. Maybe it was easy to have that kind of faith when you've grown up going to church every Sunday, surrounded by people singing and clapping and speaking in tongues. But Ivy and I hadn't gone to church. And now, I don't know what to believe.

What I do know, standing here in front of her right now, is that the belief I'd held on to all these years that there would always come a time when we'd sort things out has been well and truly smashed to pieces.

My palms dampen as memories float up in my mind from our childhood: walking to the primary school at the end of our road together on the first day of term with our buckle-up patent leather shoes and play-acting along to *Gladiators* on a Saturday afternoon in the living room. Sharing a flat together as adults, with our film nights and the atmosphere Ivy created just by being in the same space. With so much history behind us, I can't understand any more what could ever have been so important that we no longer spoke. Not Finn, or the fight at Dad's funeral, none of it.

'I'll leave you alone for a bit,' Ruth says, gently placing her hand on my back.

I shake my head, wiping the back of my hand under my eyes. 'I'd like it if you stayed.'

In this otherwise cold and lifeless room, Ruth's warmth beams out towards me and I let myself lean into it. My breath is shaky as I look at Ivy for what will be the last time. Ruth said she believes that none of us really die, that we all just merge into the space around us. But Ivy hasn't. She isn't in *this* space. I can't feel her. But still, I lower my head and drop a kiss onto her forehead, squeezing my eyes shut at the coldness on my lips. I wish I could tell all her the things I really wanted to say, and have wanted to over the years. But now that I'm here, there's only one thing that's worth saying.

'I'm sorry.'

Three hours later, I'm sitting in the front row of a crematorium a few miles away. It feels like the time between driving back to Ruth's from the funeral home and getting here has passed by in a blur. Getting dressed in the simple, long-sleeved black dress I'd bought especially for today, twisting my hair up and securing it in place with the gold leaf-shaped hair clip that Ivy had bought me one Christmas, coating my lips with nude lipstick – all of it seems to have happened without me really being in my body. We'd followed the hearse with her coffin in the back of it, and traffic had stopped as the small cortege passed by. Snaking along the coastal road to this little building up the hill has culminated in this. A room packed with people, bunches of wild flowers and a cardboard coffin.

An entire wall is made from glass windows, facing out to the sea. Outside, the sky is blue and cloudless. The sun is shining. My eyes keep glancing to the plain cardboard coffin just a few feet away from me and the picture of Ivy that's been blown up and framed. It's a copy of one from her house, where she's sitting in the grass with Duke in her lap and a big smile on her face. The vitality of it, the colourfulness of it, the wildness of the flowers in the vases on either side of it all merge together as a reminder that this wasn't just someone. It was Ivy. A thirty-five-year-old woman who, no matter how fully she'd lived, still had a whole life in front of her.

I cross my legs and the soles of my shoes scrape along the blue carpet. My fingers pick apart the tissue in my lap as Ruth stands up on the small, raised platform, talking about Ivy and the impact she'd made on the community she'd chosen to be a part of. My shoulders shiver and I look down at my hands. An arm wraps around me, but I don't look up because I know that, if I do, Ivy's smile will be beaming back at me again. Finn's hand closes around my shoulder and the other lands in my lap, taking mine in his. He'd been one of the coffin bearers and the look on his face as he'd brought her in had taken my breath away. I'd almost forgotten they'd had their own shared history, not just at university but also here. I can tell from the way he's holding my hand that his heart is hurting too, but I daren't look at him. I don't know if it would help either of us to see that look reflected back at us so closely, but the simple act of physical contact feels like a hug to the soul and I try my best to send that feeling back towards him.

Ruth steps down from the podium, and the celebrant asks if anyone else wants to share. Ruth's eulogy was the only one of two on the order of service and I realise that nobody here knew Ivy *before*. This isn't a funeral surrounded by family members who'd known her from the year dot and had memories of her growing up. It seems unjust for the people who were here not to know who she'd been before coming here. I squeeze Finn's hand before letting it go and he frowns as I go to get up.

'Are you sure?' he whispers at me.

I nod back, holding my breath as I stand and put my hand up meekly at the same time. I'm no stranger to public speaking. Since starting our business, I've done plenty of expos and trade shows, and given countless presentations. But as I step up onto the platform, I know this is different. I don't have a speech prepared to talk about my sister and the person who, apart from Maddie, I would have said was my absolute best friend until a few years ago. The microphone juts out towards my face as I stand in front of the room full of people and realise how many people are actually here. Every seat is taken, with people standing around the sides of the room and crowded by the closed doors. There are people in suits and regular clothes, from young kids to a few elderly people and, as I stand there looking at them, I remember what Ruth had said about the work Ivy had done to become part of the community.

'Um, I'm Jess,' I say tentatively into the microphone. 'I'm Ivy's older sister.'

Surprise flickers on a few faces, but I continue. 'Ivy and I weren't so close these last few years. We weren't close at all, actually.' I look down at the wooden stand and the copy of the order of service lying on it. 'I've asked myself a lot about what she'd been up to over the last few years. I never would have imagined that she'd have ended up here.'

I look back up at the room and my eyes pull right back to Finn and Ruth, seeking out familiarity.

'I'd always thought she'd end up in a big city somewhere, surrounded by people and traffic and the opportunity to do whatever she wanted, at whatever time of day. Ivy was always so *much*.' I shake my head a little with a smile. 'It was like she came into this world on a mission to leave her mark. Every kid in our school knew who she was, and after she'd got banned from the after-school club, her reputation as a wild child was pretty much set in stone, and she'd lived up to it ever since.'

A few people in the crowd chuckle and I press my hands into the wooden support in front of me.

'Our mum died when we were young. Ivy was only eleven and I was twelve, and it hit her hard. Both of us really, but especially her. She became so scared of losing people that she'd always have one foot out of the door so that she could be the one to leave first. It's been amazing to hear how much she settled herself here. That my sister, who had no tequila limit and the biggest, wildest personality I've ever known, found a calm place by the sea, chose a job where quietness is a virtue and surrounded herself with people who simply loved her for who she is is something I'd never have guessed at but am so happy to know. She found community, and a family to replace the one she didn't have any more. And I'm really proud of her for that.'

Tears fall from my eyes as I step down from the podium and shakily make my way back to my seat. A sob pushes up from my solar plexus as I'm faced with the enlarged image of her again and music starts playing.

Seeing this room packed with people who are all here to celebrate Ivy makes me realise how brave she was. At Dad's funeral, she'd said I was jealous of her because she actually lived her life while I swaddled myself with responsibility. Maybe she was right. I've spent my whole life doing everything right, taking supplements and doing all kinds of crazy things to keep myself healthy. It's protected me from nothing. But Ivy? She'd been brave enough to do everything she'd wanted to do.

Ivy's smile beams at me from the photograph and I realise, *really* realise, that I won't ever see it again.

And I break.

Chapter Thirty-Eight

Jess

Present day

Finn and I have just pulled up to a huge tent in the middle of nowhere and music is pounding through the air. It matches the pounding in my head that had set in as soon as Ivy's coffin had been drawn behind the curtain. I close the car door behind me and my heels sink a little into the grass.

I wedge my clutch bag under my armpit and look at Finn with unease. 'I don't know about this. Doesn't it feel weird to you to have a rave as a wake?'

Finn shakes his head. 'Not at all. Ivy was still massively into clubbing. She even started a whole sober rave scene here.'

We walk across the grass towards the big white circus-style tent with multicoloured lights strung up along the outside of it. There's already a load of people here, many more than were at the funeral. It feels like a small festival, with people dancing on the grass and milling around the tent. The sun has gone down, leaving just a few bright orange streaks blazing through small, thin clouds. A crescent moon is already hanging in the sky and the air has that hazy, end-of-summer feel to it. The music, the sky, the smell of grass and earth in my nose, the guy who's just walked out of the tent with his face painted with dots . . . it all adds up to make this day even more surreal than it already has been.

I follow Finn inside. A DJ is standing behind a table at the far end and there's already a cluster of people dancing in the middle. The pole at the centre of the tent has been layered with strips of material and branches reaching up to the conical roof to look like a tree. The entire ceiling is covered with a sheet painted in a design of interconnected circles and triangles, which all seem to culminate in a massive lotus flower at the centre. More strips of material hang down from the tree-pole branches, lit up in neon pinks and greens. The whole thing is wild and psychedelic, and, I have to admit, it's much more Ivy than a sit-down do in the pub.

'This is . . .' I shake my head, not quite able to put my thoughts into words. 'Who organised all this?'

He points towards Joe who's just walked in from the open tent flaps directly opposite the ones we came in through. Finn raises his arm and he nods in recognition. The two of them hug in that big, bear-like, manly way. I thought I'd cried all the tears I could for today at the service, but seeing them hug like this brings another lump to my throat. They pull away from each other and we hug too, something we didn't seem able to do at the service. We'd both been our own private pockets of grief and in the formal setting of the crematorium, it felt like we didn't know each other well enough to hug. But here, in this darkened tent that, for all intents and purposes looks like a festival, it feels like things are somehow different.

'What do you think?' Joe asks, nodding to the space around us.

'It's great,' I say, surprising myself but realising that it really is. 'It's very Ivy.'

'Yeah, I think she'd approve.' His shoulders and chest puff under his shirt, as if he's taking a huge breath, and then he turns back to look at us. 'So. We've got a little face painting station over there because she loved all that. And that's the bar over there. There's no booze, just water, juice and soft drinks. And some tea, I think.'

'You did good,' Finn says, slapping him tenderly on the back. 'Almost as good as she did herself.'

Joe shrugs with a grin. 'I had help. Hannah's the one who actually pulled it all together, I just did the heavy lifting.'

'Hannah's Ivy's best friend,' Finn explains. His use of the present tense makes me smile a little. It feels absolutely appropriate in this setting. 'She'll be around here somewhere.'

'So, which one of you wants to go first?' Joe asks, holding up a pen lit up in neon fuchsia pink by the blacklights. 'Jess?'

My instinct is to pick one of the excuses that have instantly reared up in my mind. There'll be an insane amount of chemicals in those things. My skin won't react well. They put all sorts of stuff into face paints – parabens, mercury and even formaldehyde. Plus, I'll look silly. Joe's face is covered in stripes of bright green and blue, with red dots in the middle. The lines of colour only seem to emphasise the sadness behind his eyes. I internally shake my excuses away and nod.

'Sure,' I reply. It'll wash off, and this is Ivy's party after all.

Finn goes to the drinks table while Joe and I make our way over to the side of the tent where I sit on a wooden stool, holding my bag in my lap.

'So, what will you be turning me into?' I ask. 'A cat? A mouse?'

'Oh, I'm not doing it, unless you want to end up looking like a clown.' He picks up a small box. 'The idea is that everyone does their own. It's kind of like an individual expression, or something. It was always like that at the raves here.'

I look into a box of face paints.

'This reminds me of a box of felt-tip pens Ivy and I shared as kids. We'd lie on the carpet in the living room and open up a colouring book – her with one page and me with the other,' I look at Joe. 'And when I'd take a pen, it'd nearly always be dried out because she'd never put the caps on properly.'

Joe laughs. 'Sounds like Ivy.'

His smile stays on his face, but his eyes are so sad. I try to imagine what it must be like to wake up to your partner like that, and it makes me shudder inside. He's holding the box in his hands so I take it from him and set it on my lap. My feet are balanced on the footstep of the stool, and I rummage through the box.

'That was really nice, what you said at the service,' Joe says. 'She'd have liked that.'

I look up at the surreality of his stripy painted face framed by messy curls. 'Were you together for long?'

Finn had told me already, but I've barely spoken to Joe and if there's one thing I know, it's that processing grief happens by talking and sharing memories.

He smiles sadly. 'It felt like a lifetime in a way, but it wasn't anywhere near long enough.'

I balance the box on my thighs and give him my full attention.

'We'd been to a friend's wedding, that day,' he continues, the lines on his face twisting and contorting as he talks. 'It was a good day, too. A really good one. I'd looked at my mate, newly married, and thought to myself, *I could imagine this*. It had felt kind of thrilling, you know? To be able to picture myself settled like that, with her. I felt so lucky.'

The sadness in his voice brings a lump to my throat, but I can't help but smile, too.

'I know that feeling,' I say. 'I reckon Ivy felt it too. If things would've been different between us, I can imagine she'd have told me so herself.'

I smile at him as the music pulses in the air around us, and he smiles back. They weren't just hollow words; I really do think she felt the same. Everything I've seen and heard about her tells me so. Plus, the fact that she'd been in a relationship with him at all speaks volumes.

'Maybe.' He looks down and shakes his head for a second before looking back up at me. 'It would've meant a lot to her, you being here. She spoke about you a lot.'

I half-grimace, half-smile, and rifle through the box as a way to keep my eyes busy. 'Yeah?'

'I think you were her big, unfinished thing. The one that got away.'

I frown at his choice of words. 'You know that's usually for the big, tragic loves in life, right?'

'Yeah.' He nods. 'I know.'

The way he says it fills my heart with warmth. His voice is calm and kind and sure, as if he's certain that Ivy would have described me as just that. *The one that got away.* My eyes sting. I want to believe him, but the truth is, we'll never really know. I blink the tears away and smile as Finn comes back with bottles of water. I take one from him, grateful for the coldness of it in my hands in this extra warm tent.

'So,' Joe says loudly. 'I'm going to dance for a bit. Ivy always said it was better than therapy for the big feelings you don't know what to do with. See you in a bit.'

He smiles again and leaves the two of us to go to the cluster of people dancing in the centre of the tent. I unscrew my bottle and watch him as he rolls the sleeves of his shirt up to his elbows.

'He seems like a nice guy,' I say before taking a long sip of water. 'I'm glad she ended up with someone like him.'

Finn nods in agreement. 'Yeah, he is. They fit together really well.' He looks down at the box. 'What's the deal with that?'

'It's self-face painting, apparently. How that should work without a mirror though, I'm not so sure.' I look at the ground around us and twist on my stool to see if there's a hand mirror somewhere before shrugging. 'I'll use the camera on my phone.'

'I can do it if you want?'

'Like I do yours, you do mine?'

He nods. 'Exactly. But only if you know what you're doing.'

'How hard can it be?' I raise an eyebrow and give him the box as I step down from the stool.

My knee-length dress has hitched up a little, and I tug it back down before pulling off my shoes. The heels will only sink into the grass and get wrecked, and after being in them all day, my feet are grateful to be on flat ground.

'Colour requests?' I ask, rifling through the box as he shuffles himself into a comfortable position.

He shakes his head, so I take out a mix of green, yellow and purple and he opens his knees wide so I have space to stand in front of him. I take the step forwards, enclosed by his inner thighs. Finn has sat by me almost all day today. He's hugged me I don't even know how many times. But this is the closest we've been.

I take a little breath and even though my hair is pinned up, I imagine I could shake it back anyway, and uncap my pen. I've never painted a face in my life. I have no idea what I'm doing, and no idea what I'm drawing, but I put the purple pen on his skin and draw a line starting at the middle of his hairline, down over his forehead, the bridge of his nose, over his lips and into the bristle of hairs across his chin.

'Are you painting me as *Braveheart*?' he asks with a grin while keeping absolutely still.

'I've never seen it,' I say, taking the cap off the second pen.

'Travesty.' His eyes flick towards mine.

My lips curve into a smile. 'Ssh.'

My eyes narrow with concentration as I step a little closer and draw horizontal, wavy lines across his forehead. His skin twitches as I glide across it. The memory of the last time we'd woken up together comes up into my mind. I'd known before going to bed the night before that I was going to tell him to go to Sweden, and remember trying to memorise all the features of his face. I'd drawn a line across his forehead with my finger, just like I'm doing right now with the pen. I wonder if he remembers that too.

I'd told him to leave, but I'd also been angry with him for not putting up more of a fight. And for jolting back into my life that day in Pret, only to disappear right back out of it like a phantom of my imagination. I'd been angry at him for coming into my life at all and having that thing about him that had made me reach and yearn for him like I had. My hand trembles as I draw on his face. I only know I was angry with him back then because I don't feel it any more. Maybe it's the sadness of today, the strange, other-worldliness of this tent or the music that seems to be tapping away at something deep inside me, but all I feel is a space where that frustration used to be. I swallow and step back. The colours on his face glow under the blacklight.

'All done,' I say, putting the caps back on the pens and handing them over.

'Your turn.'

His eyes bore into mine and my body flushes under my dress as we switch places and I hitch up onto the stool. I probably could've done this myself, even without a mirror, but I have to admit there's something nice about handing over control. It's just face painting, it's nothing huge. But the act of saying to someone *you take care of it* isn't something I do very often. I take another quick sip of my water before holding the bottle in my lap and sitting up straight on my stool, watching Finn as he rummages through the box.

He has to crouch a little to have his face level with mine. He holds one of the painting pens vertically in front of the middle of my face, and then horizontally as if he's an artist, sizing up my proportions. I laugh and swat him away with my hand, a smile resting on my face. The tent is filling with more and more people, and the rhythm of the electronic music pulses out in a kind of trance-like beat. I push the long sleeves of my dress up to my elbows and tug the material away from my lower back.

Finn's eyes come back to being level with mine, his face a few inches away.

'I wish I'd brought different clothes,' I say, feeling my body flush again.

His green irises seem to dance as they take in my face. 'You look great.'

I meant in terms of comfort, but I don't correct him. I forgot how the iris of his right eye has a speckle of brown by the pupil, like an inkblot. It's impossible not to stare into them when he's this close to me, crowding out my peripheral vision.

Finn shakes the pen in his hand, uncaps it and then slowly brings it to my left cheekbone. The moisture of the paint lands on my skin, warm and thick, almost like foundation. He sweeps the pen from the inside to the outside of my eye, and his knuckles graze my skin. My breath catches in my throat. He moves the pen a bit lower, making the same sweeping movement, and again, the touch of his skin on mine is so light that I wonder if I'm imagining it, if the burning trail that's being left behind is from the chemical paint or the recognition of his touch. His eyes skip across my face, the short, dark hairs of his eyebrows pulled together in concentration. I don't know whether to close my eyes or let them stay wide open to take him in.

I keep them open, drinking in the light smattering of freckles across the bridge of his nose. The delicate indentation of his eye sockets. The curl of his lashes. The curve of his lips. It feels like this is the first time I've really seen him since getting here, and my heartbeat quickens until it's almost matching the music. I close my eyes as the direction of his strokes change, deepening and slowing my breath, bringing it back to normal. Finn stops painting for a second, but I keep my eyes closed. I might not be able to see, but I can feel him in front of me and I guess he's changing colours. And then a spot of warmth and softness lands on my bottom lip and I snap my eyes open to see his staring back. For a moment, I'm stunned, until I realise it was the pen and not his lips on mine.

He's so close to me, I can smell him. I can feel his breath landing on my skin and I have no idea if I'm imagining things, or if it's as shaky as mine is. I snap my eyes shut again. The music floating around us, the darkness of the tent and the intimacy of him being this close, tracing lines over my face with the paint, is swirling together and landing in the pit of my belly in a way I haven't felt in a long, long time. His pen strokes my upper lip, the tip of it lightly dragging the skin. A breath leaves my mouth in a whisper. My belly somersaults as his knuckles track across my bottom lip. My body actually trembles, and I hold my breath to stop myself from moving any more than strictly necessary.

I'd always wondered why people would impulsively kiss some-one, or even sleep with someone, after being in an emotionally intense situation. Why would someone who's crying suddenly kiss the person closest to them? Why, after hearing about the death of a friend or family member, would someone feel the need to have sex? It had never made sense, until now.

These feelings coursing through my body feel big. So big. Grief, regret, sadness, nostalgia . . . they just feel so huge and the only thing that seems to be counteracting them in any way is the tenderness of Finn's fingers on my face. The light whisper of his breath on my skin. And there couldn't possibly be a less appropriate time than now to be feeling these feelings.

I keep my eyes closed until he's finished, managing a smile as he helps me down from the stool. From the moment I saw him in the pub, he's been nothing but friendly. He hasn't been overly nostalgic about us. But from the fire in his eyes as he holds my gaze, I know his feelings and thoughts can't be very far behind mine. We both take sips from our bottles, and I use it as an opportunity to look away from him and towards what we're here for. What was it Joe had said about dancing being a way to get rid of those big emotions?

I close my eyes for a second and tilt my head back. I can't remember the last time I danced. Maybe at my wedding, but even then, it wasn't *dancing*. It wasn't letting loose and being taken somewhere by the music. The last time I was in a club was years ago, maybe even as far back as university. I concentrate on the music that had sounded like one big messy ball of noise when we'd walked in, and let myself start to move. If this is what this party is for – to let the big emotions go – then that's what needs to happen.

I open my eyes again, grab Finn's hand without a word and head to the centre of the tent. We thread through the crowd that's moving together like one big mass, hands up in the air, feet stomping on the ground. I know that Ivy would go right to the very heart of it and, even though it's not what I would usually do, I let myself be drawn there. The colours, the strips of material hanging from the ceiling, the way everyone is dancing around the man-made tree in the centre with faces full of paint in all colours and designs makes me feel like I'm in some surreal, psychedelic rainforest in the Amazon. It's all so far from reality, that, somehow, it feels safe to let myself get into it. Into the music, into the heat pouring from everyone around me, and into the feeling that, for the first time all day, if Ivy is anywhere right now, she's here.

I let go of Finn's hand, and I dance.

Chapter Thirty-Nine

JESS

Present day

The sound of Duke's whining breaks me from a foggy, surreal dream about chasing after Ivy down the corridor of our primary school, and I open my eyes with a start. For a moment, I'm disorientated at my surroundings and the sound of impatient whining before throwing the covers back and getting out of bed. My eyes are bleary and I squint as I make my way to the front door. Duke shoots outside and I cross my arms over my chest, cold in my t-shirt and shorts. I have no idea what time it is, but since getting in from Ivy's wake, the sky outside has changed from night to day. I peek my head around the door to look outside. Duke is peeing at the hedge and the sky is grey. It could be early morning, but late afternoon is more likely, given the length of time Duke has his leg cocked up for. I feel an attack of guilt. I'd told Ruth and Finn I'd look after him, and he's been cooped up inside all this time without being able to go to the toilet.

He finishes up and trots back towards me, heads straight back inside and sniffs at his empty food bowl.

'Alright, let me get dressed first,' I say as he sits and watches me.

I quickly go back to the bedroom, take a hoodie from the back of the door and pull it on. I'm immediately wrapped in the scent of musky incense and it brings up the tiniest snatch of a dream from last night, but it slips away before I can catch it, like oil sliding through water. I pull the hood up over my head, cross my arms over my chest and make my way back to Duke, who gets up on all fours, as if he knows food is coming. He watches intently as I open up a can of dog food from under the sink.

'Wild venison with quinoa, carrots and fennel,' I read from the can, looking at him with raised eyebrows. 'She really spoiled you, didn't she?'

I could laugh at the way his focus is entirely fixed on my every move. His happiness over such a simple thing like eating lights me up a little, bathing me with warmth in the otherwise cold cottage. As he tucks into his food, my stomach growls at the lack of any. I look through Ivy's cupboards, and pull out a pack of dried pasta and a jar of red pesto. Until now, I've either eaten at Finn's pub or Ruth's house, but I don't really want company. I've got Duke for now and the only other person I'd like to see is the one person who isn't here, at least not physically. Hazy snatches of my dreams of Ivy float in front of me like wisps of smoke. I don't know if it's simply tiredness, grief or the vacuum that's been left after stamping my feet into the ground and waving my arms in the air for hours, but it's as if I've woken up in a void that I'm not quite ready to come out of yet.

As my pasta cooks, I wander around the living room with the cold air against my bare legs. I sniff at the candles Ivy had amassed since being here, remembering the Jo Malone one from a guy she'd dated that's now in storage, along with everything else of hers from the flat we'd shared. I put the candle down and run my fingers across the back of the sofa, picturing her curled up and reading with

Duke by her feet – something I'd never have been able to imagine until coming here.

I take my bowl of pasta and haul myself back into bed where I prop the pillows behind my back and pull the duvet over my legs. I've no idea if Ivy let Duke sleep in her bed, but I don't stop him as he jumps up and nestles by my feet. My phone buzzes on the small bedside table. I'm amazed there's still battery in it after being unplugged for so long but I've barely used it, apart from the photos I'd taken for Maddie yesterday. My screen is full of notifications: emails, missed calls, reminders and messages. I should unlock it and start picking away at them to stop myself from getting over-whelmed, or check for anything urgent at the very least. Instead, I spear a couple of pesto-coated twists of pasta with my fork. I know that Maddie has everything covered and, honestly, the idea of poking my head into the world of work right now feels like an intrusion I don't want.

The tomato sauce is oily on my tongue and the pasta lands in my stomach with stodgy satisfaction. I stop chewing for a moment, remembering the small bag in the kitchen, full of vitamins, adapto-gens and the new asparagus root pills I'd bought online last week to help regulate my hormones. They cost almost a hundred pounds and I haven't taken one since I got here. But instead of moving from the comfort of Ivy's bed, I stay right where I am, settling further into the pillow. And even though it's nowhere near the same, the feeling I have right now reminds me of the Sunday film nights we would have back in our little flat. We didn't always speak as we put face masks on our skin or painted our nails, but then again, it was never really about talking. It was simply about spending time in each other's company. And, really, there isn't a better place to feel like spending time together than right here, in her tiny little cottage bedroom.

The next day feels a little like emerging from a cocoon. The haziness of yesterday feels thinner, like wispy clouds that only keep the sun away for a second, instead of big, thick ones that hide the sky completely. I know I can't spend another day in bed, not least because Ruth had asked if I'd start helping her go through some of Ivy's things today. I get up, groaning at the tightness of my body from the break in my religious workout routine. The only time I've worn my running clothes was on my walk with Finn, so I pull them on. Duke sits on the bath mat as I brush my teeth, watching me with his dark eyes. I wonder if he knows that I'm Ivy's sister. His dog-aunt. The term makes me smile. He's been a constant companion the last two days. Hearing his gentle breath as he sleeps has been surprisingly reassuring and I actually feel like last night was one of the best night's sleeps I've had since Nick and I split.

When Ivy left after Dad's funeral, I'd started to run with headphones in my ears, using the music to distract me from myself. Today though, I keep them in their little case in my bag as I close the cottage door behind me. I clip Duke's leash to his harness before zipping up my jacket. It's fresh out, in that way that already makes you miss the summer before it's even over, and the grass under the tree is sprinkled with fallen apples. As obsessed as I am with eating organic and fresh whole foods, I don't think I've ever eaten something that came from my own garden. I've never even had a garden. I pick one of the apples up and put it in my pocket. It's ironic that she'd ended up here, in a garden with herbs and big leafy greens, doing yoga and having a dog, while I was still in London, working much more than was healthy or even necessary and popping pills to keep myself in balance. I tie my hair back with the hairband around my wrist and set off.

I haven't planned out a route, but find myself following the path that Finn had led me on for our walk. I start off slow, unsure of how Duke's little legs will keep up with a full-on run, and enjoy the feeling of uneven terrain under my feet that's unlike the smooth tarmac I'm used to. For the next half an hour, we run through fields and down to the beach along the water's edge until I see The Anchor pub up ahead. I think it's too early for it to be open, but I could do with a drink and I'm sure Duke could, too.

Music is playing inside so loud that the wood under my palm vibrates as I push the door open. Chairs are stacked upside down on the tables and hard rock is blasting from the speakers. For a second, I'm taken back to the day Finn had turned up to cook Ivy dinner at our flat and I'd been introduced to his love of hardcore music. I let the door close behind me and stand in the middle of the room as my heartbeat steadies out after my run. It trips over and speeds up as the door behind the bar swings open and Finn emerges with two crates of beer in his arms. From the look on his face, his choice of music matches his mood and I feel suddenly stupid for dropping in unannounced before the pub's even open. He doesn't see me as he drops the crates on the surface of the bar, so I turn to leave. I can make do with a bottle of water from the shop instead. But before I get to open the door, the music is turned down.

'Jess?' His voice cuts above the guitars and growling, and I stop for a second before turning around.

I smile weakly. 'Morning.'

'What are you doing here?' He rests his arm on one of the crates with a frown.

'I went for a run and just thought I'd stop by to say hi.'

He opens one of the fridges behind the bar and starts filling it with bottles from the crate, avoiding my eyes. 'How are you?'

'Oh, you know.' I shrug lightly.

Maybe I remembered it differently, but at the rave-wake, I thought we'd bridged some kind of gap. We'd danced side by side the entire time and, even though we hadn't spoken much at all, it hadn't felt anywhere near as awkward as this.

'We thought you might've left already when you didn't reply to any of our messages,' he says.

Is that why he's being so weird? Because I didn't reply to his message? I hadn't replied to any and, truth be told, I hadn't even seen his name on my screen when I'd quickly scrolled through it yesterday.

'Ruth wanted to know if you were alright,' he adds.

'I'm fine. I was just a bit exhausted and slept most of the day.'

He nods gruffly with his eyebrows pulled tightly together and a slight slick of sweat across his forehead.

'Are *you* okay?' I ask.

Finn lifts the second crate and hauls it down the bar before setting it back down again.

'I'm fine,' he replies, in a way that tells me he absolutely isn't but also doesn't want to talk about it.

He yanks open the fridge and the growling music stops for a second before the tapping of drumsticks introduces yet more angry guitar strums. Everything about Finn's body language is making it clear that, whatever he has going on, I'm a huge distraction. My face flames. Maybe I'd confused everything. Maybe he'd just been compassionate with me in the lead-up to Ivy's funeral, and at the wake. I'd been certain that something had passed between us as we'd painted each other's faces. Then again, it doesn't really matter. It's not like anything could've happened between us anyway.

'You know what, I think I'm going to go,' I say, pointing my thumb over my shoulder. 'Get myself some breakfast and him some water.'

'We have water. And breakfast.'

'You're not open.'

'I can make you something.'

'I'll just get something from the shop.'

'Since when did you become the type to have a pasty for breakfast?'

The tiniest of laughs drops from my mouth. 'I was thinking more along the lines of cereal.'

'Come on.' Finn sighs. 'I'll make you something.'

I tilt my head to one side. 'Really? Because to be honest, you're acting like you can't get rid of me quickly enough.'

Finn puts his hands on the now empty crate, bowing his head. He sighs and looks up, picking up the crate and walking back over to the other end of the bar.

'I'm sorry.' His mouth pulls to one side as he chews the inside of his cheek. 'It's not you.'

'Really? It's not you, it's me? Is that what we've come to?'

He smiles at the dry humour in my voice and stacks the second crate on top of the first. His long fingers curl under the handles and he lifts them both to set them onto the floor.

'Really, it's not you. I had a shit sleep and we're understaffed, and . . .' He tails off and shakes his head before taking a cup from the top of the coffee machine. 'Want one?'

'You know I don't do proper coffee. I'll have a decaf?'

I'm weak, I know, but sometimes there's no alternative and I doubt they do matcha here.

Finn pulls a face. 'No way. I don't serve that crap, it's awful. You know what they have to do to the beans to make it decaf?'

I shake my head.

'Let's just say that *you* would run a mile. I can do you herbal tea, if you want?'

I'm intrigued, and make a mental note to google *why is decaf bad for you?* Finn hadn't really understood my strange food rules

308

when we were together. He'd put my water fasts and daily doses of charcoal down to being strange character quirks. It feels nice that he's warned me over something he knows I'd care about. He always had been observant like that. I watch him press a shot of espresso beans into the coffee sieve and throw caution to the wind.

'You know what,' I say, hoisting myself up onto a stool, 'screw it. I'll have a cappuccino.'

Finn raises an eyebrow. 'Really?'

'But only if you've got soya or oat milk.'

'We've got both.'

'Okay. Then oat.'

He goes to take another cup and looks at me again. 'You sure? Are you going to get coffee jitters or anything like that?'

I unzip my jacket and shrug it off with a smile. 'I'm sure I'll be fine.'

Finn makes my drink and I find myself watching him pour perfect foamy oat milk into the cup with eagerness. My first coffee in years. He hands it to me and I hold the cup between my hands while he fetches water for Duke.

'Cheers,' he says with a smile.

I smile back, hovering the cup under my nose for a second to take in that unique burnt aroma before taking a sip. It's creamy and frothy and even with the knowledge of that article I'd read, it's delicious. It's like a smile landing in my chest. I've no idea how I'd managed to stick to my matcha lattes all this time. I obviously have stronger willpower than I'd thought.

'Good?' he asks.

'Good.' I smile before taking another sip. I smack my lips together to lose any milk moustache, and look at him over the rim of my cup. 'So. What's going on? Is there a reason you're listening to the world's angriest music?'

He sighs and leans his forearms on the bar, holding his cup between his hands. Our arms are so close that they almost touch. He looks down into his cup.

'It's Em's birthday soon and I thought . . . I don't know.' He sighs again and looks up at me with a shyness in his hooded eyes. 'The conversation you and I had on the beach got me thinking about things a lot, and then Ivy's funeral just intensified it all. I started getting into how short life is and all that usual existential crisis stuff.'

He laughs a little, but it's shallow. I get it. Grief has a way of making you question everything about your life and the decisions you've made.

'It just got me thinking, what if it had been me that died. I haven't spent enough time with Emilia as it is and it won't get easier with me being here.' He shrugs. 'I guess my mind was just getting the better of me when you came in. I'd woken up thinking I should ask Maia if Em could come here, or if I could go there and then . . . I dunno.'

My heart pulls at the way he shrugs his shoulders again, as if it was a stupid idea to have.

'It sounds like a great idea,' I say with a small smile.

'You don't know Maia,' he replies, looking back at me with a sceptical face. 'It'd probably start world war three and a re-hashing of all the things I did wrong and God knows what else. And anyway. Em's got a new dad now, so.'

'*You're* her dad, Finn. Come on, we've both lost ours and I'm guessing you'd do anything to have had extra time with him.'

He twists his cup in circles with the thumb and index finger of his right hand. 'Yeah. I would.'

'Exactly,' I reply. 'So maybe this is a good reminder to make the most of things while we can. I mean, imagine if I'd got in touch with Ivy years ago, or her me. Who knows how different things could've been.'

He plays with his cup and I stare at his forearms, pressing down into the bar. *Who knows how different things could've been* is something I'd stopped letting myself think too much about years ago. It had felt too sad, the whole thing – always wondering *if only*. If only I'd told Ivy about Finn straight away, the morning after. If only I'd have insisted on going with her to Tenerife. If only I'd have had the courage to believe that what Finn and I had was real instead of going into self-protection mode by telling him to go. I might never have met Nick and dragged him into a marriage that could never have worked. Finn might have never gone to Sweden. Ivy might still be alive. I drain the last of my coffee, already feeling the slight buzz in my nervous system.

'Are you ready to be a dad?' I ask and he nods carefully after a couple of seconds.

'I have no idea *how* to be one, really. But I'd like to at least try.'

'Then that's all you need to say. I'm sure she'll understand.'

I put the cup back down onto the saucer and look at him. It's still crazy to think he has a daughter. That there's someone walking around who he had a hand in creating. My body mixes a cocktail of feelings and emotions. I miss him. On some level, I've always missed him.

'Maybe you're right. Maybe I can make it over there for a couple of days,' he says, nodding as his eyes hold mine. 'I guess there's only so long you can keep punishing yourself for, right?'

It sounds good in theory, but in practice, I know it's not always quite so easy. I look down into my empty cup, ringed with a stain of coffee. The words *if only* float across my mind again and I brush them aside as Finn pushes himself away from the bar and puts his hands behind his head. The double-folded edges of his white t-shirt sleeves sit flush against the delicate skin of his inner biceps as he stretches.

'Thanks for the pep talk,' he says with a smile. 'What do I owe you?'

'You can put it on your tab.' I smile back.

The crown of my head buzzes with the caffeine and my heartbeat turns a little faster. It's not quite the jitters I'd been worried about. If anything, the floaty feeling is kind of nice.

'I'd better get back,' Finn says, hoisting the crates up and holding them against his body. 'It's the last weekend of the summer holidays and I'm short staffed. It'll be a long day.'

I turn away to look around at the empty pub. I worked as a waitress while I was at university and it was always so stressful when someone couldn't make it for their shift. There were seven tables in Finn's pub, as well as the long bench I'd sat at when I'd first got here. Add standing room at the bar and the sofas in the corner by the big screen television, and it added up to a fairly big space.

'I can help you out,' I say, turning back to look at him. 'If you want?'

Finn's eyebrows raise an inch. 'Really? Don't you have to help Ruth today?'

'Yeah, but it might be nice to have something to do afterwards.'

I have things to do already, like getting on with my own work – as much as I can from here anyway – but I'd planned to do that before Ruth comes over. Starting the process of clearing Ivy's cottage won't be an easy thing to do. Serving tables would be a good distraction for whatever might come up that doesn't involve me sitting on my laptop until my eyelids droop with tiredness.

'Plus, it's my last night here. It beats sitting in alone,' I smile weakly as he repositions the crates in his hands.

'You're leaving already?'

'I have to get back to work next week and it's a full day's journey back, so . . .' I tail off and we stare at each other for a few seconds.

I wish this reunion had happened because of something else, something joyful like a wedding, or totally coincidental like bumping into each other again somewhere far removed from Ivy at all. Just having him around has helped these last few days in ways I'm not even sure I understand, but I suppose it's enough that we've come full circle. I'll go home and he'll stay here and we can get on with the rest of our lives knowing that this chapter has been closed. Properly, this time.

'Right, makes sense.' He nods. 'Well, I won't say no to giving you a good send-off, or a hand for tonight. If you're sure you're up to it?'

'I'm sure. I'll come around seven?'

'Sounds good.'

He smiles at me and I hop down from my stool to pull my coat back on. We say our goodbyes and I leave, stepping out into the fresh morning air.

Chapter forty

JESS

Present day

After leaving Finn, I grab some fruit from the shop and make my way back to the cottage. I have a few hours until Ruth comes over, so I shower, dress and chop my apples, pears and oranges into a fruit salad that's nowhere near as zesty or satisfying as the one Finn made a few days ago, but is at least more nutritious than what I've eaten over the last twenty-four hours. I sit with my bowl wedged between my crossed legs and balance my laptop on the arm of the sofa. I click into my email inbox to scan the subject headers and my eyes stop immediately at one from Maddie.

> **From:** Maddie Johnson
>
> **To:** Jess Palmer
>
> **Subject:** WE GOT IT!

I quickly open the email and take in the words on my screen before picking up my phone. Maddie answers after two rings.

'We got into John Lewis?' I say by way of a greeting.

'I know!' she replies, and I can hear her grinning down the phone. 'I found out yesterday but didn't want to call in case you weren't feeling up to talking.'

I smile at her consideration. 'Thanks, Mads.'

'How are you?'

'Up and down. It's been a strange couple of days,' I say, and fill her in on the funeral and wake.

'It sounds like a really beautiful day,' Maddie says.

'It was. And now I've got her little dog with me, which actually really helps.'

'You should bring him back with you.'

I laugh a little. 'I don't think that's going to happen, but it's a nice idea. I'll be coming back alone.'

'You know you don't have to rush back if you're not ready to?'

'I'm ready. And we've just got our biggest contract ever. There's a lot to do.'

One of the strangest things that happens when someone dies is that life really does goes on and, I suppose, in a way it's comforting. That feeling of getting swept away by grief hasn't just disappeared. I'd had a moment earlier when it had hit me again that Ivy was really gone. I wasn't here on holiday, visiting her or looking after her house until she got back from somewhere exotic. She was gone. That remembering had literally taken my breath away. And then Duke had sniffed at my feet and I'd seen my laptop on the sofa, and those two things had pulled me back. Keeping busy helped.

'I just thought you might want to stay there and catch up with things a bit,' Maddie says.

'Things?'

'Okay, Finn. You did say you had a moment.'

I groan. I wish I hadn't said anything about the wake now. I can admit to myself that the simple memory of his feather-light touch while painting my skin had felt delicious. But it was nothing more than a moment. A blip in time. Digging into it with Maddie now would be like opening Pandora's box.

'It was nothing,' I reply lightly. 'Things feel good with him. It feels like we've straightened things out and we can leave things on good terms.'

'Fair enough,' Maddie concedes.

I know she's disappointed in my closing the subject, but we go back to talking about the John Lewis deal and work instead. After hanging up, I stand in the middle of the living room, looking at all of Ivy's things. Nick had helped me clear out our family home after Dad died. I'm usually pretty good at throwing things out, but it's different when someone dies. My ruthlessness had disappeared and I'd attached meaning to everything, like the chipped mug Dad had drunk his tea from becoming a treasured keepsake that just had to be kept. All of the things Ivy had left behind when she'd gone are in a storage unit in an obscure corner of north-west London, and I realise that I'm going to have to sort through the remnants of her life again when I go back home.

Duke barks at the sound of a car pulling up, and when I open the door, I see Ruth stepping out of her black Mini Cooper. She starts hauling flattened cardboard boxes from the back seat and I shove my feet into my trainers to go help her. I take the boxes and she pushes her oval sunglasses up into her grey hair. We hug hello and her warm palms spread across my shoulders as she holds me for a second. Ruth isn't small by any means. She's actually an inch or two taller than me and much stockier. She's got good bones, as my nan would say, but today, she feels smaller than before. It must be tough to have lost her brother and Ivy in the space of a few short months. We pull apart and I hitch the boxes under my armpit as she takes a basket out from the passenger seat of her car.

'How are you?' I ask and she sighs, looking at the house.

'Well, I'd be happier if today wasn't something that had to happen but since it is . . .' She smiles tightly. 'What can you do?'

'We can leave it for today, if you want?'

I'm not sure if the offer is more for her benefit or mine, but it does feel a bit early to be doing this. It had taken until over a month after Dad's funeral for me to start the process of clearing the house.

Ruth shakes her head. 'I think it's better to do these kinds of things sooner than later. And you're here now. There might be some things you want to take with you. Finn told me you're leaving tomorrow already?'

News travelled fast in this town. I feel a pang of guilt as I nod. 'That's the plan.'

If I'd have managed to get that Airbnb, I would have actually left this morning. As it is, I'm glad for the extra day to spend more time with them, not to mention little Duke who has basically become my new best friend.

We head inside and I make us some herbal tea. Everything I can see through the kitchen window is lush and green and, even though I can't see the sea from here, I can hear it in the distance.

'It's beautiful here,' I say, more to myself than to Ruth.

'You know, you could stay a while longer.'

'Thanks, Ruth,' I reply, and I mean it. 'But I have to get back to work. We just got a new contract and there's so much to do.'

'All the more reason to stay on a couple of days and refill your tank then. I'd certainly like it and so would he.' She nods to Duke.

I smile weakly, trying to fight the feeling that I'm somehow letting her down.

'No pressure,' she adds. 'I'm just letting you know it's an option, that's all.'

We drink our teas side by side in easy silence. Birds chirp outside and the faint smell of grass wafts in through the open windows. It's easy to let myself drift along with the idea of another day or two, but it's only putting off the inevitable. With the John Lewis confirmation through, work really will get busier.

'So,' Ruth says with a sigh after draining her cup. 'We should get on.'

I nod reluctantly. 'Do you have someplace you wanted to start first?'

'I thought kitchen first. The crockery and things like that can stay – they're likely mostly mine anyway – but giving it a sort through is a good idea. And then we can tackle the other rooms together.'

It makes sense. The kitchen is the most impersonal room in the house and we make quick work of sorting through the cupboards and drawers. We both circle around and avoid the cork board full of photographs hanging on the wall as if we've telepathically sent the message that we don't have to go quite so deep just yet.

'Are you a bookworm? If any of these are interesting for you, you can take them,' Ruth says as we move into the living room.

Most of the books are about yoga, but I run through the rest, my finger trailing along the spines as I go. I pick out a few novels and put them to one side.

'How come you didn't come to the wake?' I ask.

Ruth looks up from her seat on the floor but continues to wrap one of Ivy's bronze statues in newspaper.

'I'm too old for raves, I wanted a quieter way to say goodbye. I have my own little ritual for such things.'

'What kind of ritual?'

She shifts from kneeling to sit with her legs crossed and untucks her white button-up shirt from the front of her leggings. The skin at the top of her chest is lightly wrinkled and slightly red behind the white crystal pendant hanging from her chain.

'Well,' she says, pushing her hair back. 'I meditated and I thought about her. I remembered things about her. How she looked, how she spoke. It was like spending time together. It's something I've always done. I suppose it's what we all do, really. That's what funerals are for. I just do it in my own way.'

'I felt her. At the wake.' I pause and watch for any signs of a critical response, but Ruth's expression widens a bit as if I should continue. 'I can't really explain it. I just had the weirdest, strongest feeling that she was there somehow. Does that sound mad?'

She shakes her head. 'Definitely not. Jess, what you feel is what you feel. Just because someone else doesn't have the same experience or it sounds weird doesn't mean it's not true.'

'The feeling I've had from the moment I got here was that if Ivy were alive, she'd have been happy to see me. At the wake, it felt like I was able to bury all that had happened between us. Like being there had somehow made things okay.' I shake my head and swallow against the reality behind my words. 'But I know that's not true. The way we split from each other was *not* good. Imagining that things somehow magically fixed themselves is just deluded.'

The words tumble from my mouth with a breath that feels heavy. Like, if it were visible, they would drop down and melt into the ground.

'We never got to sort things out, and that's something I know I'm going to have to live with. I hurt her, a lot.'

'She hurt you, too,' Ruth says. 'She told me so herself.'

'Maybe, but it was my fault she left. I should've understood why she acted like she did instead of just being annoyed.'

Ruth puts the paper-wrapped statue on the floor next to her. 'One of my teachers told me something once that really shifted the way I think about things. He said that nobody ever does anything because of you. You can trigger a reaction – anger, jealousy, whatever it might be. But the way they *act* on that emotion is *always* down to them and never down to you.'

She makes it sound so simple and clear-cut, and a flash of irritation scratches at me because of it. Ruth is someone who seems to have such a wise world view but her explanation feels like something I'd open in a fortune cookie. My face obviously isn't able to hide the way I feel, because she gets up from the floor and tells me to follow her. We walk into the bedroom and she stands in the centre of the small room by the foot of the bed.

'What do you see?' she asks, and I look around, shrugging my shoulders.

'Ivy's bedroom.'

'Is there anything in here that stands out to you?'

I hide a reluctant sigh against the irritation that's followed from the living room and look again at the space around us. Nothing seems out of place. There's her bed, with its iron frame and cream covers, a chest of drawers with jars and bottles standing on top of it, a mirror and a wooden chair stands in the corner. My suitcase is lying open on the floor – maybe that's what Ruth wants me to see. I go to shrug again before noticing the wall hanging. It's the only bit of decoration in here, which I guess makes it stand out. Plus, the cream strands of thick, cream-coloured cotton are interwoven with strands of a dusky pink colour, which is never something I'd associate with Ivy. I was the pink lover. Always had been and still am, with my laptop and phone cases, purse and planner in the same shade of blush pink.

I shrug a little and gesture to it. 'This, I guess.'

'Why?'

I sigh again, a little louder this time. I have the feeling that I'm being tested and I'm not really getting it. 'I don't know?'

Ruth turns to look at me. 'You have one too, don't you?'

My eyebrows crease together. 'How do you know that?'

'Because Ivy made them. She made a sun for herself, and a moon for you.'

My throat immediately tightens with a strange, almost sickly tingle. If this were anyone other than Ruth, I'd have the feeling that I was being played somehow. Her eyes bore into my face, so much like Finn's with their laser-pointed focus. I look back at the wall hanging, half-expecting it to have changed. Of course, it hasn't. It's the very same as it was a second ago – a round sun to my crescent moon.

'I don't understand.' I shake my head.

'When I first met Ivy, she told me about your wedding and how she didn't know if she should go because she didn't want to ruin your big day. She wanted to sort herself out and, as you've seen, she did. But she still didn't feel ready by the time your wedding came around and so she wanted to send something. A gift.' Ruth looks at the hanging. 'It was her way of extending an olive branch, I suppose.'

I blink and a tear falls from my eye. 'But I'd thought it was from a magazine.'

It feels stupid now to have assumed that a magazine would randomly send such a thing, but the explanation had fit together at the time. Understanding now that it had come from Ivy, for my wedding, creates such a pain in my chest that I actually put a hand against it.

'Well, why didn't she write a card or something to go with it?' My voice rises a little as the irritation I'd felt earlier comes back. 'If I'd have known it was from her . . .'

The decoration hanging on my living room wall was an olive branch. And I'd had no idea.

'I don't know,' Ruth replies with a shake of her head. 'She had a lot going on. Maybe she just forgot.'

I go to ask myself who would forget to put a card with a gift, but I already know the answer. It was classic Ivy, and the tears fall freely from my eyes.

'Jess, I know you think that Ivy died hating you.' Ruth takes my hand in hers and squeezes it. 'But this should tell you that she didn't.'

I wipe the tears away with my free hand and look at the wall hanging. All this time, I'd thought that Ivy had ignored the invitation because she hadn't wanted to sort things out. Now I find out that the opposite is true.

If only I'd have known, it could've all been so different.

Chapter Forty-One

Jess

Present day

Finn's pub on a Friday night is clearly the place to be. There are families and singles, older people, kids who tried, and failed, to order booze with fake IDs and the ninety–ten split of diversity I'd expect to find at the seaside.

'You good?' Finn asks, and I nod, glugging back a glass of water.

I'd almost wanted to cancel and take back my offer of helping. My heart had felt so heavy after learning the truth about my wedding gift, but I couldn't have done that to Finn. Besides, I knew that it would do me good to be around people and do something active, and I'd been right.

There's a family at one table who are all looking down into blue-lit screens, and another with sunburnt parents and boisterous, restless twins. Finn has just finished making a bunch of mojitos and Moscow mules for a group of girls who must be going to the closest big town with a club afterwards if their short dresses and made-up faces are anything to go by. The cook puts a plate with a juicy burger filled with crispy lettuce and mushrooms next to a stack of chips in the service hatch. I readjust the paper Union Jack folded around the toothpick that's been stuck into the centre of the burger and carry it out to the packed beer garden.

It looks like a TV advert for a fancy cider brand, with groups of people sat at picnic tables under the glow of soft lights strung up in the trees. My feet crunch on the gravel and I smile as I give the plate of food to one of the girls in a big group. I'm pretty sure I recognise her from the rave-wake, but with a purple beanie hat over her long brown hair instead of a neon-painted face, I'm not entirely sure. Reef's 'Place Your Hands' is just starting up inside and the group of guys standing by the door break out into a cheer, spilling slops of Guinness over the tops of their glasses and onto the ground. They look more like city types in their Ralph Lauren shirts and jeans than the sun- and sea-bleached-haired lot at the table next to them, but it all seems to work.

I head back inside. The pub is filled with music, chatter and laughter and I stop by the door as a feeling I can't quite place floods through me. It has the sensation of relief, mixed with a current of nostalgia and, as my eyes land on Finn, a flush of warmth and pride. He looks completely at ease with his fingers curled around the beer tap, drawing amber liquid into a pint glass while chatting to a man with the longest, bushiest beard I've ever seen. The tendons in Finn's forearm flex under his skin and his cheeks have a slight rosy tint to them. I know that being here instead of back in Sweden or running his own restaurant somewhere wasn't part of his plan, but he's done good with it. Walking in here feels like entering a place that's been made entirely for fun and the lighter side of life. It's exactly what you'd want from your friendly local pub, and I'm pretty sure that's down to Finn and how he runs it. I'm fairly certain his dad would be proud.

He catches my eye as I make my way behind the bar to stand next to him and take the next person's order. We weave around each other as we work, instinctively and intuitively making space in the narrow confines of the gap behind the bar. It's like a dance I've never done before but have somehow been practising for my whole life. I find myself smiling as we go, cracking jokes as I ease into it, feeling more familiar with where things are and how they're done. Every time the super-speed dishwasher finishes a cycle, billows of steam rise up from under the bar as we unload slippery, hot glasses. My jeans are smeared with beer and wine, the humidity has turned my hair into a frizzy mess and my cream vest has specks and splashes on it that I can only hope will wash out. I try my best. I really do. But the more we move around each other, the harder it is not to notice the contours of the muscles on either side of Finn's spine, or the shape of his shoulder blades flexing under his t-shirt. The back of it is tucked into his jeans and the denim hugs the curve of his bum as if they were made just for him. His face is soft and relaxed, his eyes bright and shining – the complete opposite of this morning. And he grins widely every single time he looks at me. Which is often.

Somewhere above the music, I hear a phone ringing.

'Jess, can you get that?' He calls over to me as I pour a Malibu and Coke.

He shrugs and gestures to his hands, both of which are busy pulling separate pints from separate taps. I put the bottle down and look at the phone receiver by the till, but it's empty. Finn turns his hips a little and I see the top of the handset sticking out from his back pocket.

'What do I say?' I shrug.

He rolls his eyes with a smile. 'You could always try *hello*?'

I smirk and swat his arm playfully before reaching around to prise the phone from his pocket. My fingers graze the denim of his jeans and it's like a current of electricity running up the length of my arm. I turn away and plug a finger into my ear as I answer the phone, but it rings out before I can say anything.

'Too late,' I say, putting the handset back in the receiver base.

'They'll call back if it's important,' he replies nonchalantly, putting the glasses onto the bar before turning towards me.

His eyes lock onto mine, those green irises with a rim of brown at the edges that have always managed to disarm me. His gaze flicks down to my neck, and I feel it with a jolt of tingles right in the base of my throat. He steps towards me and I look at his arm stretching out in my direction. My brain processes it in slow motion, taking in the way his fingers stretch, the small, raised scar on the soft skin of his inner forearm and how his t-shirt pulls ever so slightly against his abs. My breath stops in my throat as his hand lands on my hip with a weight that feels stabilising and firm. I feel his fingers closing around the curve of bone, landing on the outer edge of my lower back one by one. Little finger, ring finger, middle, index and thumb. I couldn't move, even if I wanted to. It feels as though we've shifted into a completely different space, where we're alone instead of in a pub packed full of people.

My heart is pounding so loudly that it almost drowns out the music and my hand instinctively goes to move to his chest, until his eyes shift to refocus on the space behind me. And I catch myself as I realise he's just reaching for a packet of crisps. My cheeks flame like two hot chunks of coal under my skin. I don't know what that was, but when he looks at me, I know he felt it too. His eyebrows pull together in the same bewildered look I'm sure I have on my face, and he shakes his head an inch before going back to his customer. I try to shake it off and go back to the Malibu and Coke I'd been making before the phone rang. The feel of his hand on my hip is still there like an imprinted memory, and a smile tugs at my insides against my will.

Fuck.

◆ ◆ ◆

I try to keep a distance for the rest of the shift, but it's not easy when he's standing right next to me, reaching across me and smiling at me all the time. As the customers begin to leave and the pub slows down, so do I. Suddenly, I become aware of the fact that we've been on our feet, rushing around for the past five hours with almost no pause, only a few snatches of water and not a single toilet break. The last person to leave is the bushy-bearded man who finally gives Finn a long, boozy hug before leaving. Finn bolts the door behind him and drops his forehead onto it with his shoulders slumped and rounded under his t-shirt. He turns around, leaning his back against the door and looks at me.

'You. Are. A. Lifesaver.'

I shrug with a smile as if to say it's all in a day's work. 'It was fun.'

'You're pretty good, you know.' He pushes himself away from the door. 'Fancy a job?'

'I'm too old for this. My back's aching.' I laugh, but it is actually a little sore, and I arch it slightly, squeezing my shoulder blades together.

It's a completely innocent movement but I'm quickly aware of how the silky material of my vest strains against my chest. After whatever that exchange was with Finn, I feel like my senses are on red alert, which is dangerous territory to be in. It feels like that day when I'd stood in my kitchen with the urge to text him and tell him to come over while Ivy was at Carnival. I settle for using a hand to rub one of my shoulders instead and glance around the now empty pub. We've been clearing up as we've gone along in the last forty minutes. The tables are already cleaned and the bottled drinks have been restocked.

'What do we do now?' I ask as he comes to my side of the bar.

'We drink. What do you fancy?'

Finn takes out a bottle of fancy cola from the fridge and I point to a red bottle from the same brand.

'That one. Hibiscus and what was it?'

He deftly taps it under the wall-mounted bottle opener and hands to me. 'Apple.'

I take it from him, trying, and failing, not to get caught in his gaze again. He's appeared totally innocent in 99 per cent of his actions tonight, but it's that 1 per cent that's making my spine shiver. His fingers brush against mine as he lets go of the bottle and linger for just a fraction of a second longer than they really ought to. We lean against the bar, sipping at our drinks. It feels like I've been twirling around in a circle for the last few hours and the world around me is slowly starting to come back into focus. It really was fun, and after the time spent with Ruth earlier, it was exactly what I needed.

I yawn and Finn turns to face me, resting his elbow on the bar's surface.

'Tired?'

I nod and my body melts a bit at the admission of being powered out. 'But we've got to clean and stuff, surely?'

He shakes his head. 'I'll clear up the rest but the cleaner will do most of it in the morning.'

I look at the clock and smile. 'It's already morning.'

'So it is.' He smiles back but then it fades a little. 'What time are you heading off?'

I haven't thought about the long journey back home – the drive to the station, the two trains and hours of sitting and thinking and replaying and absorbing everything that's happened over the last few days. It feels overwhelming and exhausting.

'I don't know,' I reply. 'Not too late, I suppose.'

He looks down at his bottle. 'You could stay? I'll need another hand tomorrow if Jodie's still sick.'

When he looks up at me, the smile on his face is light and breezy, but his fingers pick at the label on his bottle.

'Two nights in a row might just kill me,' I joke.

I can't lie. It's tempting. Making a repeat of tonight, being in a warm little sea-scented bubble where troubles are left at the door. Where *my* troubles are left at the door. Being here means I don't have to be back in my sterile apartment. Life in Treppin Bay is so far away from my failed marriage and unnecessarily long work hours, and so much closer to Ivy.

'Well, you'd better make sure you say bye before you go,' he says. 'No sneaking out of town.'

I cross my fingers across my heart. 'Of course. I'm counting on you for a decent breakfast. Or brunch, if I can't get up so early.'

I look at the wall, the glasses stacked behind the bar and anywhere other than Finn, because it's becoming more and more difficult to stop myself from slipping into what feels like a sense of panic at the thought of going back to my real life tomorrow.

'I'm glad we got to see each other again, Jess. I really did always feel like a total shit for not meeting you that day.'

I turn back to him with a smile. 'It's alright. Your excuse was a pretty good one, so you're off the hook.'

'Being off the hook,' he repeats with a shake of his head. 'You make it sound like it was really okay that I stood you up, when we both know it wasn't.'

'You had good reason. And it's in the past. Don't worry about it.'

'It wasn't just because of Emilia though,' he says after a couple of seconds.

I pause. 'So what was it then?'

'I'd actually seen you before you'd seen me that day in Pret. I'd walked past and seen you and wanted to just keep on walking, but I couldn't. I'd told myself I could just drop in, grab something real quick to check if it really was you and leave without you even noticing me.'

I shake my head as his cheeks redden.

'I'd been struggling in Sweden. Things with Maia were totally fucked and she'd been calling and messaging every two seconds. And you were sitting there all cool and collected and happy about starting your new business and it was like being taken back to when we first met.'

I remember exactly how I'd felt, sitting there in front of him. It isn't far off from how I'm feeling right now, how I've been feeling all evening. If he could see what was going on inside me, he'd see that I am, and was, anything but cool or collected.

'But meeting for a drink was your idea.'

'I know.' He nods. 'And I wanted to. But I didn't want to mess your life up. Things were so complicated and I was technically still with Maia and it just felt safer not to meet you.'

'What do you mean *safer*?' My heart is beating in the strangest of ways and I can almost feel it pulsing in my throat.

'I saw you and I knew that I wasn't over you. Not at all.'

'Finn . . .' I groan, shaking my head.

'I know. I didn't plan on telling you any of this, but I can't *not* say it.' He puts his bottle on the bar and stands up tall, shoving his hands in his back pockets. 'The last few days have been all kinds of fucked up and weird and sad. Hell, the last few *months*, even. And then you came and it's been so . . .' He shakes his head as if he can't find the words and I hold my breath. 'And then at the rave, it felt like there was something between us.' He looks away for a few seconds before turning back towards me. 'I don't know, Jess. Am I nuts? Am I the only one who's feeling this?'

I let go of my breath and shake my head because of course he's not nuts. My insides flicker with joy at the knowing that he's felt the same things I have. His eyes are holding me in place, just like they always do.

'Nothing's changed for me, Jess,' he says, shrugging his shoulders to his ears and keeping them there. 'I still feel the same way about you that I always have and I would be so ready to give this another try if you were too.'

We stare at each other for a few seconds and my heart thumps in my chest. The words he wants to hear are bubbling in my throat but I can hear the voice screaming at me from the back of my head.

Leave. Right now. Before you do something stupid.

I open my mouth to say something, but before the words come out, something shifts inside that makes me reach for him at the very same moment that he reaches for me. Our lips collide and my entire body comes to life as he wraps his arm around my waist. One of my hands is in his hair while the other splays across his back, pressing his body against mine until we stumble backwards against the bar. I've forgotten how to breathe. Or maybe I just don't need to. The feeling of his lips on mine and his tongue flicking in my mouth is like oxygen in itself.

It's been eight years, nine months and twenty-six days since my body has felt *this* and I drink it in as he hoists me up onto the bar. My legs wrap around his waist, and it's a movement that somehow jolts me back into reality. I pull my head away and push my palms into his chest.

'Finn, stop.'

'What, why?' He shakes his head, bewildered, as I jump down from the bar.

My feet land on the ground with a thud and my heart is ricocheting in my chest. I shake my head, blinking and trying to get my bearings as I push him away from me.

'God, Finn. We can't do this.'

'Why not? I meant what I said.'

'Okay, then *I* can't do this.'

I shake my head and look at him. His cheeks are flushed and his eyes busy searching my face. I breathe out through my nose and my entire body sags. Everything feels too raw and intense. His kiss

331

had made my whole being come alive, but it had taken me back to those few weeks we'd had together.

'I can't go through this again,' I say, pulling my arms across my chest.

'Through what?'

'Come on, Finn. We've been here before. We know how this ends.'

He scrunches his face and shakes his head. 'Jess, things are completely different now.'

'Are they? What's changed? You have a whole life here, and mine's in London.'

'So we'll make it work.'

Finn says it as if it's easy and obvious. But it isn't, and it makes my heart hurt. This conversation feels infinitely harder than the one I'd had with Nick a few months ago, despite us living together and having exchanged vows.

'Please, Finn.' I hold my hands up and steady my breathing, feeling the easy bubble we'd built up over the course of the evening shatter and disappear. 'Just, don't.'

I fight the tears clawing their way through my eyes and grab my bag from the hook by the door to the kitchen.

'Come on, Jess. Don't go.'

I hear his voice behind me but I don't stop walking away. My fingers tremble as I unbolt the door. The simple fact is that it's all much too late, and the price of all of this is has always been too high. I've missed out on so much of Ivy's life, and I can trace the unravelling thread all the way back to that house party nine years ago. Being here with him again, in the middle of the remnants of her life, feels like a higher price than it ever had been before.

Chapter Forty-Two

JESS

Present day

I sit on the mustard-yellow sofa, turning my phone over and over in my hands. The cottage feels different today. Less homely and welcoming, as if it knows that I'm leaving. Which is ridiculous, of course. It's a house, not a person. I tip my head back and sigh, looking up at the ceiling and the delta-like network of cracks emanating from a place where the wall begins. I know Finn made me promise to say goodbye properly, but after our kiss I just can't do it and I'd chickened out with a text instead.

Right at that moment, my phone rings and Maddie's picture flashes on my screen.

'Hey,' I answer the phone, flooded with relief that my best friend is as much of an early riser as I am.

'Alright. Start from the beginning.'

We both know that there is absolutely no room for greetings after the text I'd sent her as soon as I'd got in from the pub, so I start from the top. I tell her about the way we'd worked together, in total synchronisation and that moment when I'd been sure he was about to kiss me, right up to the part where he actually had. Or I had. I'm not sure who reached for who first.

'Bloody hell, Jess.' Maddie gasps, and I can easily imagine her eyes as wide as saucers.

'I know,' I reply, my heart beating faster just from recounting it all over the phone.

'So then what?'

'I told him I couldn't do it and I left.'

'You did what? Why?'

'Oh, God. Not you as well, come on Maddie. You know why, and you're supposed to tell me I did the right thing.'

'I can't tell you that, Jess. I know you want me to remind you about all the reasons you split up first time around and how he stood you up, but you loved him. And he loved you. And clearly, that hasn't changed. I can't sit here as your best friend and tell you you're not making a huge mistake. Because you are.'

I shake my head, shocked. 'So what should I have done? Slept with him and pretended the last nine years never happened?'

'No, but you don't have to keep on punishing yourself. It's sad as fuck that things happened the way they have, but it's not like you haven't paid enough for it. You're getting divorced because you married someone who wasn't right for you, the man who *is* has just told you he still loves you and you're running away from it.'

My throat chokes with tears. Maddie is never aggressive or opinionated like this, and it's hard not to let my hackles rise. 'That's not fair.'

'Isn't it? You have *got* to stop holding yourself back from your life. Ivy had moved on and made a happy life for herself, and so should you. You can't keep running away from the things you're scared of. I can't and I won't let you.'

'What do you mean you won't let me?' I reply hotly with a little laugh at her uncharacteristic blatantness.

'I'm pregnant again, Jess. And if this baby is the miracle one that finally goes full term, I want its godmother to be someone who can prove that good things can come out of shitty situations.'

I blink, shaking my head for a few seconds as a fresh wave of tears jabs at my eyes. 'You're pregnant? Maddie, that's amazing.'

'Yeah, it is.' She sighs down the phone. 'But I mean it, Jess. If you leave without giving things a chance, you'll never live with yourself.'

I rub my forehead as my phone buzzes against my ear. I take a quick look at the screen to check who it is.

Finn: This doesn't have to be a goodbye.

I press myself into the arm of the sofa. I can't type anything back because Finn's wrong, and so is Maddie. This has to be goodbye.

I spend the next ninety minutes packing up my things and gathering up the parts of my life that had blended in with Ivy's – my planner on her coffee table, my toothbrush in the glass next to hers. I look at the pill box that I fill with my weekly doses of vitamins, minerals, elixirs and promise-to-cure-and-prevent-alls. I'd put it next to the kettle, exactly like I do at home, but unlike back in London, I haven't taken anything since my first night here. Haven't even thought about it, in fact. It wasn't a conscious decision either, just like it hasn't been a conscious decision not to look at my phone as much, check my inbox less or only open my laptop twice in the entire time I've been here. There's a weighty feeling of grief in my chest and I find myself wishing it was yesterday again so I'd have an extra day and relive it all, until the point where I'd pulled away from Finn's kiss.

It's already way past eleven, and I still have to go to Ruth's to say goodbye and drop off the key. After my first dose of caffeine in years yesterday, my body is already nagging for another, especially after a night of no sleep and constant rides on an emotional rollercoaster. A headache is building, which doesn't exactly make the prospect of hours of travel ahead of me any more bearable.

I zip my suitcase and pull it to stand upright, hitching up the handle and standing in the middle of Ivy's living room before going to the cork board full of photographs. It doesn't feel like just a few days ago that I'd looked at it and broken down in tears. My eyes skip over the collection of photos again and I smile a little at the one that had been copied for her funeral. I carefully unpin in it and slip it into my handbag. I look around at her house for one last time and walk out.

I close the door behind me, keeping my eyes down as I lock it, as if looking back up at this cottage would be the straw that breaks my composure. A wasp buzzes lazily somewhere in the eaves above my head and the scent of grass fills my nose. I take a full breath of it as I go to the little hire car where I've already put the box of things I'm taking back with me – some books, a statue of some Hindu god I have no idea about but somehow made an impression on me, her bathrobe and a few candles, beauty products and, of course, that macramé wall hanging. I put my suitcase in the back and as I get into the car, I look at the apple tree with its low-hanging red fruit, the plants that have been left to grow wildly in their pots and the mosaic painted pathway leading to the front door. I swallow and turn the key before making a three-point turn and driving out onto the road.

It only takes two minutes to drive around to Ruth's place on the other side of the field and I can already feel my eyes threatening to spill yet again when she opens the door.

'Tea?' she asks, cocking her head to one side as Duke runs out and jumps up at my feet.

I look down at my watch. I'd love nothing more than to go into her kitchen, with its all white everything and completely relaxed energy, but I can't.

'I'd love to, but I have to get the car back on time,' I reply apologetically and cross my arms over my chest.

Ruth nods. 'Alright.' She hands me a box with some cans of food and a few toys in it. 'Oh, there's a second leash as well, hold on.'

She disappears inside and I resist the urge to step over the threshold, afraid that if I do, I won't want to come out again. Duke sits by my feet with his tail swishing on the ground, as if he knows he's coming with me. I know Ruth, Finn and Joe love him, but it's not good for him to be shipped around so much and I'm sure it's a relief for them too. Besides, I couldn't imagine going back to London and leaving him behind.

She comes back with a leather leash and a laptop in her hands. 'Are you sure you want to take him with you?'

'Sure. He can come with me to the office and I'll be glad of the company at home.' I nod towards the laptop. 'What's that?'

'It was Ivy's. I thought you might want it. I don't know what to do with it otherwise,' she replies. 'I haven't even opened it – I don't know the password but it feels strange to just get rid of it.'

I have no idea what I will do with it either but I nod and she puts it into the box in my arms along with everything else.

A sad smile spreads on her face. 'Are you sure I can't change your mind? I've a vegan quiche with your name on it.'

I laugh a little, shaking my head. 'It really means a lot, but I can't.'

I put the box down and she reaches out to pull me into a hug. Just like a few days ago when I'd met her for the first time, I breathe in that maternal feeling. The feeling of someone who cares for you, just because. Her body is warm and her hug tight, and I clench my eyes shut, wishing that things could be different. We both laugh a little and sniff as we pull apart, and I wipe one of my cheeks with my knuckles.

'Thanks, for everything – letting me stay at the cottage and organising the funeral.' I take an envelope from my back pocket. 'I wanted you to have this.'

I know words aren't enough and funerals are expensive. As much as Ivy seemed to have changed, I'm sure she wouldn't have had any insurance for that, so I withdrew the maximum on my three cards and put the cash in a card for Ruth.

'Open it later, though,' I add quickly before she can get into it. I'm pretty sure she'd only try to give it right back to me.

Suspicion pinches at her face, but she nods anyway. 'Ivy was like family. So you are too.'

I smile as a ball of warmth spreads in my chest. It means the world to hear something like that when you don't have any more family of your own.

'I'm definitely going to miss you,' she says, crouching down to rub a palm across Duke's little head and play with one of his ears. She picks up the box with his things and Ivy's laptop, and stands back up with a smile. 'Don't be a stranger.'

'I won't,' I reply, taking the box from her.

It doesn't feel like a lie as I say it. It feels like a nugget of truth that helps me to get in the car and drive away without looking back.

Epilogue

I place the small monstera plant down onto the pale birch wood surface of a display unit. Its deep green leaves provide a stark contrast to both the white pot it's growing from, as well as the bright neon, Miami-inspired palette of ring binders on either side of it.

'Alright, that's the last of them,' Maddie says, and I turn to see her carrying an identical plant and placing it on a tiered display unit on the other side of our shop.

Our shop. It still blows my mind to think that we actually have one. Maddie runs her fingers across the plush coral leather of one of our planners and looks at the space around us with wide eyes. The white, tiled floors gleam under the lights and every corner of the shop is split into a different colour scheme – black, white and gold by the entrance, brown, beige and earth tones in one corner and bright primary colours in another. Pastels are in the other corner by the door and the middle of the shop has everything else.

'Mad, isn't it?' I say as she comes over to stand beside me. 'It's hard to believe this is really ours.'

I look at the big, black letters fixed to the wall behind the payment counter: XOXO, and shake my head with a tinge of disbelief.

'No it isn't,' Maddie says with a grin. 'We've worked bloody hard to get here. Think about all those hours in the office, going to expos and 4 a.m. Zoom calls with some supplier in the States.'

I almost laugh. 'I'd forgotten about that.'

'We've earned this, Jess.' She threads her arm through mine and squeezes it. 'Every last little bit.'

She's always talking about mindset, and how it wasn't enough to get the things you wanted – you had to feel you deserved them too. I've always been able to know that certain goals were achievable, it's the deserving part that's needed more work, especially over the last week. It had taken longer than expected to finally get the keys to this place and even though we could've waited to open until the New Year, we'd both wanted to push for the pre-Christmas rush. What Maddie calls Imposter Syndrome, and I call self-doubt, has been blowing up everywhere and getting more and more intense as the shop fit-out was done. Those thoughts of *who was I to think I could own my own a shop?* have been tapping away in the back of my head. But now, standing here in the middle of all of it, there's a welling feeling of pride in my chest. Tomorrow, XOXO will officially open in the offline world.

'Yeah.' I grin and squeeze her back. 'We have earned it, haven't we?'

'You bet we have.' Maddie groans, tipping her head back with a yawn. 'Oh, God. I don't think I can keep my eyes open any more.'

I look at the clock as she lets go of my arm. It's just after eight thirty, still pretty early for me, but way past her bedtime these days.

'I really wanted to go for dinner tonight to celebrate, or at least for a quick drink of pretend wine.' Maddie looks at me with apologetic eyes and puts a palm over her lower belly and the little bump that's just about visible under her jumper. 'I'm sorry.'

'What? Don't be silly,' I reply with a laugh. 'I'm bushed too.'

We've been putting in full days at the office and then coming here in the evenings. I've been really trying to keep the more relaxed vibe I'd fallen into in Cornwall when it comes to work – no phone in bed and no checking emails until after breakfast. So far, it's actually working and I'm pretty proud of myself.

'I don't think I could eat anything anyway,' Maddie says. 'I don't know why it's called morning sickness if it still goes strong at night. Or why I've still got it in month four.'

It sounds like she's grumbling, but the affection in her voice is clear. Despite the nausea and tiredness she's had so far, this is the happiest I've seen her in years. All signs are pointing towards a healthy pregnancy, but she's rightly cautious about taking things easy.

'Go home,' I say with a smile. 'Get some sleep.'

She raises her eyebrows. 'Only if you go too. I'm not leaving you here to hang around and find things to do.'

'Don't worry about that. My sofa's calling me and it's past this one's dinner time.'

I nod towards Duke, curled up on his little travel blanket, and feel a burst of affection. I think he's happy not to be split between the lives of three different people. He comes with me to work and I've kept Ivy's tradition of giving him the absolute best of everything. He's definitely made the last few months easier, that's for sure.

Maddie yawns openly and widely, adding on a big groan at the end for emphasis. I guess it's tiring work, growing a human, something that I'm starting to realise I might never get to do. Being single, almost divorced and fast-approaching thirty-seven years old is something I hadn't anticipated for my future, but I don't let myself dwell on it for too long.

'Do you want a lift?' Maddie asks, wrapping herself in a woolly winter cape that fastens at her neck.

I shake my head and pick up her oversized handbag, holding it out to her. 'We'll get the bus.'

Her face is sceptical, but we live in opposite directions and she doesn't insist as we head outside and say our goodbyes. The air is blisteringly cold, but there's something about London that always feels hopeful in the run-up to Christmas. Especially now, with the smallest flakes of snow skirting around on the pavement and festive lights stretching from lantern to lantern. I look through the glass doors at our shop with a satisfied smile before walking with Duke to the bus stop. It's not as comfortable as Maddie's car would have been, and Duke hates the Tube. He was so traumatised after the first and only time I'd tried that I've come to accept that our trips home from anywhere beyond our office will involve the upper deck of a bus.

I sit with him on my lap, and rest my head against the fogged-up window. I use the back of my hand to smear away a strip of condensation and watch the world outside. The streets are packed and the traffic is heavy as we get to Trafalgar Square. I wish I'd brought a book to distract my mind from using the quiet time to think about Finn. The memory of our kiss is so strong I can still feel the scorching heat of it on my lips.

I've thought about what he said every day. That he still felt the same way about me that he always had. It makes my heart leap with the madness of it all, even though it's the same for me too. Sometimes, I even let myself build up a fantasy of what would have happened if I hadn't stopped that kiss. I construct a whole life where we're together – here or in that little cottage in Cornwall – and we have something that works for us. Where neither one of us are making a compromise that feels too big and there are no shadows of the past to cling to us.

I swipe at the window again. I miss him, and I've given up pretending I don't. I'd tried for a few days after getting back, and it hadn't worked. I'd seen a quote on Instagram, saying *it will hurt until you let it hurt*. Maddie had been right. I'd been punishing myself for years instead of really moving on from it all. So I've started to let myself feel the hurt when it comes to Finn in the hope that, one day, it won't be quite so acute.

The woman sitting beside me stands up to get off and is immediately replaced by another with expensive-looking shopping bags. It's funny how you can sit in such close proximity to someone and have no connection to them at all, but you can go through years of your life tied to someone who's miles away. My phone vibrates in my pocket and my heart takes a triple beat at Finn's name on my screen. There's no message as such, just a silly meme about human-looking carrots. I smile and send back a laughing emoji, followed by a green heart. The goodbye text wasn't quite goodbye, in the sense that we've maintained contact. It felt too weird not to. We keep things light, swapping funny memes and photos of what we're looking at in that moment, like snapshots into the life of the other. It feels nice and keeps a smile on my face for the rest of the ride home.

After feeding Duke, I reheat a bowl of yesterday's pumpkin and ginger soup and eat it, curled up on the sofa with re-runs of *Friends* on the TV. One of Ivy's candles flickers with a small orange glow on the windowsill and, with the central heating on full blast and the scent of soup in the air, the flat doesn't feel quite as alienating as it used to.

Once I'm done eating, I leave my bowl on the coffee table. Little by little, and after half a year, my flat is starting to feel like home. I've committed myself to unpacking all of the boxes and bags before the New Year. As Duke cleans his paws on the other end of the sofa, my eyes fall to the bookshelf. I've hung curtains at the windows, unpacked blankets and bought plants, but the bookshelf is still half-empty. I'd given a load of novels to the charity shop when I'd left the flat I shared with Nick, but a full shelf of books has always felt like the finishing touch to a room for me. I get up and make my way to the bedroom to get the box I'd brought back from Cornwall. The books of Ivy's I'd chosen won't fill all the empty space, but it'll be close enough.

I pick the box up, feeling the smooth cardboard under my hands, and stop for a second to look at the two macramé wall decorations now hanging side by side on my bedroom wall. Moving the one I'd had from the living room to the bedroom was one of the first things I'd done when I'd got back, and they are the first things I see when I get out of bed in the morning. They complement each other perfectly, the sun and the moon, very different from each other but also very much the same. I think I've come to terms with the fact that we never got the chance to personally put things right, and take what I can from her wedding gift instead.

I blow hair from my face and head back into the living room, dropping the box and kneeling on the floor. I take out the books one by one and slide them into place, grouping by colour until the box is empty apart from Ivy's laptop. I take it out and put it on my lap. I'm really not sure what to do with it. Without knowing her password, it's completely unusable but I don't want to sell it. I unzip the black foam cover to look at it. Even if I did want to sell it, it's so ancient I doubt anyone would want it. It's clunky and heavy, and covered with random stickers. There isn't even a charging cord, and when I open it and press the power button, nothing happens. It's totally empty so I close it and slide it back into its case. There's a small pocket on the inside, so I pull the zip back and take out a small pile of papers and a notepad. I instantly recognise it, because it's one of ours – black with silver star-like paint splotches on it. I shake my head. It has to be one of those strange but lovely coincidences that Ivy carried around and used something Maddie and I had designed and produced.

I rearrange myself to sit with my legs crossed, clenching and releasing my toes against the prickle of pins and needles. The papers are bills for the cottage, and I make a note to send them on to Ruth in case she's not already seen them, before flicking through the notepad. The pages are full of Sanskrit words and little stick-figure drawings of people in different yoga poses. My fingers trace over Ivy's small handwriting, neat on some pages and scribbled on others. She'd always complained of having a hand that was too slow for her brain when it came to writing, resulting in whatever she wrote being almost illegible, even to herself sometimes.

An envelope is wedged between the last page and the cover, and my heart jumps to my throat as I flip it over to see my name.

Jess Palmer

c/o XOXO

13 Cottington Street

London, SW9 1AT

There's a stamp on it, but the envelope hasn't been sealed. My blood pulses in my ears as I pull out the paper inside and unfold it with shaky hands. It's filled with Ivy's handwriting, all of it neat and precise. The skin on the tops of my arms and the back of my neck ripples, and tears sting at my eyes before I even begin to read.

15th August

Hey, Jess,

I know this has taken a long, looooooong time to come around. Seven years . . . it feels mad to think about that. I'm embarrassed it's taken so long to get in touch, especially after your wedding invitation. I wanted to reply and even wrote out responses to you a few times, but it always felt a bit impersonal and if I'm being honest, I wasn't ready.

But first of all, congratulations! I hope you're enjoying married life. I know I wasn't all that nice to him but Nick's a nice guy and I'm sure he's treating you well. Your invitation really did mean a lot, but I needed to sort a few things out and I didn't want to ruin your big day.

There's so much to say, and I'm really not sure where to start. When you wrote, I was in India. I'd been travelling a long time and your email came right when I knew I needed to change things. I hadn't been happy for a long time and reading about your wedding was a bit of a wake-up call. I know you probably thought I'd end up somewhere far flung and foreign, but I'm actually here, in England, in a little village in Cornwall.

I've been here for a couple of years now. I live in a cottage (don't laugh) and I have a dog! I know . . . me, who couldn't keep a cactus alive, owns a pooch. His name is Duke and he's the sweetest, most adorable thing ever. I brought him back from India, which cost both arms and both legs but was totally worth it! And, more importantly, he's still alive (haha). I'm also a yoga teacher now. Yep. Who'd have thought it LOL. But I really love it. It's helped me a lot to process things and I don't really know what I'd have done without it. My teacher and boss is amazing, and I owe her an awful lot (the cottage I'm writing this to you in for starters!) And you'll never believe it, but it's Finn's aunt! It was one of those weird random things that don't make much sense but it's all worked out so well, I know it was fate.

It's been a pretty wild ride these last few years, but I thought, life's too short and beautiful to hold on to hurt. We're going to a friend's wedding tomorrow and it's got me thinking about life and love and all of that. Oh, by we, I mean Joe :) If you can believe it, I've got an actual boyfriend. He's a surfer and gorgeous and I actually got to find out what love really is . . . who knew it was so . . . well, you know! Which is what got me thinking, really. About the whole Finn thing. And I'm going to say what I should've said years ago: I'm sorry.

It was so ridiculous of me to blow up like that, and ban you from our holiday. I still can't believe I did that . . . I really was a brat, wasn't I?! You were right, about me being pissed off that he'd chosen you. Not because you didn't deserve it, but because I was jealous. Finding Joe has made me realise there's more than enough love to go around. I feel awful for making you feel bad about falling in love. And as for Dad's funeral . . . I'm really embarrassed about that. I know it's no excuse but I was just in a really crap place, and you were absolutely right about everything. FYI, I don't touch drugs any more, haven't smoked for two years and get tipsy from even sniffing alcohol! I just want you to know that nothing was your fault. It was mine. And I've got the yoga and Joe to thank for being able to see that. And Finn. He lives here too, by the way. His dad died and he moved back a few months ago.

Anyway, as I said, this wedding has made me think about life and love and how maybe, if you two had stayed together, it could've been you and Finn who got married. And because life has shown me that the things that are meant to come to you eventually do, I'm sure I would have still met Joe, maybe from travelling or visiting you both here – who knows!

Wow, I hadn't meant for this to get quite so deep. I'd love to talk properly, it's been such a long time. Maybe on the phone or even in person? My cottage only has one bedroom but it has a super comfy sofa if you don't want to share the bed, and if not there's loads of Airbnbs around. We could take doggy walks by the beach and you can come try out my yoga class. It's a pretty special place, and I think you'd like it here.

I totally get it if you don't want to reply though, or if you need more time . . . I haven't exactly made things easy so if it's too much, that's ok. But if you do want to, then I would love for you to come. You could meet Ruth and Joe.

And of course, Finn. I know he'd love to see you again too.

Lots of love,

Ivy

xoxo

◆ ◆ ◆

My eyes stream as I read Ivy's letter, once, twice and three times. She's told me everything that Ruth and Finn have said but it means so much more, because it's coming from her. I try to picture her sitting on the sofa or in a cafe, carefully writing this letter. And I wonder what would've happened if Ruth hadn't given me the laptop or if I hadn't opened up that side pocket.

I swipe my cheeks with my palms, leaning back against the wall with Duke sniffing at my face and his paws on my chest. She really was happy, and knowing that floods my body with relief, even after seeing it with my own eyes. I scoop Duke up in my arms and kiss his head until he fidgets and jumps back down. She really had forgiven me for Finn too.

I look at my phone on the coffee table, and crawl over to it, taking Ivy's letter with me. My hands shake as I take photos of it, and send it to Maddie. I find my way to the chat with Finn and my heart flutters, remembering what he'd said again. He was ready, if I was.

Am I?

I bite my bottom lip, frowning as I look at his tiny profile picture in the corner of my screen. And then I send the photos. I watch as the first tick appears on the chat box. It's sent. And the second. It's delivered.

My heart beats faster as I flick my gaze to the top of the screen and under his name, his status changes to online. The two ticks in the box turn blue and I bite on the skin of my thumb, staring intently at the screen. I don't even know if this can work. He's got his business and life in Cornwall and I've got mine here. And now there really is the possibility of there maybe, truly being an *Us*, my belly free falls as I wait for his response.

I watch as his status changes to *typing* . . . and every time it stops, so does my heart. After stopping and starting and stopping and starting, I find myself typing too, unable to wait for his answer and too afraid it might not be what I want to hear. Before I can think twice about it, I press send.

> **Jess:** If you're still ready and willing to give us another try, then I am too . . . Do you have space for one more at Xmas? xoxo

ACKNOWLEDGMENTS

The story of Jess and Ivy has been four years in the making, and I'm so thankful for the Lake Union team for helping it to happen. Thank you to Sammia Hamer and Victoria Oundjian for believing in me, and to Sophie Wilson for being such a great editor. A special shout-out goes to Nic Wharmby for the holiday rep gold and Jodie for naming Jess and Maddie's company: XOXO. So much of this story was inspired by the passing of my beloved grandad, Ronald Martin, and I'm so grateful to have the family I do. I love you all. Finally, to Simon, thank you for cheering me on and taking care of all the adulting things in the last weeks of writing. From Goa to Bavaria and still here. You're amazing.

ABOUT THE AUTHOR

Natalie K Martin was born in Sheffield and grew up with a fascination for human relationships. After leaving her corporate career to travel and write, her novels became Amazon bestsellers on release.

Writing emotionally led contemporary fiction about life, love and the tricky parts in-between, Natalie's books are relevant and relatable to the everyday woman and have been featured in the *Daily Mail*, *Woman's Own* and *Pride Magazine*.

A dedicated advocate for women's empowerment, Natalie also works as a Menstrual Cycle Coach, and teaches yoga. She lives in Bavaria, Germany, with her boyfriend and their rescue dog.

BOOK CLUB QUESTIONS

1. Jess and Ivy are incredibly close sisters, but very different in their approach. How much do their differences lead to their separation?

2. Is Ivy's decision to travel and live a more nomadic lifestyle actually more about running away from responsibility and having to grow up?

3. Why does Jess follow her dreams when it comes to business, but settle for a relationship that doesn't make her happy?

4. How do the losses that Ivy and Jess have experienced inform who they are as sisters and people?

5. What characters did you find yourself identifying with? Are you more of a Jess or an Ivy?

6. How different do you think their stories would have ended up if Ivy or Jess had been able to apologise and forgive each other? Would they still have found themselves in the same place in their lives?